A LANCASTER *C*AMISH *C*HRISTMAS

4 Romance Novellas

A LANCASTER AMISH CHRISTMAS

ANNE BLACKBURNE, AMY CLIPSTON,
AMY LILLARD, MINDY STEELE

BARBOUR
PUBLISHING

Lucy's Christmas Sunbeam ©2024 by Anne Blackburne
A Bird-in-Hand Christmas ©2024 by Amy Clipston
Christmas Lily ©2024 by Amy Lillard
Leaving Lancaster ©2024 by Mindy Steele

Print ISBN 978-1-63609-931-6
Adobe Digital Edition (.epub) 978-1-63609-932-3

All scripture quotations, unless otherwise noted, are taken from the King James Version of the Bible.

This book is a work of fiction. Names, characters, places, and incidents are either products of the author's imagination or used fictitiously. Any similarity to actual people, organizations, and/or events is purely coincidental.

Cover design © Kirk DouPonce, DogEared Design

Published by Barbour Books, an imprint of Barbour Publishing, Inc., 1810 Barbour Drive, Uhrichsville, Ohio 44683, www.barbourbooks.com

Our mission is to inspire the world with the life-changing message of the Bible.

Member of the
Evangelical Christian
Publishers Association

Printed in the United States of America.

LUCY'S
CHRISTMAS
SUNBEAM

by Anne Blackburne

CHAPTER ONE

*C*ome out, come out, wherever you are!"

Lucy Beiler paused to listen carefully, hoping for a clue as to where her baby sister, Mildred, was hiding. She'd been solely responsible for Millie's care since their mother died giving birth to the child on Christmas Day nearly three years before. And while she loved the tiny little girl, a special gift from *Gott* delivered into her hands even as their *maem* was delivered into Gott's, at times Millie's love of games tested her patience.

A peek behind the couch revealed nothing but dust bunnies and a small stuffed pig. Stretching, she nabbed the toy by one scruffy ear. "Millie! Look who I found! Pinky Pig was hiding behind the couch."

She heard a small cry of "Pinky!" coming from the kitchen.

"Come on, *liebling,* we need to go to the hardware store so I can caulk the shower."

She grinned at the sound of a giggle coming from under the kitchen table.

She peeked beneath the hem of the sage-green tablecloth. "Gotcha!"

Millie burst into giggles, her slightly tip-tilted eyes sparkling with mischief as she regarded her older sister from above chubby little hands pressed over her mouth in an attempt to contain her mirth.

"Found me!" the child signed and then chuckled.

"*Ja*! So now you have to be a *gut* girl and get ready to go out with me, okay?" Lucy used both signed and spoken language when addressing her sister, because she wanted Millie to learn to speak as well as sign.

Lucy reached down and tickled Millie on her round tummy. Millie giggled and signed. "Okay, Lucy."

"Can you say it?"

"Okay!"

Lucy scooped the mite up in a big hug. "You're so smart! Come now. We'll need sweaters." The late September days were turning cool in central Pennsylvania, where she and Millie lived in the *dawdi haus* on the farm where Lucy had grown up.

She popped a pink hoodie over her sister's head, lifting her braids out and straightening her little prayer *kapp*.

She smiled into her sister's open, loving face, her heart melting a little bit at how much she loved the child, who was more like a daughter than a sister.

"Ice cream?" Millie signed with a winning smile.

"First, the caulk. We'll see about ice cream."

"Okay!" she yelled.

"Okay!" Lucy answered.

She strapped her *schwester* into her car seat in the buggy she'd inherited from their maem. Not all Amish used the contraptions, but she wasn't about to take chances with Millie's safety. She could be quite impulsive, and Lucy wanted to be certain the child couldn't fall out of the moving buggy.

As she pulled onto the back road and pointed the horse toward Bird-in-Hand, she thought about what else she should do while she was in town.

I could use some more pink yarn for Millie's Christmas sweater. It'll be here before I know it! And maybe some candlewicks. I want to try making up some nice candles for my other sisters. She smiled at the thought. She enjoyed making simple gifts for the people she loved.

Half an hour later they were exploring Fisher's Hardware in Bird-in-Hand.

"Now, where do they hide the caulk?" she muttered as she made her way down the aisles in the store.

"Caulk!" Millie shouted.

Turning around the end of an aisle, Lucy heard a startled exclamation and realized she'd run into a man who'd been coming the other direction.

She watched helplessly as he stumbled against the cart, shoving it into a display of stacked paint cans.

"Millie!"

The stranger twisted his body between the cart and the toppling cans of paint, wincing as heavy one-gallon cans bounced off his shoulders and back.

Between their efforts the cart was righted.

They stared at each other, momentarily speechless, the man's feet planted squarely in a spreading pool of white primer.

They spoke simultaneously.

"I'm so sorry! I'll pay for the spilled paint! And maybe new boots." Lucy flushed as she stared at the handsome Amish man whose boots were probably going to be ruined.

"*Ach*, I'm sorry! I should have been watching where I was going! Is your little girl *oll recht?*"

They stared at each other for another beat before once again speaking at the same time.

"No, no, it was my fault!" he insisted. "No need to pay for anything. I'm just glad your daughter wasn't hurt."

"She's fine, but what about you?"

After a few seconds the corner of the man's mouth tilted up, and an amused snort escaped him.

Lucy's mouth dropped open, but then the ridiculousness of the situation hit her, and she covered her mouth as giggles escaped her.

Then they were both laughing right out loud.

"Oh my, I haven't laughed like that in ages!" Lucy wiped tears of mirth from her eyes.

The stranger grinned. "Me neither. I'm just glad you're both okay."

Millie looked from one to the other and grinned. "Ice cream!" she signed, causing Lucy to chuckle again. "My schwester wants ice cream."

"Schwester? She's not your daughter?"

"Well, she's like a daughter to me. I've raised her since our maem died when she was born. I'm Lucy Beiler. You're sure you won't be in trouble for this mess? I really do think I should pay for the open cans."

He shook his head firmly. "*Nee.* It's obvious now that the display wasn't safe."

A store employee hurried up to them, his eyes widening as he took in the scene. "Ach! What happened?"

"Just a little mishap, and some paint cans fell," the man, whose name Lucy still didn't know, told his coworker. "Would you please clean it up for me while I take these ladies back to the soda fountain for ice cream?"

"Ja, of course. I'm just glad nobody got hurt. Someone told me paint cans were hitting you in the head!"

The first man shrugged. "I may have a few bruises, but it's nothing more than I deserve. *Denki*, Jacob."

Jacob left, presumably to gather cleaning materials. The first man looked down at his boots with a regretful air and then bent down and untied them before stepping out of them and taking big steps away from the spilled paint.

"Let's get ice cream!"

Lucy unstrapped Millie from the cart, which was also standing in the spreading pool of paint, and soon they were sitting at the soda fountain at the back of the store.

A young Amish woman hurried over to them, glancing at Amos' feet as she slipped behind the counter. "Amos! Where are your shoes? And who are your friends?"

"Hi, Rebekkah. This is Lucy Beiler and her little sister, Millie. We met in the paint section when I clumsily upset the endcap display of primer. My boots didn't make it. We need ice cream to recover from our trauma."

She grinned at him and smiled at Millie. "What kind of ice cream do you want, *lieb*?"

Millie looked at Lucy with big eyes and signed, "Chocolate."

Lucy kissed her sister's head. "Sure, Millie." She smiled at Rebekkah. "Chocolate soft serve for Millie. And I'd like a strawberry shake."

"Coming right up. And your usual, boss." She got busy scooping ice cream as Lucy turned to regard the stranger on the stool beside her.

"Boss?"

He quirked an eyebrow and grinned back at her. "Ja, didn't I tell you? I'm Amos Fisher. My family owns Fisher's Hardware.

That's how I know I won't get into trouble for spilling the paint. Well, as long as my *dat* doesn't find out."

Amos accepted his root beer float from Rebekkah and watched as Lucy Beiler settled her young sister in her lap and tucked a napkin into the neck of her pink hoodie before handing her a spoon. The little girl tucked into the small dish of ice cream, and her sister smiled as she took her first taste of her milkshake. "Yum!"

"Rebekkah makes them right." He took a big sip of his float before sighing with satisfaction. "I've always loved these, ever since I was a kid and it was my *grossmammi* behind this counter. She always gave me extra cherries. Hey, Rebekkah, where are my extra cherries?"

"I forgot what a big kid you are, boss." Rebekkah pulled a jar from a small fridge behind the counter. "Move your glass over here so we don't get cherry juice all over the counter."

Grinning like a kid, he complied, and Rebekkah dumped several cherries and quite a bit of juice into his glass.

"Perfect."

They finished their treats in companionable silence. When they were done, Amos glanced at Millie and chuckled.

"There's as much chocolate on her face and the napkin as in her tummy, I'll bet."

"Oh, ja. Hence the napkin."

Rebekkah handed her a dampened paper towel, and Lucy cleaned her sister's face and hands before removing the makeshift bib. Amazingly, there was no chocolate on her pink hoodie.

"She's adorable. And I like her pink piggy. How old is she?"

"My sister or the pig?" Lucy's dark brown eyes twinkled mischievously, and Amos fought to catch his breath. Lucy was quietly stunning, with her chocolate eyes and hair to match, tucked up into her heart-shaped prayer kapp. He struggled to remember the question.

"I figure your sister is the elder of the two?"

"Ja, but not by much. Millie will be three on Christmas Day. The pig was a gift from our sister-in-law, Neva."

He frowned, trying to remember the various Beiler siblings. "Neva is married to Mose, ja?"

Lucy nodded. "They're much older than I am. Mose is forty-two. He and Neva have six *kinner*, and they live in the big house on our farm. Millie and I live in the dawdi haus."

"I don't know him well, although I do know several of your siblings—the ones who live in Shipshewana, Indiana. I just moved back from there a few months ago, when my older *bruder*, Sam, died."

Lucy paused to think for a moment. "Ach, ja. Sam Fisher was your bruder. I knew him from services."

He nodded. "He took over the store from our parents years ago, but he recently died of cancer. I came home to run the business when he got too sick."

"I know how hard it is to lose someone close. My parents died within a year of each other. My daed in a farming accident and then my maem when Millie was born. I'm sorry for your loss."

"It's Gott's *wille*."

"Ja, and that is a comfort. But I'm still sorry for your loss. Like I said, I know how hard it is."

He smiled at her. "Denki, Lucy. I appreciate it."

"But you grew up here, ja? It wonders me that I don't remember you."

"I'm considerably older than you. I'm twenty-eight. When I turned eighteen, right after I was baptized, I moved to

Shipshewana and started learning the carpentry trade. To be honest, while I loved Sam, we got along better with a little distance. I didn't want to work for him. We would have banged heads about everything. So I accepted an invitation from a cousin there, and I've been there ever since."

"That explains it. I'm twenty-one. You would only have been in school for about a year after I got there, and you certainly wouldn't have had time for a little girl only six years old!"

He laughed. "I think I remember you, though. Long brown braids and big brown eyes. And I seem to recall you liked to catch bugs. The teacher didn't appreciate your scientific curiosity, as I remember."

"That was me! Poor Amber Coblentz! She hated bugs, and I was always taking one inside to show her. I still like bugs, but now my audience consists of Millie, who also thinks they're very cool."

"Lucky you!"

"Ja, and lucky Amber too. She married a shopkeeper from Ohio. I ran into her at a wedding a couple years ago. They live in his hometown above their dry goods store—fewer bugs than on the farm!"

Millie tugged on Lucy's bonnet string and signed, "Down."

Lucy sighed. "I think we've pushed our luck far enough when it comes to this little girl's patience for sitting still."

He offered her a hand down from the stool. She accepted, her eyes shyly meeting his, and she blushed.

Amos was surprised to feel a little tingle in his hand as Lucy briefly held it while she climbed down from the stool. Not only had he enjoyed his time with the lovely young woman and her adorable sister, but he was finding that he wished they could spend more time together.

What are you thinking, man? You just got back after being away for years. You're not looking for an entanglement right now!

But Amos didn't feel like listening to his subconscious. "It was very gut getting to know you a bit, Lucy. And you too, Millie," he told the little girl who was gazing at everything they passed with wide eyes. "I hope to run into you both again soon. Except maybe not literally next time."

Lucy laughed, appreciating his twinkling hazel eyes and the way his sandy-brown hair, just a bit too long, brushed the collar of his green-and-white-striped Fisher's Hardware shirt.

"Well, maybe I'll see you at services? I attend here in Bird-in-Hand."

He considered the idea. "I've been attending services in Lancaster with my cousins. Maybe I'll check out the services here. Is this a church Sunday coming up?"

"Ja, we're meeting at my neighbor's place, just a mile or so from my home." She gave him the address and then, saying goodbye, started toward the door.

Millie tugged her hand, and she looked down at the child. "What is it, lieb? You've still got Pinky."

Millie signed, "Fix shower."

Lucy slapped her forehead. "Oh, ja! Denki, Millie. I almost forgot what we came here for in the first place!"

"You mean, it wasn't to spill paint and eat ice cream? I'm crushed."

"Ha ha. Those were definitely bonuses, but we actually came here to buy caulk so I can make the shower usable in the dawdi haus. It's leaking into the basement now."

"Well then, follow me." He led her to the plumbing section, pulled a tube of caulk from the shelf, and held it out to her. "I believe this is what you need."

She looked at the label. "That looks like what Mose told me to buy. Denki."

"I strive for excellent customer service."

"Well, you've achieved it today. The ice cream didn't hurt." She grinned at him, revealing a set of dimples and strong, even teeth.

Uh-oh, she just sparkles. I'm in trouble. "Come on, I'll check you out so you can go caulk your shower." He led her to the checkout and indicated to the woman standing there that he'd take care of the sale. "Go ahead and take a break, Melba. I'll keep an eye on things for a bit."

She looked with open curiosity at Lucy and Millie, then winked at him and turned toward the back of the store. "Okay, boss, see you in fifteen minutes!"

"Did she just wink at me?"

"Ja, she did," Lucy confirmed. "You ate ice cream with an unmarried Amish woman. You are in big trouble now."

He threw back his head and laughed. "Does anything ruffle your feathers?"

"When you're a single woman raising a child, you need to develop a thick skin."

His smile slipped. "You don't mean people think Millie is your daughter?"

"You did."

He frowned. "Huh. I did. But I also assumed you were married." He stared at her for a few beats, then blurted out, "You're not, are you? Married?"

She shook her head. "Nee. Single woman raising a child, remember?"

"Ach, ja." He felt himself blushing a bit. "And people have judged you?"

She shrugged. "Some people assume I'm an unmarried mother.

And even among people who know the situation, there are those who think it isn't proper for a young, single woman to be raising a child alone."

He rang up her purchase and bagged it, but when she reached for it, he drew it back. "I'll carry this heavy package out to your buggy. Just part of the service!"

"Really? You'd do the same for anyone, hmm?"

He grinned. "Ja, of course! Ah, here comes Melba, back from her break already. I'm going to walk out with the Beilers. I'll be right back."

"Take your time!" She winked again.

He stared at her, then turned and followed Lucy and Millie out of the store. "Did she wink at me again?"

"I'm afraid so."

Amos shook his head in mock sorrow. "I can see I'm going to have to have a talk with her about respecting her boss. Sure, she may have changed my diapers when I was a *boppli*, but that doesn't mean she can just be winking at me left and right!"

Lucy strapped Millie into her car seat and then climbed up into the buggy. Taking the reins in her hands, she looked at Amos. "Are you sure? She seems to think she can."

He handed her the small bag containing the tube of caulk and was about to ask if he could see her again when a man's voice interrupted them. Amos saw Lucy's face at the sound of the voice, and the alarm on it raised his hackles.

He turned and saw a young Amish man and woman standing together next to an old buggy. The woman looked uncomfortable, and she put her hand on her *mann's* arm, as if urging him away. The man, a burly fellow with a brown beard showing a couple of years' growth, and an unpleasant look in his eye, shook off his wife's hand.

"Aren't you going to answer me, Lucy? Or are you too gut for me now?"

"Come on, Johnny, let's go inside. I need to get those jars and get back home."

"I'll go when I'm ready." The man didn't even look at his wife, who glanced uncertainly between him, Lucy, and Amos before putting her head down and hurrying into the store.

"Is there a problem here?" Amos asked cautiously, keeping himself between the obviously angry man and Lucy's buggy.

"What business is it of yours?"

Raising his eyebrows at the man's surly attitude, Amos crossed his arms over his chest. "I'm Amos Fisher. This is my store. Everything that happens here is my business."

"Well, ain't you fancy? Lucy, you're keeping company with fancy Amish folk now?"

Lucy bit her lip and glanced back to check on Millie, who was busy with her piggy.

"Johnny, you made it perfectly clear last time I saw you that you had nothing else to say to me."

He laughed, an ugly sound, and spat on the parking lot by Amos' feet. "I just wondered how you and the kid are getting on. Is she still alive? Or did you give everything up for nothing?"

At Lucy's gasp, Amos decided he'd had enough. "I don't know who you are, but you need to do your shopping and then leave."

The man eyed Amos speculatively and spat again. "I'm John Zook, Lucy's ex-fiancé."

Lucy sat up straight and glared at the man. "For the record, we were never engaged. In case you've forgotten how it was, we courted for almost a year, but when I told you I'd be raising my schwester, you said you weren't interested in that, and dropped me like a hot brick and married someone else. I have nothing to say to you."

Zook sneered at Lucy and spat again. Amos realized he was chewing tobacco, a habit he considered disgusting.

"It's your fault I married that mouse. You should have given the brat to one of your married kin, not tried to raise it yourself! You had no business ruining my plans! After all the time I invested in you too. You're an ungrateful, selfish woman, Lucy Beiler. And you look haggard. No wonder you're *en alt maedel*."

Amos stepped forward and took the man's arm, turning him toward his buggy and marching him over to it.

"That's it. You leave now. We'll find your wife a ride home."

"Hey!" Zook sputtered, "Take your hands off me!"

"Get into the buggy. Now."

The two men faced off, Lucy's pale face watching from inside the buggy, where Amos knew she stayed to protect Millie.

"I'll show you what happens when you push John Zook around." But at that moment, a police siren squawked, two short blats, and a Lancaster County sheriff's cruiser pulled up next to the buggies.

"Great, I'll be hearing from the bishop about this, for sure and certain," Amos muttered, stepping back from Zook, who turned to face the deputy.

"Everything okay here, folks?" the young deputy asked. "Oh, Amos, I didn't realize you were part of this. We got a call about a possible fight in your parking lot." He eyed John Zook. "Why am I not surprised to find you where there's trouble, Mr. Zook?"

Zook's face turned beet red above his beard, and Amos watched him attempt to gain control over his anger. He could tell by the way the deputy shifted away cautiously that this wasn't the first time he'd interacted with Zook.

"I wasn't doing anything, just catching up with an old friend," Zook spat, looking up at Lucy in the buggy. The deputy followed his gaze and saw Lucy sitting, white-faced, in the vehicle.

"Ma'am," he nodded politely. "We got a call that this man was harassing you. Do you want to file a complaint?"

Lucy lifted her chin and gave a decisive shake of her head. "No, denki. He was unpleasant, but I just want him to leave me alone."

The deputy nodded slowly. "What about you, Amos? He looked like he was getting ready to swing at you when I pulled in."

Amos briefly considered having Zook hauled off to jail but decided it would be more trouble than the satisfaction would be worth. And it wasn't the Amish way. Regretfully, he shook his head. "Nee, Tom, denki. I doubt he will be a problem again, because he is no longer welcome in my store."

At that moment, Mrs. Zook came hurrying out of the store, a bag clutched in her arms. Taking in the scene, she looked horrified. "John! What's going on? Why is an *Englisch* policeman here? Are you in trouble again?"

"Get in the buggy, *fraa*," Zook snarled at his downtrodden wife. "We're going home."

Amos felt sorry for the woman, who clambered into the buggy and sat staring straight ahead, making eye contact with no one.

Zook spat on the pavement again. "I don't want to shop in your store anyway. Your selection is no gut!" He climbed into his buggy and jerked his gelding's head roughly around. The horse snorted in protest, and he yelled at it, driving it out of the parking lot and into the street without another word.

"He's a troublemaker, Amos. Watch out for him," the deputy said. Then, nodding again to Lucy, he climbed back into his cruiser and drove away.

"He is a *druvvel-machah*, but I doubt he'll trouble me again," Amos said, walking back to Lucy. "You were engaged to him?"

"Nee! Well, almost. I'll. . .I'll tell you about it another time, okay? I'm not going to be able to talk calmly right now, and I need to get Millie home. I'm sorry I brought trouble to your place of business, though."

"You didn't make him show up here."

"Nee. I haven't seen him since he dumped me and left the district. I heard he'd found a fraa in a neighboring one, and assumed he was living and working there. I've never seen her before. Oh, this is so upsetting!" She covered her face, and Amos realized she was crying.

"Hey! No need for tears! The guy didn't hurt anyone."

"But it's so embarrassing!"

"Why should you be embarrassed? You didn't do anything. He's the one who should be embarrassed. And his wife, unfortunately."

"But everyone will hear of this! They'll talk about us. I hate that."

Amos started to say nobody would find out from him, but he followed Lucy's eyes and saw that they had a small audience of English and Amish standing outside the store, watching.

"Oh bother," he muttered. "Okay, show's over, folks, everyone go about your business, please."

"Just making sure you didn't need help, Amos," Melba called from where she stood, halfway out the open doorway of the shop. The others nodded, and Amos realized they weren't snooping as much as having his back.

"Denki, we're fine. I'll be in soon." He turned back to Lucy, his face serious. "Lucy, I am very sorry all that happened, but none of it was your fault. I want you to know, I really enjoyed my time with you and Millie. I would like to spend more time with you both. If I come to services here Sunday, will you sit with me afterward, during lunch?"

Lucy brushed tears from her eyes and looked at him as if trying to figure out whether he was sincere. He smiled reassuringly, and after a moment a soft smile flitted across her lips. He sent up a quick prayer that she would say yes. After a few moments, she nodded, putting him out of his misery.

"Ja, Amos, I believe Millie and I would both enjoy that."

Amos' grin split his face. "Really? That's wonderful gut! So, I'll see you in a few days." He stepped back from her buggy. "Keep an eye open for Zook. If you see him anywhere near you, I want to know, okay?"

"I don't think he'll be a problem. It's been almost three years, and this is the first time I've seen him. But, if I do, I'll tell you."

She smiled tentatively again, then gently turned her horse toward the road.

Watching the compelling pair drive away, Amos offered up a prayer.

You know I haven't been looking for romance, Vader. *I'm still not sure I'm ready for anything like that. But, I guess I'm plenty old enough to think about finding a fraa and settling down. Please, keep Lucy and Millie from harm, Vader. I guess I'll just wait and see what You have in mind for us. Your will be done.*

He watched Lucy drive away toward her farm and smiled wryly. *My* brieder *will have a gut laugh at my expense, after all the girls I ducked in Shipshewana! I guess Gott does work in mysterious ways!*

CHAPTER TWO

That should hold us for the week." Neva Beiler washed her hands to remove flour and dough while Lucy slid the last four loaves of bread into the oven.

"Ja, even with your hungry hoard eating it almost faster than we can bake it!" Lucy laughed as she walked to the door between the living room and kitchen in her brother and sister-in-law's home.

Her nieces Emma, eighteen, and Linda, sixteen, were playing on the floor with Millie. They had spread plastic animals across the rug and built pens for them with wooden blocks.

Emma gave her a thumbs-up. Lucy smiled and nodded and withdrew into the kitchen.

"Have some *kaffi*." Neva set a couple of mugs on the table, then sank into one of the kitchen chairs with a deep sigh. "Ah, a gut day's work. And doesn't it smell heavenly in here?"

Lucy nodded, inhaling the scents of coffee and fresh, hot bread. "Ja, I love baking day."

Lucy had joined Neva in baking for their two households shortly after Millie's birth. Having taken on the responsibility of raising a child on her own—let alone a disabled child— she'd found she often didn't have time for everyday chores.

Neva had suggested simplifying things by combining household chores such as baking and washing, and Lucy had readily agreed.

"It's a lot more enjoyable since you and our little sunbeam started coming over to spend it with us!"

Lucy smiled at her sister-in-law, whom she loved as dearly as any of her sisters. "Honestly, Neva, I don't know how I'd have managed otherwise. Your kinner are so gut with her! And since I spend a lot of time alone with a little child, it's very nice to come here and be with adults."

"Well, we love having you both here. Now, grab the tin of cookies. The girls will be ready for a snack soon enough."

Lucy grabbed the cookie tin from the counter. They had filled it that morning. They'd also made enough bread for both households for a week.

She stirred some cream into her coffee and took a small sip, her mind on the incident at the hardware store the day before.

I'm going to see what Neva thinks about the whole thing. She always has gut advice, and she won't blab my business to everyone in the family.

"You look like your thoughts are too heavy for your neck," Neva observed, choosing a couple of cookies from the tin.

Lucy sighed again. "There is something I'd like to run past you, if you don't mind?"

Lucy explained about her trip to Fisher's Hardware and how much she'd enjoyed meeting Amos. She related the mishap with the paint cans, which caused both women to laugh.

"It sounds as if he's a very nice man. Will he come to services Sunday, do you think?"

Lucy shrugged. "I'm hoping he will." She smiled shyly, and Neva grinned back.

"Well, it's about time you showed some interest in a nice, eligible man! You haven't looked at anyone since that no-good Johnny Zook walked away just when you needed him most. Good riddance."

"It's not as if any eligible man has really looked at me. Men my age seem to think twice about taking on a fraa who comes with a child, especially one who needs so much medical care."

Neva wrinkled her nose. "Puh, I knew the right man, a man who can see past his own nose, would eventually come around and see what a jewel you are. The fact that it's taken three years is probably gut. You've had time to really learn how to care for Millie's needs. You've figured out the English medical system, and that child is simply thriving! You are an excellent mother and an excellent catch."

Lucy's mouth had dropped open somewhere in the middle of Neva's impassioned speech, and she simply stared at her sister-in-law, humbled and amazed she had such a high opinion of her.

"Well, close your mouth before a fly gets in!" Neva smiled and drank some coffee. "Why are you surprised that I think you're doing a gut job? Don't you think your bruder and I would have said something if we didn't think so?"

Lucy considered. *Mose and Neva are both straight-talking people you could trust to tell you the truth. I guess they would have said something a long time ago if they didn't think I was doing a gut job with Millie. After all, Millie is Mose's little schwester too!*

She smiled at Neva warmly. "Denki, Neva. I know you'd have said something. But thinking I'm doing okay is a far cry from all those nice things you just said!"

Neva shrugged and pushed up from the table to gather together dishes for a snack for Millie and her two babysitters. "I guess I didn't think you needed to hear it before. So, now you can be confident when you're with Amos—no second-guessing yourself, *fashtay?*"

"Ja, I understand," Lucy said. "Um, there is something else that happened yesterday, though. Speaking of Johnny Zook. . ." She told Neva about her run-in with Johnny in the parking lot, and Neva's generous mouth grew grim.

"Goodness, do you think Amos would have fought with him? That would go against the *Ordnung!*"

"Nee. I don't think so, but Amos kept Johnny from coming near me. Johnny was saying really rude things. I was happy when Deputy Miller showed up."

Neva nodded. "Gut. I know we usually prefer to avoid the English police becoming involved in our affairs, but if Johnny was threatening you and our sister, then I can't say I'm sorry they came. Let's hope he stays away from Bird-in-Hand from now on."

Lucy agreed, but inside, she worried. Johnny had been very unreasonable about blaming his own unhappy life on her choices.

"He made me uneasy. If you see him around, please don't try to talk to him."

Neva planted her hands on her generous hips. "If I see him around, I'll let your bruder know. He'll take care of it. Now, let's get those girls in here so we can wrap up snack time and I can start supper. Will you and Millie be staying?"

"Denki, we'd love that." Lucy loved being included in her oldest brother's large family. It got a little lonely in the dawdi haus sometimes. But she valued her independence too much to move in with any of her brothers or sisters. So the arrangement with Neva and Mose was just right.

CHAPTER THREE

*S*unday after services, Lucy carried a sleepy Millie outside and took a seat at one of the picnic tables already set up under a large tent in the side yard. The men and boys were carrying benches outside, and the women were setting up the food tables.

She looked around, hoping to catch sight of Amos, who, along with one of his cousins, had attended services that morning.

"Ach, there you are, Lucy! We're wonderful busy, but you need to watch this little one, as I know she has the wanderlust!" Their sister Katie set two cups on the picnic table.

Lucy handed the sippy cup to Millie and drank deeply from the other cup. "Mmm. Did you make this? It's really gut!"

Katie smiled and ran her hand over Millie's braids. "Ja, it hits the spot. Well, you two stay here and save me a few seats. I'll be back with Isaiah and the boys in a few minutes." She hurried away, and Lucy enjoyed another sip of sweet lemonade.

I'm blessed to have such a thoughtful sister, which is what I'll remind myself of when my three boisterous nephews join us.

Katie was married to Isaiah Schrock, whose father, Elam, was the bishop of their church district. Isaiah also served as a minister for the district. Their three sons, Levi, ten; Zeke, six; and Carter, four, never seemed to lack energy.

Lucy noticed that the men were going through the food line, and she watched for her brother-in-law and nephews, ready to wave at them to come join her when they got through the line.

"*Guder mariye,*" a deep voice said, making her jump a little. "Is there room here for us?"

Lucy looked up and saw Amos and another man standing across the table from her, both carrying plates laden with food.

"Ach, you startled me! Ja, I'm saving seats, but there's plenty of room."

The men sat down across from Lucy. "This is my cousin, Reuben Lambright. He came with me to see if there are any pretty *maedels* in your district. Reuben, this is Lucy Beiler, and her little sister, Millie."

"Well look, I found two pretty maedels right away!" Amos' cousin was a big man with crinkly laugh lines beside his ice-blue eyes and white-blond hair under his hat.

"Too bad for you I saw them first, cousin," Amos joked.

Reuben chuckled and smiled at Millie. "And who do we have here? Millie? Is that your pig?"

Millie smiled at the man and held Pinky out for his inspection. He made appropriate noises of admiration, which pleased the child, who giggled and hugged her pig. Reuben picked up his fork and began to eat.

"Oh boy, Amos, I think I may switch districts for good. The food here is much better! Don't tell my *mudder* I said so."

Amos nodded, his mouth full of fried chicken. He swallowed. "This is *appeditlich*. I may need seconds."

Lucy chuckled. "You have to take them with your firsts around here. The food disappears too fast to go back!"

"Ach, *vell*, I'll just enjoy what I have then. These noodles are also wonderful gut!"

"Ja, they are!" Reuben took a big bite of his serving.

Lucy blushed. "Denki. I made the noodles."

Reuben nudged Amos with his elbow. "There you go, Amos. Better snatch her up. Pretty, and a gut cook!" He wiggled his eyebrows and took another bite of Lucy's noodles.

Lucy wasn't sure how to react, having little experience with flirtatious men. She glanced uncertainly at Amos, who gave her a reassuring smile. "Don't let Reuben's teasing bother you. He was raised in a barn and doesn't know how to behave in polite company."

"Hey! My mudder wouldn't like you calling her house a barn." Reuben sent his cousin a mock glare, causing Lucy to giggle. She decided Reuben meant nothing by his flirting. It must just be his nature.

At that moment, Katie bustled up with her brood. "Oh, you have company, Lucy! Did you save us seats?"

"Ja, there's just enough room for all of us. The table seats eight."

Isaiah eyed the two strange men, then settled down next to Lucy, gesturing for his boys to sit beside him on his other side. He nodded at the visitors to his district. "*Willkumme*, I'm Isaiah Schrock, Lucy's brother-in-law. Are you visiting our district?"

Amos swallowed his food and blotted his lips with a napkin before answering. "Ja, at Lucy's invitation. I'm Amos Fisher, and this is my cousin, Reuben Lambright."

"Fisher…ach, ja, now I know why you look familiar. I've seen you at your store. Welcome to our district."

Amos and Reuben smiled and resumed eating.

Katie set her drink in the place beside Amos and looked at

Lucy. "The men are through the line. We'd better get our food before it's gone."

"I'd be happy to hold Millie, if she'll let me. I started eating before Isaiah. I'm almost finished." Amos smiled at the child, who grinned openly back at him.

Lucy looked uncertainly at Millie. She was usually easygoing, and she obviously liked Amos, but you never knew. "Would you like to sit with Amos, lieb?"

Millie nodded happily, and Lucy stood and handed her across to Amos. "I'll be right back with your lunch, Millie."

She and Katie started across the yard.

"My, he's a handsome man," Katie said, gesturing back toward Amos with her chin. "Where's he been hiding?"

"He's been living in Indiana, working as a carpenter. But he came home recently to run the family store in Bird-in-Hand after his brother died."

"Ach, ja! Of course. They've always gone to services in Lancaster. I guess they live in between, so I really don't know the family well. But I remember hearing about the brother. Cancer, right? So sad, but Gott has His plan."

They filled their plates with good food. Lucy carried two—one for herself and one for Millie.

Katie gave a glad little cry. "Oh gut! There's some of Joanna's rhubarb pie left! She makes the best filling, though I think my crust edges hers out." Joanna was Lucy and Katie's sister. At twenty-six, she was a widow with two young kinner. It was an open secret in the family that she was seeing Tom Stutzman, a young man in the district who had lost his wife and was raising their three kinner by himself. Lucy suspected that it wouldn't be long before they decided to turn two families into one. "You do make very gut piecrust, Katie, but I love Joanna's too. Grab me a piece too, please."

Katie put two slices on her plate, and they walked back to their picnic table.

Lucy sat down and placed Millie's plate next to her own. "Denki, Amos, you can hand her over."

"I'm done eating. Why don't you let me hold her while she eats? That way you can enjoy your own food."

She wondered when she'd last been able to eat without a squirmy toddler in her lap. "If you're sure?"

"I think that's *wunderbar* nice of you, and Lucy accepts," Katie said, picking up Millie's plate and handing it across the table to Amos.

Lucy raised her eyebrows and looked at her sister, who made a face and indicated Lucy should eat. "Let the man help you out. He's obviously gut with the little girl!"

"I've had plenty of practice with my nieces and nephews. I like kinner, and Millie is a gut little girl."

"Not always," Lucy muttered, and Amos grinned.

Millie dug into her favorite food, macaroni and cheese.

Katie sat down and smiled at Amos. "You look very natural holding the boppli, Amos. You'll make someone a gut mann."

Lucy gave her sister a toothy smile. "Katie, why don't you tell us about your latest quilting project?" Turning to Amos, she explained, "Katie is an award-winning quilter. Her original designs have taken first place several times at the county fair, and once at the state fair!"

"Really? That's impressive, considering how many gut quilters there are in Pennsylvania."

Katie blushed—something you didn't see every day, and Lucy quickly took a sip of lemonade to hide her smirk. *That'll teach you to matchmake, sis!*

"My passion is in designing new takes on traditional patterns. I'm working on a log cabin variation right now. Actually, Lucy is a very gut quilter in her own right. She's sold many quilts at the tourist shop in town and some in shops in Lancaster, Ronks, and Intercourse."

Lucy blinked. She hadn't expected Katie to turn the tables on her. "My quilts will keep you warm in the winter, but they're nowhere near the works of art that yours are."

"It's nice when something can be both practical and attractive," Amos said, wiping a bit of cheese from the corner of Millie's mouth. "I'd love to see your quilts, Lucy."

"Really?"

"Ja, why are you surprised?"

"I don't know. Nobody has ever asked before."

"Well, I'm asking now. Where do you quilt?"

"Not in my cottage. There isn't room. Neva has a nice big room in the main house where we can set up two quilt frames at once."

Katie nodded. "Ja, it's very handy. Her Mose set it up for her. She's quite a gut quilter too."

He looked thoughtful. "I've been thinking I'd like to expand and offer local crafts at the hardware store."

"You're really serious?" Lucy asked.

"Ja, of course."

"That's probably a very gut idea. I'm sorry, I'm just not used to a man asking about quilting, I guess."

"I think it can only be gut to help people in our community have more opportunities to thrive, ain't so?"

Lucy nodded. "Of course. When would you like to come?"

He looked at Reuben, who grinned at him and shrugged. "Why not today, cousin?" Reuben asked. "You could drive her home and take a look at her work."

"How would you get home?" Amos asked, frowning at his cousin.

Maybe he was just being nice. It doesn't look like he wants to come, Lucy thought, watching the byplay between the two young men.

"That's a gut idea," Katie interjected. "Actually, I think Isaiah and I are driving to Lancaster this afternoon, to see his Aunt Amelia and Uncle Ben, aren't we, Isaiah? We could drop you home, Reuben. It would be no trouble."

She looked expectantly at her mann, who turned and slapped Amos on the shoulder. "Why not? I haven't seen Aunt Amelia and Uncle Ben in a few weeks, and they're always happy to see the boys."

"Did I hear there is to be a singing later?" Amos asked.

"Ja, but usually I don't go, because it's too late for Millie to stay up." Lucy tried not to think about how much she liked the idea of attending the singing with Amos.

"I'm sure Neva wouldn't mind keeping Millie this evening so you can attend the singing, Lucy," Katie gave a firm nod of her head that sent her kapp strings swinging. "Goodness, you never ask for anything! It's time you had a little fun."

Amos smiled across the table at her. "Well, what do you say? Up for a little fun in the form of a singing?"

Lucy swallowed nervously. "Ja, I am, if you're sure it's not going to interfere with other plans you have?"

"I'm sure. I'm secretly hoping for more of that rhubarb pie!"

She laughed. "Well then, count me in, as long as Neva doesn't mind watching Millie."

"So it's a plan! I'm sure Neva will be very happy to watch Millie." Katie grinned happily. "Boys, we're going to see Aunt Amelia and Uncle Ben!" She jumped up from the table. "Come, Lucy, we'd better tell Neva you're stopping by with Amos, and ask her about this evening. She'll want a bit of warning."

Katie jumped up and hurried off to find their sister-in-law, and Lucy looked helplessly at Amos. "She's a force of nature. If you have something else you need to do, it's really fine."

Amos stood, snuggling a drowsy Millie against his chest. "Don't try and get out of it now. I'm determined to see your quilts. Then we'll go to the singing and eat pie."

Isaiah stood as well. "Come, boys, let's find your mother. Reuben, we'll gather up our dishes and be ready to go in a few minutes. I want to tell my vader where we're going too."

"I'll be out here," Reuben told Isaiah. Then he turned to Amos and Lucy. "If you want to get going, I'll tell your sister you're headed home."

"I'll wait and be sure it's okay with Neva first," Lucy said. "Here she comes now with Katie."

Neva bustled up to the picnic table with Katie and looked between Lucy, Amos, and Reuben. When no one spoke, she put her hands on her hips. "Well? Isn't anyone going to introduce me?"

"Sorry, Neva! This is Amos Fisher and his cousin Reuben Lambright, from Lancaster."

"Nice to meet you both. I understand you want to drive our Lucy home and look at our quilts, of all things?"

"Ja, if you don't mind. I'm thinking of carrying local crafts at the hardware store."

She squinted at him for a few moments, then gave a nod. "Okay, that's fine. And then you want to drive our Lucy to the singing?"

"Neva, I'm right here," Lucy said, waving at her sister-in-law.

"I'm acting in place of your parents, Lucy. I'm sure Amos understands."

"Um, yes, of course," he said, squirming a bit. "I'll drive her to the singing and then home again. If that's oll recht with you and your mann, that is."

"Excuse me, but as I'm twenty-one years old, I believe I can accept my own invitations. I do appreciate your motivation, though, Neva. So, do you mind watching Millie tonight for me?"

"Of course not! The child is no trouble. I was just checking." She turned and started back to the house. "You two go on ahead in Amos' buggy. One of the kids will drive your rig home, Lucy. We'll see you at the house in a few minutes."

Katie gave a satisfied smirk. "That's settled, then. Have a gut time! Reuben, are you ready? Our buggy is just over there. See you later, Lucy!"

Reuben stood and followed Katie, giving Amos and Lucy a little wave. "Have fun. See you later, cousin."

And then it was just the two of them and Millie, and suddenly the moment seemed awkward.

"So," he started at the same time as she said, "Well."

They looked at each other and laughed. "Here we go again!" She grinned at him. He grinned back, but then his smile faded as something between them snapped. Her eyes widened, and he reached out a hand. She wasn't sure what would have happened if Millie hadn't chosen that moment to reach for her older sister, leaning out of Amos' arms precariously.

"Millie! Be careful! You'll fall!" Lucy cried, reaching out and taking the child from Amos. She snuggled her sister close then chanced a glance at their new friend. She thought she caught a regretful expression flickering across his strong face before he said, "I wouldn't have let the boppli fall, Lucy. You can trust me."

She considered him a moment. "Ja, I think I can."

Millie leaned back and whispered, "Pinky?"

"Oh! Where is Pinky?" Lucy looked around but didn't see

the toy. Millie's bottom lip quivered. "Pinky," she said, her big blue eyes filling with tears.

"It's okay, lieb, we'll find her."

"The pig was just here." Amos looked underneath the picnic table. "Here it is!" He leaned down and snagged the toy and handed it to Millie, who squealed with excitement. "Whew! Close call." They moved Millie's car seat to Amos' buggy, and a few minutes later they were on their way. "She's going to be asleep before we're out of the driveway."

"Well, she can use a nap. Although it'll make things harder later for Neva." She shrugged. "Oh well! Nothing we can do about that!"

They drove the short distance to Lucy's family farm in companionable silence, just enjoying the crisp fall afternoon.

"Nice place," Amos commented as they turned into the driveway and headed for the main house. "Your bruder and sister-in-law take gut care of it."

She nodded. "Ja, just like Dat and Maem did before us."

"I respect that continuity," he said. "It's important to me and my family too, which is why I'm home running the hardware store instead of building furniture in Indiana. Family is the most important thing, after all." He looked around in appreciation as they neared the house.

She pointed to the small dawdi haus set back in the trees about a hundred feet from the main house. "There's where Millie and I live. It used to be my *grossdaddi* and grossmammi's house. Now it's mine."

"It looks nice and tight," he commented. "And I like your flowers."

"I love flowers. They make me happy. In fact, the quilt I'm working on right now is a wall hanging with a dogwood pattern, representing God's love for creation."

"That sounds lovely."

"Denki. I just finished a pair of matching twin quilts in green and red, with appliquéd fir trees in each block. That sort of thing sells very well this time of year."

He nodded. "My mudder switches out the quilt on her bed each year around Christmas to a pretty snowflake patterned quilt made by her sister in Illinois."

"That sounds pretty. And a nice connection to your aunt who lives so far away."

They pulled up to the hitching post, and Amos jumped out to tie the horse. Lucy climbed out and went to lift Millie from her car seat, but Amos stepped up beside her and put a hand on her arm. "Let me, will you? You show me where to put her when we get inside."

She nodded and watched as he carefully unstrapped and lifted the car seat out of the buggy, with all the care she imagined a dat would exhibit.

He smiled at her. "Okay! Let's go inside. I'm looking forward to seeing your work, and Katie's and Neva's!"

She led the way to the house and turned to wave as she heard Mose and Neva's buggy come up the driveway, followed by her mare, Athena, pulling her buggy, driven by Emma.

Her family was around her. Her belly was full of gut food. She had spent the morning worshiping with her church community. Her baby was sleeping the sleep of a child who knows she is safe and loved. And an interesting man was spending time with her.

Life is gut! Lucy thought. *Gott is gut!*

CHAPTER FOUR

$\mathcal{T}$uesday morning Lucy was up early, getting her barn chores done before Millie awoke.

"There you go, Athena, all clean." She laid the pitchfork aside and dug into her pocket for a carrot she'd brought for the mare.

Her milk cow, Tansy, was contentedly chewing her cud, while that year's calf, Noodles, snoozed in the straw near her feet.

"Just the chickens left, and I'm done." She looked around to be sure she hadn't missed anything, then turned out the battery lantern and let herself out the side door into the cold twilight of predawn.

She was about to walk across her small yard to the chicken coop when movement in the shadows caught her eye. Uneasy at the notion that it could be a coyote, she called, "Shoo! No chicken breakfast for you today!"

She waited another moment, and when nothing moved, she let out a shaky laugh. "Probably just a possum."

She'd nearly reached the coop when a large form detached itself from the shadows and stepped into her path.

She gasped and stumbled back. "Who is that? Mose?"

"No, it's not Mose, it's John."

"John Zook? What are you doing here?"

He gave a nasty laugh. "No 'guder mariye' for me, Lucy? That's not very polite."

Lucy glanced over at the main house, where a cheery light shone in the kitchen window—evidence that Neva was up making breakfast, which probably meant Mose was in the barn doing his chores.

John raised his hands in a calming gesture. "I'm not here to hurt you. I just want to talk, like I said the other day before that jerk Amos Fisher blew everything out of proportion."

She shook her head, wondering if they were remembering the same incident. But she decided it probably wasn't the best time to point that out. "Er, guder mariye, Johnny."

"John. I'm not a boy anymore."

She swallowed. "Sorry. John."

He crossed his arms and glared at her. "Look, I made a mistake three years ago. I should have taken you with the kid. Too late now. And now I'm stuck in a bad marriage with a stupid woman." He took a step closer to her and reached out to catch one of her kapp strings in his work-roughened hand. She took an involuntary step back, and her kapp came off, pulling pins with it and swinging from his hand, strands of her hair escaping to twist in the morning breeze.

He stared at her. "You are still beautiful, Lucy. Maybe we could still be. . .friends?"

"Friends?"

"Ja, you know. I could come over here sometimes in the evenings."

She shook her head. "I'm busy with Millie in the evenings."

He gave an impatient grunt. "After she falls asleep. Late. You know, after my fraa falls asleep."

Her mouth dropped open, and she didn't know what to say to him. "This. . .this is what you wanted to talk to me about at the hardware store?"

"Nee. Running into you there was an accident. But then I saw Fisher flirting with you, and I got angry at the unfairness of it all. So I came over here this morning to tell you that you aren't any better than I am! And I was watching you do your chores, and it just sort of occurred to me that you're a woman alone, and you're not likely to marry while you have that brat. Maybe you'd like a man's company?"

"What? Nee! That wouldn't be right! You're married!" She reached for her kapp. "John, give me my kapp! You shouldn't be here. You should be home with your fraa! I don't want anything to do with you. I would have married you three years ago, but you made your choice. And calling my sister a brat isn't likely to make me sorry for that choice! Now leave, before I call Mose."

His face darkened, and an ugly look came into his eyes. He took a step toward her, and she danced back several steps, stumbling and nearly falling over an exposed tree root. She looked around desperately, but there was no escaping the fact that if she ran, he might go into the cottage and hurt Millie.

He advanced another step. "You think you're too gut for me, don't you, Lucy? After all I did for you and your family? Remember how I helped you and your mudder move into this house after your dat died in that farming accident? Remember the gut times we had? The plans we made? And when your mudder found out she was *ime family weg*, I even agreed to wait for you when you decided you couldn't leave her until after her baby was born. Who could predict she'd join her mann in heaven so soon? I did everything you wanted! Then you ruined it all by deciding to raise your sister instead of giving her up to one of your siblings as you ought to have done! You owed me! So now it's time to pay up."

Before she could answer, Neva called, "Lucy? Are you oll recht? Who is that with you? Mose! Mose! Come out here!" Lucy knew that somehow Neva had seen that she was in trouble.

The barn door crashed open, and Mose ran out, looking around. "What is it?"

"It's Lucy! Someone is bothering Lucy!"

Mose looked over and started their way at a quick trot, and John took a step back. "Think about what I said, Lucy." He turned and ran into the woods behind her small barn as Mose reached her.

"Lucy! Are you oll recht? Was that John Zook?" Mose reached out and took her gently by the arm, and she turned from where she'd been staring into the woods to look at him.

"Ja, but I don't understand. He made the choice to leave, not me."

"Come, lieb, you're shaking. Where's your kapp?"

"He pulled it off. I don't know where it is."

At that moment, Neva reached them, panting with the exertion of running across the farmyard. Behind her were Linda and Abram, the sixteen-year-old twins.

"Here's her kapp!" Linda said, reaching down and picking it up from the dirt, where John Zook had apparently dropped it.

She offered it to Lucy, who shook her head. "Nee, I don't want that. I'll get a fresh one." She looked toward the dawdi haus. "Millie! Is Millie oll recht?"

Abram looked at Mose, and the two hurried over to the dawdi haus and inside. Neva, Lucy, and Linda followed, and they entered the kitchen as the men returned from checking on Millie.

"She's still sound asleep in her crib," Mose said.

"What was that about?" Neva asked, steering Lucy to the

kitchen table and pushing her gently into a chair.

"I'm not sure."

"I'll make kaffi. You sit," Neva said.

"Maem, she's shaking," Linda said. "Are you cold, Lucy? Do you want a blanket?"

"Ja, please, there's one on the back of the sofa."

Linda got the colorful granny square afghan Lucy had crocheted the previous winter and handed it to her aunt. "Here you go, Lucy."

"Denki," Lucy said, wrapping herself in the warm blanket.

Neva took a seat and nodded to Mose to do the same. "Lucy, what did he say to you?"

Lucy looked at the twins and frowned. "Um, maybe the twins could go back to the main house? I don't want to talk about it in front of them."

Neva and Mose exchanged alarmed looks, and then Mose said, "Abram, Linda, go finish the chores. We'll all be along soon with the boppli."

Although obviously loath to leave, the twins knew better than to argue with their parents, and with a final glance at their aunt, they went out the back door.

"Did that man hurt you, lieb?" Neva softly asked, taking Lucy's hand in hers.

"Nee, not physically. But he said mean things about Millie again, and he. . .he suggested something improper to me."

Mose's eyes narrowed. "He did? What?"

"He suggested that he could come over here at night after his wife fell asleep and we could. . .could. . .keep company."

Neva's mouth dropped open in shock, and Mose turned and glared in the direction of the woods where John Zook had made his cowardly retreat.

"Well, I never!" Neva breathed. "Mose, what on earth do we do about this? We need to protect Lucy, but we don't want the whole community to hear about it!"

"I didn't do anything wrong, Neva."

"Of course not, lieb. But people can jump to wrong conclusions."

"I will speak with the bishop. We will handle this with the minimal amount of fuss possible." He ran his fingers through his beard. "Though in this community, that may not be saying much."

"Great. People have just gotten used to the fact that I'm raising Millie, and now a man I used to be associated with is going to ruin my reputation?" Her eyes flooded with tears. "Can't we just pretend this didn't happen?"

Neva and Mose again exchanged looks, and Mose regretfully shook his head. "Nee, child. I'm afraid he has proven to be potentially dangerous. We need to take steps to ensure he doesn't bother you again. That means intervention by the bishop."

Lucy sighed. "Oll recht. But I hate this. Why can't he just leave me alone?"

Neva gave her a hug. "Who knows why people do what they do? You just trust in Gott, and your big bruder, to make sure you're safe." She stood up and brushed invisible dust off her pristine white apron. "Now let's get that precious baby up and head over to the main house for some breakfast. All this will come out however it will come out. Fussing about it won't change a thing. I'll go get Millie, if you don't mind?"

"She'd love that. I'll gather up a few things," Lucy said, standing up. Mose stood as well.

"I'll wait for you all, just to be safe. Not that I expect John Zook to return today. But. . .I'll feel better."

Lucy nodded, and Neva went to get Millie.

As she readied herself and the baby to go to the main house,

Lucy couldn't help but fret just a little. Who made an indecent proposition like that? Not the young man that she thought she'd known. *Thank Gott I didn't marry him!*

Sometimes things did work out for the best, even if you couldn't see it at the time.

As they walked through the crisp morning sunshine to the main house, with Millie bundled up in Mose's arms and Neva chatting about their day, Lucy thought about Amos and wondered if there might be something there.

"We'll just have to wait and see!" Neva said brightly, and Lucy turned toward her sister-in-law in shock. Had she spoken her thoughts out loud?

At the sight of Lucy's face, Neva laughed. "You should see your face, Lucy! I don't know what you were thinking about, but what I said was, we'd have to see if we have enough flour on hand for next week's baking. If not, we'll have to run into town."

"Oh, I thought you'd read my mind."

"A mind reader, I'm not. Come, let's just enjoy some simple time together as a family. I'm sure the girls have breakfast ready, and I'm hungry! We're having dippy eggs!"

"Sounds like just what I need, Neva. Denki."

"Of course! Meanwhile, I want to run into Bird-in-Hand later and drop a couple quilts off at the tourist shops. Do you want to come along and take those two beautiful twin Christmas tree quilts?"

"Ja, I need to deliver them to Sarah at Just Plain Quilts. She called and said my queen-sized double wedding ring quilt sold, and she has a check for me."

"Wunderbar!" Neva smiled at Lucy. "That is a gorgeous quilt. I'll bet it was a hard one to give up, ja?"

Lucy nodded. "Ja, but I need the money, with Millie growing

so fast. I need to buy fabric for clothes for her, for one thing."

"Okay, then it's settled. We'll go over after we have breakfast. Lucy, I'd like us to stick close together until this business with John Zook is resolved, okay? Mose and I would rather you didn't go anywhere alone right now."

She looked like she expected Lucy to argue, but Lucy felt grateful that she had family who cared enough to put themselves out for her. "Denki. I really appreciate it. And I'd rather not run into him while I'm alone again." She shuddered. "He was very angry and frightening."

Neva put Millie into her high chair and then turned and gave Lucy an impulsive hug. Lucy felt herself tearing up, and she hugged her sister-in-law back tightly. "Denki for being so great, Neva," she whispered.

Neva pulled back, and Lucy saw that there were tears in Neva's eyes too. "Well, then!" the elder woman said, turning and briskly beginning to get breakfast onto the table. "Enough worry! Sufficient unto the day is the evil thereof!"

Smiling to herself, Lucy helped Neva prepare the meal with the twins, who hurried into the kitchen from the root cellar carrying jars of peaches and pears. Lucy took comfort in the simple family chore and the feeling of togetherness and safety it brought her.

Denki for my family, Vader, she thought. *And please, keep us all safe from harm, and let things return to normal. Thy will be done.*

CHAPTER FIVE

$\mathcal{A}$mos was taking a breather at the soda fountain in the hardware store, having just finished helping to unload a truckload of Christmas inventory ordered the previous spring. He'd been thinking about the idea he'd had about selling local crafts, and where they could put them in the store. After seeing the wonderful needlework at the Beiler farm, he realized he'd been missing out on an important market niche.

Rebekkah had just set his customary root beer float in front of him when a cheerful voice interrupted his reverie about whether he'd guessed right at the hardware spring market as to what would be popular this Christmas season.

"So! This is what the boss does while everyone else works."

He spun around on his swivel stool and smiled at the sight of Lucy's sister Katie standing there clutching one of her wriggly sons by the hand, the other two boys peering out from behind her skirts, eyes wide at the sight of the ice cream.

"Katie! *Wie gets?* Hello, boys."

"Boys, say hello to Mr. Fisher."

A chorus of "Hello, Mr. Fisher" sounded, and Amos grinned

because all their eyes were locked on his ice cream.

"I don't suppose anyone has time for ice cream? My treat."

Katie smiled. "That's very kind, but you really don't have to do that."

He laughed out loud, because at his question all three boys had nodded eagerly, but at her words, they'd all turned crestfallen faces toward their mudder.

"I'd love to, really."

Looking at her boys' hopeful faces, she smiled wryly and relented. "Well, then, denki. We accept."

"Rebekkah, these boys need some ice cream."

She came over, drying her hands on a towel, and smiled at the boys. "Ja, of course. What will it be?"

Soon all three were happily tucking into bowls of ice cream with colorful sprinkles scattered on top.

"Denki again, Amos. That was very nice of you."

"I recognized fellow ice cream lovers. How could I keep all the ice cream to myself?"

She giggled and took a sip of her Coke. "So, did you hear about the excitement over at Neva and Mose's this morning?"

He shook his head. "Nee. Is everyone oll recht?"

"Oh ja, sure. But Lucy was plenty shook up over it all, I'll tell you! That Johnny Zook is going to have to answer for himself this time!"

Amos sat up straighter and looked at Katie, waiting for an explanation. When she said nothing else, he cleared his throat. "Katie, you can't just say something like that and then stop. What happened?"

"Oh! I heard he was waiting outside the barn this morning before first light, and when she came out after doing her chores, he got in her way, and grabbed her prayer kapp and said some very improper things. Neva and Mose heard the fuss and chased him off."

"What kind of improper things?"

She shrugged. "I didn't get the complete rundown, but I guess he suggested they might, you know, keep company at night after his wife was sleeping. And when she told him to leave, he grabbed her kapp and it came off."

Rebekkah came over, a concerned look on her face. "Is everything oll recht, boss? You look upset."

He scrubbed a hand over his jaw. "Ja, but I have to go do something. Please stay and enjoy your treats, Katie. Rebekkah, please tell Melba she's in charge."

He headed for the back door, grabbing his jacket on the way out.

"What would possess a man to behave in such a way?" he fumed when he was alone. He knew he didn't really have a right to go over and demand to know what was being done about John Zook and that Mose would be within his rights to tell him to leave without any answers. But he felt compelled to go, anyway. As he hitched his gelding to his buggy, he began to pray.

"Vader, I've only known Lucy for a short while, as adults, anyway. But I feel strongly drawn to her, and to her little Millie. Please, if it is Your will, give me the right words to say so that they will let me help. Help me to remain calm, for I am feeling anything but. Most of all, help me to be a comfort to Lucy. I can't understand how my feelings for her are growing so fast, but they are. And I want to be there for her. Denki, Vader."

He drove down the road toward the Beiler farm a little faster than was prudent, hoping he could get answers about what they planned to do to keep Lucy and Millie safe from an unstable man, in what looked to be a deteriorating situation.

CHAPTER SIX

$\mathcal{M}$ose took one look at Amos' face and held up a hand. "We'll talk outside, if you don't mind, Amos."

Amos nodded and walked back down the steps to wait in the yard as Mose firmly closed the door behind him. He joined Amos and raised an eyebrow in query.

"You must know why I'm here."

"I assume you heard we had a visit from John Zook this morning. Word travels fast."

"Well, it was your sister Katie who told me when she and the boys stopped in the hardware store. But ja, people will have heard. If you don't mind me asking, Mose, what are you doing to make sure this doesn't happen again?"

Mose studied the younger man for a few seconds, and Amos had to force himself not to fidget. Finally, Mose sighed. "I'm going to speak with the bishop. He'll have to intervene."

Amos nodded. "And the sheriff? Did you call him to report what happened?"

Mose looked at Amos sharply. "Nee, we don't want to involve the English authorities unless we have no choice."

"But Mose, he came on your property, found Lucy alone, and insulted and frightened her!" He took a step closer. "Are you aware that John Zook is not unknown to the sheriff and his deputies? Deputy Miller called him a druvvel-machah. I think the man is dangerous, and you should report this, at least to ensure it's on record, in case he tries anything else."

Mose looked troubled. "I hadn't considered that. You think he'll try something else? Even if the bishop speaks to him?"

Amos huffed out a frustrated breath. "I don't know. But are you willing to bet Lucy and Millie's safety on it? I know it's not our way to call the police, but sometimes, I think we need to be willing to deviate from our ways."

"You feel very strongly about this."

Amos sucked in a deep breath and puffed air out of his cheeks to give himself a moment to ratchet down his intensity. Then he met Lucy's brother's eyes squarely, man-to-man. "I've come to care for them both."

Mose thrust his hands in the pockets of his black barn jacket and stared at the ground for a full minute while Amos struggled for patience. Finally, Mose sighed. "I can see the wisdom of your suggestion. I confess I am not comfortable speaking to the sheriff. Perhaps you are?"

Amos nodded slowly. "Ja, I'll talk to Deputy Miller. He is discreet."

Mose nodded. "Gut. You speak to this Deputy Miller, and I'll speak to Elam. He'll need to contact the bishop in Zook's community. I believe he and his fraa reside near Intercourse."

Amos steepled his hands together, pressing them to his lips as he thought. "I wish there weren't so many steps to getting this done."

Mose shrugged. "I know. But it's how it works. I've already

sent a message to Elam asking for a meeting. I expect to see him tomorrow. Maybe you don't need to wait that long to speak to this Deputy Miller."

Amos nodded. "I'll go do that now." He glanced at the house. "Please tell Lucy that I'll stop in and say hello to her soon but that I couldn't this afternoon."

Mose smiled. "I'll do that. Denki for your concern about my sister, Amos. I appreciate it."

"I'm glad. I was afraid you'd send me packing."

Mose chuckled. "I guess I thought about it."

Amos smiled wryly. "I'll let you know what Deputy Miller says."

As Amos was pulling into the road, he saw another buggy heading toward the Beiler farm and recognized Bishop Elam driving.

I guess Mose won't have to wait until tomorrow to speak with Elam after all.

On the way to the sheriff's office, he reflected that if it hadn't been for Katie's coming to the hardware, he might not know about Zook's visit.

Why would they think to tell him, an outsider?

He decided it was time to change that. He was interested in Lucy Beiler, and there was no point in dragging his feet.

It was time for him to tell Lucy he'd like to court her in earnest, so they could see for themselves whether they might have a future together.

And so he'd have the right to protect her if John Zook decided to pay another visit.

CHAPTER SEVEN

$\mathcal{T}$he next morning Lucy's thoughts were reeling from the bishop's visit the night before. Katie and Isaiah had accompanied Bishop Elam.

While the men spoke quietly in the living room, the women shared a cup of coffee in the kitchen, and Katie had confessed that she'd told Amos Fisher what had happened.

Of course, Lucy had already known about that since Mose had to explain why Amos had come by yesterday afternoon but hadn't come inside to say hello. Today she had hitched up Athena and headed to town, Millie strapped in the back, to speak to Amos about the situation.

"I can't decide whether to be annoyed with Mose and Amos for 'handling' things as if I were a child, or grateful to them for looking out for us, Millie."

As soon as Lucy entered Amos' store, she spotted him standing behind the counter with Melba going over some paperwork. Melba poked Amos on the arm. "Hey, boss, look who's here!"

Amos glanced up, frowning, but his frown transformed into a smile when he saw Lucy and Millie. "Lucy! Guder mariye!

Hello, Millie, how are you this morning?"

Millie grinned and reached for Amos, nearly falling out of Lucy's arms as she flung herself at him. He laughed and caught her, lifting her high in the air before settling her into his arms. "Well! I'm glad to see you too, little sunbeam."

Lucy's heart clutched at the sound of her nickname for her sister on Amos' lips. Catching sight of her arrested expression, he raised an eyebrow. "Everything okay?"

"Oh ja, it's just. . .I call Millie 'sunbeam' too."

He smiled tenderly at her. "Well, she's one of Gott's special sunbeams, ain't so?"

Lucy nodded, her throat too tight to speak.

Millie signed something to Amos, who glanced at Lucy for a translation. She gathered herself. "She asked for ice cream. Not today, lieb."

Millie pouted, and Lucy held out her stuffed pig. "Here's Pinky. Amos, do you have a few minutes to talk?" She glanced at an obviously eavesdropping Melba and added in a whisper, "Privately?"

Amos led Lucy into his office near the back of the store and gestured for her to sit in one of the utilitarian chairs facing his desk. Rather than sit behind the big, cluttered desk, he took the other chair and faced Lucy.

"I can guess why you're here."

She sighed. "John Zook."

He nodded grimly while handing a container of colorful paper clips to Millie to keep her occupied. "I thought he was a hothead before. But now I think he's unhinged. What kind of man ambushes a woman outside her home in the dark?"

She shook her head. "He didn't used to be like that. At least, not so I noticed. And I think alcohol may have played a part in his visit yesterday. I smelled it on his breath." She shuddered. "I'm so grateful Neva looked outside and saw what was happening. John ran away before Mose got there."

"So he's also a coward, who only picks on people he sees as weaker than himself."

"He seemed ready to throw a punch at you in the parking lot the other day, and you're obviously not weaker than Johnny."

He grinned. "Oh? You think I look strong?"

She rolled her eyes in mock exasperation. "Don't fish for compliments."

He chuckled and bounced Millie on his knee. She giggled and showed him a pink paper clip. "Very pretty, lieb," he crooned.

Lucy was enchanted by his easy interaction with her sister. Amos was a natural with children.

"So, I'm guessing you'd like to know how my conversation with Deputy Miller went?"

Lucy nodded. "Ja. What does he think?"

"He didn't seem very surprised. He's going to come out to your farm and take your statement, probably today. And he said he was going to go have a talk with John yesterday afternoon. But I don't think he expected it to do much good. He did mention that John drinks too much, so that meshes with the alcohol you smelled on his breath."

Lucy played with her kapp strings, pondering Amos' words. "Elam said he's going to talk to John's bishop. But I'm worried that a person who would do something like that in the first place isn't quite right. And that no warning will persuade him to stay away." She realized her hands were shaking, and she clasped them tightly in her lap.

He regarded her seriously for a few moments, then nodded. "I figure you're right about that, Lucy, which is why I'm going to go talk to John Zook myself, just so he understands we are all supporting you—the whole community is—and maybe he'll think twice before venturing to Bird-in-Hand again with troublemaking on his mind."

Lucy was alarmed. What if Amos went out to the Zook place and John attacked him? Who would be there to help him? "I'm not sure that's such a gut idea. If you do that, then you'll be the trespasser, and maybe you could be seen as the aggressor. He might feel threatened and do something."

"Like what?"

She shrugged helplessly. "I don't know! Please, Amos, promise me you'll be careful. In fact, please take someone with you. If there are two of you, he'll think twice about doing anything. And you'll have a witness."

He considered this and decided it was a sound idea. "Ja, okay, I'll take my cousin, Reuben. He has a calm way about him."

"Okay, if you have to go, I feel a little better about it. Surely, with his bishop, you and Reuben, and Deputy Miller all telling him to stay away from us, he'll have to listen, ain't so?"

"I guess we'll see." Then he looked at Lucy in a way that made her feel a little funny.

"What is it? You look kind of odd."

He threw his head back and laughed. "Oh, great. That's sure to impress you and make you take me seriously when I tell you I want to get to know you better, Lucy. You and Millie, that is."

"Get to know us better? Why?"

A slow smile spread across his lips. "Why else would a single man want to get to know a single woman better? I'd like to court you."

"You would? Why?"

"Don't you know how appealing you are?"

She shrugged. "All I know is I don't have time for things like courting."

"You're too busy for courting?"

"Taking care of Millie is a lot. You have no idea."

"Then why don't you fill me in?" He sat back, snuggling the little girl in his lap, and Lucy saw that her sister's eyelids were beginning to droop.

She reminded herself it wasn't Amos' fault he had no idea what raising a child with a disability was like. She sure hadn't known what she'd been getting into when she'd insisted on doing it. Not that she'd had a moment's regret!

"Okay, fine." She glanced at Millie, who was now asleep, her head pillowed on Amos' chest. "So, Millie has Down syndrome. Do you know anything about that?"

He shook his head.

"It's a genetic disorder. There are a lot of medical conditions common in people with Down syndrome. They can develop childhood leukemia, thyroid issues, heart issues, hearing and vision issues. And those are the serious things." On a roll, she gestured wildly with both hands. "There are smaller, everyday things too. For example, Millie is almost three, and she isn't potty-trained yet, simply because her body isn't ready. It'll probably be another year or two before she can master that skill."

When he simply nodded, she took a calming breath. *Lucy, he's not challenging you. Maybe he really wants to know.*

"What else do you and Millie deal with?" he asked gently.

"Well, thank Gott, her eyes and ears are fine, at least for now. But speech, obviously, is an issue. Many children with Down syndrome don't learn to speak as early as other children. So I decided to take the advice of some of her therapists and work with her to learn a special kind of sign language called Makaton, for people with speech delays. She's smart. She picked it up easily." Lucy felt a bit defensive of her sister, as some people looked at her and saw her different facial features and thought that meant she was unintelligent.

He just nodded. "I've seen her sign. It's impressive. But I've heard you asking her to speak, so I know you're also encouraging her to learn that skill."

"Ja! And she's resistant, let me tell you. Some of the other parents of children with Down syndrome warned me against teaching her sign language, saying it could delay her speech development because it would remove the need to learn to talk in order to communicate her needs. And they're not wrong. The problem is, most people can't understand sign, so her ability to communicate is limited. That's not a big deal now, but later when she goes to school, or gets a job, it could be."

He nodded his understanding. "I see. But once you get her talking—and I have no doubt you will—she'll have both skills, and that will give her an advantage, nee?"

She couldn't believe he actually got it. "Ja! Exactly. Plus, some people with Down syndrome develop hearing problems as they age, and if she does, the signing will come in handy then."

"It all sounds reasonable to me."

Lucy felt herself tearing up as emotion grabbed her. In ten minutes, Amos had grasped what some people who'd known Millie her whole life still couldn't.

"Tell me about what other things you and Millie deal with." He handed her a box of tissues.

She laughed as she dried her tears. "I'm sorry, Amos. It's just that few people are as understanding as you are. You act like this is all just normal."

"Isn't it?"

"Well, ja, for us. But not for most people."

"My grossmammi used to say that it's none of our business what other people think of us. I try to remind myself of that when people get nasty."

She smiled. "I like it."

He nodded, encouraging her to continue her story. "Well, Gott was gut to us, and Millie doesn't have most of the serious medical problems common to people with Down syndrome."

"Most? What does she have?"

"So, children with Down syndrome often have congenital heart defects. In fact, around 50 percent of children with Down syndrome have some kind of heart issue, compared to around 1 percent of children in the rest of the population."

"Wow. That's a high percentage."

She nodded. "In Millie's case, she has the most common type, AVSD. The long name is atrioventricular septal defect. Basically what it means is that Millie has a hole in the wall that separates the chambers of the heart. The top two chambers are the atria, and the bottom chambers are the ventricles. We got lucky. Millie has one hole between her atria. Usually, surgery is required to correct this. We've got a checkup in a couple weeks to see if the hole has closed on its own, like it should have before she was born. If not. . ." She felt herself in danger of tearing up again, and she stopped talking.

He reached out and took her hand. "If not, Millie has to have surgery to correct the problem?"

She stared at their joined hands, distracted from her worries by the lovely warmth flowing from his hand into her own cold one. Recalling herself, she nodded. "Ja, surgery. The surgery has a nearly 100 percent success and survival rate, but still, it's pretty scary."

"If she needs surgery, your family, your church community,

and, if you'll let me, *I* will all be there praying for you and Millie, helping you through it. Remember, our heavenly Father loves us. He loves Millie, and He wants her to thrive."

Tearing up yet again, Lucy waved her free hand in the air. "Oh! I never cry, and here I am constantly weeping in front of you!"

"Well, the subject is pretty dear to your heart, so it's understandable, ja?"

She nodded and grabbed another tissue to blot her eyes and nose. "Well, that's the serious stuff. There's more, but those are the main things."

"You can fill me in on the other things as they come up."

She looked at him then—really looked. He seemed sincere in his interest, and that was after hearing all the hard stuff and dealing with her tears. What kind of man was he, that he could hold her fears and worries gently and give her comfort?

"Why aren't you married?"

He laughed. "I wasn't ready to think about it before."

"And. . .now you are."

"Now I am."

"You're really serious about courting us? We're a package deal, Amos. If you want me, you get Millie too."

"I'm perfectly serious, Lucy. If only you could see what an amazing woman you are, you'd understand why I want to get to know you better. I'm afraid you've let other people's criticisms affect your self-view. But I'm here to tell you not only are you beautiful on the outside but on the inside as well. And that's the really important thing, ain't so?"

She let out a shaky breath. "Ja, that's what we're taught. But I'm going to confess to you that I like both your inside and outside, Amos. I think you're very handsome."

He laughed and she blushed. Millie stirred and blinked her

eyes open and, seeing Lucy, reached for her big sister. Amos leaned over and placed the child in Lucy's lap, and Lucy snuggled her precious little schwester.

"Then ja, I agree to let you court us. And we'll see how we all get on. You haven't seen my little darling in a bad mood. Just wait."

"I'm looking forward to it. And Lucy, I'd like to go with you to that doctor's appointment in a couple weeks, if you don't mind?"

She nodded slowly. "Okay. Neva will go too. We hire an English driver."

"Good. So, now that we've got the serious stuff behind us, let's celebrate. How about some you-know-what?" He pointed with his chin toward the part of the store where the ice cream fountain was located. Millie sat up and signed, "Ice cream?"

Amos laughed. "She's no slouch!"

"I could go for some ice cream. But then we need to go to the yarn shop. I have some knitting to do for Christmas."

"I'll walk with you. I want to go to the post office, and it's right next door."

As they walked toward the soda fountain, she felt more optimistic than she had in a long time.

Was it the promise of ice cream? Or was it the handsome, remarkably understanding Amish man walking by her side?

CHAPTER EIGHT

*T*wo weeks later Lucy, Millie and Amos were strapped into the middle row of a van headed to Philadelphia for Millie's appointment with the pediatric cardiologist. Neva had developed a nasty cold and decided to stay home.

"After all, with the two of you courting now, there's nothing odd about him accompanying you and Millie to her doctor's appointment, is there? If things work out, he'll be her dat soon enough!" Neva had said with a wink, followed by a mighty sneeze. Lucy sighed, remembering, and was grateful Neva hadn't said such a thing where Amos could hear. Whether or not the statement was technically true didn't make it any less cringeworthy, in Lucy's opinion.

The early November morning had still been dark when Lucy plucked a reluctant Millie from her warm bed, dressing and feeding the grumpy child before the van was due. The driver had picked up Amos first before stopping at the Beiler farm near Bird-in-Hand, which was between Lancaster and Philadelphia.

The first part of the trip had been spent entertaining Millie, who was a bit cranky due to the change in her morning routine.

About an hour into the two-hour trip, Millie had fallen asleep, and Lucy rested her own eyes, grateful for a short respite before they arrived in the city.

Amos heard soft snoring and glanced over at Lucy to see that she'd fallen asleep. He smiled as he thought about the last couple of weeks, which he, Lucy, and Millie had spent getting to know each other. He had to suppress a chuckle as he remembered some of the outrageous comments he'd overheard her relatives make when they thought he couldn't hear. Comments about how happy they were that their dear Lucy had finally found herself a nice man to court her. And how they'd never thought the day would come, and Lucy getting older every year.

Again he had to stifle a laugh, because at twenty-one, Lucy was hardly long in the tooth! But Amish girls tended to marry young, and many men her age or older were already off the market. Some men might wonder what was wrong with her, that she was still available.

Lucky for me! The men around here must be slow not to see how wunderbar she is. And Millie is a little sweetheart too. If Lucy accepts me, I'll be a very blessed man.

His smile of satisfaction at how their courtship was proceeding—slowly but surely—dimmed as he considered the problem of John Zook. Although the man had stayed away, Amos was not convinced the fellow wouldn't be a problem yet.

Deputy Miller had told him that Zook had tried to deny even going to the Beiler farm. Then he'd said he'd had business with Mose, and he'd tried to claim that Mose had attacked him, unprovoked, and frightened him away. He denied any wrong-doing toward Lucy. Amos snorted. What else could you expect from such a man?

He knew that Bishop Elam had spoken with Zook's bishop, who hadn't been surprised to hear Zook was causing trouble. He'd promised to speak to Zook but hadn't held out much hope of reaching the man.

Amos and Reuben had decided to wait and see if his bishop got through to him before paying Zook a visit.

The driver spoke, breaking into Amos' thoughts.

"We're about there, folks. Just about five more minutes."

Amos sent up a quick prayer for a good outcome to the day's appointments.

Lucy tried to concentrate on her knitting in the waiting room at Children's Hospital, without much success. Millie was happily playing with toy cars and trucks on the floor with other children.

They'd already gone through several tests that morning and had grabbed a bite to eat in the cafeteria before reporting to Millie's doctor's office.

"It's going to be oll recht, no matter what. I'm here for you, and so is Gott." Amos spoke to her in Pennsylvania Dutch to give them a bit of privacy, as they were the only Plain people in the waiting area.

Lucy attempted a smile. "I know you're right. But I'm *naerfich*. What if she needs surgery? What if I lose her? Oh, Amos, I don't think I could handle it!"

He reached out, caught one of her hands, and squeezed gently. "I can't promise that nothing bad will happen. But I can promise that whatever happens, you won't face it alone." He stared into her eyes, and she blinked a couple of times to clear away the tears that threatened. Slowly she nodded.

"Okay. Denki."

He nodded firmly, just as the waiting room door opened and a cheerful nurse clad in bright pink scrubs called, "Millie Beiler?"

"Do you want me to wait here?"

"Nee, please, come with us."

He scooped Millie from the floor, allowing her to keep hold of a red convertible she was clutching in her hands. "Come on, lieb! You can bring the toy. We'll return it after you see the *dokder*."

They followed the nurse, a tall, striking Black woman named Irene whom they'd met with several times before, to an examining room, and she asked Amos to place Millie on the table. He and Lucy stood by as Nurse Irene checked Millie's eyes, nose, mouth, pulse, temperature, reflexes—the works. And Millie, who'd been through it all a thousand times, just kept pretending to drive the little car around on the table and in the air.

"Okay, Miss Millie, you seem healthy and fine this morning! How do you feel?" Irene directed her question to the child, which made Lucy smile slightly. She loved the way the people here treated patients, even young children, with respect.

Millie smiled and signed her response. Lucy was about to translate when the other woman surprised her. "You feel good?"

Millie nodded and signed some more, asking the nurse if she liked her red car. "Yes, it's very pretty. Can you say 'car' out loud?"

Millie shook her head no, and Lucy felt disappointed. But Irene wasn't done. She pulled a red lollipop from her pocket, and Millie's eyes grew large and round. "This lollipop is the same color as your car, isn't it?"

Millie nodded and reached for the lolly, but the nurse pulled it back a bit, smiling mischievously. "Do you like the color red?"

Millie nodded shyly and held out the car. Nurse Irene frowned a bit and looked confused. "Wait, do you like the car, or the color red?"

Millie held out the car and signed with one hand, "Both!" They all laughed, and Irene said, "What do you like better than the red car?" She held out the candy. "Maybe this red lolly?"

Millie nodded emphatically and reached for the treat, but the savvy middle-aged nurse smiled and pulled it back again. "Okay, it's all yours. But you'd better make sure I understand what you want, or I might accidentally give you this..." She pulled a green broccoli floret from her other pocket and held it out to Millie. "Do you want the broccoli or the lolly?"

She kept putting one hand forward then the other, and Millie giggled. Then to Lucy's surprise, she shouted, "Lolly!"

"Aha! Thanks for telling me, Millie. I guess I'll eat the broccoli." She handed the lollipop to the child, who squealed with glee and handed it to Lucy to open.

Lucy did so, staring at the nurse. "That was tricky."

"I do have my little ways." They watched Millie lick the candy, and Irene turned to Lucy and Amos. "She's coming along nicely, Lucy. I'd say right on target. It's obvious you've been working hard with her. But I'm not surprised. I knew you would. You've always struck me as the determined kind."

"What about her heart?" Lucy asked quietly, glancing at her sister.

"The doctor will be in to discuss that in just a bit. Then stop in the lobby on your way out to make another appointment. You can continue at home with your physical therapist. And I think it's time to add a speech therapist, as I believe Miss Millie will soon be chattering away."

Lucy blinked tears away from her eyes, and Irene gave her a hug. "You're doing fine, Mama. It'll all be okay, you'll see."

Then she smiled at Amos and patted Millie on the head and left.

Lucy turned to Amos. "What do you think she meant that the doctor will discuss the heart test with us? If it was okay, wouldn't she just say so?"

"She simply may not be allowed to talk about that. You'll find out soon enough."

She took a deep breath and closed her eyes, sending up a silent prayer. *Vader, please let Millie's heart be fine now. But we'll face whatever we must, with Your help.*

Amos was watching her when she opened her eyes. "He hears our prayers, Lucy. Keep the faith."

She nodded shakily, as a brisk knock on the door heralded the arrival of Dr. Linn.

He smiled at Lucy and Amos and beamed at Millie. "I see you scored a red lolly from Nurse Irene. That's my favorite flavor!"

Millie grinned a sticky grin and yelled, "Lolly!"

Lucy gasped. "That's twice!"

The doctor smiled at her. "Yes, she's doing fine. Speaking single words comes before phrases and, later, sentences. My nurse tells me she recommended you start seeing a speech therapist back home in Lancaster?"

Lucy nodded, and he looked satisfied. "Good. Millie is right on track for what I'd expect of her developmental stage. And you're probably pretty anxious to hear about her heart?"

"Oh ja, please, put me out of my misery!"

He smiled gently at her. "I am very happy to tell you that the hole between her heart chambers has closed on its own, Lucy. We won't have to do surgery."

Lucy's reaction to that was to burst into tears. She sat down and covered her face with her hands and let the fear and grief pour out as sweet relief. After a few moments, she felt a tentative hand on her shoulder, and she opened her eyes. The doctor was standing off to the side, smiling, and Amos was squeezing her shoulder reassuringly. Millie was standing in front of her, lollipop forgotten, looking very concerned. She reached sticky hands up to cup Lucy's face. "Mama okay?" She asked in her bright, childish voice, and Lucy started crying all over again.

It was the first time she'd heard the word *Mama* on Millie's lips. She hugged the sticky child tightly to her and said, "Ja, Millie. Mama is okay. I'm better than okay. I'm great!"

And she knew that it was true. With the question of Millie's heart condition answered so very satisfactorily, she suddenly felt optimism flood her soul and knew that Gott was so very gut, and with Him, anything at all was possible.

CHAPTER NINE

*L*ucy spent the next few weeks working on secret Christmas gifts for her family.

She was knitting Millie little pink mittens and a darling pink hat with the tiniest kitty ears. She'd also made her a new quilt for the toddler bed she was getting for Christmas. Lucy had discussed the pros and cons of keeping Millie in her crib versus moving her to a toddler bed with the group of mothers with disabled children she met for coffee each month, and they agreed that the possibility of Lucy climbing out of the crib outweighed the very real worry about her being able to simply wander off from a toddler bed.

Lucy sighed. A mudder's worries were never done! She glanced at the row of brown paper bags, each tied up in a pretty red or green ribbon, arrayed on the counter of her Hoosier cabinet in the corner of the room. Her lips curled upward as she thought of her family's pleasure when they opened the simple, useful gifts she'd made them. Then a thought struck, and she frowned. There was nothing for Amos. Should she make him something?

Lucy decided to worry about that later and instead put her energy to use making hot chocolate to warm up her fingers. She was stirring it on the stove when a quick knock was followed by Neva stepping into the kitchen and pushing the door closed quickly behind her.

"Brrr! It's gotten cold out there! We may have snow by Thanksgiving at this rate."

She stopped and stared at the line of gift bags arrayed on the cabinet, then grinned at Lucy. "Are those Christmas gifts? Is there one for me?"

Lucy quickly glanced at the bags to be certain nothing of their contents showed. "Maybe."

"Isn't it a little early?"

Lucy shrugged. "I start making my gifts in January each year."

Neva blinked. "I haven't even started everything I plan to make. Some people may have to content themselves with a tin of cookies."

"I'd be happy to be one of them. I love your cookies."

"I'll keep it in mind. Now, I'm sitting down, and you can offer me some of that hot chocolate. My feet are aching like nobody's business!"

Lucy made a second cup of hot chocolate and put out a plate of pumpkin bread she'd made the day before. Neva busied herself spreading cinnamon cream cheese on a slice of bread, all the time not saying anything or meeting Lucy's eyes. Finally, Lucy could take it no longer. "Neva. I know you. What's up?"

Neva looked up as if surprised. "What do you mean? Can't I come visit with my little sister without raising suspicions about my motive?"

Lucy gave her a skeptical look. "Sure, and you often do. But tonight something is off. So, spill."

Neva bit her lip and slowly pulled a letter from her apron pocket.

"You're making me nervous. What's that letter?"

"Now, before I tell you, I just want you to keep an open mind."

Lucy frowned. "When don't I have an open mind?"

"And remember we all love you and only want what's best for you and Millie."

Now Lucy was becoming alarmed. "What's Millie got to do with that letter? Neva, you're scaring me."

"Oh, I told them this was a bad idea, but would they listen?"

"Neva!"

"Fine, fine! Lucy, you've done a wonderful job raising Millie. But some of your sisters think that now that you've got a man interested in you, maybe it would be best if you gave Millie over to one of them to raise, so you don't lose another man who doesn't want to take on. . ."

She didn't get to finish her sentence, because Lucy jumped to her feet, her face white and drawn, and gasped, "Who is *narrish* enough to think I'd give Millie up to catch some man?"

Neva pointed at Lucy and exclaimed, "See? That's just what I told them you'd say!"

"Who?"

Neva cleared her throat. "Well, actually, it's Barbara and Arleta. They feel that with their experience, either of them would be suitable to take Millie and raise her."

"What, like a puppy someone got tired of? They're both mudders, so either of them will do?"

Neva bit her lip again and looked miserable. "It's not quite like that. They mean well."

Lucy's head was swimming. She had to sit down, because she was afraid she might fall. Barbara was married to her brother Daniel, and the couple had eight kinner. Arleta was married to her brother Mark, and they had five. Both women were in their late thirties and, undeniably, had a great deal of parenting experience. But that didn't mean they'd be better mudders to Millie than she!

"They may have more general parenting experience, but neither has experience with a disabled child! I've spent nearly three years learning how to care for Millie's needs!"

"Now, Lucy, don't get upset," Neva began, and Lucy's head snapped up and she glared at her beloved sister-in-law. "Don't get upset? How would you feel, Neva, if someone suggested they would do a better job than you of raising your kinner?"

"I hadn't thought of it that way." She wrung her hands. "Barbara and Arleta thought that maybe they'd been wrong not taking her from the beginning, but you were so insistent, and they both had so much on their plates, and everyone agreed that with Mose and me right across the farmyard. . ."

Lucy couldn't believe what she was hearing. "Am I hearing this correctly? They feel guilty, and now they think they can take my baby from me after I've been raising her for nearly three years?" Then a terrible thought occurred to her. "Neva! Do you and Mose resent us for causing you more work?"

"No! Never. You and Millie are a joy to us."

"But Barbara and Arleta think they can just announce they're taking her, and I'll be fine with that?"

"Er, well. . .ja. That's what they think. But I don't think they mean any criticism of the job you're doing, but rather they feel guilty that you've spent your youth raising your sister instead of finding a mann of your own and starting your own family. I see where they're coming from. I should maybe have offered to raise Millie too. I guess I feel a little guilty myself. Except I've been here helping you, so I feel gut about that."

"Has this been something you've all been discussing behind

my back for years?"

"No! You obviously love Millie, and she's thriving. Which I told Barbara and Arleta, but they're pretty insistent. They've decided that they'll all come here for Christmas and when they leave, they'll take Millie home with them to Shipshewana."

Tears streamed down Lucy's face, but she could do nothing to stem the flow. Her brothers and sisters meant well, she was sure. But how could they be so clueless as to her feelings?

Neva handed her a tissue, and she blotted her face and blew her nose. "Can they do this? Can they just take Millie from me?"

Neva looked helpless, and she shrugged. "If you're asking about your legal rights, I just don't know. We've just kept it in the family, as is our way, ja? I never thought anyone would object to the arrangement once it was settled."

"And now? Do you support this, Neva?"

Neva stared at her lap for a few seconds, then looked Lucy in the eyes and shook her head. "I wasn't sure before, but now that we've spoken? I see that you love Millie as much as any mudder who had given birth to the child would. Our sisters would give her a gut home, sure, but they wouldn't love her as much as you do. So no, I don't support this, and I'll tell them as much. But child, I think they'll still come to see for themselves and make up their own minds. You—we—may have a fight on our hands."

Lucy took a deep breath, then nodded. "Fine. I can fight for what I love. Especially if you and Mose, and maybe Katie and Susanna and their husbands are on my side?"

"We'll see what the other local family members think. They would be powerful allies if they'll back you up. And I don't see why they wouldn't, as they've all seen what a wunderbar gut mudder you are to little Millie."

Lucy managed a small smile, and Neva pushed her cup of

hot chocolate toward her. "I'll help you stand up against our well-meaning family. But you might want to talk about all this with our heavenly Father and ask Him to be sure to guide you in what is best for you and Millie."

Lucy sipped her hot chocolate. She would certainly be talking to Gott about all of this, as well as praying for a clear head and a calm heart. And also for a way to make her family see that Millie was right where she needed to be—in Lucy's arms and in her home!

CHAPTER TEN

$\mathcal{T}$he next day Lucy was washing up after lunch while Millie took what would probably be a short nap. She pondered again what Neva had told her the evening before, and though it still upset her, in the clear light of a new day she realized her sisters only had her best interests at heart.

She reflected that it had been several days since she'd seen Amos, who had said he was having a busy week but would try to get by one evening after work.

"I hope he comes by tonight. I really want his opinion on this situation." As she dried and replaced the last of the lunch dishes, a knock sounded on her kitchen door.

Hoping it was Amos, she hurried to dry her hands and open the door, but her smile of greeting changed to a look of puzzlement when she beheld four elderly women from her community standing outside. Before she could recover from her surprise, Elvira Leham quirked a bushy silver eyebrow and said, "Well, Lucy, will you make your elders stand outside in the cold, or are you going to invite us in?"

She quickly stepped back and gestured for the women to

enter. "Sorry! Please come in."

Elvira stumped into the kitchen, leaning heavily on a black cane. She sat heavily in one of the kitchen chairs, followed in slow motion by her cronies, Clara Miller, Haddie Lapp, and Karen Weaver. All four women unwrapped heavy woolen capes and removed warm black bonnets, handing them to Lucy to hang up.

She put kaffi on and paused a moment to think about what baked goods she had to offer her intimidating guests.

"I made pumpkin bread the day before yesterday, and I have some cinnamon cream cheese I made." She placed the coffee and food on the table, then stood looking at the women as they all fixed it the way they liked it.

"Sit, child! Don't make us crane our necks looking up at you." Elvira sank her large, square teeth into a slice of bread. Her eyes grew round as she chewed. "Mmm! This is appeditlich! Is this your grossmammi's recipe, child?"

"Yes, it is, denki."

"Elvira, tell the girl why we're here. She's nervous as a long-tailed cat in a room full of rocking chairs!"

"I'm getting to it, Karen. Don't rush me," Elvira groused. Then she gave Lucy what she no doubt felt was a reassuring smile but which Lucy found a bit terrifying.

"The fact is, Lucy, we came to tell you how pleased we are to hear your wunderbar news!" Elvira said.

Lucy blinked as she tried to think what news she could mean.

"Goodness' sakes, Elvira, be more specific!" Clara Miller instructed, poking her friend in the arm. Elvira glared at Clara, brushing her hand away. "What else could the child think I mean other than the fact that she's being courted by that nice Amos Fisher?"

"And high time too," piped in Haddie Lapp. "We'd all started to lose hope that you'd find a mann, after you let Johnny Zook get away three years ago."

"That's not exactly what happened," Lucy began, but before she could elaborate, Clara interrupted with, "I'm sure you tried to hold on to him, but you made your choice, and it wasn't him, was it?"

All four women made tsking sounds and looked at one another, sorrowfully shaking their graying heads.

"Well, actually, I felt I had no choice, really. If you'll recall, my mudder died delivering Millie, and I felt called by Gott to raise my little schwester."

"Of course, of course!" Clara crooned. "And a gut girl you were! But shame on all your older siblings for not stepping up and taking that child so you could get married and have kinner of your own!"

Lucy shook her head and tried again to explain. "Nee, I didn't want that. I wanted to raise Millie myself!"

The women made sympathetic sounds until Elvira thumped her cane on the floor. "Lucy, nobody is saying you did wrong by taking your sister on. But we can all agree you sacrificed the life you should have had as a result. So we're here to tell you we are very pleased that you are being courted by a nice man like Amos."

"Um, thank you," Lucy said.

"Ja, and also that we are very pleased that your sisters have finally come to their senses and will be taking Millie back to Shipshewana to raise, as is proper."

"I'm not sure where you heard that, but I'm not going to. . ."

"We heard it from the bishop's wife! She heard from your sister-in-law Barbara's mudder, whom she knew as a girl. Barbara will come take the child at Christmas. And then Amos will marry you!" She sat back and beamed at Lucy, obviously very pleased.

"Actually, Amos is very fond of Millie," Lucy started to say but was interrupted by Elvira.

"Sure, sure, but now he can look gut for being willing to take the child, at the same time he doesn't need to! Win-win!"

"Nee! He knows Millie and I are a package deal. I don't want a mann who doesn't love Millie."

All four women blinked at her, struck dumb by her outrageous claim. Clara recovered fastest.

"But Lucy, that's nonsense. Every maedel wants to get married!" All the other women chimed in with their agreement to that statement, and Clara continued. "Besides, surely you've heard the gossip?"

Lucy stared at her a moment, and when she just looked at her cronies without elaborating on her statement, Lucy shook her head. "Nee, I don't usually listen to gossip."

"Well, there's your mistake! I know, I know, we aren't supposed to listen to loose talk, but it can be so useful to know what people are saying, right, ladies?" Her friends all nodded emphatically.

Karen leaned forward, the front of her dress dipping into her coffee mug unnoticed. "I heard that Amos Fisher doesn't really want to be Millie's vader. He just didn't want to disappoint you by saying so."

Lucy's mouth fell open in shock, and Elvira dove right in with, "Ja! It's true!"

"Ja, ja," Clara said, reaching out and patting Lucy's hand. "I heard he told his cousin, the Lambright boy from Lancaster, that he was relieved he wouldn't have to tell you that it was him or the child."

Tears filled Lucy's eyes, and she swallowed hard to keep the tears at bay. Elvira thumped her cane again. "Now look! You've upset her! This just shows what a gut heart you have, Lucy, caring so much for that little girl. But rest assured, Barbara and her mann will give her a gut home, and, after all, you've done the hard part! We heard her health issues are all cleared up and she won't be needing heart surgery. So now raising her will be just like raising any child, ain't so?"

Lucy gathered her wits. "Nee! Raising Millie is not just like raising any other child! She has all kinds of needs that I've spent years learning. I love my sisters and brothers, but they have no idea how to care for Millie. And besides, Millie is my child! I won't give her up for Amos, or any man." She stood, walked over to the door, and opened it. "Denki for bringing me this news of how Amos really feels about. . .about Millie," she gasped. "I almost made a terrible mistake! Now, if you don't mind too much, I need to be alone."

The four women looked at each other, then rose and collected their capes and bonnets from the pegs.

"Well," Elvira said disapprovingly, "we didn't mean to upset you, girl. We thought you'd be relieved!"

The four elderly friends made their careful way down the steps to the yard, bickering all the way.

Lucy pressed her back against the closed door as the tears fell, unchecked, down her cheeks. How could she have been fooled again as to the true nature of a man who had seemed to be genuinely interested in her?

"Oh, Vader!" she cried, "Can this be true? Can Amos have been lying to me all this time?" She sat at the table and put her head on her arms, letting out all the heartbreak. After a few minutes, she splashed her face with cold water, drying it on a dish towel. Feeling a headache coming on, she got up to take some acetaminophen. She leaned against the sink, sipping cool water. And a firm resolve grew in her heart. Nobody was going to take her child.

"Better to know the truth than to go on in ignorance of Amos' true feelings and fall even deeper in love with him." She sighed. "I'll go talk to Neva when Millie wakes up. She needs to know that the news of our sisters' plan is public knowledge now. And I'll tell her about my near miss with Amos! Nothing has to change. I haven't lost anything. Everything will be just as it was before I met him. I should be happy!"

Lucy was carrying Millie across the farmyard toward Neva's place when a buggy turned into the driveway. She recognized Amos' horse and rig and steeled herself for an unpleasant confrontation. She'd hoped not to have to face him that day, but better to get it out of the way.

He climbed down from the buggy and hitched the horse to the rail, then trotted over to where she stood holding Millie. When the child cried out gladly and reached for him, Lucy pulled her back. He looked at her, surprised, and when he saw the grim expression on her face, his own smile slipped away.

"What's wrong, Lucy? Has something happened?"

She narrowed her eyes at him. "You could say that."

"What do you mean?"

She couldn't believe his audacity, pretending to care for Millie that way. "I know!"

He blinked. "You know. . .what?"

"Oh! It makes me so mad that you keep pretending! I know how you really feel about Millie! Some of the elder women from the community came by today and told me the truth, about how you told Reuben you didn't want Millie, and you were going to tell me I had to choose between you and her!" Tears were starting to roll down her face, and Amos looked bewildered. He tried to speak, probably to tell more lies, she thought, and she couldn't stand it.

"You're even worse than Johnny Zook, because you led me to believe you were coming to love me and Millie, and it was all just a game to you! Please just leave. I won't believe anything you say!"

Amos looked gobsmacked. "Lucy, please, I don't know where those women heard that, but it isn't true! You need to listen to me."

"Nee! I do not need to listen to anyone! My sisters want to take Millie away, but I won't give her up, and even if I did, I wouldn't accept you after this. Go! And don't come back. We are done."

"Your sisters. . .what?"

Lucy clutched a whining, confused Millie to her chest and ran the rest of the way to the house, where Neva was standing on the stoop, looking concerned. Lucy rushed past her sister into the kitchen, calling, "Close the door, Neva! I don't want to hear anything he has to say!"

Neva looked outside at Amos, who was standing in the driveway looking lost. When he saw her, he started forward, but she shook her head. "Not now, Amos. We'll get to the bottom of this, but I advise you to be patient. I'll let you know when you can come over."

Lucy heard all of this as she sat rocking Millie back and forth. Emma and Linda had come into the kitchen, and Neva gestured for them to take Millie to play. Emma gently lifted the child from Lucy's arms, and Neva sat down next to her.

"It was all a lie. Elvira told me." And she burst into tears and clutched Neva as the elder woman held her and allowed her to cry it out.

Neva's eyes narrowed thoughtfully. "Elvira, is it? Well, that may explain a few things. For now, you just cry it out, lieb. And pray. It will give you peace of mind. Everything is going to be fine."

But from where she was sitting, Lucy didn't see how anything would ever be fine again. All she could do was pray that things would work out for the best, somehow. And since she couldn't begin to see what "the best" was, she'd have to trust her heavenly Father to guide her way.

CHAPTER ELEVEN

$\mathcal{A}$mos stewed over what had happened on his way home.

Can Lucy really believe that I'm a liar, no better than John Zook?

The more he thought about it, the more his bewilderment turned to hurt that Lucy would believe anything about him without asking him first. This morphed into anger and righteous indignation.

"I thought we had something special," he muttered. "But if she has so little trust in me, how deep can her feelings run?"

Lately he'd started imagining a place in town, somewhere he and Lucy picked out together. He'd thought about making sure the place they chose had a room big enough for a quilt frame.

He'd even imagined having enough bedrooms that their family could grow.

If Lucy's feelings were real, she would never believe rumors about me. Or at least she'd have the gumption to ask me if they were true, instead of hurling unfounded accusations at me and booting me off her property!

He took care of Starlight and then stomped into the kitchen, where his mother and father sat quietly reading with pie and coffee.

His dat looked up in surprise. "Amos? What's stuck in your craw?"

"Nothing!" He opened a couple of pots that were keeping warm on the stovetop but decided he was too upset to eat.

"Don't want dinner?" his maem asked casually.

"I'm not hungry."

His father raised an eyebrow at his mother. "Now I know it's serious."

Amos slumped into a chair and crossed his arms over his chest. "I don't want to talk about it."

His mother quietly placed a plate of food on the table in front of him then poured him a tall glass of cold milk. He stared at the food for a bit, then took a bite. "It's gut, Maem. Denki."

She smiled as he commenced eating, and as his plate emptied, she cut a large chunk of cherry pie and added a dollop of vanilla ice cream.

Once he'd cleaned his plate and was sipping coffee, he'd calmed. Examining the matter, he just couldn't understand what had happened.

"Are you ready to share what's troubling you, son?" His dat asked quietly.

He turned and stared into the kitchen fireplace and sighed, long and low. "Ja. I suppose so."

He explained what had transpired at Lucy's place.

His maem looked at his dat, eyebrow quirked, and he shook his head and combed his hand through his long, salt-and-pepper beard. "Well, obviously someone's tongue has been wagging."

Amos frowned. "I didn't see anyone leaving her place when I got there. But she was so angry it seemed like she'd just heard the gossip. She said I was no different from John Zook. She thought I would make her give up her child! I know how much she loves that child. I would never behave that way. Why did she believe that? Why didn't she talk to me?"

He blinked back tears of hurt and anger, and his mother patted his arm. "Son, don't be too hard on her. Remember, that's exactly what you told us John Zook did—gave her an ultimatum about choosing between him and the child. So she believed gossip in the moment, and hadn't had time to reason through it. If you hadn't stopped by until tomorrow, I imagine you'd have met with a different reception."

His father nodded his agreement. "Ja, I think that is probably what happened. You need to go back and talk to her tomorrow. But it would be helpful if you had an idea who has been spreading rumors and could talk to them first."

Amos shook his head, unable to think of anyone so mean. But suddenly, he remembered something. He sat up straight, a thoughtful expression on his face.

"What have you remembered?" his mother asked.

"It may be nothing, but about an hour before I got off work, Elvira Leham and her three gut friends came into the hardware store. I greeted them, and all four of them glared at me and walked by without speaking. I figured they had something in their craws, but I never thought it might be me!"

His mother nodded. "That's a good clue, Amos. Those four are the biggest gossips in the county. Between them, they know everything about everyone—or think they do."

"And what they don't know, they make up," his dat added.

Amos stared glumly at the table. "It doesn't really make a difference, does it?"

"Why not?" his dat asked.

"Because, Lucy doesn't trust me. So we really don't have anything worth fighting for, do we? It was all just an illusion.

Really, it's a gut thing this happened, before I did something really stupid like propose to her."

His father and mother exchanged looks, and he sighed again. "Okay, what?"

"Your vader and I think you should sleep on this. Ask Gott to guide both you and Lucy, and help you see clearly through the web of rumor and innuendo laid down by others."

"Ja, sleep on it," his father concurred. "And maybe you could go talk to Elvira Leham. See what helpful advice she gave to Lucy today."

"Actually, I wouldn't start with Elvira," his mother said with a thoughtful look. "I'd go for an easier target. Start with Clara Miller. And use flattery. She's very proud of her silver hair."

"Iris! That sounds downright slippery," his father said.

"Denki," his mother said with what he would have sworn was a blush. "I do try to keep up with the local gossips!"

"That's what I admire about you, Iris. No moss grows on you," his father said with a gleam in his eyes for his wife of more than thirty years.

"Why, Aaron, what a lovely thing to say."

"Okay, I'm going to bed. Thanks for the advice, and all." Amos got up and placed his dishes in the sink. But his parents had eyes only for each other.

"That is what I want," he told himself as he climbed the stairs to the boyhood room he'd reclaimed upon returning home from Shipshewana earlier in the year. "That's what I thought I'd found with Lucy."

He showered, tossed his clothes in the laundry hamper, brushed his teeth, and pulled on sweats and a T-shirt. As he grabbed his Bible, thinking he'd look for a little inspiration, he sent up a silent, heartfelt prayer.

Vader, maybe I was rash this afternoon in my judgment of Lucy. Maybe I let my emotions rule my logic. Please, help me get to the bottom of what happened. And please, help me discover whether I was right about Lucy in the first place. And if so, then please, Vader, help Lucy see that she was also right about me. Your will be done.

He found solace in God's Word for a time, then shut off his battery-powered lantern, deciding to sleep on it as his parents had suggested. Tomorrow he would find out what was what.

CHAPTER TWELVE

The next morning Amos was stocking shelves at the hardware store when Clara Miller walked in carrying a small yellow dog. *Can it be this easy?* He'd been worrying about how he would get her alone to pose his questions, and here she was.

He smiled broadly and exclaimed, "Guder mariye, Clara! Is that a Chihuahua?"

Clara scratched the little dog's ears. It trembled continuously. "Ja, this is Bitsy. Heard you'd taken over the store, Amos. Shame about your bruder, but how can we understand Gott's will?"

He cleared his throat. He did not want to discuss that. "It's a coincidence seeing you here today."

"Why is it a coincidence? Where else would I be going to buy new lantern batteries?"

"Well, you do have choices, so I appreciate you bringing your business here. The coincidence is that just last night my mudder was saying how much she admires your hair. It is a beautiful shade of silver."

"Oh?" The old woman preened, patting her prayer kapp and smiling broadly at Amos. "Well, denki! I am blessed." She leaned in conspiratorially. "Tell your mudder to use a shampoo with a bluing agent. It helps keep the hair from going yellow!"

He blinked. "Right. A bluing agent. I'll tell her. So, I heard a rumor about myself recently, and I wondered if you might have heard it too?"

Her face closed up, and she looked at him guardedly. "A rumor? About you? What on earth could you have heard, Amos?"

"That I'm not interested in raising little Millie Beiler as my own and planned to tell her schwester, Lucy, that she'll have to choose between me and the child. Can you imagine where such a rumor might have started, Clara?" He looked at her steadily, not allowing her to break eye contact.

"Goodness, no! You're planning on marrying little Lucy Beiler? That's wunderbar news!"

He looked at her sadly and shrugged. "Maybe yes, and maybe no. It depends. This story that is being spread about has put her off, and she is very understandably upset with me."

"But if it isn't true, where would Elvira have heard. . . What I meant to say was, if it isn't true, where would Lucy have heard it, and why would she believe it?"

He nodded and gave her his most helpless look. "That's just it! I don't know. But it isn't true, Clara. I would never court a woman with a child and then say I didn't want the child. That would just be wrong, ain't so?"

She nodded eagerly. "Oh ja! Of course, who would have thought such a thing? I'll be sure to tell Elvira. . .er, I'll be sure to stamp out that nasty rumor if I hear anyone else mentioning it." She turned and hurried back out the front door.

"Forgot her batteries," Melba said from behind him.

He turned and looked at the older woman. "I guess you

heard all that?"

"Oh ja. But I'd already heard the rumor about you from another of Elvira's little friends, Haddie Lapp. You need to squash this one fast, boss."

"I assumed you set Haddie straight?"

"You bet I did. Now, I imagine you have some damage control to tend to. Go on ahead, and I'll mind the store."

"Denki, Melba. I'll be back as soon as I can."

When he arrived at Elvira Leham's farm, he found his quarry taking advantage of the sunny day, removing laundry from her line outside the kitchen doorway. She shaded her eyes to see who was visiting, and he was close enough to see her ruddy complexion pale when she recognized him.

He smiled to himself as he drew up to the hitching post. Now, if he could just stay calm while he spoke to her. *Gott, give me the right words to make this woman tell me the truth. Please help me be patient and calm, and to remember that she is also your daughter, whom you love. Although it isn't going to be easy, Vader, I confess.*

❧

Lucy climbed out of her buggy and looked around the parking lot at Fisher's Hardware. She pulled her black wool cape more tightly around her shoulders. It was sunny, but the breeze made the day chilly. As she approached the front door of the business, it opened, and Melba Burkholder stood there grinning knowingly at Lucy.

"Guder mariye, Lucy," Melba chirped. "Would you be looking for Amos?"

Lucy stopped a few feet away. "Ja, I am. Is he here?"

"Nee, sorry. He's out doing an errand."

Lucy waited, but when Melba didn't volunteer when her boss

might return, she smiled tightly. "Do you expect him back soon?"

Melba folded her arms across her chest and looked up at the sky as if trying to remember. "Hmm. That depends."

Deciding to play along, Lucy asked, "Depends on what, Melba?"

The older woman grinned. "On whether he decides to wait for you to get back to your place when he finds you gone. He was going to look for you to clear up a little misunderstanding I hear you two had."

Lucy's mouth dropped open. "A misunderstanding?"

"Ja. Elvira was here earlier. And you just missed Clara."

"I see. Well, I'll head home. If Amos returns you can tell him that's where I'll be if he has something to say to me."

She turned on her heel and headed for her buggy. "Lucy!" Melba called, and Lucy turned to find that the older woman's expression had lost all levity. She waited to hear what Melba had to say.

"Don't be too quick to believe gossip. Especially from professionals. That's all I have to say." Melba turned and went back inside, closing the door firmly behind her. Lucy stood there a moment, pondering what Melba had said. *Maybe I was too quick to do just that. I hope this can be fixed.*

CHAPTER THIRTEEN

*W*hen Amos spoke with Elvira, she had acted amazed that the information she'd obtained from "someone completely reliable" wasn't true.

Despite his efforts, he could not pry the source of the rumor from the old woman.

He'd taken his leave and prayed that Gott would work in her heart and prevent her from doing any more damage with her wagging tongue.

He guided Starlight to the hitching rail at the Beilers' and secured him. Then, seeing nobody around, he headed for the dawdi haus. His knock on the kitchen door was answered not by Lucy but by a flustered Neva, who stepped aside saying, "Come in! Oh, we have such a situation on our hands!"

He entered, not sure what he'd find, and was greeted by the sight of Lucy sitting at the kitchen table crying her eyes out. "Is this my fault?" he asked Neva, who shook her head in disgust. "Nee! I don't know where to lay the blame for this new disaster, but certainly not at your feet."

"Can I talk to her?"

Neva shrugged helplessly. "You can try. Something terrible has happened, Amos, and I honestly don't know where to turn."

Before he could ask any more questions, Lucy lifted a tear-stained face to stare at him bleakly. He gasped at the look of despair in her eyes and took an instinctive step toward her before remembering that he wasn't in her good graces.

But she stood up and reached for him, fresh tears spilling down her face. "Oh, Amos, they took my baby away!"

"What? Who did, lieb?" He wrapped Lucy in his arms and held her while she sobbed, and looked at Neva in an attempt to make sense of what Lucy was telling him. Neva was wiping tears from her own eyes. "Did someone take Millie?"

"It was Children's Protective Services. They said someone had reported that Millie was being neglected, possibly even abused, by Lucy! I saw a car pull into the driveway, and I hurried over to see what was going on. They were very curt, and when I asked them whether it was usual to take a child from her home based on a single report, they said not typically, but in this case they were doing it because of the fact that Millie has Down syndrome and might not be able to advocate for herself if she was being mistreated. How could anyone look at that child and think she was being mistreated?"

Amos scowled. "What toddler can advocate for herself? This is narrish. All they had to do was look around and they could see she is very well cared for."

"It may be crazy, Amos, but they did it regardless." Neva sat beside Lucy, who had stopped crying and was staring into the fireplace and hiccuping occasionally, her eyes dull and hopeless.

Amos knelt on the floor beside her and took her cold hands into his large, warm ones. "Lucy," he said softly, waiting until she focused on his face. "Do not give in to despair. Remember what

Psalms says about it. 'I waited patiently for the LORD; and he inclined unto me, and heard my cry.'"

Neva put a hand on Lucy's shoulder and continued with the next verse. "He brought me up also out of an horrible pit, out of the miry clay."

Neva and Amos waited, watching Lucy quietly, patiently.

Finally, Lucy whispered, He "set my feet on a rock, and established my goings." The sigh that followed was long and ragged, and it tore at Amos' heart.

"Lucy, we will find out who is behind this. And we will get Millie back," Neva vowed.

Lucy wiped at her cheeks and eyes. "But. . .where do we even begin?"

Amos cupped her cheek in his hand and tenderly brushed a last tear away with his thumb. "We find out who is telling lies. And we convince them to tell the truth instead."

⁓

Lucy walked with Neva and Amos to the farmhouse as if in a dream. Amos interrupted her grim thoughts. "I think I know where to begin asking questions. I just came from seeing Elvira, and I'm certain she knows who is behind this."

Lucy put a shaking hand on his arm. "I'm going with you."

"I don't think. . ." Neva began, but Amos interrupted. "Nee, I think it is a gut idea. Elvira can face Lucy and see what she's done with her gossiping."

"If she confesses, maybe we can have Millie home by bedtime! Come, let's get going!" Lucy felt as if she were crawling out of her skin with worry.

Twenty minutes later they pulled into Elvira's driveway. Before they came to a stop, the door opened and Elvira stepped outside, followed by her friends.

Lucy walked over and looked slowly from one woman to another, saying nothing. They began to squirm a bit, and Elvira cleared her throat.

"Well! It looks like the two of you have worked everything out! Gut, gut! So we can just forget the whole thing, ain't so?"

"We cannot forget anything, Elvira," Lucy said through gritted teeth. "Your gossip has caused real harm today, and you're going to make it right."

"May we come inside and discuss this?" Amos asked politely. "Something has happened, and I think it is more than you bargained for. You'll want to help us set things straight."

After a few moments, Elvira gave a jerky nod and allowed Lucy and Amos to precede her into the house, followed by the other women. "Come into the kitchen, where it's warm."

They entered a depressingly dark kitchen, and Elvira gestured for everyone to have a seat. "Clara, please get out the cookies I made the other day," she said. "I'll make coffee."

"No, denki. We have no time for that," Lucy said. She quickly explained what had happened, stopping once or twice to marshal her emotions. When she finished, all four older women looked chastened.

Elvira cleared her throat. "I shared the rumor about Amos not wanting to raise Millie. I thought it was true. At least I can defend myself that much. But, maybe I should have considered the source before being so quick to believe it."

Lucy didn't know what to say. Amos had no such problem. "You wouldn't tell me who your source was before. Will you now?"

"Ja. It was John Zook."

"How did you come to be speaking with him?" Amos asked.

"I was at the market the other day, and he bumped into me.

Struck up a conversation. I remember him from when he was a boy here in Bird-in-Hand. He was an odd boy. Some people said he was sensible and responsible, but I saw through his acts. You were fortunate that he walked away like he did, Lucy."

"I guess I was. But you haven't explained how you came to believe Amos would do the same."

Elvira looked a bit uncomfortable, and Clara nudged her. "Go on, tell them the rest."

Elvira glared at her friend but gave a small nod. "Ja. So, he casually mentioned that he'd run into you two at Fisher's Hardware, and then he said he didn't expect it would lead to anything permanent, as he'd heard you, Amos, weren't interested in raising Millie."

Amos nodded slowly. "Makes me wonder what else he may have done."

Clara poked Elvira again, and she swatted her friend's hand. "I'm getting to it!"

"What is it?" Lucy asked, eyeing the women with a growing feeling of trepidation.

"I don't know for sure and certain, but I strongly suspect he's the one who called Children's Protective Services on you," Elvira said, all in a rush. "He seemed really bitter toward you, and now I realize he was out to cause all the harm he could, without actually getting his own hands dirty."

"He had you four to do the dirty work," Lucy commented quietly.

"I know we deserve that. It's true, we enjoy a little gossip, but we don't mean any trouble," Karen Weaver, quiet until now, said with a look of shame on her face.

Lucy sat back and looked at Amos. "Well, now we know who started the rumor. What do we do about it?"

Elvira sat back and folded her arms with a smug look. "Now,

that happens to be something I know my friends and I can help with."

Amos narrowed his eyes at the woman. "Oh ja? And just how can you do that?"

"Simple. I tell the truth. Are you with me, girls?"

All four women eagerly agreed to do what was right.

Lucy stood up and looked around. "What are we waiting for? Let's go!"

CHAPTER FOURTEEN

Fröhliche Weihnachten, Lucy!"

"*Frohe Weihnachten*, Barbara! I'm so glad you could all come for Christmas." She gave her sister-in-law a hug and offered her a cup of apple cider.

"Denki, Lucy." Barbara savored the warm cider. "Where's our little Christmas Sunbeam?"

Lucy smiled at the endearment. The Amish considered children with disabilities to be extra special gifts from Gott, and they felt that by accepting such a child, a person would learn much about perseverance, character, and, most importantly, love. They sometimes called such children sunbeams. Lucy silently thanked Gott once again for bringing Millie home in time for Christmas, which was also her third birthday.

After Elvira and her friends had told the authorities what they knew, John Zook had been brought in for questioning by the authorities. Lying about such matters and wasting the time of already overburdened agencies was a criminal act. John had confessed, and Millie had been home within a day.

The biggest surprise came when Lucy received a letter from

John apologizing for his behavior and promising to leave her and her family alone in the future. He'd said that he was seeking help for alcoholism, and he and his wife were getting marriage counseling. Lucy had shown the letter to Amos, and they'd said a prayer for the Zooks.

Now it was Christmas, and her whole family was celebrating together.

"Millie's with Amos in the living room," Lucy told Barbara and Arleta.

"Ah, what a nice young man. You do know that when Arleta and I came up with the idea of one of us taking Millie back to Shipshewana to raise, we only had your best interests at heart?"

"Except, we had no idea what we were talking about, did we, Barb?" Arleta asked with a laugh as she came up behind Barbara.

Barbara had the good grace to chuckle. "Nee, obviously. Neva explained that you and Millie are truly bonded and that you are her mudder in every way that counts."

"We never would have suggested it if we'd understood," Arleta added, a look of remorse crossing her pretty face.

"It's okay, as long as you never suggest such a thing again!" Lucy said with a stern look at her well-meaning sisters-in-law.

"We promise! So aren't you blessed to have found a man who wants you both?" Barbara wiggled her eyebrows.

"I'm the one who is blessed." Amos walked up carrying Millie, who was waving a crocheted yellow duckie Neva had made her. "Somebody was looking for her maem."

Lucy reached for the precious child who had changed her whole life with her mere existence.

"Come here, my little sunbeam," she crooned. Millie threw herself into Lucy's arms, and all the adults laughed.

"So," Barbara grinned mischievously. "When are the two

of you getting married?"

"Barbara!" Neva, who had joined the group, chided.

"I just wondered if we should be planning another trip to Pennsylvania anytime soon, that's all, Neva."

"Well, then," Lucy said with a glance at Amos, "maybe you should plan on a little trip next November, if you can fit it into your schedule."

"I knew it!" Barbara cried, pulling Lucy into a hug.

"We couldn't be happier for you, Lucy," Arleta beamed. "Everyone in the family feels the same."

"Denki, from all of us," Lucy said, her loving smile the very balm of forgiveness. Barbara and Arleta smiled back, a little bit misty-eyed.

Millie yawned and laid her head on Lucy's shoulder. "Are you ready for bed, lieb?"

"Can I help you get her down?" Amos asked, tenderness shining from his hazel eyes.

"That would be nice, denki." A portable crib had been set up in a spare room so that Lucy and Amos could stay later to celebrate with their family. Lucy got Millie into her pajamas and then sat in a rocking chair with the child.

Amos handed her Millie's favorite picture book. "Let's read about *Spot the Dog* tonight."

"Spot!" Millie said, popping her thumb into her mouth. As Lucy read, Millie's eyelids grew heavy.

"It's time for bed, lieb," Lucy said softly. "I love you, honey. Merry Christmas."

Millie reached up and cupped Lucy's face in her small hands and planted a wet kiss on her mudder's cheek. "Love you, Maem," she clearly said.

"Amos! Did you hear that?"

He smiled and placed a soft kiss on Lucy's forehead. "Ja, I heard it. And I share the sentiment 100 percent."

Her eyes damp, she watched as Amos gently placed the sleepy child into the crib, and then he took her hand and led her to the window. The stars shone God's love and commitment down onto His creation. Amos cupped her face and leaned in to place a soft kiss on her lips. "I love you, Lucy. And I love Millie, with all my heart. Never doubt it."

Smiling through sudden tears, Lucy stood on tiptoe and returned the kiss. She tenderly brushed his slightly-too-long blond hair back from his face. "Oh, Amos. I love you too. With all my heart. Merry Christmas!"

From the portacrib came a small but clear voice. "Mewy Cwissmas, Maem! Mewy Cwissmas, Dat!"

Their eyes huge, they hurried over to look down at Millie, but the child's eyes had drifted closed, and she sucked her thumb as she snuggled Pinky.

"Did she just. . . ?" Amos whispered.

"Ja!" Lucy said, awe in her voice. "This is truly the best day ever!" Overcome with emotion, they shared another soft kiss before tiptoeing out of the room to share their happiness with all their loved ones, gathered together in God's name.

∽

Fröhliche Weihnachten!

Anne Blackburne lives and works in Southeast Ohio as a news-paper editor and writer. She is the mother of five grown children, has one wonderful grandchild, and has a spoiled poodle named Millie. For fun, when she isn't working on Amish romance or sweet mysteries, Anne directs and acts in community theater productions and writes and directs original plays. She also enjoys reading, kayaking, swimming, searching for beach glass, and just sitting with a cup of coffee looking at large bodies of water. Her idea of the perfect vacation is cruising and seeing amazing new places with people she loves.

A BIRD-IN-HAND CHRISTMAS

by Amy Clipston

Dedication

For Joe, Zac, and Matt with love

GLOSSARY

aenti: aunt

aentis: aunts

appeditlich: delicious

bedauerlich: sad

boppli: baby

bruder: brother

bruders: brothers

bruderskinner: nieces/nephews

bu: boy

daadi: grandfather

danki: thank you

dat: dad

daadihaus: small house provided for retired parents

dochder: daughter

fraa: wife

Frehlicher Grischtdaag!: Merry Christmas!

froh: happy

geh: go

gegisch: silly

gern gschehne: You're welcome

Gude mariye: Good morning

Gut nacht: Good night

gut: good

haus: house

Ich liebe dich: I love you

kaffi: coffee

kichlin: cookies

kinner: children

kuche: cake

liewe: love, a term of endearment

maed: young women, girls

maedel: young woman

mamm: mom

mammi: grandmother

mei: my

nee: no

onkel: uncle

onkels: uncles

schee: pretty

schtupp: family room

schweschder: sister

schweschdere: sisters

sohn: son

Was iss letz?: What's wrong?

Wie geht's: How do you do? or Good day!

wunderbaar: wonderful

ya: yes

CHAPTER ONE

New Wilmington, Pennsylvania

Makayla flipped through her cookbook until she came to the casserole section. She found the recipe for the spaghetti-and-meatball casserole and smiled. It was her five-year-old son's favorite, and the page was spotted and a little bent. She'd promised to make it for Lukas tonight. Besides, her fiancé, Thomas, was coming for supper, and he said it was her best casserole.

She began gathering the ingredients—spaghetti noodles, a jar of marinara sauce, a can of golden mushroom soup, meatballs, shredded mozzarella cheese, and parmesan cheese. When giggles exploded, she peeked out the kitchen window to see her son running toward the mailbox with his cousin Leah, who was six.

She was so grateful her in-laws had insisted she and Lukas move in with them after her husband, Markus, passed away in an accident almost two years ago. He'd been fixing a leaky roof for an elderly neighbor after a snowstorm when he slid on a patch of ice, fell off the roof, and died instantly. Since her brother-in-law and his family lived on the same property, Lukas and his cousins could play together and help with the chores on the dairy farm.

Lukas and Leah each took a handful of letters from the mailbox and then charged toward the house. The early November sky was clogged with white clouds, and the bare trees swayed in the gentle Friday afternoon breeze.

The back door opened with a thud before Lukas and Leah scrambled into the kitchen, their laughter bouncing off the pine cabinets.

"We got the mail!" Lukas' blue eyes sparkled. He and his cousin dumped the pile of envelopes onto the table.

Makayla touched her son's cold, red nose. "*Danki.*" She sifted through the pile, picking out the letters addressed to her and her in-laws before handing Leah the letters belonging to her parents. "Please take these to your *mamm.*"

"I'll *geh* with you." Lukas followed Leah out of the kitchen, and the back door banged shut again.

Makayla examined the letters and found one from Freida Hertzler in Bird-in-Hand, Pennsylvania—Mamm. She smiled, so grateful that she and her mother exchanged letters and phone calls regularly, given that they lived in opposite ends of the state. She sank down onto a kitchen chair and opened it.

> *Dear Makayla,*
>
> *I hope you're doing well out there in New Wilmington. It's gotten cold here in Bird-in-Hand. I've been working on some heavier shirts for your* dat *to wear while he's in the stables.*
>
> *I can't believe the holidays are coming soon. Your dat is making blocks for Lukas for Christmas. I can't believe it's been six months since we last visited you, and it's been too*

long. We love coming out to New Wilmington to see you, Lukas, and Markus' family. Stella and Simeon are always so kind to host us in their home.

I've been thinking a lot about when you were home with us seven years ago. I really miss having you here. I understand you have a life in New Wilmington, but I was wondering what you would think about coming home for Christmas this year instead of us coming to see you. You haven't been home in seven years, and we'd love to show Lukas where you grew up. You could stay for Thanksgiving and Christmas. We have plenty of room in this big, old house.

What do you think? Let me know.

Love,
Mamm

Memories overcame Makayla. It seemed like only yesterday that she had left Bird-in-Hand and traveled more than five hours by bus to New Wilmington to help her cousin Delilah, who was seven years older than Makayla and had just given birth to her fourth child.

But there was another reason she'd left her home community. An image of her ex-boyfriend's handsome face filled her mind. After nearly a decade she could still recall Wyatt's striking honey-brown eyes and hear that laugh that always sent a warm glow through her. But he was a cheater. He had broken her heart, and she'd packed up and left for New Wilmington soon after receiving Delilah's letter, never looking back.

And when Markus Blank had asked her to marry him after only dating a few months, Makayla had jumped at the chance, especially since he had helped her mend her broken heart. He had been so kind, patient, and loving. She had been so surprised when he'd noticed her at a youth gathering. Having a family had always been her dream—and his too. Their engagement had been short, and after they married, they'd settled in a house not far from his father's dairy farm. He ran a roofing business with his best friend and business partner, Thomas Graber.

She had hoped to raise a large family with Markus, but God had other plans. She'd never imagined becoming a widow two years ago at the age of twenty-eight, but she was grateful Markus' best friend, Thomas, had proposed to her earlier this fall. Giving Lukas a stable life and father was her top priority, so marrying Thomas made sense.

There was only one problem. She didn't love him. But she was confident that she would. . .eventually.

She studied her mother's neat, slanted penmanship. She could envision in her mind her father's horse farm and the large white home where she'd grown up. Her heart swelled as she recalled cooking with her mother in the large kitchen, helping her father muck stalls in his stables, attending church with friends in her district, laughing with her best friend, Becky, and playing volleyball with her youth group.

She missed her friends, and she was always eager for her parents' visit. But if she went home, she'd risk running into Wyatt.

Stella, her mother-in-law, entered the kitchen. "Did you get a letter today?"

She pushed the letter over to Stella. "*Mei* mamm wrote and asked me to bring Lukas home for the holidays."

"Isn't that nice?" Her mother-in-law perused the letter and then focused her hazel eyes on Makayla. "You don't want to go?"

"I was just thinking about going home, but I'm not sure."

"Why?"

She sat up straight in her chair. "It would be better if my parents came here. After all, this is Lukas' home."

Stella shook her head. "They've come here to visit Lukas every year since he was born. It would be nice if you took him to Bird-in-Hand to spend time with them."

"But Lukas would miss his cousins."

Stella tilted her head. "Wouldn't it be fun to show Lukas where you grew up?"

"*Ya.*" Makayla nodded. "But what about Thomas?"

"He'll be here when you get back, and your wedding isn't until February. You'll have plenty of time to prepare."

"But I promised Barbie I'd be here to help her when her fourth *boppli* comes," Makayla added, grasping for another excuse. "She'll have her hands full and—"

Stella rested her hand on Makayla's. "Barbie is due in January, and if the little one decides to come early, I'll be here." She gave her hand a gentle squeeze. "Why are you so hesitant?"

Makayla shrugged. When her mother-in-law studied her, she felt itchy under her stare.

"What are you afraid of?" Stella asked.

Makayla and her best friend, Becky, never discussed Wyatt in their letters, and she'd never asked her parents about him. Yet Makayla had always assumed he'd married that other woman and they'd started a family. Surely he'd found someone who was much prettier and more interesting than she was. Yet even after all this time, the idea of seeing him made her stomach twist.

But why should she care? Wyatt was the one who had cheated, not her.

"I'm not afraid of anything." Pushing the chair back, Makayla stood. "I need to get the casserole put together. Thomas will be here at five." She returned to collecting the ingredients.

When she felt a hand on her shoulder, she stilled.

"Makayla," Stella began, "you blessed Simeon and me when you and Lukas moved in after we lost our precious Markus." Her eyes sparkled with tears. "Losing our second *sohn* was more painful than we ever imagined, but it's not our way to question God's plan."

Makayla nodded and sniffed.

"We love having you here, but our gain has been your parents' loss. Spending the holidays with your family would be such a blessing to your folks. It's their turn to enjoy Lukas and you."

Makayla wiped her eyes. "You're right. I'll discuss it with Thomas tonight."

"*Gut.*" Stella's expression brightened. "Now, how can I help prepare supper?"

"Did you climb a big ladder today?" Lukas asked Thomas while they sat at the supper table later that evening.

The delicious aromas of the spaghetti-and-meatball casserole drifted over the kitchen.

Thomas' dark eyes turned toward Lukas. Without smiling, he gave the boy a curt nod. "We patched a barn roof. So ya, we had to use the tallest ladder."

"Wow." Lukas' blue eyes widened. "When I get bigger, I'm going to climb on that ladder too."

Makayla shared a smile with Stella before they each forked more casserole into their mouths.

"How's business?" Simeon asked.

"We're set up with roofing jobs until later in the month. I'm grateful since business always slows down in the winter." He ate another bite of casserole. "This is *appeditlich*, Makayla."

"Danki."

"Mamm made it because it's my favorite," Lukas announced.

Thomas frowned at her son. "Lukas, don't be prideful."

Makayla bristled, and Lukas' smile flattened as he turned his attention to his plate. If only Thomas could find some patience with her son. Maybe after they were married, he would soften more. At least she prayed he would.

Lukas remained silent while eating during the rest of supper. Thomas and Simeon discussed business until their plates were empty, and then Makayla served vanilla cupcakes and coffee for dessert. After they finished, Makayla and Stella began cleaning up the kitchen. Stella wiped down the table while Makayla washed the dishes.

"Say good night to Thomas and take your bath," Makayla instructed her son.

Lukas waved to Thomas. "*Gut nacht.*"

Thomas nodded at him, and Lukas scampered toward the bathroom. He turned toward where Makayla scrubbed utensils at the sink. "Danki for supper."

"*Gern gschehne.*" She dried her hands on a dish towel.

"Makayla, why don't you visit with Thomas, and I'll finish the dishes?" Stella asked.

"Right." It was time to tell her fiancé about the letter she'd received. "Let's visit by the fire."

Simeon excused himself and headed out to the barn while Makayla and Thomas sat in rocking chairs in front of the fireplace. She turned toward Thomas and recalled two months ago when they'd relaxed by the fire and he had proposed to her. He had the same stoic expression on his face when he'd said, "We should get married, Makayla. I'll take care of you and Lukas, and you can run my household. How does that sound to you?"

That was Thomas. Everything was matter-of-fact. He was attractive with his dark brown hair and dark eyes, and he was stocky, standing a few inches taller than her height of five foot five. Although he felt more like a brother than her fiancé, she was thankful that he had offered to marry her and be a father to her son.

"Is there something you wanted to talk about?" he asked.

She moved her fingers over the wooden chair arm. "I received a letter from mei mamm today, and she invited me to bring Lukas home for the holidays. Stella thinks I should go."

Thomas rubbed his chin, and Makayla held her breath. Maybe he would tell her no, and she'd have an excuse to not go home and risk seeing Wyatt again.

A few moments ticked by before he finally nodded. "We can celebrate Christmas when you return. Just be back before our wedding."

"I will."

A hush settled between them, and she breathed the smoky scent of the fireplace.

"I made progress on the addition this week," he said. "I'm sure the *haus* will be ready in plenty of time before you and Lukas move in."

"Gut."

They sat in silence for a few more moments. "Was there anything else you wanted to discuss?" he asked.

She shook her head. "That was it."

"Well, it's getting late." He stood. "Gut nacht."

She shook his hand. "I'll see you at church on Sunday."

She walked outside and leaned on the porch railing while he traipsed toward his waiting horse and buggy, his lantern guiding his way. Once again, she tried to imagine what life would be like when she married Thomas. Although she and Lukas would move into his house across town, she would have the same chores she had in her in-laws' house. But she would be a wife again, and that would be an adjustment. Yet she was convinced God was calling her to do this.

The storm door opened and closed with a click before Stella joined her. "I wasn't eavesdropping, but I looked out the window and saw Thomas heading toward his buggy."

"It's okay." Makayla smiled at her mother-in-law.

"What did he say?"

"He thinks I should go."

Stella patted her shoulder. "That's gut."

"I'll call mei mamm tomorrow." She dreaded having to see Wyatt Mast at church after what he had done to her. But she pushed that thought away. She would enjoy seeing her parents, showing Lukas around her community, and reconnecting with her friends.

Surely Wyatt was married by now, so she wouldn't have to deal with him.

At least, she hoped so.

CHAPTER TWO

Bird-in-Hand, Pennsylvania

The following afternoon Wyatt pulled out a flyer from the pocket of his winter coat. He surveyed the bulletin board in the Lancaster Hardware and Supply store and moved a few business cards before choosing a pushpin. Then, with a sigh, he hung up his flyer.

This was the fourth business he'd visited today to display his work-for-hire signs. Surely there was someone in Bird-in-Hand who needed a handyman, and it would be even better if they needed someone long-term.

His shoulders slumped. He couldn't believe he was thirty-two years old and unemployed. But if Menno Yoder hadn't left the kerosene lantern burning, then the shed shop would still be standing.

Wyatt shook his head and started toward the exit. Since he had a handful of flyers left, he would stop by the grocery store and farmers market on his way home.

When he heard someone call his name, he turned to see

Omar Hertzler hurrying toward him.

"*Wie geht's?*" Wyatt rolled up the flyers and slipped them into his trouser pocket.

"I thought that was you." Omar shook his hand. "I heard about Jonas Flaud's shed business burning down earlier this week. Thank the Lord no one was hurt."

"That was a blessing." But the man had lost everything, and because of that, Wyatt no longer had a job. Still, he was sympathetic toward Jonas' plight. He was irritated with Menno, but not Jonas. Wyatt handed the older man one of his flyers. "If you know anyone who needs a handyman, please give them my number."

Omar brushed his fingers over his graying, light-brown beard while examining the flyer. Then his gray eyes met Wyatt's again. "What do you know about training horses?"

"I helped mei *onkel* train horses when I was a teenager. I'm a little rusty, but I'm a fast learner." Wyatt's brow wrinkled. "Why?"

"Would you consider working for me?"

Wyatt was speechless for a moment. "You're hiring?"

"My farmhand moved to Ohio last week. He's been writing a *maedel* there, and they're getting married in the spring. So I need a farmhand, and you need a job." Omar smiled.

Wyatt stroked his clean-shaven chin, trying not to frown. Never in his wildest dreams did he imagine he'd work for his ex-girlfriend's father. Last he'd heard, Makayla had moved to New Wilmington and gotten married, and there was a rumor that she hadn't been back to visit her parents at all during the past seven years.

Not that it mattered.

Being at her parents' house when they hosted church still conjured up memories of her, and that was difficult enough.

Could he stomach working at her house every day and being faced with the reminder of how she'd left without an explanation and completely destroyed him?

On the other hand, his rent wouldn't pay itself. . .

"I know you're a carpenter," Omar said, "and I understand you're looking for something in your field. But what if I made it worth your while? Would you consider working for me until you found something else?" Then he quoted a salary that made Wyatt reel back in shock. It was more than twice what he had made working for Jonas. The older man chuckled. "You look surprised."

Wyatt opened and closed his mouth. "That's very generous, Omar."

"What do you say?"

Beggars couldn't be choosers. He shook the man's hand. "When can I start?"

"How does Monday sound?"

Wyatt couldn't help but grin. "Perfect."

"*Wunderbaar.*" Omar pointed to the bulletin board. "Now take down those flyers."

"I sure will."

"And if you find another carpenter job, just give me a couple of weeks' notice if you can."

After retrieving the flyer from the bulletin board, Wyatt headed out the door with a little spring in his step. His unemployment had come to an end.

Thank You, God!

Wyatt just had to get back into the groove of working with horses, but he could do it. Omar had always been a kind and patient man.

He just hoped it wouldn't be awkward working for his ex-girl-friend's father. *Surely it won't be.*

～

The following Friday night the taxi drove down the dark two-lane highway, and when the sign advertising Hertzler's Belgian and Dutch Harness Horses sign came into view, Makayla's stomach swooped with excitement.

"Wake up, sleepyhead." Makayla gently nudged her son while he snored softly in the booster seat beside her. "Lukas, you need to rise and shine. We're at *Mammi* and *Daadi*'s haus."

His sky-blue eyes fluttered open as he yawned. "Already?" He peered out the window as the Prius steered up the winding rock driveway.

When they reached the top, the headlights swept across her father's line of red barns and stables, along with the white split-rail fence lining the enormous, rolling green pasture where his beautiful horses frolicked during the day. The large, two-story, whitewashed house where she had been born and raised looked the same.

The taxi stopped at the top of the driveway, and Lukas clapped his hands. "I can't wait to see Mammi and Daadi."

"I'm sure they're excited to see you too." She unbuckled his seatbelt, and he jumped out the door before scooting up the front porch steps, where two lanterns glowed. She pushed open her door. "Don't run!"

The front door opened, and Mamm appeared on the porch, pulling her grandson in for a hug.

Tears stung Makayla's eyes as she joined them on the porch. "Mamm."

"Oh, Makayla." Mamm sniffed, and her light blue eyes

brimmed with tears. "He's gotten so big the past six months." She reached up and cupped her hand to Makayla's face. The lines around her eyes and mouth seemed more pronounced, and more strands of gray streaked the blond hair peeking out from under her prayer covering, but Mamm still was as lovely as Makayla recalled.

She pulled her mother in for a hug. "I've missed you."

"Wow." Lukas said. "The haus and the farm are so big!"

Makayla and her mother shared a smile. Then she looked toward the long stable and spotted lanterns glowing in them. "Dat is still working?"

"He should be in soon. He's going to be so excited. I didn't tell him that you were coming."

"You didn't?"

"No. I thought it would be a special surprise since he's been talking about how much he misses you and Lukas."

Makayla's chest squeezed. How could she have ever doubted coming home?

Mamm took Lukas' hand. "Do you like cinnamon rolls?"

Her son gasped. "Ya!"

"I thought so. Come with me." Mamm mussed his light brown hair with her free hand before steering him in the front door.

Makayla paid the taxi driver and retrieved their two suitcases. When she walked into the house, she was swept back in time. The large family room was just as she recalled with the same brown sofas, matching wing chairs, propane lamps, and dark wood end tables and coffee table.

She turned toward the hallway that led to her parents' bedroom and a bathroom and glimpsed up the staircase that led to her former bedroom, along with a bathroom, her mother's sewing room, and two spare rooms.

She hugged her arms to her middle. It seemed like just yesterday when she'd made the decision to leave both Bird-in-Hand and her heartbreak in the rearview mirror while a taxi drove her to the bus station. But here she was, back in her childhood home after seven long years.

The scent of cinnamon rolls and the sound of giggles drifted out from the kitchen, and she felt drawn to her sweet son's laughter. She left the suitcases by the stairs and joined her mother and son at the large kitchen table, where cinnamon rolls and a cup of tea awaited her.

"This is so yummy, Mammi." With his mouth covered in icing, Lukas held up his half-eaten roll.

"Enjoy, mei *liewe*." Mamm wiped his mouth with a napkin and turned to Makayla. "How was your trip?"

Makayla covered her mouth to shield a yawn. "Gut. Long."

Lukas finished a cinnamon roll and then chose another one.

"Slow down, Lukas, or you'll get a tummy ache," Makayla warned.

Her son took another bite and licked his fingers. "Where do we sleep?"

"Your mamm's room and your room are upstairs. Your mamm lived here when she was a little girl."

Makayla sipped her tea.

The front door opened. "Freida," Dat called from the foyer. "It smells delightful in here. Why is there luggage by the stairs?"

Mamm smiled. "Come see, Omar."

Dat appeared in the doorway, and his face broke out in a grin. "Makayla! Lukas! What a surprise!"

"Daadi!" Lukas bolted across the kitchen and into his grandfather's arms.

Dat lifted him up as if he were weightless and hugged him.

"Oh my goodness." He balanced Lukas with one arm and reached his other arm out to Makayla. "Come here, *Dochder*."

She joined their group hug and, closing her eyes, enjoyed the comfort and security of her father's arms.

"Are you surprised, Omar?" Mamm asked with a chuckle.

"Ya! Why didn't you tell me they were coming, Frieda?"

"I prayed Makayla and Lukas would join us for the holidays, and when I wrote her, she said yes. So here they are!"

"We're staying until after Christmas." When Makayla opened her eyes, she peered out toward the hallway and stilled. For a moment she thought she was dreaming. She blinked her eyes but the scene in front of her didn't change.

Her ex-boyfriend, Wyatt Mast, was standing by the front door, staring at her.

She swallowed and sucked in a breath.

Her father released her from his bear hug, and she stepped back, her gaze locking on Wyatt while her belly clenched. She hadn't expected to see him at all, but now he was in her house—her parents' house. Confusion swamped her.

Wyatt studied her, shifting his weight on his feet while his expression became stony. She was certain she had stepped back in time since he looked just as she remembered with his light brown hair, his bright and intelligent honey-brown eyes, and his tall, fit, muscular build.

But then she noticed his features were more mature than she recalled. His jaw was somehow more chiseled, and his shoulders were broader. It hit her—Wyatt was clean-shaven, which meant he was still a bachelor. How was that possible?

"Wyatt," Mamm's voice sounded from behind her, "join us for cinnamon rolls. I'll put on a pot of *kaffi* too."

Wyatt shook his head, his stare not leaving Makayla's. "No,

danki. I should get going."

"Don't be *gegisch*," Dat told him. "You worked hard today. Everyone who works hard deserves at least one cinnamon roll and a cup of kaffi."

Worked hard?

Lukas rushed over to him. "I'm Lukas Blank." He pointed to his chest. "And I'm five and a half."

Makayla sucked in a breath while Wyatt peered down at her son.

"Hello there, Lukas Blank." He crouched down, holding his hand out to him. "I'm Wyatt Mast."

Lukas shook his hand with vigor. "We came here on a bus today. It was a looong ride. It was so long that I fell asleep."

"Really?" Wyatt asked, and when his lips tipped up into a genuine smile, Makayla blew out a relieved sigh.

"Ya." Lukas pointed to Makayla. "That's mei mamm. Her name's Makayla."

Wyatt stood up to his full height, several inches taller than she was, and his smile flattened. "Makayla. It's been a long time."

For a moment she couldn't find her voice. "It has," she finally said, her words scratching out of her throat.

"The rolls are getting cold," Mamm announced from the kitchen.

Lukas grabbed Wyatt's coat sleeve and tugged. "Sit by me. I'll share my cinnamon roll."

"I'm sorry, buddy." Wyatt smiled down at him. "I have to get home, but I'll see you soon."

"Okay." Lukas disappeared into the kitchen.

Makayla swallowed her shock. Why was her son being so outgoing and friendly toward her ex-boyfriend? The scene was so unexpected that she couldn't comprehend it.

"Gut nacht, Omar." Wyatt looked toward the kitchen and then added, "I'll see you Monday, Freida."

"Goodbye!" Mamm called from the kitchen.

Dat grinned. "You mean you'll see us all at church on Sunday."

"Right." Wyatt adjusted his hat on his head, cast his eyes toward Makayla once more, and then slipped out the front door.

Once he was gone, Makayla spun toward Dat. "Why was Wyatt here?"

"He works here."

"He works here?" she asked, and he nodded. "Since when?"

"Since Monday." Dat retreated into the kitchen.

She followed him, and the aroma of coffee and cinnamon rolls filled her senses. "Why would you hire my ex-boyfriend?"

Dat washed his hands at the sink. "Abner moved to Ohio, and the place where Wyatt worked burned down. I needed a farmhand, and Wyatt needed a job." He said the words as if he were simply ordering dessert at his favorite restaurant. Then he sat down beside Lukas and grinned at him. "Are you going to share that cinnamon roll with me?"

"Sure!" Lukas pushed the plate toward him, and Dat beamed.

The sweet scene overwhelmed Makayla, bringing happy tears to her eyes.

Mamm carried the coffee carafe to the table. "Relax, Makayla. Tell us the news from New Wilmington."

She took her seat and began updating them on her in-laws, but inside she was reeling. Not only was Wyatt single, but he was working for her father.

It suddenly didn't feel like home anymore.

Wyatt squeezed the reins with such force his hands ached while he guided his horse home. The whir of the buggy wheels and the *clip-clop* of his horse's hooves filled the space while his thoughts whirled like a cyclone.

He couldn't believe Makayla was back. When he'd seen her, he was almost certain he was imagining her, but she was as real as the cold evening air seeping into his buggy. She looked just as he remembered with her sunshine-colored hair, bright blue eyes, flawless ivory skin, high cheekbones, and pink lips.

He had considered backing out the door, but instead, he couldn't move, feeling as if he'd been dipped in cement. He was suddenly plunged into a barrage of memories of their happier times—laughing with friends while playing volleyball, holding hands and sitting on the porch watching the sun set, and whispering how much they loved each other while riding in his buggy.

But that had all been washed away when she slipped off to the western part of the state without any explanation.

Wyatt guided the horse onto the road that led to his family's land. He contemplated what he would do now that Makayla was back. For a moment, he was tempted to quit, but the logical thing to do was to stay since he needed the job. Besides, he was thirty-two years old. Surely he would be able to stomach seeing her on a daily basis for two months. She'd said she planned to leave after Christmas.

And Wyatt liked the job more than he'd thought he would. In fact, he enjoyed working with the horses more than building sheds.

He steered the horse onto the rock driveway while he thought about Makayla's son. He had heard that she'd married, and Omar had shared that her husband had passed away a couple of years ago. Before Makayla had left, Wyatt had planned to ask her father for permission to marry her and then take her out to their favorite picnic spot and propose to her. But she hadn't wanted a future with him. She'd certainly made that clear.

Wyatt had to admit Lukas was adorable. Meeting her son had sent grief twining through him. He felt sorry for the little boy who didn't have a father. Lukas was such a likable kid and not shy at all. He smiled while he thought of his own niece and nephew. Wyatt relished time with them—playing ball, fishing at the pond at the back of the property, and sharing stories about when he and his brother were kids. He had thought he'd be a father by now, but it seemed that permanent bachelorhood was God's plan for him.

After steering to the barn, Wyatt unhitched the horse and considered how he was going to handle working for Omar while Makayla was there. All he could do was be civil. She had hurt him once, and he couldn't permit her to do it again. He would focus on his job, because right now, that was all that mattered.

CHAPTER THREE

*S*unday morning Makayla smiled as her father guided his horse up the Zook family's long driveway toward their farm. She was excited to see her former church district members and couldn't wait to reconnect with her old friends. She'd kept in touch with her best friend, Becky King, and she looked forward to seeing others.

Dat halted the horse near the sea of buggies before Makayla and Lukas climbed out of the back.

"Can I help Daadi with the horse?" Lukas asked.

"Of course." Dat waved him over.

Mamm took Makayla's arm. "Everyone's going to be so surprised to see you."

She steered Makayla up Miriam Zook's back steps. A buzz of conversations wafted over them, and Mamm led her into the group.

A gasp sounded before someone grabbed her arm. "Makayla!" Becky King, her best friend since first grade, yanked her into a hug. "I didn't know you were coming home."

Makayla held on to her friend and squeezed her tight. "It's

so gut to see you! I'm sorry I didn't have time to write you before I came. Mei mamm invited me, and the plans came together quickly."

"How are you?" Becky grinned, and her green eyes twinkled. She looked just as Makayla recalled with her angelic face, her light brown hair tucked under her prayer covering, and her lovely smile.

"I'm sorry my letters haven't been as regular as I'd like, but you know how it is when you're running a household. How are your *kinner*?"

"Lily just turned five. She's playing with a toy in the corner, and Perry's mamm is holding Jake. He's fifteen months." Becky touched her abdomen and then leaned in closer. "We haven't told anyone, but we're expecting another this summer."

"Oh praise God!" Makayla hugged her friend again. "What a blessing."

"Danki. Where's Lukas?"

"He's with mei dat."

"I can't wait to meet him." Becky's smile brightened. "Are you back for gut?"

"No, I'm going home after Christmas." Makayla hesitated. "I'm getting married in February."

Becky's brow wrinkled. "You haven't mentioned anyone in your letters. Who are you marrying?"

"Markus' best friend, Thomas. He proposed—"

"Makayla!" one of her mother's friends interrupted her words.

Soon a group of women surrounded her, wanting to know about her life in New Wilmington. She answered their questions until the clock struck nine, and they headed toward the barn for the service.

Becky held her five-year-old's hand and looped her other arm with Makayla's. "Sit with me during the service."

They made their way into the barn and sat on a bench in the married women's section, with Makayla between her mother and Becky. A whiff of animals lingered in the air, and Makayla surveyed the congregation, finding familiar faces in the crowd. When she spotted Lukas sitting next to her father, he waved before turning to say something to her father, who grinned as he replied. Happiness buzzed through her. Not only did she feel comfortable in her home church district, but so did her son.

Her eyes darted around the barn, and when she found Wyatt sitting in the unmarried men's section, her stomach sank. He was handsome in his black-and-white Sunday suit while he spoke to Levi Kurtz, whom she recognized from school and youth group. She tried to force her eyes to look away, but when Wyatt glanced over, their gazes locked.

Her breath caught as they stared at each other, and memories of their joyful time together as a couple replayed in her mind. But it had all been a lie, a facade, since he'd been seeing someone behind her back.

When the song leader started the first line of the opening hymn, Makayla picked up her hymnal. She dismissed her confusing thoughts and turned her attention to worshiping the Lord. After all, she'd return home to Thomas soon, and Wyatt would go back to being part of her past.

❧

"Do you like working for Omar?" Levi asked Wyatt while sitting across from him during lunch.

After the service had ended, Wyatt and Levi had helped the other men convert the benches into tables for the noon meal. The congregation ate in shifts, with the men enjoying lunch first while the women served it, and then the women eating after the men were done. Once the benches had been set up, Wyatt and Levi found a place to sit. His older brother, Eli, and his father sat nearby talking to friends.

Although he and Levi had grown up together, attending the same one-room schoolhouse and youth group, they hadn't gotten close until a few years ago. Since they were both in their early thirties and single, they had a lot in common, and Wyatt was grateful to have a bachelor his age to sit with during the church services.

Wyatt placed lunch meat and cheese on a piece of bread and folded it in half. "Ya. I trained horses with my onkel before I got into building sheds, and a lot of what I learned came back to me."

"Do you think you'll keep working for him?"

"Ya, I like the work, and the pay is gut too." Wyatt peered around the barn, taking in the hum of conversations.

Women moved around the rows of men, distributing plates of food. Makayla and Becky walked into the barn carrying coffee carafes, and he hoped she'd fill cups at a different table. He took another bite of his sandwich and attempted to expel all thoughts of Makayla from his mind. He'd had a difficult time keeping his eyes off her during the service. No matter how he tried to concentrate on the minister's words, his eyes kept defying him and seeking out her pretty face in the congregation.

"I saw Makayla sitting with her mamm and Becky King."

Wyatt stopped chewing, and his gaze snapped to his friend's.

"From the look on your face you saw her too."

Wyatt wiped his mouth with a paper napkin, hoping to appear casual. "Ya, I did at her parents' place Friday. She's just visiting for the holidays."

"Huh. I guess it will be uncomfortable for you to work for your ex-girlfriend's dat with her there."

You have no idea. "I'll just avoid her."

Levi's brown eyes focused on something behind Wyatt. "Oh, here she comes."

Wyatt craned his neck over his shoulder while Makayla worked her way down the table, filling coffee cups. His body tensed as she approached.

"Kaffi?" she asked, holding up the carafe. He was almost certain her hand quivered with the motion.

He handed her his cup, careful not to allow his fingers to brush hers. He tried to ignore how her blue dress complemented her eyes—those eyes he'd once gotten lost in.

She filled the cup and handed it back to him.

"Danki," he muttered, his lungs constricting.

She gave him a solemn nod before her baby-blue eyes focused on Levi across the table. "Kaffi?"

"Thanks." Levi gave her his cup.

She poured the hot liquid into Levi's cup and moved on.

"Awkward," Levi whispered the word before sipping from his cup.

Wyatt snorted.

After lunch, Wyatt walked out into the cold, early November afternoon and shoved his hands into his pockets. The sky above them was bright blue and cloudless, and Wyatt breathed in the fresh fall air.

"What are your plans for this afternoon?" Levi asked while they strolled toward the stable to collect their horses.

Wyatt rubbed his cheek. "I was thinking a nap might be in order. I may even start that mystery novel I picked up at the library last week. How about you?"

"Same."

"Wyatt!"

He turned just as Mamm hurried over to him, pulling an attractive brunette who looked to be about his age along with her.

Oh no.

Levi patted his shoulder. "Have fun." He chuckled to himself before continuing toward the stable.

"Wyatt, this is Judy. She's Miriam Zook's niece, and she's visiting from Lititz." Mamm's grin widened. "And she's *single*, just like you."

Wyatt pinned a bright expression on his face. "Hello." He nodded.

The young woman responded with a shy smile.

"I invited Judy to visit with us this afternoon."

Not again. "I was planning to rest this afternoon."

"Nonsense." Mamm gestured between them. "Judy is coming home with us to visit and you can bring her back here later."

"Wunderbaar." Wyatt swallowed a groan. There went his peaceful Sunday afternoon.

If only he could convince his mother to stop trying to find him a wife, but that would be impossible.

Later that evening Wyatt guided his horse down the road after dropping Judy off at the Zooks' farm. He blew out a resigned sigh, and his posture sagged.

He had spent the afternoon sitting at his parents' kitchen table, trying to make conversation with Judy. Although she was lovely and lit up when she talked about working as a nanny for her neighbor, they had nothing in common. Wyatt had tried discussing books, but she preferred crocheting to reading. He mentioned a few of his friends who had moved to the Lititz area, but she didn't know any of them. He'd even brought up the weather as a last-ditch effort to pull her into a conversation, but Judy spent most of the afternoon discussing recipes with his mother while Wyatt and his father talked about work. He would have preferred to spend his afternoon resting and reading, but he couldn't be rude and embarrass his parents—as much as he longed for some solitude.

The journey to take her back to her aunt's house had been just as uncomfortable as their afternoon. He tried to think of something to say and wound up babbling on about Omar's farm while she nodded and occasionally cupped her hand to her mouth to cover a yawn. When they finally reached her aunt's house, she looked just as relieved as he felt when she shook his hand and rushed up the back steps.

During the short ride home, he found himself pondering the young women his mother had tried to encourage him to date during the past several years. He hadn't had anything in common with them. Nor had he felt any connection to them. Each and every encounter had been stilted, which he found frustrating. In fact, he hadn't connected with a woman since. . .*Makayla.*

He groaned and tried to shake off that truth. But it remained. When he'd been with Makayla, they'd never run out of words. She seemed to always understand him, and on the rare occasion that they hadn't talked, they sat in comfortable silence and held hands.

But that connection had been a farce. He gritted his teeth.

After stowing his horse and buggy, Wyatt jogged up the back steps at his parents' house. He spotted a lantern glowing in the kitchen and scrubbed his hand down his face, preparing himself for his mother's inquisition.

Wyatt pulled in a deep breath that seemed to bubble up from his toes and then hung up his coat and hat in the mudroom before kicking off his boots. He found his mother sitting at the kitchen table reading a book, just as he'd expected.

Mamm looked up, her expression hopeful. "How was the ride?"

"Fine." He leaned back on the counter.

Her brown eyes glittered. "Did you make plans to see her again?"

He touched the stubble on his chin. He didn't want to hurt her, but he also refused to commit the sin of lying. "Mamm, I'm sure you noticed we had nothing in common and—"

"Now, Wyatt," she began, "this was your first meeting. My first date with your dat was awkward, but then we fell in love. We were engaged six months later and married that following spring. You shouldn't give up so easily. You're thirty-two. It's time to settle down and start a family."

He suppressed the urge to roll his eyes. "Mamm, I appreciate that you want me to be like Eli, but I believe God has chosen this path for me. And I'm *froh*."

She walked over to him, barely coming up to his shoulder. "Wyatt, how can you be happy when you're alone?"

"I'm not alone." He gestured around the kitchen. "I have you and dat, Eli and his family, and I have a new job. My focus right now is my work. I don't have time for—"

"You need to *make time* for dating, Wyatt." She shook a finger at him. "When your dat and I are gone, you'll truly be alone."

He blew out a resigned sigh. "You're right, Mamm. I need to make time." He'd been down this road more times than he could count. Arguing was futile. "We both need to get up early tomorrow. Gut nacht." He started for the stairs.

"Did you see Makayla at church today?"

He stopping moving at the sound of her name. He pivoted to face his mother. "Ya."

"Freida said she'd be here through the holidays." Mamm seemed to study him. "Are you going to be okay working at the farm with her there?"

"Why wouldn't I be?"

Mamm took a step toward him. "Don't let her get to you, Wyatt. She hurt you once."

"I'm fine, Mamm. Really."

"If you say so." Mamm paused. "I worry about you, Wyatt. That's why I'm so determined to find you a *fraa*. I don't want you to be alone." Her voice quavered. "Every mother's dream is to see her kinner happy."

His chest compressed. "Danki, Mamm, but you don't need to worry about me."

"Okay." She patted his cheek. "Gut nacht, Sohn."

He hugged her and then jogged up the stairs.

CHAPTER FOUR

"Are there any kinner for me to play with?" Lukas asked the next morning.

Makayla glanced around the kitchen table at her parents, who were eating eggs, bacon, and home fries she had prepared. She had set her alarm to be up before her mother, determined to do her part to help while she was at home.

Today she planned to help her mother with chores. But first she needed to find a way to keep Lukas occupied. "No, there aren't any kinner," she told her son. "Mammi and Daadi's neighbors don't have any kinner your age, but you could help me with the sweeping."

Her son's little shoulders drooped. "Okay."

"Do you like to work in the barn, Lukas?" Dat asked.

His expression brightened. "Ya."

"Well then, you'll come out to the stable with me." Dat lifted his cup of coffee.

"Okay."

Makayla smiled at her father, and he winked.

After breakfast Dat led Lukas outside while Makayla and

her mother cleaned up the kitchen and started baking bread.

Staring out the window above the sink, Makayla saw Dat say something to Lukas before he hurried into the stable while Dat continued toward the barn, where the phone was located. She assumed her father had sent Lukas to find Wyatt while he checked the messages. Would Wyatt let Lukas help with his work? Surely he would.

"Makayla?"

She jumped with a start. "What?"

"*Was iss letz?*" Concern flickered over her mother's face.

"I was just thinking about Lukas. I hope he has fun working with Dat."

Her mother's expression warmed. "Your dat and I are so froh that you and Lukas are here. I'm sure they'll have a ball doing chores."

Makayla returned to the dough and hoped her mother was right.

◦○◦

"Do you need any help?"

Wyatt turned toward the entrance to the horse stall, where Lukas stood. "Hi, Luke."

"My name is Lukas."

"Is it all right if I call you Luke?"

The boy shrugged. "I guess so." He pointed toward the open stable door. "Mei daadi told me to ask if I can help you."

Wyatt grinned and leaned on his pitchfork. "Have you done farmwork before?"

"I help mei daadi and onkel back home." He pointed toward the wall as if New Wilmington sat on the other side.

"You said you're five, right?"

He stood a little taller. "Five and a half."

"Uh-huh." Wyatt rubbed his chin.

The boy pointed at him. "You don't have a beard."

Wyatt moved his fingers over his neck and shook his head. "Golly, you're right. I sure don't. I hadn't noticed it before."

Lukas grinned. "Do you have any kinner?"

"No, I can't say that I do." Then he tilted his head. "Do you?"

The boy chuckled. "No! I'm still little." He pointed to Wyatt. "You're funny."

Wyatt grinned. This kid was a hoot.

"Do you have any *bruders* or *schweschdere*?"

Wyatt leaned against the stall wall and set the pitchfork next to it. "I have an older brother. His name is Elijah, but he goes by Eli." He crossed his arms over his middle. "He's married to Gloria. They have a *bu* named Benjamin, but we call him Benji. He's eight. You'll like him. And Benji has a younger *schweschder* named Liz-Beth. She's six. And that's my family, not counting cousins, *aentis*, and *onkels*, but they don't live nearby."

"You're not married?"

"Nope, not as far as I know."

Lukas giggled. "You'd know if you were married."

"Ya, I guess so." Wyatt shook a finger at him. "But there might be some people who don't know if they're married or not."

Lukas snorted. Then his smile faded. "I don't have any bruders or schweschdere."

"Oh." Wyatt stood up straight.

"I live with mei mamm and mei other mammi and daadi. Mei onkel and *aenti* have a haus there too, and I have three cousins." He counted them off on his fingers. "Rosemary is seven. Leah is six, and Zeke is three. Aenti Barbie is having another boppli soon. I heard mei mamm say we have to be back before the boppli comes so she can help her."

Wyatt didn't want to think about Lukas and Makayla leaving, which made no sense to him. Why would it bother him? He barely knew Lukas. He shoved away the thought and gestured around the barn. "Do you like working on a farm?"

"Yeah." Lukas smiled. "The animals are fun."

"I suppose they are—most of the time."

"Are you a farmer?"

"I was a carpenter, but the place where I worked burned down."

"Wow." Lukas' eyes widened, and Wyatt noticed they were the same color as Makayla's. "Did you see the fire?"

"No. It happened in the middle of the night, so no one was hurt. But I needed a job, and your daadi offered me one. So here I am."

Lukas looked around the horse stall. "Are we going to stand here and talk all day? Or are you going to give me a chore to do?"

"Wow, Luke." Wyatt sighed with pretend annoyance. "You're just as demanding as your daadi." Then he held out his pitchfork. "How about we muck the stalls?"

"Okay." Lukas puffed out his chest before grabbing the tool. "I'm ready."

They set to work. Wyatt gave Lukas instructions, and soon they were each mucking a stall.

A little while later, Omar joined them in the stable. "How are things going in here?" he asked.

Wyatt shook his head and wiped the back of his hand across his forehead. "Well, Luke is working circles around me. I just can't keep up with him."

Lukas snickered a few stalls down. "Wyatt's a slowpoke."

"Now you're just being a bully," Wyatt teased, and Lukas' laughter became louder. He grinned at Omar. "He's a great kid."

Omar's face lit with happiness. "I think so too. I'm so glad Freida convinced Makayla to come home for the holidays."

Lukas bounded toward them, a grin on his little face. "Are you two going to work or what?"

"I'll tell you, Omar," Wyatt joked with a sigh. "This bu is making me work harder today than you have all last week. I might have to take a nap after lunch."

"A nap? Are you a boppli, Wyatt?" Lukas chortled, and Wyatt couldn't stop his laughter.

Omar joined in and mussed his grandson's hair.

Makayla glanced out the kitchen window at noon. It must have been the dozenth time she'd looked out the window hoping to catch a glimpse of Lukas working with Dat and Wyatt. She'd even swept the porch more than once, but she hadn't gotten a chance to see them. She hoped Lukas had had a good time working beside his grandfather and Wyatt.

Lukas finally exited the stable, and Wyatt appeared beside him. Her son gestured widely while telling a story, and Wyatt laughed.

"What are you looking at?" Mamm appeared beside her.

"Lukas."

"Aww." Mamm patted her shoulder. "How sweet. It looks like Lukas and Wyatt have become gut friends."

Dat joined them, and they all ambled toward the house.

"Here they come for lunch." Mamm opened the refrigerator and retrieved the pitcher of water.

Mamm filled their glasses, and Makayla brought a platter of lunch meat and a basket of rolls to the table before adding condiments.

The back door opened, and Lukas scampered into the kitchen

with his coat hanging off one arm. "Mamm! Mamm!" He jumped up and down and began to talk at a fast clip. "Me and Wyatt mucked the stalls. He's so funny, Mamm! He asked me if I had any kinner. And he also said that I made him work so hard that he needed to take a nap like a boppli!" He guffawed, bending at his waist.

Makayla felt someone watching her, and she turned toward the doorway, where Wyatt studied her with a sheepish expression. Not sure how to react, she swiveled toward her son. "Lukas, you need to hang up your coat and wash your hands. It's time for lunch."

He stopped laughing. "Can I work with Wyatt after lunch, Mamm? Please? Pleeease?"

Makayla hesitated for a moment and then nodded. "Ya, of course. But please go hang up your coat in the mudroom and then wash your hands." She shook her head while he darted toward the mudroom. "He's wound up."

"Sorry." Wyatt moved a little closer. "Didn't mean to get him going too much."

"*Nee*, it's. . .fine."

Mamm came up beside her. "Lukas is quite the eager beaver."

"That he is." Dat scrubbed his hands.

Makayla stole a glance at Wyatt. She tried to decode his pleasant expression, but it seemed genuine, which surprised her after the stoic look he'd given her Friday night.

After Wyatt washed his hands, he and Dat took their seats.

Lukas rushed over to Wyatt. "Can I sit by you?"

Wyatt's face shone with affection for her son. "Sure you can, buddy." He patted the chair.

Makayla was speechless and confused not only by how quickly her son had warmed up to Wyatt but also by how her ex-boyfriend seemed to have a sudden bond with him. She sank down onto a chair on the other side of Lukas before they all bowed their heads in prayer.

After the prayer, they all began making sandwiches.

"Mamm, can I have a sandwich like Wyatt's?" Lukas asked.

"Ya." Makayla met Wyatt's gaze. "What are you eating?" she asked.

"Roast beef." He placed the sandwich on Lukas' plate. "Here you go, bud. It's yours."

"Wyatt you don't have to—" she began.

"It's okay. I can make another one," Wyatt said, and Lukas smiled up at him.

"Danki." Makayla made herself a sandwich and began to eat it while her father and Wyatt discussed their plans for their afternoon chores.

Lukas chimed in, asking questions about the horses and the farm.

After lunch, she and Mamm started cleaning up while the men retrieved their coats.

"Mamm," Lukas began while buttoning his jacket, "Wyatt isn't married but he has a niece and a nephew around my age. Maybe I can meet them. Maybe you and me can go over to his haus, and I can play with them. What do you think about that?"

Makayla halted and shared an awkward glance with Wyatt. "Ya. Maybe."

"How about today?" Lukas divided a look between Makayla and Wyatt.

Makayla's gaze locked on Wyatt's, and heat began to crawl up her neck. "Oh Lukas, honey, I don't think today would be a gut day for that."

"Your mamm's right, Luke," Wyatt added. "But I'm sure we

can all get together sometime soon."

"Okay!" Lukas sang before rushing out the back door.

Wyatt grinned toward the door and then turned back to Makayla. "He's a great kid."

"Danki," she said.

Wyatt nodded and then headed outside.

Later that evening Wyatt knocked on the Hertzlers' back door. He stuck his hands in his pockets and rocked back on his heels while awaiting someone to answer the door. The evening air was cool, and he looked out toward his waiting horse and buggy.

He waited a few moments before knocking again. When he didn't hear any footsteps coming toward him, he hesitated and turned the knob before gingerly pushing it open.

After wiping his boots in the mudroom, Wyatt entered the kitchen, where Makayla stood at the counter. The delicious aroma of meatloaf floated over him, and his stomach growled. It had been hours since lunch, and his belly felt empty.

Wyatt remained in the doorway for a few moments while she gathered a stack of dishes from the cabinet. She turned toward him and jumped with a start before pressing her free hand to her chest and breathing deeply.

"I'm sorry." He held his hands up. "I didn't mean to startle you."

A blush tinged her cheeks, and her expression flickered with embarrassment. "It's my fault. I didn't hear you. I was deep in thought." She looked lovely, clad in a blue dress that complemented her baby-blue eyes, along with a black apron. He'd always thought that blue was her color.

He shook himself. Makayla was his ex-girlfriend, and he shouldn't be admiring her.

"Did you need something?" she asked, placing the stack of dishes on the table.

"Ya." He cleared his throat. "I wanted to tell your dat I was leaving for the night."

"He's in his office." She started toward the doorway. "I'll get him."

"No, that's fine. You can deliver the message if you don't mind."

She picked up a dish towel from the counter. "Okay."

"Please just tell him I finished my chores, and I'll see him in the morning."

"Sure."

Silence stretched between them, and they stared at each other. For a moment, he considered asking her what he'd done to cause her to leave without any explanation. He wanted to ask if she'd meant it all of those times she'd said she loved him and wanted a future with him. Or had she been lying to him? Had she been waiting for someone better to come along?

"Is that—" he started.

"Danki for—" she began.

They started to speak at the same time, and then they laughed. The sound of her happy lilt took him back in time once again and sent a strange warmth rushing through him.

"You first," Wyatt said.

She shook her head. "No, you." When he shook his head, she made a sweeping gesture and said, "I insist."

He licked his lips and gathered his thoughts. Then he pointed to the stove. "Are you making your superb meatloaf?"

"Ya, I am." She seemed to study him. "How'd you know?"

"I would never forget that appeditlich smell. I always looked forward to it."

She began fiddling with the dish towel. "We have plenty if

you want to stay. I'll just set another place." She tossed the dish towel onto the counter and opened the cabinet, where she chose another dish and added it to the stack.

"No, no." He held his hands up. "I wouldn't want to impose." He took a step back toward the mudroom. "You already fed me lunch." But for some stupid reason he wanted to stay.

"It's no imposition, Wyatt." She paused. "But I understand if you need to go. . ."

That was his cue to leave. "Right." He stroked his neck and started toward the door.

"Wyatt, wait," she said.

He spun to face her again and was stunned to find her standing next to him, her expression open.

She paused, swiping her hands down her apron. "Thanks for being so nice to Lukas."

He grinned. "That's not difficult. I meant it when I said he was a great kid."

"I appreciate it."

"You're very blessed to have him for a sohn, Makayla."

They stood only a breath away from each other, and his pulse began to zoom. He could almost reach out and touch her.

He moved his fingers over the zipper on his coat. "Well," he began. "I guess I'll see you tomorrow."

"Ya," she said.

Wyatt strode to his waiting horse and buggy and tried to ignore his stampeding heart.

CHAPTER FIVE

$\mathcal{W}$yatt hammered a nail into the split-rail fence Friday morning. The mid-November air was cold, but the sun was bright, a stark contrast to the brown meadow and leafless trees. He scanned the vast pasture where the horses stood and turned his attention back to the fence that desperately needed mending.

When he'd walked the pasture earlier in the day, he had spotted the broken rails and wondered what Omar's previous farmhand had done for chores. The fence should have been repaired in the spring and not left for late fall. He'd asked Omar if he had any planks, and his boss had been delighted to offer the supplies for the job. Wyatt would make a note to paint the fence for him when the weather was warm.

"Wyatt!" Lukas came running toward him with a big grin on his face and his arms flailing about.

Wyatt pushed his hat back on his head. "What's up, buddy?"

"Look at this rock I found." Lukas held his hand out, and his blue eyes sparkled while he presented the small, flat rock as if it was the most precious prize on earth.

Wyatt's lips twitched. All week long Lukas had followed

him around like his miniature shadow, and he had enjoyed every minute with the kid, working on chores together and discussing everything from the horses to what it was like when Wyatt was a boy. "Wow." He examined the flat, brown-and-gray stone. "That's the coolest rock I've ever seen."

"You can touch it."

Wyatt picked it up and turned it over in his hand. "Where'd you find this?"

"Daadi said I could go exploring." Lukas pointed toward the far end of the pasture. "I was just walking around and I saw it. It's almost as neat as the rock me and Leah found when we were exploring back home." He scrunched his nose. "Did you ever go exploring when you were a kid?"

"Plenty of times, but I never found a rock this great." He held the rock out toward the boy. "Danki for showing me."

Lukas pushed it toward him. "You can have it."

"I wouldn't want to take your very cool rock, Luke."

"It's yours." The boy grinned. "I'll find another one."

"You sure?"

"Positive."

"Thank you. I'll cherish it." Wyatt dropped the rock into his pocket. He'd be sure to leave it for Lukas later.

The boy pointed to the hammer. "Can I help you with the fence?"

"You can be my supervisor," Wyatt told him. "How about you point to the rails that need to be replaced, and I'll change them out?"

"Okay!"

For the next hour, Wyatt worked to fix the rotten planks while Lukas kept him entertained with stories about his grandfather's farm back in New Wilmington. He couldn't help but notice how different Lukas was from his mother. While Makayla was always a woman of few words, her son was a chatterbox.

When they finished the last rail, Wyatt loaded up the rotten ones in a wheelbarrow and put Lukas in charge of carrying the hammer and box of nails while they headed back to the stable.

"Look." Lukas pointed to the porch. "There's mei mamm!"

Makayla waved to them. "Lunch!"

"Is it lunchtime already?" Wyatt muttered. The morning had flown by. After depositing the wheelbarrow and supplies in the barn, they strode toward the house.

"Are you hungry, Wyatt? I sure am." Lukas took off toward the house.

Wyatt chuckled. If only he could bottle that energy. Once inside the house, he kicked off his boots and hung up his coat and hat on a peg in the mudroom before finger combing his thick hair. He entered the kitchen and was greeted by the scrumptious smells of chicken potpie. He nodded to Makayla and Freida before scrubbing his hands at the sink. The table was already set for five, and a chicken potpie casserole sat in the center.

When he turned toward the table, he found the only empty seat left was between Makayla and Freida. He sat down and bowed his head before Omar scooped chicken potpie casserole onto his plate and passed the dish to his wife.

"Mamm," Lukas began, his face full of excitement. "I went exploring on the farm today and found the best rock." He pointed at Wyatt. "Show mei mamm the rock."

Wyatt fished it from his pocket and held it out to Makayla.

"Oh my goodness." She took the rock from Wyatt and examined it, turning over in her hand. "What a special rock."

"I know," Lukas gushed. "I told Wyatt he could have it, and I'll find another one."

She handed the rock back to Wyatt. "That was very kind of

you." She gave him a sweet smile.

He put it back into his pocket, and his heart did a silly little jig. Then he swallowed a groan. He couldn't allow her to get to him.

While Lukas went on and on about the fence work, Wyatt scooped casserole onto his plate and began to eat. He turned toward Makayla beside him, and she studied her son with love sparkling in her eyes.

For a moment, he wondered what could have been if Makayla hadn't run away to the western end of the state. Would she have married Wyatt, built a house with him, and had a family with him, maybe had a son about Lukas' age?

Wyatt shook off the thoughts and studied his lunch. He had to stop allowing Makayla to sneak under his skin. He had to keep his guard up.

"Well, it sounds like you and Wyatt make a gut team," Omar said.

Wyatt looked up at his boss. "We sure do." He winked at the kid, who gave him a thumbs-up. When he felt someone watching him, he cast his eyes toward Makayla, who studied him with appreciation. He quickly looked away.

After lunch, Wyatt headed back outside, pushing all thoughts of his ex-girlfriend from his mind.

"Wyatt!" Lukas trailed after him. "What chores are we going to do now?"

He rested his hand on his friend's little shoulder. "How about we gather up our supplies and then check the fence in the far pasture?"

"Let's go!" Lukas took off running, and Wyatt grinned.

⁓

The trill of the sewing machine filled the room later that afternoon while Makayla sewed another pair of trousers for Lukas.

She hummed to herself and enjoyed the quiet time alone to pray. Her encounters with Wyatt were getting easier, but the past still stood between them.

A knock sounded on the doorframe, and she turned to see her mother standing just outside the room.

"You've been busy." Mamm pointed to the small pile of clothes Makayla had already made for her son.

"Ya." Makayla leaned her elbow on the sewing table. "Lukas has gotten taller. I thought I'd make him a few shirts and trousers, along with another Sunday suit."

Mamm sat on a chair beside the sewing table. "Kinner grow so fast. It seems like only yesterday you needed a stool to reach the kitchen counter." A thoughtful look overtook her face. "It's nice how close Lukas has gotten to Wyatt. Your dat mentioned they start first thing with mucking stalls together and then Lukas follows him around all day, ready to help him with every chore. They feed the horses together, and he's even learning how to train them. He wants to shoe them too. Of course, he's too little, but he can watch."

Makayla rested her chin on her palm. "Lukas talked about Wyatt nonstop last night when I put him to bed." She found it curious that Lukas seemed more excited to see Wyatt than he'd ever been when Thomas had come over to visit.

She had been contemplating that while sewing earlier. She couldn't stop herself from contemplating the admiration she'd found in Wyatt's eyes when he looked at her son. She'd found the same fondness in her son's eyes when he saw Wyatt. It baffled her. In fact, Wyatt had done nothing but bewilder her since she'd arrived home. She kept wondering if he'd changed or if she'd misjudged him when she decided to leave.

But if she'd misjudged Wyatt, then why had Fern Lehman

told her that she'd seen Wyatt kissing and holding hands with another young woman at the ice-cream parlor all those years ago?

"When's your wedding?" Mamm's question yanked Makayla back to the present.

"February."

"I'm surprised you're not waiting until the spring."

Makayla shrugged. "Thomas is almost done making some renovations to his haus. He added on another bedroom and bathroom for Lukas and me since he lives in the *daadihaus* on his schweschder's farm. We thought about getting married sooner, but it made sense to wait until after the holidays. And there was no reason to wait until spring since second marriages aren't a big deal. We'll only have a few family members there."

"I'd love to help you with your wedding plans, and your dat and I would be honored to come."

"You don't need to travel all that way for one day." Makayla waved off her mother's offer. "Like I said, it will be small."

Mamm seemed to study her. "Is everything okay?"

"What do you mean?"

"Are you excited to marry Thomas?"

"Of course I am," Makayla insisted. "Why wouldn't I be?"

"Well..." Mamm hedged. "When you talk about him, you're very matter of fact."

"I don't mean to be that way. I'm just grateful Thomas offered to marry me. I'm blessed that two men were ever interested in building a life with me."

"Why would you say that?"

"I'm so plain and boring. It's a wonder I ever—"

"Hold on." Mamm held her hand up, silencing her. "Why would you call yourself plain and boring?"

Makayla swallowed as the cruel words from Fern Lehman

echoed in her mind. *"You'll never find a husband. Wyatt would never marry anyone like you!"* The familiar sting overtook her.

"Mei liewe, you're a talented artist, you have a kind and generous heart, and you're *schee*. Any man who knows you would be blessed to have you in his life."

Makayla sat up straight and turned her attention to the trousers she was working on. "I need to get back to this sewing. Lukas will need these trousers for helping with chores, and I need to start working on Christmas gifts for Thomas, Barbie, Tim, Stella, Simeon, and the kinner—"

"Sweetheart, I'm worried about you." Mamm's voice was full of compassion. "Do you think maybe you're marrying too soon after Markus' death?"

Makayla pursed her lips. "No."

"Listen to me." Her mother's voice pleaded with her. "You shouldn't marry Thomas if you don't love him."

Makayla stilled for a fraction of a second but returned to sewing.

Mamm touched her shoulder and retreated from the room.

Makayla stopped the machine, closed her eyes, and sighed. Her mother made it sound so simple, but nothing was that simple. Her son needed a father, and Thomas had offered to be his father.

And that was that.

But if it was so cut and dry, why did doubt fill her at the thought of marrying him?

Wyatt led his horse toward his father's stable the following Monday evening. He set his lantern on the stall and took care of his horse. He had spent another day doing chores for Omar with his little buddy Lukas following him around the farm. Today he'd started showing Lukas how to train the horses, and the boy had seemed to enjoy every minute.

He couldn't help but think that he would miss the kid after he returned to New Wilmington in a month and a half. Would he miss Makayla too?

He shoved away the thought. He and Makayla had only traded greetings and a few smiles since their talk a week ago, but it was just as well. What more could they say since they'd both moved on?

"Wyatt." His brother sauntered toward him.

"Eli. Wie geht's?"

"I thought I heard your horse coming down the driveway. I wanted to check in and see how you're doing." Although Eli was three years older than Wyatt, he was a couple of inches shorter. But they'd often been told that they had similar facial bone structure, along with the same light brown hair and golden-brown eyes as their father.

Wyatt gave him a confused look. "I'm fine. You?"

"Gut. How's it going at Omar's farm?"

"Great." Wyatt leaned back on the stall. "I like the work a lot."

Eli nodded slowly. "It's not uncomfortable for you with Makayla visiting?"

Aha! So that's what his brother was really asking. "It is, but it's just temporary. She's heading back to New Wilmington after Christmas." He brushed his hands down his trousers. "I'll miss her sohn." He explained how Lukas was his unofficial assistant on the farm. "That reminds me. I wanted to build him a swing. Don't we have some wood around here?"

"I think there's some in the back of the barn by Dat's workbench."

"Danki." Wyatt started back there.

"Hey, Wyatt," Eli called after him. "Don't get too attached to the kid."

Wyatt looked over at his brother. "Why not?"

"Just. . .be careful."

"What do you mean by that?"

Eli moved his hand over a loose piece of wood on the stall wall. "I remember how rough it was when Makayla took off. I don't want you to go through that again."

"What does having a relationship with her sohn have to do with her hurting me again?"

"I think it's kind of obvious." Eli shrugged. "If you get too close to her sohn, you're opening yourself up to her again."

Wyatt studied his older brother while irritation coursed through him. "It's been a long time since she hurt me. I won't fall for that again. I think I'm smart enough not to make that mistake twice." He kicked at a small pile of hay with the toe of his boot. "Besides, I'm not interested in a relationship right now."

Eli held his hands up as if to calm him. "Just listen to me, Wyatt. You and Makayla have a history. You once told me that you wanted to build a future with her. It wouldn't be difficult for you to fall for her again."

"Danki for your concern, but I can handle my own relationships." He slipped past his older brother and started for the back of the barn.

"Wyatt," Eli called after him. "I'm only saying this because I don't want you to get hurt again."

"How about you stay out of my business?" Wyatt went to find supplies so he could build Luke a swing.

CHAPTER SIX

$\mathcal{T}$he following morning, Makayla smiled over at her mother. "I've missed making Christmas cards with you."

"I have too."

After finishing their chores, they had set to work creating the cards. Makayla drew a covered bridge in snow on the front, and her mother wrote a message on the inside before addressing and stamping the envelopes. Makayla had always loved to draw but hadn't had much time for it since becoming a mother. It was a treat to be able to create the cards.

"Do you think Lukas would like to help us?" Mamm asked.

"Absolutely." She tapped her pen against her chin. "That's if we can get him away from Wyatt long enough."

Mamm chuckled.

"We should save some for him to color. He'll be disappointed if we don't."

"Lukas is very artistic like you. I've enjoyed the drawings you sent me."

Happiness filled Makayla. "Danki."

They worked in silence for a few moments.

"I love seeing Lukas interact with your dat. I know your dat would love to keep the farm in our family."

Makayla chewed her lower lip as guilt swirled in her chest. Her father had always said that he wanted to leave the farm to her heir, but that would be difficult if she was living on the other side of the state.

"I'm not saying that to make you feel bad, Makayla," Mamm hedged. "But if you ever decided to move back home, you know your dat would be froh to build you and your family a haus here, and then you, your husband, and your heirs could take over the farm and he could eventually retire."

She nodded. "I know." But she doubted Thomas would ever consider leaving New Wilmington since his family was there. She started drawing another card. "I can't believe Thanksgiving is next week."

"The month has flown by too quickly."

Makayla nodded. She was savoring her time with her parents and her community.

They continued creating cards for almost an hour, and then Mamm stood. "I think we've done enough for today. I'm going to go work on a Christmas gift I'm making for Lukas. I started a quilt for him."

"He'll love that." Makayla stretched her wrist. "I think I'll write a few letters before I make lunch."

"Okay." Mamm patted her shoulder on her way out of the kitchen.

Makayla wrote to her in-laws and then to Barbie. Now she needed to write to her fiancé. She stared down at her notepad and wrote, "Dear Thomas." She fiddled with her pen. Why was it easier to write to Markus' parents and her sister-in-law than to her fiancé?

Mamm's words from last week echoed in her mind: *"You*

shouldn't marry Thomas if you don't love him."

She groaned. It was her business whom she chose to be Lukas' stepfather.

She poised her pen and began to write:

I hope this letter finds you well. It's cold here in Bird-in-Hand. Lukas is having fun helping with the chores on the farm. He likes working with the horses. My parents are enjoying every moment with him. I had to make him more shirts and trousers since he's outgrowing his clothes so quickly.

It's also been nice to see old friends at church. I can't believe Thanksgiving will be here next week. My mom and I made Christmas cards like we used to when I was at home. I always loved drawing a farm scene or a covered bridge with snow on the front of the cards and writing "Merry Christmas from our family to yours" on the inside.

Makayla stared down at the notepad and racked her brain. She reread it and frowned. The letter was really bland. Stilted, actually. Why couldn't she think of something more interesting to stay to the man who would be her husband in a couple of months?

She considered telling Thomas about how Lukas was enjoying every minute with Wyatt, but what would Thomas say? Would he even care that her ex-boyfriend worked for her parents? She considered that question and couldn't come up with an answer. She wasn't sure if he'd care or not, and she wasn't sure how she felt about that either.

She began writing again:

I hope you're having a good week. Be sure to be careful on the roofs. Please tell everyone hello for Lukas and me.

> *Fondly,*
> *Makayla*

She folded the letter, slipped it into the envelope, and addressed it before sticking a stamp on it. Then she gathered up the three letters, pulled on her shawl, and stepped out onto the porch.

She started down the steps but stopped when she heard Lukas laughing nearby. She followed the sound until she came to the side of the barn, where Lukas played on a swing hanging from a tall oak tree. He pumped his legs high into the air while Wyatt stood nearby, grinning.

"Mamm!" Lukas hollered. "Look at how high I am. I'm going to touch the clouds!"

"I see that," she exclaimed.

Wyatt waved to her and then closed the distance between them.

"Did you put up the swing?" she asked him.

"Ya." His expression became sheepish. "Mei *bruderskinner* have an elaborate swing set with a fort and slide that I built for them. I could build one for Luke, but it would take me a while, and I have so much to do here." He gestured around the farm. "But I thought he might like a swing. I found some rope and a piece of wood last night, and I hung it earlier today." He jammed his thumb toward Lukas and then shielded his mouth with his hand and lowered his voice as if sharing a secret. "And I have the sneaking suspicion that he likes it."

He grinned, and she couldn't help thinking that he was handsome. *Really* handsome. And he truly cared for her child. At that moment she was so overwhelmed that she couldn't speak.

His smile flattened, and he held his hands up. "Whoops. I should have asked you first. Since it could hold my weight, I thought it was okay. But if I was out of line since I didn't—"

"Nee, nee, nee," she interrupted him. "Wyatt, it's fine. I mean, it's better than fine. It's actually pretty amazing that you did that for him. Danki."

He blew out a puff of air and wiped his hand over his forehead.

"Whew. I thought I was in trouble."

They both were silent for a moment while they watched Lukas continue to pump his legs and glide up toward the blue sky.

"Does he have a swing set at home?"

She turned toward Wyatt, who watched her with interest. "His cousins do." She swallowed as memories rippled over her. "Markus had built him one at our former haus. Lukas liked to play on the slide. He was only three when Markus. . ." Her voice trailed off. "Anyway, I know he'll enjoy this very much. Danki, Wyatt."

"I'm sorry about Markus," he said before he paused.

The empathy in his honey-brown eyes took her by surprise.

"I've stayed friendly with your folks, and Omar told me when he passed away."

At that moment, she felt close to him—closer than she'd ever felt to Thomas. She trusted Wyatt, and she was comforted by his words.

But she couldn't allow him to worm his way back into her heart. Not only had she made a promise to Thomas, but she couldn't risk Wyatt hurting her again. She needed to put some space between herself and Wyatt—*fast*. Holding up the letters, she started toward the path leading to the driveway. "I need to take these to the mailbox."

"Wait, Mamm!" Lukas dragged his feet along the ground until he came to stop. "I want to take letters and push up the flag." He leaped off the swing and held out his hands.

She gave Lukas the letters and then looked up at Wyatt. "Lukas loves to put the mail out and then pick it up after the mailman comes."

"Who are they for?" Her son examined each envelope.

"Mammi and Daadi, Aenti Barbie, and. . .Thomas."

Lukas grasped the envelopes. "Did you tell them that I'm

working on the farm?"

"Ya." She gave his shoulder a gentle squeeze before he ske-daddled down the path. "Don't run, Lukas!" she called after him. "You'll fall." When he continued to race away, she clucked her tongue. "Always in a hurry." Then she looked over at Wyatt. "Thanks again."

"No problem."

She nodded and then ambled toward the house.

"Makayla!" Dat beckoned her to join him in the barn. "Becky King left you a message asking if she can come to visit today."

She hurried toward the barn as excitement filled her. A visit from her best friend was just what she needed.

Later that afternoon Wyatt peered out from the stable to where Lukas played with Lily King. He folded his arms over his chest and smiled while Lukas pushed Lily on the swing, and the little blond giggled while pumping her legs.

He recalled how he and Makayla used to spend time with Lily's parents, Becky and Perry, when they were in youth group. They had started dating at the same time, and Makayla and Becky took turns hosting dinners for Wyatt and Perry. He and Perry had been best friends, but it all changed when Makayla left and Becky and Perry were married. He and Perry didn't have much in common after that. In fact, it seemed like most of Wyatt's friends had moved on and gotten married, and he was the only one out of their group who was still a bachelor and living with his parents.

Lukas spotted him and waved. "Wyatt! Come push us!"

He hesitated. He was caught up with his chores at the moment. And Omar was busy with a customer interested in a horse for his sixteen-year-old son.

"All right." Wyatt couldn't resist that boy. He jogged over and pushed Lily, who responded with a squeal as she pumped her little legs faster.

Lukas clapped, and Wyatt grinned over at him. He had relished the joy he had seen in the child's face when he'd hung up the swing for him. And the appreciation in Makayla's eyes had sent tenderness tumbling through him as well.

Throughout the morning he'd pondered the letters she'd written and wondered who Thomas might be. She hadn't called him a brother-in-law, and it would be strange for her to write to her brother-in-law anyway. He could be a friend, but it would also be unusual for her to have a friend. Unless he was her boyfriend. . .

Not that it was any of his business.

"My turn!" Lukas exclaimed. "My turn!"

Lily dragged her feet along the ground and then hopped off the swing before Lukas climbed on it.

"Push me up to the sky, Wyatt!" Lukas ordered.

"Hold on. . ." Wyatt pushed him, and giggles erupted from him again.

Wyatt laughed and kept pushing.

⁓

Makayla gazed over at Jake sleeping in the portable crib Becky had brought for him. "It seems like only yesterday Lukas was that small."

"They grow so fast." Becky sighed and touched her abdomen.

Makayla smiled over at her friend. "I'm so glad you came to visit today. I've been thinking about you and meaning to call."

She and Becky had spent the past hour baking cookies and

getting caught up, discussing their lives as well as friends in the community.

"I've wanted to connect with you too." Becky picked up her mug of tea. "You said something interesting at church, and we never got to talk about it because I couldn't get you alone. You were practically mobbed while we were helping out in Miriam's kitchen." She leaned forward. "You said you're marrying Markus' best friend."

Makayla pushed the ribbons from her prayer covering behind her shoulders. "That's right."

"When did he propose?"

"A couple of months ago." She moved her fingers over her warm mug.

"A couple of months ago?" Becky looked incredulous, and Makayla nodded. "That means we've traded a letter or two since the proposal. Why haven't you mentioned it in your letters?"

"I—I guess it slipped my mind."

Becky snorted. "Okay, Makayla. A proposal doesn't just slip your mind. When Perry proposed to me, I wanted to climb up on my parents' roof and shout for joy. Why are you acting like it's no big deal?"

"Thomas isn't like that. He doesn't get excited about things." She took a sip of tea. "It just makes sense for me to marry him since he'll be a gut dat for Lukas."

Becky studied her.

Makayla needed to change the subject. "I was surprised when I got home and found out that Wyatt's working for mei dat."

"How's that been?"

"Fine. He's been very kind to Lukas." Makayla explained how Lukas talked about him constantly and followed him around like a little apprentice. She also told her about the swing he'd set up for Lukas.

Becky picked up an oatmeal-raisin cookie from the plate in the center of the table. "Wyatt hasn't dated much since you left. Mei mamm talks to his mamm at church, and she said Wyatt's mamm is constantly trying to set him up with a maedel. She's determined to find him a fraa."

"Interesting." Makayla couldn't imagine why Wyatt wasn't married. He was hardworking, kind, thoughtful, great with kids, handsome...

"Maybe he never got over you." Becky said the words so matter-of-factly that Makayla gasped. "Why are you looking at me like that?"

"How could that be true when Fern Lehman said she saw him cheating on me?"

"Perry always insisted that was a lie."

"But she was our friend, and lying is a sin."

"Fern may have been a member of our friend group, but I never trusted her. She never seemed genuine to me. I also felt like she was using us. I have to admit I haven't missed her since she moved to Colorado with her husband a few years ago." Becky broke the cookie in half and ate a small piece. "Anyway, I *strongly* suggested that you ask Wyatt about the rumor, but you insisted on leaving even though I said it might not be true."

Makayla nodded. "You're right. Sometimes my stubbornness gets the better of me, but Fern was so convincing." She could still hear Fern telling her that she'd never be good enough for a man as hardworking and handsome as Wyatt.

"Have you ever asked Wyatt about it?"

"No, and it doesn't matter now. The past is the past."

Becky looked at the clock above the stove and frowned. "I'd better call my driver. I need to get home and start supper."

Makayla walked with Becky to the barn. When they ambled back toward the house, they stopped by the tree where Wyatt pushed a giggling Lily on the swing.

Lukas rushed over to Makayla. "Mamm! Me and Lily are having so much fun."

"That's great." Makayla rubbed his shoulder.

"Lily," Becky called, "we have to get ready to go now. Thank Wyatt for pushing you on the swing."

The little girl brought the swing to a stop. "Danki," she told him before she bounced over to her mother.

Becky waved to him. "Danki, Wyatt."

"No problem." He waved to the children and smiled at Makayla. She nodded and took Lukas' hand.

"He's always been gut with the kinner," Becky said while they walked toward the house.

Makayla opened the storm door and looked over to where Wyatt sauntered toward the stable. "That's why I don't understand why he isn't married."

"Maybe God hasn't led him to the right woman yet," Becky quipped. "We never know what God has planned for us."

Makayla nodded. "That's true."

❦

That evening, Lukas snuggled under the covers. "I'm having so much fun with Wyatt and Daadi. And I really like Lily."

"She likes you too." Makayla handed him his teddy bear.

"You know what, Mamm?"

"What, Lukas?"

"Wyatt is my best friend."

Makayla's heart tripped over itself. "Why is he your best friend?"

"Because he's really funny. He makes me laugh all the time."

Her son grinned. "And he's also really nice. I love that swing he made me. And he teaches me things. He taught me how to use a hammer and a measuring tape today. He's going to show me how to train horses." His expression became serious. "Do you think Wyatt could come with Mammi and Daadi the next time they visit us?"

Makayla moved her hands over the quilt while trying to think of a response. "I doubt it, sweetie."

"Why not?" Lukas whined.

"Well, Daadi would need someone to stay here and take care of the horses. If he didn't, they wouldn't have any food to eat. You wouldn't want that, would you?"

"No, I guess not." Lukas scrunched his nose. Then his face brightened. "Maybe Wyatt could come and Daadi could stay home. They could take turns."

"We'll see." Makayla leaned over and kissed his cheek. "Sweet dreams. Don't forget to say your prayers. *Ich liebe dich.*"

"Love you too, Mamm."

Makayla picked up the lantern and carried it out into the hallway, where she gingerly closed her son's door. Then she leaned against the wall and took a deep breath. Her son had gotten too attached to Wyatt, and she didn't know what she would do about it.

CHAPTER SEVEN

$\mathcal{M}$akayla climbed out of her father's buggy Sunday morning and scanned the Mast family's farm before the church service. She took in their spacious white farmhouse, row of barns, large pasture dotted with cows, and second white farmhouse at the other side of the pasture. The scent of animals and moist earth hung in the cool morning air. The men in the congregation lingered by the pasture fence, and the women filed into Eleanor Mast's kitchen, carrying pies they would share during lunch. The younger men and women visited near Eleanor's garden.

Makayla silently marveled at how spending time with Wyatt—and especially seeing him with her son—had reduced some of her anxiety about being reunited with him. She'd been silly for worrying she couldn't handle seeing him at church when for some crazy reason it felt normal to interact with him on an almost daily basis.

"There's Wyatt!" Lukas announced before bounding toward his friend, who stood by the pasture fence talking to a group of men.

Makayla gasped. "Lukas!" she called after him. "We need go to the kitchen with Mammi."

She called him again, but he continued trotting toward Wyatt and the other men around him. She glanced behind her and found her father taking care of the horse.

"Let him go," Mamm said.

Makayla shook her head. "Nee, he belongs with me. Please take my pie to the kitchen, and I'll meet you there," she said before she reluctantly chased after her son.

She met up with him just as he approached Wyatt, who stood talking to Levi. He and Wyatt looked to be the oldest bachelors in the congregation, and she wondered why Levi hadn't found a wife either.

Lukas charged over to him. "Wyatt! *Gude mariye!*"

Wyatt and Levi looked down at Lukas.

"Hey, buddy." Wyatt gave him a high five and then jammed his thumb toward Levi. "This is my friend Levi." He nodded at Levi. "Have you met Luke?"

"I'm Lukas Blank, and I'm five and a half."

Levi grinned. "Gut to meet you."

"This is mei mamm." Lukas tapped Makayla's arm. "She's Makayla."

Heat climbed her neck when Levi and Wyatt turned their eyes to her. She lifted her hand in an awkward wave.

"I work on mei daadi's horse farm, and I help Wyatt with chores." Lukas began telling Levi the details of his chores.

"As soon as he saw you, he took off running," she said to Wyatt.

He leaned back on the pasture fence and smiled.

She glanced around the property and spotted Wyatt's sister-in-law standing by the back porch with a little girl by her side. "Is that your niece with Gloria?"

"Ya, that's Liz-Beth. She turned six a few weeks ago."

"She looks just like her mamm."

Wyatt pointed. "Benji is standing over there with Eli. He looks just like him too."

She followed his stare to where his brother and nephew stood with his father. "He sure does."

Wyatt chuckled.

"He's tall for his age, ya?" she said. "I would imagine he'll be tall like you."

"I guess we'll see."

She pivoted to face him, and the sparkle in his honey-brown eyes sent warmth rushing through her. "I'll take Lukas to the kitchen with me." She tapped her son's shoulder. "Mei liewe, we need to go see Mammi."

"I want to stay with Wyatt and Levi." Lukas frowned. "Please."

Makayla's cheeks were so hot she feared they might catch fire. "No, Lukas. You need to come with me."

"Please, Mamm?" He stuck his lip out, giving her his puppy-dog look. "I don't want to sit with the ladies."

"Come to the kitchen with me to visit for now. Then you can sit with Daadi." She looked to her left and right. Where was her dat when she needed him? He must have led his horse to the pasture.

"It's okay, Makayla. He can sit with me."

She turned toward Wyatt, and the earnestness in his eyes caught her off guard.

"Danki, Wyatt." Lukas beamed.

"No." She shook her head. "It's not appropriate."

"Why not?"

"Because we're not family. You shouldn't feel obligated to entertain mei sohn."

"I don't feel obligated, Makayla." His brow furrowed.

Something resembling annoyance flitted over his face, and guilt nipped at her.

"I didn't mean to offend you." Would community members assume that she was dating Wyatt if Lukas sat in church with him? But even if a rumor started, did it matter? She sighed and turned to Lukas. "Do you want to sit with Wyatt instead of Daadi?"

Her son nodded.

"He'll be fine," Wyatt insisted.

"Danki." Another wave of attraction for Wyatt gripped her, and Makayla hightailed it toward the kitchen.

"What's going on between you and Makayla?" Levi asked Wyatt.

After the service, Wyatt and Levi sat at the long table eating lunch. A buzz of conversations swirled around them. Wyatt popped a pretzel into his mouth and cast his eyes to Lukas sitting at the other end of the table with his grandfather.

Although Wyatt had enjoyed having the boy at his side during church, he couldn't help irritation from coursing through him when he thought of what Makayla had said to him earlier that morning. As if he didn't know that Lukas wasn't his family. He was surprised she hadn't reminded him that she'd left him and married someone else too.

He'd tried his best to avoid looking at her during the service, but his eyes had continued to defy him and peer over at her frequently. She had looked effortlessly beautiful while she'd kept her focus on the minister and when she'd whispered to Becky beside her. Each time her gaze had caught his, they'd shared an awkward nod.

"You okay, Wyatt?"

"Huh?" His eyes snapped up to meet his best friend's

concerned expression across the table. "I'm fine." He lowered his voice. "And there's nothing going on between Makayla and me. Absolutely nothing."

"Then why is her sohn stuck to you like glue?"

Wyatt shrugged and then half grinned. "I suppose it's because of my magnetic personality."

Levi chuckled. "Keep telling yourself that. That's why you're still single, right?"

"Hey." Wyatt pointed a pretzel at him. "Don't forget you're single too." He added lunch meat to a piece of bread and took a bite.

"It's kinda crazy how that kid likes you so much." Levi took a sip of coffee. "Any chance you and Makayla might get back together?"

"Nope." Wyatt wiped his mouth on a paper napkin. "That will never happen."

He took another bite of his sandwich and looked out toward the barn entrance where Makayla carried a tray containing pieces of pie. He recalled the letters Lukas had toted to the mailbox for her, and he once again wondered who Thomas was. For all Wyatt knew, Makayla had a boyfriend waiting for her back in New Wilmington, and if so, that would be a relief. It made life even less complicated if Makayla had already promised her heart to someone else. She'd return to New Wilmington after the holidays and stay out of his life for good.

But Wyatt had to admit that he would miss Lukas.

And deep down, he feared he'd miss Makayla too.

❦

The appetizing smell of turkey, gravy, and rolls permeated the kitchen Thanksgiving afternoon. Wyatt ate another piece of turkey while his brother shared a story about a cow that continued to somehow unlock the pasture gate and lead the herd down the street despite Eli's efforts to try different ways to lock it.

"I saw Makayla's sohn sitting with you during church on Sunday," Mamm said. "He looks like he's gotten awfully attached to you."

Gloria nodded. "I thought that too."

"Luke is a gut kid." Wyatt shrugged.

His mother and Gloria seemed to share a knowing look.

"Makayla might be looking for a dat for him," Gloria said. "You need to be careful."

Mamm's expression became stern. "I agree. She's hurt you once, Wyatt."

He fought the urge to roll his eyes. He was so tired of being told to be careful around Makayla. "I'm not looking for a relationship," he told them. "My focus right now is doing a gut job for Omar."

Gloria tapped her fingers on the table. "That reminds me. I have a maedel for you to meet, Wyatt."

"Really!" Mamm's eyes sparkled. "Who is it?"

Oh no. . . Here we go again.

Wyatt turned toward his father and brother, hoping for help redirecting the conversation, but they still were engrossed in a discussion about the pasture fence and new locks for the gate.

"Her name is Mayme, and she lives over in White Horse. She's a seamstress," Gloria explained.

"I'm really not interested—"

His sister-in-law held up her hand, shushing him. "Just listen. She's thirty-five, and she's very outgoing. She's perfect for you. I'll invite her over for lunch one day."

Wyatt's shoulders sank.

"How'd you meet her?" Mamm asked.

"Mei schweschder Twila ran into her at the farmers market last week. They had gone to the same youth group."

While Gloria talked on about Wyatt's next blind date, he looked at his nephew. "Benji, how about we go take care of the animals after supper?"

"Sure, Onkel."

"Great." Wyatt couldn't wait to get some fresh air.

⁓

"Those are lovely." Mamm sat down beside Makayla later that evening and examined the most recent stack of homemade Christmas cards. "You're doing a great job."

Lukas grinned at her from across the table. "Mamm drew the covered bridge, and I'm coloring them."

Mamm gently bumped her shoulder against Makayla. "I told you he'd inherited your talent for drawing."

Makayla smiled. Mamm was right. Lukas was doing a great job shading the bridge while staying in the lines, which was unusual for a boy who wasn't yet six.

She and Mamm had cooked their Thanksgiving dinner earlier, and while Dat retreated out to the stables to care for the horses and Mamm had taken a nap, Makayla and Lukas had started on the Christmas cards that she and her mother had saved for Lukas to finish. She enjoyed the quiet time with her son while they drew and talked about the upcoming holidays.

"Would you like to help?" Makayla handed her mother a pen and her address book. "You can sign the cards and address the envelopes."

They worked in silence for several moments.

Mamm stamped an envelope. "Did you check the messages this morning?"

"Ya." Makayla continued to draw while she spoke. "Stella and Barbie called to wish us all a happy Thanksgiving. And there were a couple of messages for Dat."

"Did Wyatt wish us a happy Thanksgiving too?" Lukas asked.

Makayla turned her attention to her son. He looked adorable with his brow furrowed while he colored a bridge blue. "No, there wasn't a message from Wyatt."

"I miss him."

Makayla spotted her mother watching her out of the corner of her eye, and she ignored her. She hadn't been able to get Wyatt out of her mind since Sunday. She kept pondering how happy her son had been to sit with him during the service. Lukas had beamed nearly nonstop, and when he whispered something to Wyatt, Wyatt would grin at him and then put his finger to his lips to remind him to be quiet. The scene had been almost too much for her as she took in the fondness between Lukas and Wyatt.

After church she'd thanked Wyatt again for allowing Lukas to sit with him, and Wyatt had given her a curt nod before helping to convert the benches into tables. She couldn't stop herself from worrying that she'd offended him when she'd reminded him that he wasn't Lukas' family.

She found the entire situation puzzling. Her son had bonded with Wyatt too quickly, and Lukas was going to be devastated when they returned to New Wilmington. She had to find a way to stop his attachment, even though it was going to break Lukas' heart.

"You saw Wyatt yesterday," she told her son, "and you'll see him tomorrow when he comes to work." She returned to drawing another bridge on a blank piece of paper, but concern filled her. She had to find a way for Lukas to get just as attached to Thomas. And how could she do that? Perhaps she would ask Thomas to make time for him. Maybe take him fishing in the spring or work on some chores around her father-in-law's farm.

But the more important question was, shouldn't Lukas already feel close to Thomas? After all, he'd known Thomas since he was born.

The question settled heavily over her heart.

"Have you heard from Thomas?" Mamm asked as if reading Makayla's thoughts.

"No." Makayla kept her eyes trained on her drawing.

"Didn't you write him last week?"

"Ya, I did." Makayla hedged. "Most likely his response is in the mail."

"Has he written you since you've been here?" Mamm asked.

"No."

Mamm was quiet for a moment, and the sound of the clock ticking filled the kitchen. "Has he called you?"

"No."

"Have you called him?"

"I left him a message when we arrived." Makayla could feel her mother's disapproval coming off her in waves, but she continued to work on her covered bridge scene.

"Don't you think it's odd that Thomas hasn't reached out to you?" Mamm's words were measured.

Makayla released a long breath. "He's not like that."

Mamm's brow wrinkled. "Not like what?"

"He's not. . ." Makayla searched for the correct word. "He's not sentimental."

"But doesn't he want to know how you and Lukas are doing?"

"I like Thomas," Lukas chimed in.

Makayla gave her mother a pointed look, silently begging

her to drop the subject. She didn't want to discuss Thomas in front of Lukas.

"I do too." She pushed her finished drawing over to her son for him to color. "I'm sure he's just busy."

"Too busy to reach out to his fiancée?"

"Mamm, please drop it," Makayla hissed.

"I like Thomas," Lukas repeated. "But Wyatt is my best friend."

Makayla sucked in a breath. Her son certainly was going to miss Wyatt when they went home, and she dreaded how she would handle his grief.

CHAPTER EIGHT

*W*yatt shivered and glanced around Omar's horse farm Tuesday afternoon. It had transformed into a winter wonderland overnight. The first snowfall of the season had arrived earlier than usual, starting the previous afternoon, and it still hadn't stopped. They'd accumulated at least a few inches, and it gave the bare trees and bushes a serene look, reminding him of a Christmas card.

He turned toward the pasture, where the horses stood wearing their blankets while the snow continued to swirl around them. The early December air was crisp, and he could see his breath. The landscape was so beautiful that, for a moment, he was certain heaven had to be just as lovely, if not even more so.

"Isn't it schee?" Omar asked, sidling up to him.

"I was just thinking the same thing." He heard a giggle and looked over to where Lukas was building a snowman near the house. An idea struck him. "Omar, do you still have that sleigh?"

The older man rubbed his beard. "Ya, I do. It's probably somewhere in the back of the supply shed. I haven't dragged it out in years, but if you can find it, you can use it."

Wyatt entered the shed and pulled his flashlight from the

pocket of his heavy coat. He climbed past old rakes, shovels, pitchforks, a couple of brooms, a wheelbarrow, and a wagon that had seen better days. He'd almost given up hope when he came to the sleigh at the very back of the shed. The black metal sleigh, which had been built for two adult passengers, was covered in dirt and dust, looking as if it hadn't been moved in years just as Omar had said.

After shifting the other supplies and tools, Wyatt made a pathway and heaved and pushed until the sleigh was out of the small building.

Omar grinned. "You found it."

"Ya." Wyatt brushed his hand over his forehead. "Would it be all right if I took Luke out for a ride?"

Omar's expression was full of appreciation. "I believe he'd love it." He patted Wyatt's shoulder. "Take ol' Daisy with you." He nodded toward the mare in the pasture.

"Danki." After hitching up the horse, Wyatt jogged over to the house. "Luke!" he called, and the boy stopped throwing snowballs toward a nearby tree. "Want to go for a sleigh ride?"

Luke jumped up and down. "Ya!" He plodded toward the house. "Let me tell mei mamm."

The back door opened and banged shut before Lukas appeared in the doorway with his stocking cap, coat, trousers, and boots caked in snow.

Makayla closed her cookbook and frowned. "Lukas! You're tracking snow all over the haus."

He grimaced and pointed toward the door. "Wyatt asked me to go for a sleigh ride. Can I go, Mamm?"

"A sleigh ride?" She peered out the kitchen window to where

Wyatt waited by the horse and sleigh.

Memories doused Makayla. She had been around twenty-one when she and Wyatt had taken that same sleigh into town together. They had glided by colorful light displays on Englisher homes and sung Christmas carols together. Bundled up under a quilt, they had held hands while enjoying a romantic evening under the stars.

An ache radiated in her chest.

"Can I?" Lukas asked again.

Makayla leaned on the counter as the problem she'd been contemplating rose to the surface again in her mind. She needed to put some space between Wyatt and her son. Allowing him to go for a sleigh ride and spend more time with Wyatt wasn't the answer.

"Nee." She shook her head. "It's so cold out, and it's going to get dark soon. Then it will get even colder, and you'll catch a chill."

Lukas pointed to the doorway. "We can take some of Mammi's quilts to stay warm." He started toward the doorway. "I saw some in the closet."

"But the roads are slippery," she said, following him. "And Englishers always drive too fast. They won't slow down, which means it'll be dangerous out there. I wouldn't want anything to happen to you. I'll worry the whole time you're gone."

He stopped at the linen closet and faced her. "Come with us."

Makayla stilled. "What?"

"If you're with us, you won't worry about us."

She grasped for another excuse. "Nee. I need to start supper—"

"Please, Mamm." Lukas folded his gloved hands. "It'll be so fun."

"What will be fun?" Mamm stood at the bottom of the stairs.

Lukas bounced in his boots. "Me and Wyatt are going for a

sleigh ride!" He tugged on Makayla's sleeve. "I want Mamm to go with us."

"I'll make supper. Geh have fun." Mamm waved Makayla off.

Makayla shook her head. "Nee, I promised I'd make supper tonight."

"Geh," Mamm insisted.

Lukas yanked her sleeve again. "Please, Mamm."

She couldn't resist his hopeful little face or her mother's insistence. "Let me get my coat and boots."

"Yay!" Lukas sang. "I'll grab the quilts!"

After pushing her stockinged feet into her boots and pulling on her coat, gloves, and winter bonnet, Makayla carried the quilts out into the cold. She hoped she wouldn't regret this.

"We're ready!" Lukas plowed ahead of her down the stairs and through the snow to where Wyatt stood by the sleigh.

When Wyatt met her gaze, she slowed her steps. He looked handsome clad in his black coat and a black stocking cap with snow dancing around his face. Going on a sleigh ride with him was a bad idea. Not only would her son get even more attached to him, but she was getting too attracted to him too.

Lukas jumped into the sleigh as if he'd done it a hundred times. "I told mei mamm she had to come with us."

Wyatt nodded and reached for Makayla.

She paused, hugging the quilts to her middle. Staring at his outstretched, gloved hand, she stilled, and her mouth dried.

Finally, she handed the quilts to him, and he set them in the sleigh before holding his hand out to her once again. She accepted it, and he lifted her into the sleigh, where she sank down beside her son. Wyatt took his spot on the other side of Lukas and gathered the reins while Makayla arranged the quilts across the three of them.

Soon they were off, the horse pulling the sleigh through the snow.

"Bye, Daadi!" Lukas called as they zipped by his grandfather.

Makayla and Wyatt waved to Dat before they glided down the driveway. She felt the muscles in her shoulders and neck begin to unwind as Wyatt guided the horse onto the road, and Lukas cheered.

"It's a Bird-in-Hand Christmas! 'Jingle bells, jingle bells,'" he began to sing. "'Jingle all the way. . .'" He tapped Makayla's arm. "Sing, Mamm. Sing!"

She glanced over at Wyatt, and they grinned at each other. "I'll only sing if Wyatt sings."

Wyatt grimaced, shaking his head. "I'm not the best singer, but if you insist."

"C'mon," Lukas said. "'Jingle bells, jingle bells. . .'"

Makayla and Wyatt joined in, and they sang loudly while the horse clip-clopped down the road with the snow twirling around them.

When they came to a large home decorated in colorful Christmas lights, Lukas pointed. "Look at the schee lights!"

Makayla looped her arm around her son's shoulders, taking in how the lights glistened in the beautiful snow. "It's nice, ya?"

They passed more decorated homes, and Makayla enjoyed the excitement sparkling in her son's eyes. She stole a glance at Wyatt, who was smiling too.

"Did you want to go to town?" Wyatt asked.

Lukas held his hands up. "Ya!"

"Is that okay, Makayla?"

"Of course," she said.

When they reached the downtown area, Wyatt peered over at her again. "How does hot chocolate sound?"

"Oooh, appeditlich!" Lukas exclaimed.

Makayla frowned. "I'm sorry, Lukas, but I didn't bring my purse."

"Oh." Her son's disappointment was like a stab to her soul.

"Don't worry about that." Wyatt halted the horse in a parking lot and tied it up at a hitching post.

Lukas leaped from the sleigh and hurried toward a nearby bakery. "Slow down, buddy. Wait for us." He shook his head and held his hand out to Makayla. "He's excited."

"You could say that." She allowed him to help her climb from the sleigh before they plodded through the snow across the parking lot, where they met up with Lukas.

Inside the bakery, the smell of the baked goods mixed with coffee overwhelmed Makayla. They took their spot at the end of the line, and Makayla perused the cases filled with cookies, cakes, and pastries.

Wyatt touched Lukas' shoulder. "How does a hot chocolate and a doughnut sound?"

"Yummy." Lukas' blue eyes widened before they shifted to Makayla. "But I'll ruin my supper. Right, Mamm?"

Makayla bit back her smile. "I think it's okay since tonight is a special night. Right, Wyatt?"

"Exactly," Wyatt chimed in. "How often do we get to take out the sleigh?"

"Danki!" Lukas said.

Wyatt leaned over to Makayla. "Would you like a hot chocolate and a doughnut too?"

"Ya. Danki," she said, and his wide smile made her legs feel like cooked noodles.

Wyatt paid for their hot chocolate and glazed doughnuts, and they took a seat in a booth. While they enjoyed their sweet treats, Lukas discussed the Christmas lights and snow. Each time Wyatt met Makayla's gaze, she found herself remembering their fun times together, and remorse churned in her chest for the loss of what they'd once had.

They returned to the sleigh and started the journey home just as the sun was beginning to set, sending a vibrant kaleidoscope of colors across the sky. The temperature had begun to drop, and Makayla and Lukas snuggled under the quilts during the ride. When they reached her father's farm, Wyatt halted the horse at the stable.

Lukas scrambled out of the sleigh and dashed toward the house. "I need to tell Mammi and Daadi about the lights and the snow and the hot chocolate!"

Makayla chuckled to herself while she helped unhitch the horse.

"You should go in where it's warm," Wyatt told her.

She shook her head. "I want to help after all you did for Lukas. . .and also for me."

"Danki," he said.

With the aid of his flashlight, they took care of the horse and then stowed the sleigh in the shed.

"I haven't seen this sleigh in years," she admitted when they started back toward the house together. "Not since—"

"Not since we took it out years ago?"

She stuck her hands in her pockets. "Right."

"I remember it like it was yesterday. Riding through the snow, laughing and singing on the way to town. Seeing all of the Englishers' houses decked out with colorful lights. Drinking kaffi and eating *kuche* while we talked about how Christmas was almost here. . ." His eyes were focused on the sky as if their memories were projected there. "That was such a fun night."

"It was." She surveyed the farm and was overwhelmed by the beauty of not only the snow but her home. Homesickness welled up inside her and threatened to spill out. When she took another step, her foot sank into a hole, causing her to teeter and then stumble.

"Whoa." Wyatt caught her arm.

Makayla grabbed onto his biceps, and they were almost nose to nose. She breathed in his scent—soap and a musky aftershave. A shiver moved through her body, but it wasn't from the chilly early December evening.

At that moment, she realized that her heart still craved Wyatt, and she'd never felt such a heady rush of affection for anyone else—not Thomas, not even Markus.

The realization took her by surprise, and her lungs constricted.

"You okay?" Wyatt's expression was unsure.

"Ya." She started toward the house. "Danki."

Lukas appeared on the porch. "Hurry up, slowpokes!"

Makayla and Wyatt shared a chuckle before picking up their pace.

"Mamm," Lukas hollered. "We should call Thomas and tell him about the snow. Do you think it's snowing at home?"

Makayla snuck a glance at Wyatt and spotted his puckered brow.

"It's too late to call him tonight, sweetie. We'll call him tomorrow."

"Okay." Lukas disappeared into the house.

"Who's Thomas?" Wyatt asked, his voice sounding halting.

"Thomas is"—Makayla hedged—"He's...he's my fiancé." She ascended the porch steps. When she realized Wyatt had stopped moving, she spun toward him.

His eyes narrowed for a fraction of a second and then recovered. "Your fiancé?"

"Ya," she said. "He was Markus' business partner."

Something unreadable flickered over his face. "When are you getting married?"

"February." She breathed the word, and her heart began to thud.

He stuck his hands in his pockets. "Wow. So soon." He cleared his throat. "That's—that's great, Makayla. So great." He paused again. "Congratulations."

"Thanks."

They stared at each other as silence expanded between them. She held her breath and waited for him to speak, but Wyatt just studied her.

Then he took a step backward. "I should go. It's late, and I have to be back here early tomorrow."

"Danki, Wyatt. I'm so grateful for everything you do for Lukas."

He held his hand up. "It's my pleasure." He was silent for a moment. "Gut nacht, Makayla."

"Gut nacht, Wyatt."

As he headed toward the stable to collect his horse and buggy, her shoulders wilted, and she remained on the porch, wishing her heart wasn't so confused.

CHAPTER NINE

"Do you decorate for Christmas?"

Wyatt stopped brushing the horse and wiped his arm over his forehead before peering over to where Lukas worked beside him. "Mei mamm takes care of decorations."

It was Friday, and it had been a week and a half since he had taken Lukas and Makayla on the sleigh ride. He had spent the past ten days doing his best to avoid her since he'd thought they were getting close again and then she announced she was marrying another man. Every time he saw Makayla, that familiar coil of jealousy would twist up his insides, and he knew he was being ridiculous. He simply needed to find a way to ignore his feelings for her, which was easier said than done, especially since he was so attached to Lukas.

But Wyatt hadn't taken his bitterness out on Lukas. Instead, he'd continued to spend time with him. Aside from doing chores together, they had also built a snowman, had a rowdy snowball fight, and even played catch. He couldn't get enough of his little buddy. He just had to remember that his time with him would eventually end.

"Why are you asking about Christmas decorations, Luke?" Wyatt returned to brushing the horse.

"I heard mei mamm and mei mammi talking about decorating when they get back from the grocery store today." Lukas' face lit with excitement. "What if we surprised them? We could find some pine branches and put them around the *schtupp*. And I saw where Mammi keeps her special candles. They'll be *so* surprised." He held his brush in the air. "What do you think?"

As if Wyatt could ever say no to this kid. "Well, we need to finish our chores first."

"Okay!"

The scent of pine overwhelmed Makayla when she set a load of grocery bags on the kitchen table later that morning. "Do you smell that, Mamm?"

"Smell what?" Her mother dropped her bags on a counter.

Makayla padded toward the family room. "Pine." She surveyed the room, which had been decorated with pine boughs and red candles, along with pine cones. "Mamm, look at this. Someone decorated while we were gone to the store."

Her mother sidled up to her. "I would imagine my grandson did this," she said, and they shared a smile. "Why don't you find out while I put the groceries away?"

Makayla found Dat, Wyatt, and Lukas working with the horses in the pasture. She leaned on the split-rail fence for a few moments while Wyatt explained to Lukas how Dat was training the horse.

Lukas spotted her and charged toward her. "Mamm! Did you see your surprise?"

"I did." She reached through the fence and touched his red

cheek. "Danki for the schee decorations. You did a great job."

"Wyatt helped me cut down the branches and put them on the high shelves."

She felt her heart warming toward Wyatt. She was so grateful that he and Lukas would decorate the house for her. It was such a kind gesture.

She looked past her son to where Wyatt stood watching her, and a shudder raced through her. He'd been standoffish ever since the sleigh ride, which confused her. She had begun to believe that they might be friends, but now he seemed as if he couldn't stand to be around her.

"Danki for decorating the haus," she told him.

Wyatt pointed to her son. "It was his idea."

"We did great, right?" Lukas gushed.

"Ya, you did." Makayla touched his stocking cap. "I'll let you get back to your chores." She waved to Wyatt, who responded with a nod, and then hurried back into the kitchen, where Mamm arranged cans of soups in the pantry. "Let's make some Christmas *kichlin*."

"Now?" Mamm asked.

"After lunch. I want to give some to Wyatt to take home to his family as a thank-you for helping Lukas decorate the haus." Makayla found her cookbook and flipped to the dessert section. "I'll get the supplies ready, and we can start baking after we eat."

Out of the corner of her eye, she spotted her mother watching her.

"You and Wyatt seem to have gotten awfully friendly lately." Mamm paused. "Do you care for him?"

Makayla kept her eyes focused on the cookbook. "He's gut to mei sohn."

Mamm crossed the kitchen to stand beside her. "But do you care for him?"

"We're friends."

"Makayla, look at me," Mamm said.

She did as she was told and met her mother's solemn expression.

"Please answer my question. Do you care for Wyatt?"

Makayla hesitated, and her hands trembled. "I'm marrying Thomas."

"That's not what I asked you."

She shook her head. "What does it matter? I made a commitment to Thomas, and I'm going to honor it." She cast her eyes down at the cookbook. "How do sugar kichlin sound? Lukas always loves to decorate them." She lifted her eyes toward the clock. "Oh, dear. I'd better get lunch ready. It's almost noon."

Makayla fought her confusion as she pulled out a loaf of bread. She would ignore her feelings for Wyatt. As difficult as it would be, it was for the best.

⁂

"Do I smell kichlin?" Dat asked later that evening while he washed his hands at the sink.

"Ya." Makayla set a platter of roast beef on the table.

Lukas stood on his tiptoes and peeked at the cookies sitting on the cooling racks. "Can I decorate them?"

"I was hoping you would." Makayla swiveled toward the doorway. "Is Wyatt joining us for supper?"

Dat took his usual spot at the head of the table. "He said he had to get home to help his *bruder* with a project."

"Oh." Makayla tried to mask her disappointment while carrying the gravy boat to the table. Wyatt hadn't stopped in to say goodbye or stayed for supper since the night they'd gone out in the sleigh. "I guess we'll have to save his kichlin for Monday."

Lukas brought over a bowl of buttered noodles. "Why don't we take the kichlin to Wyatt tomorrow?"

Makayla hedged. That wouldn't be a very good idea. She peered over at her mother's concerned expression and then smiled at her son. "I guess we can. You can decorate them tonight, and then we'll deliver them tomorrow."

"Yay!" Lukas sang.

Makayla considered going over to the Mast family's house. But it wouldn't be a visit. *I'm just taking the cookies there. That's all it is.*

"This lasagna was scrumptious, Mayme." Gloria's tone was a little too bright while she sat between Eli and Mamm the following afternoon. "Danki for bringing it to share with us."

Wyatt sat across the table from his sister-in-law and eyed her with impatience. Gloria had casually mentioned setting Wyatt up with Mayme on Thanksgiving and then scheduled this date without Wyatt's consent. She'd sprung it on him this morning, acting as if she'd forgotten to tell him.

Since he wouldn't imagine ever embarrassing his family or hurting a visitor's feelings, he was stuck, and he wasn't the least bit happy about it. He could think of a hundred different places he'd rather be instead of sitting at his parents' table trying to make conversation with the latest bachelorette that his mother and sister-in-law had arranged for him.

Mayme's smile was wide. "Gern gschehne, Gloria. I'm so glad you all like it." She turned to Wyatt beside her. "I was going to bring a casserole, but I wasn't sure what kind. I have a huge casserole cookbook. Do you like them?"

"Of course," he said while forcing his lips into a smile.

"Perfect." She clasped her hands. "I love to make them. My favorites are tuna, chicken tortilla, shrimp alfredo, and green bean casserole." She snapped her fingers. "Oh! And I can't forget baked penne and roasted vegetable casserole." She gave him an eager expression. "Do any of those sound gut to you?"

"Ya."

"Which ones?" She tilted her head.

He drummed his fingers on the table. "You pick."

"I'll bring one over sometime."

Wyatt realized he had just committed to a second date, and he pressed his lips together. *Oh no.* The muscles in his back began to coil, and he tried to keep his frustration at bay, which seemed impossible.

Mayme was petite with light brown hair and dark eyes, a heart-shaped face, and a small nose. She seemed nice enough, but she was just a little bit too enthusiastic. Besides, he wasn't interested.

"What kind of desserts do you like, Wyatt?" Mayme asked.

He tried to quell his impatience. "Pies are always gut."

Mayme laughed a little too loudly and a little too long. "I brought a chocolate cake." She pointed toward the counter. "I hope you like it."

"I'm sure he'll love it." Mamm's expression glowed with excitement, and Wyatt was certain she was mentally planning his wedding.

Oh brother. How was he going to get out of this debacle? He looked at the clock. "I really need to get outside to do my chores."

A knock sounded on the back door.

Saved by an unexpected visitor!

"I'll get it." Wyatt jumped out of his chair and made a beeline through the mudroom. He opened the door and found Makayla and Lukas standing on the porch. Shock mixed with relief filtered through him. "Wie geht's?"

"We brought Christmas kichlin." Lukas lifted a portable food storage container. "I decorated them."

The muscles in his back started to loosen despite the tension he'd experienced with Makayla recently. "Danki."

"You left before we could give them you to yesterday." Makayla's words seemed to hold an unspoken meaning.

"Who's here?" Mamm stood in the mudroom and craned her neck to see past him. "Makayla. Lukas. How nice to see you. We were just finishing up lunch."

Makayla looked embarrassed. "I'm so sorry, Eleanor. We didn't mean to interrupt. We just wanted to drop off these kichlin." She tapped her son's shoulder. "Give them to Wyatt."

But Wyatt was determined for them to stay and break the tension. He pushed the storm door open wider. "Come in."

"We have company," Mamm said, her tone holding a warning.

Ignoring her, Wyatt make a sweeping gesture to Makayla and Lukas. "Join us."

Makayla waited for a moment, but Lukas entered the house. She finally followed him, and after hanging up their coats in the mudroom, Makayla and Lukas continued to the kitchen.

"We have more visitors," Mamm announced while sharing an exasperated look with Gloria. "I'll put on kaffi."

Mayme's smile brightened. "The more the merrier! I'll cut my chocolate kuche."

Soon the scent of coffee flooded the kitchen, while Mamm and Gloria distributed mugs, Mayme handed out pieces of chocolate cake, and Makayla added a platter of Lukas' cookies in the center of the table.

"Sit by me, Wyatt." Lukas patted the empty chair beside him.

Wyatt took a seat beside him and across from Makayla, who looked charming clad in a green dress that complemented her blue eyes.

Mayme looked over at Makayla. "How do you know Wyatt?"

"From school," Makayla said.

"This is Makayla and her son, Lukas," Gloria introduced them. "They're old friends of ours and former members of our church district. Mayme lives over in White Horse and works as a seamstress. Makayla and Lukas are visiting for the holidays from New Wilmington."

Mayme grinned. "How nice!"

Makayla responded with a thin smile while seeming to study Mayme as if sizing her up. Then she divided a look between Wyatt and Mayme. He was almost certain she had quickly put the pieces together that Mayme was Wyatt's date. Her blue eyes lingered on Wyatt for a moment before she sipped from her mug.

"This kuche is so moist," Makayla finally said.

"I can give you the recipe," Mayme offered before launching into a long explanation of why the cake was so delicious.

Lukas pushed a white envelope over to Wyatt. "Mei mamm helped me make this for you. Open it."

Wyatt did as he was told and pulled out a homemade Christmas card, featuring a drawing of a red covered bridge surrounded by snow. He immediately recognized the drawing as one of Makayla's. He'd always been impressed by her artistic abilities, and he had a few of her drawings tucked away in his dresser in his bedroom—a sunset over a farm that resembled his father's land and also a beachscape. He'd considered tossing them many times but could never convince himself to do it. "This is so schee."

"Mei mamm drew the bridge, and I colored it. Look at the inside."

Wyatt opened the card and read: "Dear Wyatt—Merry Christmas. You're my best friend. From, Luke." He studied the lopsided letters and imagined the little boy writing the note—his brow furrowed and his little tongue sticking out while he concentrated. A lump swelled in his throat.

"Mei mamm helped me write the words."

Wyatt pinched the bridge of his nose in an effort to stop his eyes from stinging. "This is real nice," he managed to say. "Danki."

"Gern gschehne." Lukas sat up taller in the seat and swiped a star-shaped cookie from the platter in the middle of the table.

Wyatt swallowed and took a sip from his mug of coffee. His gaze moved across the table to where Makayla watched him. He gave her a nod and then took a few cookies from the plate.

"I was just telling Wyatt that I love making casseroles too," Mayme told Makayla. Then she began listing her favorites.

Makayla kept her gaze locked on Wyatt, and for a moment he felt as if they were the only people in the room. Did she feel that connection too?

"Wyatt said he likes all kinds of casseroles, so I'll have to bring one over for him," Mayme continued. "Maybe you and your sohn can join us if you're still in town, Makayla." She took a bite of cookie. "Oh, these are gut. I'd love to get your recipe."

Lukas held up his hand as if he were answering a question in school. "I helped make them."

"You are a talented baker."

Lukas puffed his chest out, and everyone chuckled, which helped Wyatt relax a bit.

After a while, Lukas went outside to play with Wyatt's niece and nephew, and the adults continued to talk.

When the cake was gone, Mayme looked at the clock before glancing out the window. "Oh dear. My driver is here." She glanced around the table. "Time sure does fly when you're having fun."

"We're so glad you could come today," Gloria said, and Mamm agreed.

Wyatt nodded. Mayme was a nice maedel, and although he wasn't interested in her in a romantic away, he hoped she found a man who appreciated her.

After saying goodbye, Mayme gathered up her cake saver, and Gloria walked her to the door.

Makayla stood and carried dishes to the counter. "I should get home and take care of my chores." She shook hands with Wyatt's parents. "It was so nice visiting with you, Eleanor and Monroe. And you too, Gloria and Eli." She looked at Wyatt and hesitated. "Bye." Then she took off through the mudroom.

Wyatt's stomach dropped as he watched her leave, and his leg began to bounce. He gripped the edge of the table. He spotted Makayla's cookie container on the counter and jumped to his feet. "She forgot her container."

Grabbing it, he rushed toward the back door.

Makayla couldn't get out of Masts' house fast enough. She was so embarrassed that she'd showed up with cookies for him and managed to crash his date. And even though she was a little jealous, she couldn't be angry with Mayme. After all, she was a sweet young woman and so pretty. Of course he'd find someone like her.

But if Wyatt was on a date, why was he staring at Makayla with tenderness in his eyes?

She couldn't stop recalling Wyatt's expression while he opened Lukas' card. His Adam's apple had bobbed, and she could almost feel his fondness for her son radiating from across the table. Watching his tenderness toward Lukas, she was overwhelmed with affection for Wyatt.

Makayla wrapped her shawl around her arms and pushed open the back door, which brought in a rush of cold air before she stepped out onto the porch.

"Hold on, Makayla."

She spun to see Wyatt holding out the empty cookie container. "You forgot this."

"Danki," she muttered, taking it from him. "You could have brought it on Monday."

He studied her, and she was certain she might drown in the depths of his honey-brown eyes. They stared at each other, and heat crawled up her neck. With Wyatt's gaze locked on hers, she was certain he felt something for her too. Her pulse began to zoom, and she longed to reach out and touch his hand.

"You're it!" a child yelled nearby before a chorus of giggles floated through the air.

Just then Lukas, Benji, and Liz-Beth trotted by.

Makayla was brought back to reality. No wonder Wyatt had been avoiding her. He had a girlfriend, or at least a date, and here she was making dreamy eyes at him. But his date was none of her business, and she needed to get over his rejection of her. After all, they were adults.

Makayla shook herself and pivoted toward where Lukas played with Benji and Liz-Beth. She continued down the stairs to her waiting horse and buggy.

Heavy footfalls sounded behind her, and she turned to where Wyatt stood by her horse. "Mayme is lovely."

He rubbed his chin and remained silent.

She faced Lukas. "Lukas! Let's go. It's time to head home."

"Already?" Lukas asked as he approached. "We were having fun."

Makayla nodded. "Maybe you can play with Benji and Liz-Beth again sometime."

"Thanks again for my card and kichlin, buddy." Wyatt held his hand out for a high five.

Lukas rushed over and wrapped his arms around Wyatt's waist. The softness in Wyatt's eyes made Makayla's heart melt. After releasing Wyatt, Lukas climbed into the buggy.

Makayla waved to Wyatt, his niece, and his nephew, and then joined her son in the buggy. As she guided the horse down the driveway, she peered into the side mirror and found Wyatt watching her.

❧

Wyatt waited until Makayla's horse and buggy disappeared before heading back into the kitchen, where his mother and sister-in-law washed and stowed the lunch dishes. He stood in the doorway and scrubbed his hand over his face, while he gathered his words.

All he'd wanted to do was beg Makayla and Lukas to stay and visit with him without his family or Mayme there as witnesses. When Makayla guided her horse toward the road, he'd realized that it was time for him to have an honest conversation with her. He needed to find out why she'd been so standoffish while sending him mixed signals. He was also determined to know where he stood with her. He was going to find the perfect moment and finally ask her what went wrong between them. Then he was going to see if they had a chance to try again.

But first he had to convince his mother and sister-in-law to stop meddling in his life. He took a few cleansing breaths in an effort to stop his irritation from boiling over. He wouldn't dream of being disrespectful to his mother, but he also needed to get his point across.

Mamm turned toward him and grinned. "Wyatt. What did you think of Mayme?"

"Wasn't she schee and sweet?" Gloria gushed.

"She's perfect for you, Sohn. She'll make a wunderbaar fraa."

Gloria nodded. "Have you made plans to meet again?"

"I need you both to listen to me." He held up his hand for emphasis. "I know that you both want the best for me, but I'm thirty-two years old and capable of finding my own dates. Please stop trying to set me up."

Their smiles faded.

"I appreciate that you care, and you want to see me froh, but no more blind dates. And I especially don't want them sprung on me at the last minute." His serious expression bounced between them. "Understand?"

"Wyatt, I only—" Gloria began.

"But Mayme is perfect for—" Mamm started.

"Stop," he said, interrupting them. "I mean it. I'm done. There's nothing more to discuss." He spun on his heel and marched outside to the barn.

CHAPTER TEN

*M*onday afternoon Makayla hugged her shawl to her middle and trotted out to the barn, where she found Wyatt brushing one of the mares. She stood by the stall for a moment while he worked, taking in his tall, muscular build while he moved the brush over the horse.

After a few moments, he craned his head over his shoulder and smiled at her. "What's up?"

"Lunch is ready." She tried to ignore the heat infusing her cheeks.

"Danki. I guess your dat and Luke are still in town running errands."

"Ya. They needed to run some errands and then Dat promised him ice cream." She nodded toward the house. "I have lunch meat and rolls ready for you."

"Thanks."

They walked toward the house together, and when they reached the kitchen, Wyatt lingered in the doorway with an expectant expression. "Can I talk to you?"

"Of course."

"Alone," he said.

Makayla's stomach quivered. "Ya, that's fine." She pointed to the ceiling, where the sound of the sewing machine chattered above them. "Mei mamm is busy with a sewing project. We're the only ones here." She made a sweeping gesture toward the table, where two glasses of water, a platter of lunch meat and cheese, a few bottles of condiments, a bag of chips, and a basket of rolls waited for them. "Want to sit?"

"Ya."

They sat down across from each other at the table, and she clasped her hands. "What did you want to talk about?"

He cleared his throat. "Makayla, I've wanted to ask you something." He paused, and a tingle fizzed through her. "Why did you run off like you did?" He moved his fingers over the glass of water. "Why did you leave me without any explanation?"

"Because you"—she hedged—"Because I heard that you were cheating on me." She could hear the doubt vibrating in her voice.

His light brown eyebrows shot up. "Cheating on you?"

"Ya." She nodded. "Fern Lehman told me that she saw you in the ice-cream parlor with a schee redheaded maedel."

"What?" His eyes searched hers, and he leaned toward her. "Are you serious, Makayla?"

"That's what she told me. She insisted that you were laughing and kissing that maedel in the middle of the afternoon." Her voice trembled.

His eyes narrowed. "Fern Lehman told you that?"

"Ya, she did."

"When did she tell you this?"

"I—I don't remember. We were at youth group, and you were home that day. I think you had a stomach flu. Fern took me to the side and told me everything." She sniffed as her eyes filled with tears. "She said that you saw her and just grinned at her before kissing the maedel again." She croaked the words. "I was so upset that I couldn't breathe. My cousin had already asked me to come out to New Wilmington to help her with her new boppli. So the next day I packed up my things, bought a bus ticket, and left."

Wyatt opened and closed his mouth while staring at her, and a muscle ticked along his jawline.

She pulled a tissue from her pocket and wiped her eyes and nose. "Why are you looking at me like that?"

"I don't know what to say."

"Just tell me the truth, Wyatt." She hugged her arms to her middle and tried to stop her body from shaking like a leaf in a storm.

"You want the truth?" he asked, and she nodded. "It's not true, Makayla." His expression was fierce. "I *never* cheated on you. I never even considered it, and I'm shocked that after dating me for three years it didn't occur to you to ask me if it was true." He pointed at his chest. "How could you just run off and leave me without even asking me about it?"

"But why would she lie?"

"Why would she lie?" A humorless laugh burst from his lips. "Fern had a crush on me. Don't you remember how she used to follow me around at youth group before I asked you out?"

She pressed her lips together. "Ya, I do." Her voice was small.

He raked his hand through his hair while staring toward the kitchen window facing the barns in the distance. His expression became stoic. "I loved *you*, Makayla, and only you." He snorted. "I'd planned to ask your dat's permission to..." His words faltered, his gaze dropping to his lap.

"What?" she gasped.

Makayla's world tilted, and she cupped her hand to her

forehead. If only she'd believed the best in Wyatt. . .

And why hadn't she? Why had she been so eager to take Fern's word over the man she'd loved? If she'd asked him for the truth, they could've been married. They could've had a future together.

"Do you love Thomas?"

The question caught her off guard. "He'll be a wonderful dat to Lukas."

His intense expression sent a shiver racing through her. "That's not what I asked you, Makayla. Do you love him?"

"He's a gut man. Hardworking." She fidgeted with a paper napkin. "He'll be a gut provider." She paused and took a deep breath. "I. . .I have to do what's best. . ." Her words drifted off.

Wyatt studied her, and her heart pounded against her rib cage. She was making excuses, except for doing what was best for Lukas, and Wyatt could see right through her words.

His nostrils flared, and he jumped to his feet. "I can't believe you thought the worst of me and didn't bother to ask me if a thin rumor was the truth. Did our relationship mean anything to you?"

"Of course it did!" Anger flashed through her. "Why do you think I was so hurt? I was crushed, Wyatt. You meant *everything* to me."

His eyes narrowed. "But you ran away, Makayla! I had no idea why. What was I supposed to think?"

"You could have found out why I left," she snapped. "I never heard from you either."

He blanched as if she'd struck him.

They stared in silence for several moments before Wyatt stalked toward the doorway. "I'm behind on my chores since I'm working alone," he muttered. "And I'm not hungry." He rushed to the mudroom before the back door opened and slammed shut.

Makayla sucked in a breath as regret bubbled up inside of

her. She hated that she'd hurt Wyatt. If only she'd asked him about the gossip instead of just running away like a coward. She longed to go back in time and mend her mistakes, but it was too late now. He'd be better off with Mayme, someone who didn't have such a complicated life and so much baggage.

She couldn't do anything about the past or make amends with Wyatt. She could only focus on her and Lukas' future, and that had to be with Thomas.

Wyatt paced around his room later that evening while his conversation with Makayla played on a loop in his mind. He balled his hands into fists while frustration poured through him. He couldn't fathom how she'd allowed a rumor with absolutely no merit to get between them. Why had she run off believing the worst in him instead of talking to him and asking him if it was true?

But that didn't matter now. It was too late. Makayla had promised to marry another man, a man she didn't love. He sank down onto his bed and hung his head in his hands.

Couldn't Makayla see that he loved Lukas? And couldn't she see that he loved her too?

He froze as the truth smacked him in the face—*I'm in love with Makayla. Again.*

Closing his eyes, Wyatt opened his heart to God:

Lord, I love Makayla and I love Luke, but she's going to leave and marry someone else. Help me figure out what to do. Is it too late for us? Did we miss our chance to be a family? Or is there a possibility that we can work it out? Guide me to the right path.

He leaned back on the headboard and swiped his hands over his stinging eyes. The answer came in sharp focus—he needed to stop Makayla from leaving. He had to tell her he loved her and beg her for another chance. He prayed he could convince her that he was worth another try.

Wyatt stood. He had to go talk to her right now. Then he turned toward the clock. It was after nine. Surely she was already in bed.

Instead, he would wait until the morning and then he'd tell her how he felt and he'd beg her to break her engagement to Thomas.

Wyatt's heartbeat pounded. He would keep praying for the right words and tell Makayla how he felt tomorrow.

❦

Later that same night a knock sounded on Makayla's bedroom door, and she sat up in bed.

"Makayla?" Dat called. "Are you awake?"

She yawned and rubbed her eyes. "Ya. Come in."

The clock on her nightstand read 2:45, and she was suddenly wide awake. Only bad news came in the middle of the night.

Her door squeaked open, and the warm yellow glow of a lantern illuminated Dat in her doorway. "Was iss letz?" she asked.

"I went to the kitchen to get a glass of water, and I heard the phone ringing in the barn. I rushed to answer it, and it was your father-in-law. Your sister-in-law had her boppli." His grave expression sent worry crashing through her. "She and the boppli are fine, but your mother-in-law fell on a patch of ice on her way to visit them. She shattered her leg."

Makayla cupped her hand to her mouth. "Ach, no!"

"She had surgery and is doing well. She'll be home in a couple of days. Simeon said they have their hands full with the new boppli and Stella's injury." Dat sat down on a chair across from her bed. "He asked if you could come home and help take care of Stella."

Makayla sniffed. "Ya, ya, of course. I'll leave tomorrow." She touched her father's hand. "I'm sorry Lukas and I will miss Christmas with you and Mamm."

"I understand, mei liewe. Your other family needs you. We'll see you in February for your wedding, and when the dust settles, maybe you and Lukas can come back again. Thomas could come too." He stood. "Get some rest. You'll have a long journey tomorrow."

After her father left, she shifted under the covers, her mind racing with worry for her mother-in-law. She prayed for Stella's recovery and for a safe journey home.

Her chest felt heavy. Lukas would be heartbroken to have to say goodbye to her parents, and he would be devastated to have to leave Wyatt.

The truth hit Makayla. She would be devastated as well.

Rolling onto her side, she buried her face in her pillow as her tears began to fall.

⁓

"The taxi is here," Dat said shortly after breakfast.

Lukas wrapped his arms around Mamm's waist. "I wanna stay." A sob tore from his throat.

Makayla massaged her temples where a headache pounded. She'd been awake for hours before she finally rose—before dawn—to prepare for the trip back to New Wilmington. After leaving a message for her father-in-law, she called to verify the bus schedule and then packed her clothes. When her mother got up, she shared her plans and then her mother prepared breakfast while she packed Lukas' things and called for a taxi.

Now it was time to go. She was grateful to leave before Wyatt arrived. It was best to whisk her son away and avoid an even more emotional scene.

"Mei liewe," she whispered to her son, "we need to geh."

"Why can't I stay? Please, Mamm."

She shared a sad look with her mother. "I promise we'll come back soon."

Lukas stepped away from his grandmother and rubbed his eyes. "What about Wyatt?"

"We'll tell him goodbye for you." Dat pulled Lukas in for a hug and his face filled with a melancholy expression. "I promise we'll see you soon."

Makayla handed him an envelope containing the letter she'd written when she couldn't sleep in the middle of the night. "Would you please give him this too?"

A horn sounded from outside the house.

Makayla took Lukas' hand and led him outside. After securing him in his booster seat, she hugged her parents. "I'll call you," she promised.

With tears in her eyes, she climbed into the taxi, and as the vehicle drove away, she was certain she was leaving a piece of her heart in Bird-in-Hand.

Wyatt had a spring in his step on his way into the stable later that morning. He'd slept well and felt refreshed. He was ready to take on the day and ready to tell Makayla that he loved her and Lukas. A thrill shimmied through him at the thought of confessing his heart and asking her to stay in Bird-in-Hand. He planned to point out she shouldn't marry a man she didn't love, and there was no reason to when he loved her. He couldn't wait to see her. He spotted Omar outside and planned to tell him that he was going to talk to Makayla for a few minutes before he started his chores.

"Gude mariye," he greeted Omar on his way to the house. "How was your—" He stopped speaking when he realized Omar looked upset. "Is everything all right?"

"Makayla and Lukas left this morning."

A bolt of shock surged through Wyatt. "Left? Why?"

Omar explained about the call he'd received in the middle of the night and how Makayla had rushed off to help her family—Markus' family. "She asked me to make sure you received this note." He pulled an envelope from his back pocket and handed it to him before continuing toward the stable.

Wyatt read his name on the envelope and immediately recognized Makayla's penmanship. His hands quavered as he opened the envelope:

Dear Wyatt,

I'm sorry for believing the lies about you. I know it's too late to fix things, but please believe that I'll always regret leaving like I did. I'm sorry for hurting you.

Thank you for being such a wonderful friend to Lukas. He'll always cherish your friendship, and I will too. We'll both miss you, and we'll never forget you.

I wish you happiness in the future. You deserve the best, Wyatt.

Merry Christmas.

Always,
Makayla

Wyatt reread the letter until he had it committed to memory. He dropped down onto the cold ground and covered his face with his hands. He'd lost Makayla again.

He didn't know how he'd ever recover.

CHAPTER ELEVEN

*W*yatt leaned on his father's pasture fence and stared out toward the horizon. It had been six days since Makayla and Lukas had left, crushing him, yet it felt more like six years.

He had pushed himself through his daily routine, but he felt completely hollowed out. He'd prayed, asking the Lord to heal his heart, but it seemed like an impossible request. He'd never be the same without Makayla and Lukas in his life.

Reaching into his pocket, Wyatt pulled out the rock that Lukas had given him more than a month ago. He moved his thumb over the smooth stone. He had carried the rock with him ever since Makayla and Luke had returned to New Wilmington.

Footsteps crunched on the dead grass, and he turned just as Dat joined him. They stood in a comfortable silence for a few moments, looking out toward the patchwork of rolling farmland in the distance.

"How long are you going to sulk?"

Wyatt dropped the rock into his pocket and turned to his father. "What?"

"You've been moping around here ever since last Tuesday.

Aren't you tired of feeling sorry for yourself?"

"I'm not."

"You certainly are." Dat gave him a knowing look. "I had a feeling something was wrong when you came home from work last Tuesday, but I figured it was none of my business. When you took off after church yesterday without staying for lunch, I was concerned something serious was going on. I talked to Omar, and he explained that Makayla had left Tuesday. That's when I put two and two together."

"What makes you think I'm upset about Makayla leaving?"

His father scoffed. "Please, Wyatt. I may be old, but I'm not stupid. Every time I see you with Makayla, it's clear you still have feelings for her. I've noticed the close bond you have with Lukas too."

"It doesn't matter. She's marrying someone else." He explained how she had told him that she'd agreed to marry her late husband's business partner. "She all but admitted to me that she doesn't love him."

"And you love her and Lukas."

Wyatt paused for a moment. "Ya, I do, but I'm not enough for Makayla."

"You sure about that?"

He pivoted toward his father. "She left me, Dat. Twice." He held up two fingers. "And both times she couldn't even face me to tell me goodbye. At least I got a note this time." He snorted. "I guess I should be glad for that."

"Did you tell her that you loved her?"

He shook his head. "I didn't get the chance."

"So what's stopping you now? She's not married yet."

Wyatt froze as his father's words soaked through him.

Lead me, Lord.

Then the answer came into clear focus in his mind. Dat was right. It wasn't too late. He realized the mistake he'd made seven years ago—he'd accepted Makayla's abandonment too readily. He'd always loved her, but he'd never fought for her or for their relationship. If he had traveled to New Wilmington to talk to her, then maybe they could have worked things out and maybe she would have married Wyatt instead of Markus.

Hope took root deep in his soul, and he gasped.

"You're right, Dat." His voice was thick and reedy. "I'm going to go after her and Lukas."

"Gut." His father patted his shoulder. "God gives us second chances, Sohn. Don't let this one pass you by."

"I won't," Wyatt said. He moved his finger over the rock in his pocket as a plan began to form in his mind.

New Wilmington

The following afternoon, Makayla rested her arms on the kitchen counter and dipped her chin while exhaustion and grief doused her. She felt as if she'd been hanging by a thread since she'd returned to New Wilmington.

Lukas hadn't been himself after leaving her parents' farm. He'd cried himself to sleep every night, telling Makayla that he missed Wyatt and his grandparents, and he refused to leave his room except to come to the kitchen for meals. He hadn't played with his cousins or helped his grandfather with chores, and nothing seemed to encourage him.

Although she'd cried in the privacy of her room and begged God to heal her broken heart, Makayla had worked to keep a brave face. She was grateful that Barbie's mother had come to help her with the newborn and her older children. Makayla tried to keep her mind focused on caring for her mother-in-law, who was temporarily wheelchair bound, but she felt herself crumbling inside. She missed Wyatt so much that she was certain she'd never be the same.

When she heard the back door open and click shut, she turned her attention to the lunch dishes still soaking in the sink. She started to scrub one as footfalls entered the kitchen.

"Makayla."

She craned her head over her shoulder and saw her sister-in-law standing in the doorway, holding a bundle against her chest. "Barbie. What are you doing here?"

"I wanted to check on you and Mamm."

"We're fine. Mamm's resting, and you should be too."

"I had to get out of the haus, and I wanted you to meet your new nephew." Barbie held the baby out to her. "This is Henry Markus."

After washing her hands, Makayla took the newborn into her arms and sat down on a kitchen chair. She studied the baby's tiny face, and she suddenly thought of everything she'd missed out on with Wyatt. They could've had a family, a home, a future. If only she'd believed in their relationship—believed that he truly loved her.

Her grief suddenly bubbled up inside her, and a sob broke free, sending tears pouring down her cheeks.

"Makayla?" Barbie massaged her shoulder. "I'm so sorry. I didn't mean to make you sad. I should have warned you that we named him after Markus." She took the baby in her arms, and Makayla wiped her eyes and nose with a napkin.

"I'm sorry, Barbie." Makayla sniffled. "The name is a schee tribute, and I'm so grateful for it. But I'm not crying because of that."

Barbie angled the baby on her shoulder. "Then why are you crying?"

"I've realized I made a terrible mistake when I came here seven years ago."

Barbie's forehead crinkled. "I don't understand."

Makayla told her the story of why she left Wyatt and how they'd reconnected. She explained how Lukas got attached to him while they were visiting. "I don't regret marrying Markus, and I adore our sohn. But I keep thinking of how I abandoned Wyatt. I never should have believed gossip instead of him." She sniffed as more tears escaped her eyes. "I just don't know how I'm going to move on. I miss him." She blotted her eyes with the napkin.

Barbie studied her. "You still love him."

"Ya, but it doesn't matter." She returned to the sink and washing dishes. "I shouldn't have mentioned it."

"Makayla." Barbie paused. "You shouldn't marry Thomas if you're in love with another man."

Makayla faced her sister-in-law. "Lukas needs a dat."

"You just told me that Lukas loves Wyatt, and it's obvious you do too." Barbie adjusted the baby in her arms. "Now tell me, why are you marrying Thomas?"

She leaned against the counter. "I made a promise to him."

"Do you want Thomas to be your husband or do you only want him to be Lukas' father?"

Makayla paused. "But..."

"Listen to me," Barbie began. "You live here with Simeon and Stella, and me and Tim are next door. Lukas already has two father figures in his life—his daadi and his onkel."

Makayla was speechless.

Barbie's expression was full of sympathy. "I think you need to pray about this before you make a mistake you'll regret for the rest of your life." The infant started to cry, and she stood. "I need to feed him." She nodded toward the door. "I'll see you later, but think about what I said."

Makayla stared after her sister-in-law, her words settling over her. While she washed the remaining dishes, she silently prayed: *Lord, please lead me on the path you've chosen for me. Am I marrying Thomas for the right reasons?*

While she wiped down the table, truth rained down on her—Makayla had never thought she was good enough. When she left Bird-in-Hand seven years ago, she had believed Wyatt had cheated on her due to her own insecurity. She had never believed a man as kind, hardworking, loving, generous, and handsome as Wyatt would truly want a woman like her.

After arriving in New Wilmington, she'd quickly agreed to marry Markus after knowing him for a short time because she worried no other man would marry her. And she'd accepted Thomas' proposal for the same reason—she was afraid she'd never find another husband or a father for Lukas.

Now she realized why—Fern Lehman was the root of her insecurity. Becky had admitted that she never trusted Fern, and she'd been right to doubt her. More than once Fern had told Makayla that she'd never be enough for Wyatt, which was why he'd cheated on her.

It was all a lie. Makayla *did* deserve to be loved. She couldn't allow Fern's cruel taunts and lies to ruin her life. It was time for her to believe in herself.

Makayla didn't love Thomas, and she didn't want to marry him. And now she had to tell him the truth. A ribbon of relief unfurled in her chest.

She glanced at the clock. Thomas would arrive in a few hours for supper. After they ate, she would share the truth with him.

She hoped he would understand and she didn't break his heart.

Please guide my words, Lord.

Thomas took a sip from his coffee mug later that evening. "Stella seems to be doing fairly well considering what she's been through."

"Ya." Makayla moved her hands over her warm mug.

She had served stew and biscuits for supper and then banana pudding for dessert before Simeon pushed Stella's wheelchair to their bedroom and Lukas had gone to his room to play with the blocks her father had made for him for Christmas.

During supper she had noticed how Thomas hadn't tried to interact much with Lukas, even though they had been gone for more than a month. When Lukas detailed stories about working in the stables with Wyatt and Dat, Thomas had only given a curt nod in response. Thomas stood in such stark contrast with Wyatt, who would have been thrilled to see her son and would have hung on his every word while he talked about the farm.

Now she and Thomas sat alone in the kitchen, and it was time for her to admit her feelings to him.

"Thomas," she began while winding a napkin around her finger, "I need to ask you something, and I'd like you to be completely honest with me."

"Okay. . ."

"Do you imagine yourself falling in love with me in the future?"

His eyes widened before a nervous laugh escaped his lips. "What kind of a question is that?"

"Please, Thomas. Tell me the truth."

He scratched his neck. "I asked you to marry me, and that's that."

She shook her head. She needed to try a different approach. "Do you truly want to marry me?"

"Makayla, what are you getting at?"

Her stomach clutched. "I realized something today." She paused, gathering her words. "When you asked me to marry you, I jumped at the chance because I was so worried about Lukas needing a father. At least that's what I thought. The truth is that I said yes because I was afraid of being alone. I was convinced no man would ever want me." She held her breath, waiting for Thomas to negate her claim that no one would want to marry her.

When he remained silent, hurt pricked her. "Thomas, I'm sorry if I'm hurting you, but the truth is that I don't love you. And I don't think we should get married."

To her surprise, he blew out a deep breath. "Makayla, I'm relieved to hear you say that. I actually only proposed to you for Markus' sake."

"What do you mean?"

"When Markus passed away, I was concerned about yours and Lukas' welfare, but honestly, I felt obligated to marry you out of guilt." His eyes sparkled, and he sniffed. "I couldn't help him with that roof repair because I had a prior commitment, but he took the job anyway. For the past two years I've been punishing myself for not being there to save him. I thought"—he paused and cleared his throat—"I thought that if I took care of you and Lukas, then I'd make up for that." His voice was raspy.

Makayla was so shocked by his raw emotion that she reached across the table and took his hands in hers. "Oh, Thomas. It's not your fault that Markus died, and I never blamed you." She gave his hands a gentle squeeze before releasing them. "I appreciate your friendship and your devotion to Markus, but I still don't think we should get married."

"I agree." He swiped his fingers over his eyes. "But I'd like to remain friends."

She smiled. "Of course we will."

"Gut." He nodded. "I should get going."

She walked him to the back door and shook his hand.

"Thank you for being honest with me," he told her.

"Ya. You too."

After he left, she felt as if a weight had been lifted off her chest. She cleaned up the kitchen and checked on Stella and Lukas, who were both already asleep.

She retreated to her room, and a vision of Wyatt filled her mind. Tomorrow was Christmas Eve, and she and Wyatt were so far away from each other. She missed him so much that she ached for him.

Her eyes welled up with tears, and she pulled out a notepad and pen. Then she began to write him a letter.

CHAPTER TWELVE

$\mathcal{T}$he following evening, Wyatt sat in a taxi on Simeon and Stella Blank's driveway. It was Christmas Eve, and the trip to New Wilmington had been long. He'd spent nearly the entire time praying and asking God to guide his words when he spoke to Makayla. And now that he had finally arrived at her in-laws' home, he felt his bravery waning.

Lord, give me strength.

The driver peered over the back seat at him. "You gettin' out?"

"Ya." Wyatt paid the driver and climbed out of the SUV. Then he shouldered his backpack and pulled up all the courage he could muster from deep inside before he strode up the driveway.

When he reached the porch, his stomach bottomed out. But he couldn't—he wouldn't—turn back now. He knocked on the door and sucked in a breath.

Footsteps sounded from somewhere in the house before the door opened, and Lukas looked up at him.

"Wyatt!" Lukas launched himself into his arms. "*Frehlicher Grischtdaag!*"

"Hey, buddy. Merry Christmas to you too." Wyatt dropped

his backpack and hugged the boy. He'd missed his little friend so much. He leaned down and lowered his voice. "I have a question for you, but it's a secret, okay?"

Lukas nodded with enthusiasm.

"Would it be okay if I married your mamm?" Wyatt whispered.

Lukas shrugged. "Sure."

"Danki." Wyatt walked into the mudroom with him and pulled a small rock from his pocket. "I found this for you."

Lukas' eyes rounded. "Wow!" He turned the small, pinkish stone over in his hand. "This is the coolest rock ever. Danki!"

"Gern gschehne." Wyatt looked at Makayla standing in the doorway watching him. Her blue eyes were wide, and she was stunning clad in a maroon dress. His pulse galloped.

She took a step toward him. "Wyatt?"

"Hi." He waved at her.

She touched her son's back. "Lukas, please ask Aenti Barbie to set another place at supper, okay?"

Lukas scurried off.

"It's so gut to see you. We've missed you so much." She seemed to search his face. "Why are you here?"

He took a deep breath and said the words that had been embedded on his soul. "I'm here to tell you that I love you, Makayla." His body relaxed as a weight lifted from his shoulders.

She opened and closed her mouth, looking shocked. "You—you love me?" she asked, and he nodded. "But what about Mayme?"

"What do you mean?"

"Your girlfriend."

He shook his head. "She's not my girlfriend. I met her for the first time the day you and Lukas brought me those kichlin." He explained that his sister-in-law had set up that meeting without his consent. "I was never interested in her, and in fact, I couldn't wait for her to leave."

Her expression relaxed, and to his surprise, she linked her fingers with his. "Let's talk in private."

He picked up his backpack, and she steered him past the door leading to the kitchen, where her family was gathered for supper, and through the family room to an enclosed porch, overlooking a vast pasture.

He dropped his backpack. "Makayla, I've always loved *you*." His voice sounded husky. "I love Lukas too. The biggest mistake I made was not coming after you seven years ago." He took a ragged breath. "I'm sorry for not showing you how much I loved you, because if I had, then you never would have believed I had cheated on you."

She shook her head, causing the ribbons to her prayer covering to flutter over her slight shoulders. "It's not your fault. I was so insecure that I never thought I was gut enough for you. I was so convinced I wasn't as schee or interesting as the other *maed* in our community, so I believed Fern's lies."

"Why on earth would you think that about yourself, Makayla?" he asked. "You're the most intelligent, artistically talented, sweet, kind, thoughtful, and beautiful maedel I've ever known." He cupped his hand to her cheek, and she leaned into his touch. "You're the love of my life, and I came here to beg you not to marry Thomas."

"It's over between Thomas and me," she said, and relief rushed through him. "I was only marrying him because I didn't believe any other man would want me. That's why I married Markus so quickly. I never believed any man could love me."

"I don't know why you ever doubted yourself. You're the only woman I've ever wanted." He took her hands in his again.

"I want to build a life with you either here or in Bird-in-Hand."
He gave her hands a gentle squeeze. "I need you and Lukas in
my life. Please tell me that you'll marry me, and I promise I'll do
everything in my power to make you and Lukas happy."

"I love you, Wyatt. You're the love of my life, and yes, I'll
marry you."

With that, he kissed her. Happiness fluttered through him,
and his thoughts became fuzzy. When he released her, he reached
into his backpack and handed her a box. "This is for you."

She opened it and pulled out two linked hearts made out of
horseshoes engraved with their initials. "Wyatt," she whispered.
"This is beautiful. Did you make this?"

"I did." He traced his finger down her cheek, and she shivered.
"I'm sorry we've lost so much time. Can we start over?"

Her eyes glistened with unshed tears. "I can't think of anything I'd like to do more."

Footsteps sounded nearby, and he looked over to Lukas in
the doorway. "Hey, Luke."

Lukas pointed toward the kitchen. "Daadi wants to know if
you're going to join us for supper."

Makayla smiled. "We'll be there soon, but I have a question
for you. Would you like Wyatt to be your dat?"

Lukas divided a look between Makayla and Wyatt before his
gaze landed on Wyatt. "Is that what you meant when you asked
me if you could marry mei mamm?"

"Ya." Wyatt nodded. "That's exactly what I meant."

"Yay!" Lukas jumped up and down, and Wyatt was overcome
with joy.

Makayla looked up at Wyatt. "You asked Lukas for permission?"

"Of course I did," he said, and she beamed.

Then Lukas turned around. "Daadi!" he yelled. "Wyatt's going to be mei dat!"

A middle-aged man with a long, graying beard joined Lukas in the doorway.

Makayla made a sweeping gesture between them. "Simeon, this is Wyatt."

Simeon shook his hand. "It's great to finally meet you."

"I told my family about you." Makayla gave Wyatt a sheepish expression. "I explained that I love you, and I mailed you a letter today asking you if we could work things out."

"Really?" Wyatt asked, and she nodded. "Well, the answer is yes, we can." He looked at Simeon. "I got her dat's and Luke's permission, and I just asked her to marry me." He touched her arm. "And she said yes."

Simeon grinned. "We're so grateful you've made Makayla and Lukas so happy. Please join us for Christmas."

"Danki."

Simeon took Lukas' arm and steered him toward the kitchen. "Let's give them a few more minutes before they come to supper."

Makayla rested her hand on Wyatt's chest. "Danki for loving me and Lukas, Wyatt. I can't wait to start my life with you."

"I feel the same way," he said before kissing her again.

❧

Friday morning Makayla, Wyatt, and Lukas stood in the driveway with Markus' family. She hugged each of them and took Stella's hands in hers. "Danki for always looking out for me."

Stella's eyes filled with tears. "Oh, sweetheart, you are our dochder and always will be. I'm so thankful you and Wyatt could spend Christmas with us. It means so much."

"Me too." Makayla couldn't remember a time when she'd been so happy. "We're going back to Bird-in-Hand to start our life together, but this will always be our second home."

"Of course," Stella said. "I know your parents are grateful that you and Wyatt decided to take over your dat's farm."

"Ya. Mei dat said he'll start building our haus as soon as spring arrives."

Barbie hugged Makayla next. "I'm so froh that you followed your heart," she whispered in Makayla's ear. "We'll miss you, but we'll keep in touch."

"Ya, of course. Your mamm has been a wunderbaar help to you, and it's so kind of your schweschder to look after Stella," Makayla told her.

Barbie gave her a knowing smile. "We are well taken care of. You, Wyatt, and Lukas can go home to Bird-in-Hand and not worry about us. We'll all see you at your wedding in the spring."

Makayla's heart danced. She couldn't wait to be Wyatt's wife and for him to officially adopt Lukas.

"We'll stay in touch and come to visit at least once a year," Wyatt told Simeon and Stella. "We're all family."

"Danki, Wyatt," Simeon said. "Just make sure you take gut care of Makayla and Lukas."

"I promise you I will."

Makayla took Wyatt's hand before they climbed into the taxi with Lukas. The SUV's engine rumbled to life, and they waved as they drove down the road toward their new life together.

Then Makayla linked her fingers with Wyatt's and closed her eyes as she leaned against his shoulder. He kissed her cheek, and her happiness welled through her heart on the wings of a thousand butterflies.

She was so thankful that God had given her and Wyatt a second chance at love, and she couldn't wait to see what He had in store for their future.

Amy Clipston is an award-winning bestselling author and has been writing for as long as she can remember. She's sold more than one million books, and her fiction writing "career" began in elementary school when she and a close friend wrote and shared silly stories. She has a degree in communications from Virginia Wesleyan University and is a member of the Authors Guild, American Christian Fiction Writers, and Romance Writers of America. Amy works full-time for the City of Charlotte, NC, and lives in North Carolina with her husband, two sons, mother, and five spoiled-rotten cats.

CHRISTMAS LILY

By Amy Lillard

CHAPTER ONE

*L*ily Kate Troyer pulled her scarf a bit closer around her neck as she hurried down the sidewalk. She had heard talk that winter was arriving this week with a vengeance, and it appeared the weatherman was not kidding. A north wind seemed to cut through her black wool coat as if it were nothing more than the loosely crocheted shawl her *mammi* wore even in the summertime.

Lily Kate shivered and ducked her head against the chilling breeze. She'd much rather be at home with her cousins than running around the streets of Lancaster checking off errands as quickly as she could. But this one was important, a gift for her mother back home in New Wilmington. Not that she wouldn't be home in time for Christmas. But she wanted her *mamm* to have this new present as quickly as possible.

Truth be known, Lily Kate had bought all her family's Christmas presents and even wrapped them before coming here to Lancaster to teach school. She had been fortunate to find the opportunity. After all, who got to start a teaching job in the middle of the school year? Not many for sure, but since Mabel Esh, the teacher at the small one-room school outside

Bird-in-Hand, had fallen and broken her leg *and* her arm, the job had been a cinch to land. Especially because her uncle, Allen King, was on the school board and knew she needed a break from home.

But she wasn't thinking about that as she rushed along. Well, she was, but she wasn't about to admit it, even to herself. Right now, she had to get to the post office. If only she could remember where it was. Her cousin, Ada, had told her how to get there from the quilt shop, but she couldn't remember if there were two right turns or two left turns. And if she was supposed to turn again after that.

Goodness! Her thoughts were all over the place these days. And that would not serve her well when teaching young minds, no matter for how short a time. Though she was hoping that she could at least stay for two whole months. Her cousin even casually mentioned that maybe Mabel would give up teaching altogether, since she was growing older. Where most of the Amish schools were taught by young, unmarried women, Mabel was unmarried but with no apparent plans to wed anytime soon, even though she was somewhere in her late sixties. Never had been, never would be. She had devoted her entire life to teaching. Lily Kate wasn't as young as some. She had just turned twenty-six on her last birthday, but like Mabel, she had no plans to wed. Well, she'd *had* plans to wed, but they had fallen through. Of course, that occurrence went into the pile of things that she wasn't thinking about today.

US Postal Service. Finally. She stepped toward the familiar red-white-and-blue sign on the other side of the street.

"Look out!"

She had no sooner moved to step across when someone shouted. She didn't even have time to turn around and see what was happening before something large and solid hit her from the side. It knocked her over and backward and made her drop the stack of packages she was carrying.

"My goodness!" she cried, doing her best to pick herself back up off the ground. The mail she had—specifically the large envelope she was sending to her niece and nephew, sort of a pre-Christmas present—had come open. Coloring pages, games, and other fun activity sheets spilled out into the sidewalk. Of course, that's when another gust of cold wind swept through. The papers scattered.

"Oh no!" She grabbed for them, trying her best to recover them all—she had two of each one and it would do no good if there was only one. After all, they were for twins. She needed them all. In pairs. But some were quickly flying away, much too fast for her.

She watched them go with a sad heart, then turned back to the thing. . .er, person who had bumped into her. "Excuse y—me," she said, quickly correcting herself. It would do no good to offend the man. Though she had no idea what he could have been doing that was so important that he had to plow into her and knock her to the ground.

The man raised himself up to his considerable height. He was tall. Tall tall. And not just to her. "What do you think you're doing?" he growled.

"I—"

"Did you not see the car coming?" His voice raised once more, and he seemed to grow right where he stood. His jaw tightened and his cheek flinched under the cover of his rusty-colored beard.

"Well—"

"That's the best way to get yourself killed!" Even louder this time. Had he gotten bigger?

"See, I—" Lily Kate started, her voice meek. She hadn't meant to sound so...mousy. She didn't want to be meek and mousy. She had been pushed around her entire life, mainly because she was barely five feet tall, in shoes. And the last two days at the school, the children had tested her last nerve. Because she was small, too close to their size to be completely respected. And Christmas break was just days away. The holiday spirit was in the air and making the scholars antsy. Not that she could blame them. But she was tired of feeling picked on.

"You made me drop my packages," she fumed. "That was for someone special." She stared lamentably in the direction where her pages had flown.

"You made me drop my donuts."

Lily Kate turned back to face the man.

He was pointing at the pastry box from M&A Sweet Treats lying on the pavement, several donuts scattered around it.

Lily Kate had only been in Lancaster for a short period of time, but her cousins had already taken her there for the best donut she had ever eaten.

Not the point. "How is it my fault that you dropped your donuts when I was minding my own business and you crashed into me?"

"I can't understand how people like you manage to get around each day."

"Now hold on a minute." That was it! Lily Kate boosted up as tall as she could make herself—which wasn't tall at all—then rose to her tiptoes for a little bit extra. "I was walking along just fine when you ran over me."

"I *saved* you." He glared at her, his brown eyes dark and angry. There was something else in their depths, something that looked a little like fear, but that couldn't be. The man was big enough to take on a bear. What did he have to be afraid of?

"*Saved* me?" She shook her head. "You didn't *save* me. You practically tackled me." She had learned that word and what it meant from watching the young men at home playing football—where the elders couldn't see them, of course.

"You were about to step out into the road. A car was coming. You could have died."

"But I didn't," she countered.

"Because I saved you."

Really. The man was insufferable. "You didn—fine," she grumbled. "You saved me." Not because she believed him and what he said but because she didn't have all day to argue with him. She was getting tired of trying to prove her point. She had other things to do. The man was obviously delusional. Or at the very least, he had some misguided hero syndrome. Which was very strange for an Amish man. But the truth was some people—all people—were a varied group. Some were too much trouble to have to deal with. This man was one of those. Best leave now while she could. And while she still had some of her pages for the twins.

She turned to head over to the post office, the packages and papers still clutched to her chest.

"That's it?"

His voice stopped her in her tracks. She shouldn't turn around. She should leave well enough alone. She should walk away now. Her mother would tell her to get away while the getting was good.

But that was the thing about Lily Kate—at least according to her family. She wasn't very good at just letting things roll off her back. It was speculated over, usually at every holiday meal, if that particular trait was something she had been born with or something that had resulted from her tiny stature.

She could feel her ears getting red under the cover of her scarf. She was surprised the heat hadn't melted the yarn as she turned slowly around to face the hulking beast of a man.

He was standing, one hand on his hip, one eyebrow raised in question. A detestable smirk shaped his lips. "I'm waiting," he drawled.

Lily Kate wanted to tell him he could wait until the good Lord came back for all she cared, but it seemed that would do no good. Obviously, this man had forgotten his manners. What it meant to be a Christian had slipped his mind. Why did she have to be the one who reminded him?

How could she not? As a Christian herself it was her job, nay, her *duty* to help her fellow man. Even with helping a crotchety old man remember how to treat his fellow human beings.

"In the future if you see a woman who is crossing the road to go to the post office, it might behoove you to allow her to cross unmolested."

It was his ears that turned red now. The smirk disappeared, that jaw clinched under the full beard, and his posture straightened.

"Insufferable," he muttered.

Lily Kate raised her nose into the air and sniffed. "You most certainly are."

⁓

"What took you so long?" Lily Kate's cousin, Ada King, hopped from one foot to the other and blew on her gloved hands. "You were gone forever."

"The post office was busy." It was the truth. The post office had had a line almost to the door, but that wasn't the real reason she had taken so long to get her mail sent then return back to the buggy where her cousin had promised to meet her. Ada had wanted to look at fabric for a new dress for the upcoming New Year party that her brother Silas had been talking about nonstop. Apparently, finding the perfect shade of blue didn't take quite as long as getting accosted in the middle of the street by a strange man.

"Did you find what you were looking for?" Lily Kate asked as she started to hoist herself into the buggy. This was their last errand of the morning. Now they could go home and warm up in front of the fire with toasty mugs of cocoa in their hands and thick socks on their feet.

"Lily Kate!" her cousin gasped. "What happened?" Ada pointed, mouth agape at Lily Kate's knee. Or rather the tear in her thick winter tights and the stain of blood on her exposed skin.

Lily Kate closed her eyes and shook her head. He was the last thing she wanted to be thinking about at the moment. She had been perfectly happy with visions of warm socks and mugs in her thoughts and not hateful men who seemed to believe they knew what was right about everyone and everything. "This man—" It was all she could say before she pulled herself into the buggy. Well, almost into the buggy. Before she hit her target, her cousin wrapped a hand around her arm and pulled her back down.

"Are you okay?" Ada's voice was hushed, barely above a whisper.

"I'm fine," Lily Kate assured her cousin. "I guess he thought that I was going to walk out into the street in front of a car." No need to mention that she hadn't seen the car at the time. She hadn't been *that* close to the edge of the street.

"Go on," Ada urged.

Lily Kate had no choice but to tell her the whole story or stand out in the cold the rest of the afternoon. Lily Kate was not fond of the winter. "So, he pushed me out of the way, and I fell. I suppose I tore my stockings then."

"And this was an *Englisch* man?"

"Amish."

Ada's green eyes grew wide. "Really?"

Lily Kate pressed her lips together and nodded.

"Well, the nerve of him," Ada huffed.

"Right?" Lily Kate shook her head. "He thought he was doing something nice but now my knee is bleeding, and he wanted me to thank him!"

"I don't know, Lily Kate. You never know what a person has been through in their day. What they've had to face. Maybe his day started off poorly and he couldn't handle the possibility of you hurting yourself—because he's kind and caring deep inside."

Lily Kate resisted the urge to roll her eyes. Mostly because Mamm said it was unbecoming for a young woman to make such a face. "*Jah*," she mockingly agreed. "Way down deep inside."

Ada laughed and shook her head, her prayer *kapp* strings trapped beneath the black bonnet she wore. The motion pulled slack in either side. Lancaster women didn't tie their kapp strings like the women of her own church district, and now when Lily Kate got up in the mornings, she felt so rebellious as she left hers untied as well.

"Come on," Ada said. "Let's get home before Jamie thinks we're never coming back with his buggy."

That woman.

Simon Bontrager stomped into Riehl's Quilt Shop and did his best to push the stranger from his thoughts. But as stubborn as she was in person, she was equally so in his mind.

Didn't she understand that she had been in danger? Immediate, imminent danger. Jah, immediate and imminent meant practically the same thing, but he was serious. Even if she wasn't. She was tottering along, not looking where she was going, and then she had the audacity to get mad at him because he saved her life. Of course he had expected her to thank him, and all she did was glare at him because her mail was scattered. Mail which probably needed to be closed up before traipsing across town.

And what about his donuts? He had to abandon them to save her. They weren't even for him. They were a gift to the workers at the post office. But when he dropped them, there went that plan. Which was probably for the best, seeing as how that's where she was headed, and he couldn't imagine staying close to her for any length of time. Like standing behind her awaiting his turn. Jah, she was that trying.

"Good afternoon," Sally Yoder greeted him as he entered the shop. Her smile froze on her face. "Is everything okay, Simon?"

"Jah." Then he realized that he must have been frowning as he stepped inside. That was why she was looking at him as if he was about to explode or something. He did his best to shove thoughts of the sassy girl—or maybe she was a young woman, who knew?—that he had encountered and rearranged his face into an expression he hoped was more welcoming.

Sally, it seemed, approved. Her smile became genuine once more. "Have you brought us any more carvings?"

He shook his head. "I came in for buttons." Though he didn't know why he had to be the one with them on his list. This should have been Tamsyn's chore. But now he realized that his mother had specifically sent him into the shop so that he would be confronted with the fact that he hadn't carved much since Catherine died.

Any. The truth was *any*. He hadn't carved anything since she died. He just didn't have the heart for it. Jah, it had brought in a little extra cash and a few more dollars never hurt anybody, but Christmas was coming, and Jacob needed him. And a dozen other reasons why he just couldn't do it.

He cleared his throat. "Not today."The words came out rusty, remorseful.

One thing his mother didn't take into account before sending him in here was the time each carving required. The work had to be put in long before now. It wasn't like he could run home and carve up a bunch of does and bucks, tie a small pine bough around their necks, and throw a price tag on them. It didn't work like that. In fact, he was just coming back in to get the last one from the shop. He'd kept one for himself of course, given it to Catherine the very first year he discovered he had a talent for such matters. But he wasn't sure where it went. Catherine had taken care of all the house stuff, and he had yet to run across it.

Not that he was admitting to anything, but he didn't like going around poking in boxes unsure of what he would find. Some days it was too hard to come back from those memories. So, he'd rather take the hit, not sell this last one that Sally had, and keep those memories at bay.

"I uh. . .I came to get the last pair of deer you had on display." He had seen them through the window the day before and hustled inside, fully intending on taking them with him that very moment. But Sally wasn't there, and he didn't think anyone else would give them over to him. So, he had hidden them behind a row of those faceless dolls the tourists liked so much and some sort of contraption that he thought was used to cover up rolls of toilet paper when they sat out on the counter. Honestly, he didn't know what the problem was with visible toilet paper, but who was he to say any differently?

"Oh." Sally's blue eyes grew twice their size. "I sold them."

A weird buzzing started in Simon's ears. "You sold them?"

"Jah, just a bit ago as a matter of fact."

"To who?" He shook his head, the *who* didn't matter. It

wouldn't get them back. It wasn't that he wanted them for himself, but for Jacob. This Christmas was the first without his mother, and Simon thought he would do better without so many shake-ups.

"Here, I'll get the money for you." Sally hurried over to the register and opened the drawer, extracting several bills.

"This is too much," he said as she handed him the cash.

"We still owe you for the last three that we had on hand."

That math made more sense.

"I'm sorry," she said. And he knew she was talking about the final set of the deer he had brought in.

"Understandable." He raised the cash for her to see. "*Danki.*"

"Of course." She smiled at him, but it was a different smile than before. Everyone looked at him differently now. He couldn't go anywhere or do anything without someone asking him how he was doing or if he needed something. He knew they were only trying to be kind. It was the Amish way to take care of your neighbor. Something the young woman from earlier should have known for herself. But he hated that everyone felt that he needed their help. Maybe he did. But he hated that part as well. He hated feeling helpless, he hated that Christmas was coming and he didn't know what he was going to say to his son, and he hated that every day when he awoke, Catherine was no longer there.

CHAPTER TWO

By late afternoon, Simon was still thinking about that woman. The one who stepped out into the street without properly looking. She was a woman, he decided, instead of a girl. He figured she was just short and seemed even tinier to him since he was so tall.

And he had no idea why he was thinking about that at all. Her, her height, and the fact that she had almost died. Or been seriously injured. Most likely, anyway, if the car had hit her. Which maybe it wouldn't have. But there was no need to concern himself with that now. She was safe. For the time being.

Well, he knew why he was thinking about that, her almost being killed or maimed. Or bruised. Which made him more determined not to think about her. Which also made her stick in his thoughts like glue.

He sighed and stirred the leftover chili his mamm had sent over yesterday.

She had sent a casserole and a pie when he had stopped to drop off his sister and pick up Jacob after a morning of shopping and being disappointed over one thing or another.

The donuts, the deer carvings, being chastised by a slip of a woman half his size. There was more, he was sure, but he didn't want to dwell.

Jacob had been happy as a lark to spend half the day with his *dawdi*, helping his grandfather make the baskets that he sold in Riehl's as well. Simon's son had chatted about it all the way home, cradling one on his lap as they drove.

But even then, all Simon could really think about was the woman and her flashing, angry blue eyes. No, not angry. Indignant. That was the word. She had been indignant.

He shook his head at himself. He needed to stop with all this dwelling on her and the incident that happened. It didn't deserve any more attention. It didn't warrant so much thought. In fact, he vowed that he wouldn't let her enter his thoughts for the rest of the day. And come tomorrow he knew the sharp memories would have faded.

"When's supper?"

Simon whirled around, slinging chili sauce in all directions as he faced his son. He hadn't meant to make such a mess, but he had been caught too deep in his own thoughts.

"Not long. Have you washed your hands?"

Jacob nodded.

"Set the table with bowls and spoons, and it should be heated through by the time you are finished."

Jacob made his way over to the cabinet and started getting down the dishes.

When they had gotten home, Simon had sent Jacob upstairs to get his clothes ready for church tomorrow. There really wasn't much to do, but he liked for the boy to get his things all in one place prior to the morning, otherwise it was one big shuffle to find his—fill in the blank here with at least one missing item. Socks, shoes, vest, church shirt, hat. The list was potentially endless.

"Why are we having chili again?" Jacob asked as he placed the dishes on the table.

"Because we have it here to eat."

"But didn't Mammi send a casserole?"

"Jah."

"So why aren't we eating that tonight instead?"

Simon didn't have an answer for that. He had been thinking about a certain person that he said he wasn't going to let invade his thoughts any longer, and he had put the casserole in the fridge and put the chili in the pot.

"We can eat the casserole tomorrow."

"It's broccoli, cheese, and rice with chicken in it."

Jacob's favorite.

Simon should have realized. He shouldn't have allowed that certain person who he wasn't thinking about to ruin his thoughts on everything else so that he was behaving oddly. And putting a warm casserole into the fridge and heating up day-old chili instead. Especially when his son had probably asked his mammi to make it for him special.

"You know it's always better the second day."

Jacob nodded.

But Simon knew that he liked the casserole any way he could get it.

"So you made a basket with Dawdi?" Simon took the chili from the burner and turned the stove off. He ladled the food into their bowls as he waited for his *sohn* to answer.

"Jah. He let me make it all by myself. I got to pick out the colors and everything." Jacob was very proud of himself.

Simon realized that he had let other thoughts keep him from properly acknowledging his boy's accomplishment.

"When I grow up, I want to make baskets just like Dawdi."

"Sounds like you don't have to wait that long. So, what are you going to do with it?"

"I'm giving it to the new teacher for Christmas." Simon had only thought that Jacob was proud that he had made the basket. The fact that he was gifting it to the teacher was another matter altogether.

This new teacher must be something, Simon thought. Jacob had talked of practically nothing else since she had started this week.

It was odd that the teacher had to be replaced midway through the year, but that happened when accidents caused injury. Just like he was trying to explain to—

Anyway, Mabel Esh, the long-standing teacher at their school, had fallen and broken her arm and her leg. There had been an emergency meeting of the board to come up with a plan for the time that she would be incapacitated. Several names of young girls in the church were tossed around, but Allen King had stood up and stated that he knew someone who would be willing to start immediately, be a good influence with the children, and be more than happy to work only for the eight or so weeks that Mabel would be gone.

He was so sure of his solution that no one questioned him. He called the woman, a niece of his, and the following week they had a new teacher. Lily, Simon thought her name was. But it was Lily with something else. Lily Ann? No, that wasn't right.

Simon picked up the slightly misshapen basket that Jacob had proudly placed in the center of the table. All in all, he did a great job. Jake Bontrager was a patient and caring teacher. He always had been. Even when Simon and his sister were little.

"You're giving it to the teacher, huh?" Simon placed the basket down and took another bite of his chili.

"Jah." Jacob's eyes sparkled. "She's so nice. And very pretty. And sweet and nice."

"You said nice already," Simon pointed out, though he kept his laughter inside.

"I know. She's double nice."

"I see." He was beginning to suspect that his son had a crush on the teacher. According to Allen King, she would be going home sometime after the new year began. Then she would leave, and Jacob would be brokenhearted at seven years old.

"She's got a beautiful name too. Lily Kate."

That was it. Kate not Ann.

"It's good to have a beautiful name. If you're a girl, right?" He said the words, a dreamy quality in his voice. "If you have a beautiful name, then everybody already knows how beautiful you are."

"It's not about what's on the outside." Simon was pretty sure his son wasn't ready for the conversation about love and marriage. But he felt the need to staunch this flood of crush that was bound to sweep his son away. "You know she's not going to be your permanent teacher."

Jacob's bottom lip stuck out. "Me and some of the other boys were talking at recess. We want her to stay."

Simon cleared his throat. "It's commendable that she came all the way from—from. . .wherever it is she came from—" He had no idea, though he was sure he heard Allen say one time or another. Everything had happened so quickly that where she was coming from took a back seat to the relief and knowledge that she was coming at all.

"New Wilmington," Jacob supplied.

Of course his son knew. He probably already had her birthday memorized as well, but Simon wasn't about to ask when it was. "New Wilmington," he continued. "But Mabel Esh has been the teacher at that school for many years. Once she heals, she'll come back and teach again."

Somehow Jacob managed to look sad and hopeful at the same time. "But what if she didn't? What if Lily Kate could stay and be our teacher forever?"

"I suppose that would be okay. As long as the school board approves."

"You should come to the school," Jacob said. He stuffed his mouth full of crackers, his head bobbing up and down like it did when he swung his legs.

"Quit moving around," Simon admonished. At least it gave him something to distract the boy with. He did not want to make a trip to the school to meet this new teacher who would only be around for a short time. But he had the feeling that his son was not going to let it go that easily.

"She said any of our parents could come visit anytime."

Most schools had an open-door policy for visiting parents. They came to help out and check on their kids, to bring lunch and just observe. But he wasn't telling his son that. Jacob thought this Lily Kate was golden for offering to allow parents to come in at their leisure. Simon wasn't sure anything he could say would change the boy's mind on the matter.

"That's *gut*," Simon muttered and turned his attention back to his supper.

"You should come," Jacob said again.

"We'll see." It was the best answer he could give.

"I want you to meet her."

"I see that. Eat your supper." Simon was growing weary of Jacob's teacher chatter. It wasn't that he didn't want to meet the new teacher; he just didn't feel the need to.

Jacob gasped and clapped his hands. "I know! The program."

Simon hadn't thought much about it, but it was getting to be time for the Christmas pageant. "What about it?"

"You can meet her then." But his expression fell slightly as he said the words. "I wish you would come before that. She's so nice."

"I've heard that about her."

"Please."

Simon shook his head even as he sighed. "I'll see what I can do." But deep down inside he was hoping that his son would forget all about this double-nice teacher so Simon could get on with missing his wife.

That was it, Simon thought. That was what this was all about. This was Jacob's first Christmas without his mother, and he was doing what he had to in order to cope. Even if that meant crushing on the new teacher. Simon couldn't blame him for what he was doing. He supposed it was perfectly natural. People did what they did in order to survive, whether they were seven or seventy. He supposed he should just overlook it for now, try not to encourage it, but not put it down either. It was going to be a delicate balance of words and emotions. But he could do it. He just wished Catherine were there to help.

CHAPTER THREE

"Are you ready?" Ada stuck her head in the bathroom, where Lily Kate was putting the final touches on her hair and pinning her prayer covering in place.

"You're out of baby lotion," she told her cousin, smoothing a hand over the side of her part one last time. There. Everything was done. She was ready to go.

"I think there's some more upstairs. You want me to go get it?"

"No, I'm fine. I used this." She held up the bottle of coconut-scented hand lotion and showed it to her cousin. "It did the trick."

Ada made a face. "You're going to smell like suntan lotion all day." All day and until she washed her long, long hair again.

Lily Kate took a deep breath, inhaling the sweet scent. Amish women usually used baby lotion to keep any of their stray hairs from escaping their bob, but she sort of liked being different.

It was another topic of conversation at family holiday dinners. Why did she feel the need to stand out? Was it something she was born with, or did it come about because she was so tiny? Individuality was sort of frowned upon in Amish communities. Mainly because the community was all about community. There was nothing wrong with that. Just sometimes Lily Kate liked to do things her own way.

She had been asked once why Amish women wore black aprons over their dresses. The person who asked was Englisch of course, and Lily Kate patiently explained that some women wore white aprons to church. She didn't go into all the particulars of which women did what. She was too busy thinking about the real question. Why did Amish women wear aprons at all? She was stumped for an answer. Why *did* they wear aprons? Except the only answer she could come up with was because that's how it had always been done.

"Lily Kate! Ada! *Dat* said it's time to go." Ada's twin Amelia called to them from the doorway.

Though they were identical, Ada and Amelia seemed to look different. Lily Kate had been trying to figure out what the difference really was, but the only thing she had come up with so far was that Amelia appeared to be more reserved and Ada more confident. But that couldn't make identical twins look like merely siblings who favored each other and shared similar traits. Could it?

"Coming," Ada called in return. She linked arms with Lily Kate, only stopping to grab their purses and put on their coats before heading out to the buggy.

"Where are we going again?" Lily Kate asked.

"To the Bontragers. Irene and Jake," Amelia said from her place in the front seat. She sat there along with Jamie, the oldest of the King children, while Ada, Lily Kate, and Silas were squished together in the back. Lily Kate didn't mind. At least when they were this close it was much easier to share the blankets and keep warm on the long ride.

The Kings were taking two buggies to church today. The

other held Allen, his wife Jodie, and their four young children who ranged in age from eight to fifteen. It was a classic tale of remarriage and a second chance. Ada and her brothers and sister had lost their mother years ago. Allen, their father, had taken his time before getting married again and now was raising a second family with Jodie. It seemed to be working well. Lily Kate had only been there a couple of days, but she had never heard a cross word between them.

"But this isn't your normal church Sunday," Lily Kate said to clarify.

"Right." Silas replied. At twenty-three he was the youngest of the first set of King children, with Jamie being the eldest at thirty. Jamie reminded Lily Kate a great deal of her own brother, Cyrus. Though Cyrus was a widower, and Jamie seemed to be a confirmed bachelor. Ada had told Lily that she suspected Jamie had gotten his heart broken somewhere along the way and had sworn off love. It was a shame. He was a handsome man, with dark blond hair and green eyes like his sisters. He was good with the younger kids and appeared to be helpful in the house. But what did she know?

She couldn't say a word about someone else deciding love might not be worth the trouble it brought with it.

After all, she felt the same. She was done with it. It was not worth all the hassle and certainly not with the heartbreak it could cause when it turned bad.

She sighed and pushed those thoughts away. Back at home it was a church Sunday for her family too. They would be gathering at someone's house getting ready to hear one of the leaders speak and preach, to fill them with the Word of God. Joseph would be there, and most likely he and Amanda would be riding home together. If it was a pretty day, maybe they would take an extra drive or go down by the water. Or maybe to the park to just walk around and watch the people. All the things that Lily Kate and Joseph did together when they were a couple. But now those were all the things he was doing with Amanda. Amanda Schrock, who had once upon a time been Lily Kate's best friend.

Now everyone told her that she needed to forgive and forget. Forgive she could handle. She had been raised to forgive all, the same way Jesus forgave us, but forget. . . ? That was much harder to do.

"A penny for them," Ada said, bumping against her shoulder as they trotted along.

Lily Kate shook her head. "They're not worth near that much," she admitted.

Ada frowned. "You shouldn't be thinking about him." She said the words so that only Lily Kate could hear.

"I wasn't, really. At least I didn't start out to." But that's how it seemed to be. She could begin by thinking about canned peas, and suddenly there was Jospeh in her thoughts because he really liked canned peas. And he did! How could that be her fault? It seemed her whole world was full of Joseph's likes and dislikes and never-tried-befores. How could anything else compete?

"Well, you need to finish. And maybe you'll meet someone today who will sweep you off your feet and make it so that Joseph Beery can never be a part of your thoughts again."

That sounded fine. Except for the sweeping off her feet part. She definitely wasn't up for that. But she could do with not thinking about Joseph all the time.

"I know someone," Ada continued.

Lily Kate didn't like the tone her cousin was using. "Ada. . . No."

"He's very nice. A widower, and so you have that in common."

"Joseph didn't die." No, he just dumped her for her best friend.

"It's still a loss," Ada said.

"I don't want to meet anyone like that."

"Like what?" Ada's expression was pure innocence. "All you have to do is say hello. You don't have to date him. You're just going to meet him."

"I guess," Lily Kate grumbled. She would say hello and that was it. She didn't need a new romance, didn't want one. In fact, a romance was the last thing on her mind right now.

The Bontragers' house was like so many other Amish homes that Lily Kate had been to. White siding, barn out back. Dormant flower beds flanking everything, waiting patiently for spring.

The church wagon, which was used to transport the church benches from house to house, sat off to one side. Its gray color became less strange to her as the days passed. Maybe soon—if she stayed in Lancaster—the gray color of the buggies they drove would be as common to her as the shiny black of the ones in New Wilmington.

The barn itself was a large building, a mix of animal shelter and workshop. Ada explained that Jake Bontrager, the homeowner, made baskets and sold them in many shops all over town. Lily Kate made a note to get one for her mamm. One could never have too many baskets.

Church itself was to be held in the barn loft "bonus room," Ada told her as they waited outside for church to begin.

Though it was a normal church Sunday, where she would be at church if she had been at home, she thought that living in a district with church on the opposite Sundays meant that today she would be able to stay home and work on her lesson plan for the scholars.

No, she wasn't supposed to be working on Sunday. But she thought perhaps the good Lord would forgive her this one time.

After all, she had hardly been prepared to come in and teach classes so quickly, and it seemed Mabel Esh held all her lesson plans in her brain instead of on paper. So, the extra time would have been greatly appreciated. Had she been allowed to use it.

Oh well. Maybe this afternoon she would beg off, saying she needed a nap. She could head down to the basement and work a little. Then again, there were five girls all sleeping in the room together. She wasn't sure she would be able to get any time alone with that many roommates. Someone was usually lurking about, from Amelia, Ada's twin, all the way down to their eight-year-old sister, Barbara.

"There he is," Ada breathed.

"Who?"

"The someone I want you to meet." Ada smiled.

Lily Kate immediately started to shake her head. She had been hoping against hope that her cousin would forget this silly plan of hers. "I really do not want to meet anyone."

Ada pressed her lips together in a disapproving frown. Or maybe it was disappointed. "He's a nice man. Why shouldn't you meet him?"

"Because I am going home in eight weeks, and I told you I have sworn off love."

Ada sadly wagged her head from side to side. "That's no way to go through life," she said. Then she hooked Lily Kate's arm with her own and dragged her across the yard.

"Simon," she called as they made their way.

Lily Kate hadn't seen who her cousin had been talking about. But the closer they got, the more she thought he looked like—

"You," she breathed.

His jaw hardened just like it had the day he had shoved her down onto the sidewalk. "Hello again." His words held no ring of greeting. They were simply words.

Ada looked from one of them to the other. "Wait. You already know each other?"

"We do." Lily Kate crossed her arms and told herself to hold in her temper. It was Sunday after all, and they were about to go in and hear God's Word. Wasn't it all about forgiveness?

The man gave a small nod. "Though we have not been formally introduced."

Just then a small boy ran up, his freckled cheeks pink from the cold. "Dat, that's her. That's my teacher, Lily Kate."

It only took her a second to recall the boy's name. "Hi, Jacob."

He grinned at her, the motion as animated as his father's scowl.

"And you are?" She turned her gaze to the man before her. The man who pushed her down in a heroic move he thought would save her life.

"Simon." He dipped his chin in her direction but didn't offer his hand to shake.

"Nice to meet you, Simon." She nearly choked on the words, but she reminded herself of what Ada had said yesterday. You never know what a person has been through before you meet them. He was a widower, a single father, and apparently thought it was his duty to make sure—by any means necessary—that people didn't walk out into the street without looking.

She had lost three of the coloring pages she had printed out for the twins, and she had ripped her stockings, but it wasn't like she had to spend any time with the man. She could say hello and be on her way.

Ada was still staring at the two of them, her mouth slightly agape.

"See, Dat, I told you she was nice." Jacob tugged on his father's hand as he spoke.

At the very least she was trying to be cordial. But nice was even better. She would take it.

Though she wanted to demand a reason for his aggressive behavior. There had been plenty of time for her to get across the street without injury. She thought anyway.

And if he had been worried about her, he could have simply taken her arm and pulled her backward. He didn't have to maul her to get her attention. But she would not ask for an apology or even an excuse. That all was so yesterday.

"Jah." Simon's tone was flat as if he were suppressing all his emotions and locking them down deep inside.

Lily Kate could definitely relate. So much for the man that Ada had wanted her to meet. Just one more reason to swear off love. Like she needed another.

⁓

Simon couldn't believe the shock he had received at church. The last thing, the very last thing, he had expected was for the sassy jaywalker to be in attendance.

Lancaster was a big place with lots of Amish communities, which meant lots of Amish people. What were the chances that he would run into her again? Especially now that he knew she was a visitor in Lancaster. The interim schoolteacher from New Wilmington. Niece to Allen King. Which also meant that she wasn't staying in his church district. She was only visiting today. The last person he had wanted. . .or even expected to see.

Because seeing her again made him feel a little foolish. Perhaps he had overreacted to her stepping off the curb in front of him. Jah, there had been a car coming, and jah, she could have possibly been hit, but was it likely? Who knew?

But she was safe, he told himself as he drove home that

afternoon, Jacob chattering by his side. "Did you like her?" he asked his father for what had to be the umpteenth time.

"She seemed very nice," Simon diplomatically replied.

"She is very nice," Jacob added. "Don't you like her name?"

"It's a fine name." What else could be said about it? Lily Kate had a nice ring to it. It slipped off the tongue easy enough. But he was a little concerned about the crush his son was developing. It seemed closer to an obsession. Should he be worried? Maybe he would talk to Tamsyn about it. His sister was pretty smart about such things.

Or maybe not. She had a tendency to let things slip that were better to remain private.

"I was so excited to see her. And you got to meet her even before the Christmas program."

Jah. The end of next week. Just a couple of days before Christmas itself, the school would have its annual Christmas program. Then Jacob would have a break from the teacher. A much-needed break from the sound of it. Perhaps then when it was time to go back to school after the holiday, the crush would have burned itself out. A man could hope.

Lily Kate Troyer was scheduled to be in Lancaster teaching for at least eight weeks while Mabel Esh healed from her fall. Simon wasn't certain he could stand eight weeks of Jacob singing the teacher's praises. Not at all.

⁓

Lily Kate had only thought the previous week had been trying. But by Wednesday she was about to pull her hair out. She knew how hard it was to sit still and concentrate when Christmas break was so close. She remembered how it was. And she also remembered her teacher patiently working them through it all.

That was just what she planned to do. But first she needed a plan. All she had was the threat of talking to someone's father.

"And if you continue," she said to Andrew Schwartz, one of the three sixth-grade boys, "I will have no choice but to talk to your father."

They were the hardest, the sixth-grade boys. Maybe because there were no girls in the seventh or eighth grades, and they were taller than she was by a good three inches. Or maybe they were just mischievous that way. Though she had met Mabel Esh right after arriving in Lancaster, and she couldn't imagine the sour-faced woman putting up with any nonsense. No matter how close they were to Christmas.

Andrew nodded, but she wasn't certain that he was taking her threat seriously.

"I mean it."

He and another boy, also in the sixth grade, had decided to make a paper airplane out of the construction paper they were using to make decorations for the upcoming Christmas program. That should have been a fun enough activity, making green-and-red paper chains to hang up throughout their tiny classroom. She had even found a box of shiny Christmas garland to add a little sparkle to it all.

"Really," she said. Hoping that it emphasized and made him a believer. She honestly didn't want to speak with the boy's father.

"Jah, Lily Kate." Andrew nodded, then paused a moment before going outside with the others.

Lily Kate was on her way out the door as well, when movement on their entry porch caught her attention.

"Jacob." She smiled at the boy, wondering if he had been standing there the entire time she was talking with Andrew. "Why aren't you playing with the others?"

"I was going to," he said. "But I wanted to. . .I wanted to tell you something before. . .I started playing."

He was stuttering around with his words, and Lily Kate was beginning to wonder if he would ever get the message out.

"Jah?" she prompted.

"Danki for giving me a part in the Christmas program."

"Of course." She nodded. "Everyone has a part," she reminded him. "And then we'll all sing Christmas songs at the end."

That was something that Mabel Esh had left for Lily Kate, a plan for the Christmas program. Or rather she had dictated it to someone—word was the bishop's wife—since the hand Mabel usually wrote with was now in a cast that reached from her fingertips to nearly her shoulder.

Lily Kate was thankful for the instructions. She could look in a book and find math problems and spelling words, but she couldn't make up an entire pageant in less than two weeks.

"Are you really going to talk to Andrew's father about the paper airplanes?"

Lily Kate stopped halfway down the steps. "Jacob," she started. "You shouldn't have been eavesdropping."

He turned bright red underneath his freckles. "I didn't mean to. I was just coming in to see you and stopped at the door. I'm sorry."

She nodded. "You're forgiven. But in the future, you need to let private conversations remain private."

He nodded a little too vigorously, nearly shaking himself off the stairs.

"All right then," Lily Kate said. "Time to go play."

She smiled a little to herself as Jacob took off running to join the others in their game of baseball.

CHAPTER FOUR

By the end of school the following day, Lily Kate knew something was up with sweet, freckle-faced Jacob Bontrager. She had managed to get control over Andrew and Tommy, and now Jacob had started in. Kicking the back of the desk in front of him, pulling Lizzie Lambright's braids during lunch, during recess, during practice for the program.

She knew that he had overheard her telling Andrew that she would have to call his father if he didn't straighten up. So why was Jacob behaving in such a way? It was almost as if he wanted her to call his father in. But why?

The only thing she could think of was the fact that the boy had only recently lost his mother. If talk around town was correct, then Catherine Bontrager had died in February. Not quite a year ago. This was to be Jacob and Simon's first Christmas without her. She might not like Simon or appreciate his overzealous ways, but she did feel for him having to deal with such a loss now that the holidays were upon them. Regardless of what Ada claimed, death and breakup just weren't the same kind of loss, and she wouldn't wish the pain she knew Simon was experiencing on anyone.

And Jacob too. He probably was trying to swim through all the grief and get his father's attention. She had heard somewhere that some children couldn't differentiate between good attention and bad attention. Perhaps Jacob was one of those.

Jacob was well cared for. She knew he had loving grandparents. She checked his lunch, and it seemed good enough. Maybe a little bland. A sandwich and some crackers. A thermos of some kind of drink. There was no fruit, no dessert. Healthy enough food maybe but perhaps a little understated.

That's when she came up with the idea.

"Lily Kate?" Jacob stood before her, the cookie and the note she had slipped into his lunch cooler in one hand. "You gave me this?"

She smiled at him as sweet and patiently as a person can. "Jah. I thought you could use a treat. Do you not like chocolate chip?"

He shook his head. "I mean, jah. Everybody likes chocolate chip."

"True enough."

"But I've been—" Tears starting welling in his green eyes. His father's eyes were deep dark brown. Jacob must have inherited these from his mother.

"You know, I'm far from home right now and sometimes change is difficult. I wanted to come here and teach you kids, but I don't like being away from my mamm and dat."

"You have a mamm and dat?" The shock of that statement seemed to have staunched his tears, at least for the time being.

"Of course." She held back her laughter as much as possible at his sweetly innocent question. "And I miss them, so every Saturday I go to Immergut and get myself a treat."

"Every Saturday?" His eyes grew wide.

"We don't have Immergut where I come from. So, I'm getting them while I can."

"That makes sense," he said, nodding his head sagely.

"Soft pretzels are my favorite," she told him.

"I like them too," he admitted.

"They're kind of like chocolate chip cookies, huh?"

He grinned, showing her the gap where his front tooth had recently gone missing. "Jah," he told her. "Everyone likes them."

"It's an obsession," Ada said the following Saturday as Lily Kate marched her to Immergut.

"It's not an obsession. I just like them is all." And after the week she had teaching, she deserved two!

They entered the shop, and Lily Kate immediately drew in a deep breath. Nothing smelled as wonderful as Immergut. Yeasty and warm and comforting. Jah, okay. Maybe it was an obsession, but she wasn't willing to do anything about it.

"What kind do you want?" Lily Kate asked as she navigated between the crush of people inside the tiny shop. She wasn't the only one in Lancaster who loved an Immergut soft pretzel.

"Cinnamon sugar," Ada immediately said.

Lily Kate made a face. She was a purist. Plain pretzel—which really meant a pretzel with butter and salt—and a cup of hot mustard dip.

"Cinnamon sugar," Ada repeated as Lily Kate approached the counter.

Immergut was busy enough today that there were two lines. She managed to get to the front without a problem, though she was a little taken aback as she heard her name called.

"Lily Kate!" It was a small voice belonging to a child, and

she looked around to see that Simon and Jacob Bontrager were in the opposite line waiting to order.

"Hi, Jacob. I see you decided to get a treat today too."

She immediately regretted the words, though they seemed innocent enough. They were innocent enough, but Simon's expression darkened. Still, he managed to wave at Ada.

"Can I take your order?" the Mennonite girl behind the counter asked Lily Kate.

The Amish girl standing at Simon's register was patiently waiting for him to turn and tell her what he and Jacob wanted.

"I need a cinnamon sugar pretzel and a plain with hot mustard."

"Right away," the girl said punching in the order.

"I want the same thing," Simon said with a small frown.

"Cinnamon sugar and a plain with hot mustard?" the Amish girl asked.

He nodded.

She started for the glass counter where the pretzels were kept warm.

"Uh-oh," Lily Kate heard one of the girls say.

Then the Mennonite girl turned toward the kitchen. "How long for a plain pretzel?"

"Four minutes," came the answer.

The Mennonite girl looked to her Amish counterpart. She shrugged.

"It's going to be four minutes," she said, her words encompassing them both. "We only have one plain pretzel right now."

One plain pretzel? How did a pretzel shop run out of plain pretzels on a Saturday? Maybe because other people liked them too, she supposed.

"Here you go." She started to hand the pretzel to Lily Kate, but she found herself shaking her head. "No. Go ahead and give it to him."

"What?" the girl asked.

"I can wait for the other ones." That way Jacob didn't have to wait for his treat, and she would get a fresh pretzel. Win-win.

The Mennonite girl handed the pretzel over the counter toward Simon, but he refused to take it.

"She ordered first," he said, nodding toward Lily Kate.

"No, really," she said. "You should take it so Jacob can eat."

"It's a treat," Simon said. "It's not like he's starving. Do you think he's not eating well enough? Is that why you brought him lunch to school?"

"It was a cookie," Lily Kate protested. "Not lunch."

"Did you bring all the kids a cookie?"

"Is someone going to take this?" The Amish girl shook the package containing the pretzels.

"He is." Lily Kate gave an emphatic nod.

"She is," Simon countered.

"You know another is coming out in like four minutes." The Mennonite girl stepped in, presumably to get the line moving again. "It's not like you really have to wait."

"She should take it."

"Him."

"Two minutes," someone called from the kitchen.

She was not backing down in this. Just because he was a man who was bigger and taller than her didn't mean he got to dictate whether or not she wanted to wait on the next pretzel. She had been thinking about his son when she offered to wait. Was the man too stubborn to see that?

"Someone needs to take it." The Amish girl was beginning to get anxious.

"Dat." Jacob pulled at Simon's coat.

Apparently, she wasn't the only one.

"What are you doing?" Ada hissed in Lily Kate's ear.

"I'm trying to be cordial, and instead I'm being accused of all sorts of things."

"I didn't accuse you of anything," Simon protested.

"Favoritism." She raised her brows and pressed her lips together for emphasis. "You accused me of favoritism." One would think a parent would appreciate a teacher's measures to make a child feel welcome and loved in the classroom. One would think.

The Amish girl gave up and laid the pretzel on the counter between them. She looked around Simon to the person waiting behind him. "Can I take your order?"

"Plain's up," the kitchen called.

A second later the Mennonite girl was holding out two sacks and shaking them at Lily Kate and Simon. "Enjoy," she said. Though the word had the ring of finality.

"Come on." Ada snatched one of the sacks away and started for the door.

"I haven't paid yet," Lily Kate protested.

"It's on the house," the Mennonite girl said. "Really. Enjoy." Which seemed to be code for "just leave."

Lily Kate paused for one second longer as Simon pulled a ten dollar bill from his wallet and laid it on the counter. "Keep the change."

She was about to do the same, when Ada backtracked and pulled her from the store.

"What was all that about?" her cousin asked as they made their way down the sidewalk.

"You saw what he was like in there. I was afraid I was going to get banned all because of him." She turned as if to go back in the other direction, as if to find Simon and finish whatever had happened between them at the counter of Immergut.

How awful would it be to get banned from her favorite snack place in all of Lancaster! Even worse to be banned from her favorite snack place all because of Simon "Thinks He Knows Everything" Bontrager.

"Nuh-uh." Ada looped her arm through Lily Kate's once more and swung her back around. "We are going to the buggy. Then we're going home. And we are forgetting this ever happened."

A sudden wave of remorse washed over Lily Kate, nearly stopping her in her tracks. "Ada," she said, her voice a hushed whisper. "I'm sorry. That was embarrassing. I don't know what to say."

Ada shook her head, then smiled at her, showing all was forgiven. "You don't have to say anything. Just stay away from Simon Bontrager."

Lily Kate nodded. With pleasure.

⁓

Stay away from Simon Bontrager. That seemed easy enough. Church came and went, and the last week of school was in full swing. Some of the boys had settled down. Mostly, anyway, and for that Lily Kate was grateful. Though she had a feeling once they came back from the break, it would start all over again. Maybe by the time Mabel was able to take over her classroom once more, Lily Kate would have them all eating out of her hand. One could hope.

Mabel's injury also put them behind schedule with the Christmas program, and Lily Kate had made the executive decision right after she had come to Lancaster to push the program back a week to give the children more time to practice.

So now here they were, the last day of school before the break, before Christmas that Sunday.

Last night they had held the Christmas program for all the families, and this morning once again for anyone who couldn't come at night. The children did wonderfully. Oh, they had made their fair share of mistakes, and one first-grade boy sang the wrong words to "Jingle Bells"—loudly and horribly off-key. Where he got his unusual lyrics, she had no idea. Something about shotgun shells and a granny. But considering his sixth-grade brother was doing everything in his power not to laugh hysterically, Lily Kate suspected that brother put him up to it. That was one for the parents to sort through.

Today she was about to be off for a week. And she was thoroughly looking forward to it. Just a quick, last-minute pickup around the classroom before she left to catch the bus. She was going home for Christmas.

She missed her family terribly, but she was enjoying her newfound freedoms. All except the contention between her and Simon Bontrager. That was something she could do without. But she was proud of herself. She had survived two and a half weeks of substitute teaching. Not everyone could say that.

How special that Christmas fell on a Sunday this year. Lily Kate couldn't ever remember Christmas being on a Sunday, though she was certain it had been. Maybe it hadn't fallen on a church Sunday, and it seemed like Christmas. This was something else entirely. Almost magical.

She knew her dat would tell her that there was no such thing. That every Christmas was special and every Sunday a blessing, but it still felt different to her.

She looked around the classroom one more time, making sure everything was in its place. That was when she saw it.

A splash of yellow and green peeking out from under the

desk where Jacob Bontrager usually sat. She immediately knew what it was. His scarf. He had come in wearing it this morning. It was mostly black with balls of color sewn on one side. When she commented on it, he had told her that it once belonged to his mother.

Lily Kate was fairly certain that Catherine only wore the colorful scarf while at her own home, but Jacob needed to feel close to her and so he wore it to school. But now he had left it behind.

Once he realized what he had done, she knew he was going to be bereft, beside himself with sadness. He was proud of having found it and then wearing it to school. Her heart was torn. Did she have enough time to get to the Bontrager house and back before the bus left?

She checked the clock on the wall. Surely, she did. It wasn't that far out, and Ada was going to pick up the buggy tonight after she got off work at Stoltzfus Meats. Lily Kate could just pop out to Simon and Jacob's, hand over the scarf, then head right back into town.

It started snowing about halfway to Jacob's house. The weatherman had been calling for snow, but the clouds were holding to their moisture as if they needed it more than the people and animals below. Until now anyway. Should she turn around?

She decided that it wasn't that bad; it didn't even seem to be sticking. She could make it, and maybe in bringing the lost item to Jacob she would make some sort of progress with Simon. He would be grateful that she had gone out of her way for his son. He would thank her and smile at her, and everything would be better in the world.

Fine. She didn't like it when people didn't like her, but in her quest to be liked she had turned into a bit of a doormat. And then Joseph breaking off their engagement was the last straw.

That was when she had decided to stand up for herself, and all it had resulted in was someone actively disliking her enough to argue with her practically every time they met. It was beyond comprehension. Wasn't she allowed to stand up for herself?

She mused and mulled it over, somehow missing when the snow grew thicker. By then she was closer to the Bontragers' and figured she should just finish the errand and head back to town. She was already this far in it.

When she finally made it to the house, she set the brake on the buggy, picked up the scarf from the seat next to her, and hurried to the door. She hadn't realized how cold she was. She hadn't expected to take this long of a trip. And she really hadn't expected it to start snowing. Her warmest gloves were packed away in her suitcase in the back of the buggy. For the last few days, all the reports had been calling for snow, and it never came. Now when she had places to be, why did it suddenly start?

She raised her hand to knock on the door, but it was yanked open before her fingers touched wood.

"What are you doing out here?" Simon's voice boomed at her, and Lily Kate broke.

"Don't yell at me." Her voice was so quiet it was a little scary, even to her. Maybe even to him. Simon took a step back.

"Come in," he said, immediately changing his tone. "I just. . .why are you out in this weather?"

She held the scarf out toward him, but he didn't reach for it. She shook it a little. "This is Jacob's scarf. He left it in the classroom today."

"That's not—" Then he stopped. Reached out a trembling hand. "That was Catherine's."

"I know."

He turned the scarf over in his hands. "What was he doing with it?"

"He came to school wearing it today. I figured you knew about it and since it's his first Christmas—your first Christmas without her that he would want it with him."

"So, you brought it by in a blizzard?" The gruffness was returning to his tone.

"It's not a blizzard," she said a bit defensively. "It's barely snowing out there." But she could hear the hopeful note in her words.

They turned as one to look out the front window. The snow was coming down harder and harder as each second ticked past.

"Oh dear," she said. "I have to go." She started for the door. "Tell Jacob Merry Christmas from me, please."

Simon clasped her arm in one hand, stopping her before she could get to the door. "You can't go out in this."

She looked at him, then back to the door, then the window, and back to him once more. She bit her lip and shook her head. "I'm supposed to go home." Her words held the thickness of tears.

"We can try to call Allen later and let him know that you are safe. I have a phone in the barn," Simon continued.

"No. *Home*," she corrected. "To New Wilmington."

"There's no way," he replied.

"Lily Kate!" Jacob suddenly appeared at the bottom of the stairs.

Simon released her as if she had burned him.

"Hi, Jacob."

The boy's joy was unmistakable as he rushed toward her, wrapping his arms around her waist and hugging her tight.

She patted him on the back even though she wanted to set him from her and hurry over to the door. The snow showed no signs of letting up, and if she was going to make it to the bus stop, she would have to leave immediately.

One last pat on Jacob's back, and she pulled his arms from around her. "I'm sorry. I have to go now."

He seemed confused. "Where are you going?"

"I can't let you go out in this," Simon said.

She shook free of Jacob's hold and walked as quickly as she could to the door. She flung it open, then stopped in her tracks. Fat snowflakes raced through the air, creating a curtain of white. "It wasn't snowing like this when I started out," she explained in a mere whisper. "I was just going to run by here and then over to the bus station."

"I don't think you're going anywhere anytime soon," Simon said.

"Don't go, Lily Kate," Jacob begged. "You can stay with us for as long as you want."

Lily Kate didn't miss the sharp look father sent son. But at least Simon didn't reprimand him for the invitation. How could he, seeing as Simon himself kept saying that she couldn't leave?

"I'm sure the buses are not able to get out in this either. The weatherman is calling for feet, not inches."

"In December?" Lily Kate hated the whine in her voice. But in twenty-six years she had never spent a Christmas away from her family. Not even one!

She wanted to throw caution to the wind and head for the bus station, but she wouldn't. And she had a feeling Simon and Jacob would not allow it. The truth was anyone would be a fool to travel in this weather.

CHAPTER FIVE

"Shut the door," Simon told her. He hadn't meant to sound so gruff, but there was a blizzard out there. And the new teacher had landed on his doorstep.

"My horse."

He should have thought of that right away. "I'll go." He started pulling on his coat and his boots. Neither one would be protection enough from the heavily falling snow. But they were better than going without.

Still, he couldn't imagine why God had seen the need to punish him. Not with the snow but with the presence of the woman hovering close by.

"I'll help," Jacob offered.

Simon shook his head. "You stay here with Lily Kate."

The wind was fierce, the snow heavy and driving. Her horse balked a bit, but when the beast realized that Simon was there to help, it stopped struggling and went along to the barn.

His own horse chuffed as he led the gelding into an empty stall. Then Simon backtracked to the workroom for a towel and an extra blanket. He had already placed one on his own horse.

The weather was only supposed to get worse from here, the snow not stopping until sometime in the night.

Simon ignored the blocks of wood and half-finished carvings and hustled back over to the horse's stall. He dried the gelding with the old towel, then hung it up across the door of the stall to dry. Then he covered the beast with a blanket and patted his long, strong neck.

"Are you hungry, buddy?" he crooned. He gave the horse one last pat then made his way over to the barrel of horse kibble. He got out a scoop for the gelding and bucket of water from the workroom sink. In no time at all, he was back in the stall.

Now he had no more excuses to stay out in the barn. Besides, it was getting colder and colder. But he was dreading going back in and facing the disappointment on Lily Kate Troyer's face.

He couldn't let her go out in this. She would have to spend the night, but with any luck and a few prayers—okay, *a lot* of prayers; he couldn't leave anything to chance—she would be gone come tomorrow.

Tomorrow. Tomorrow was Christmas Eve. His first Christmas without Catherine. But his heart didn't pang so hard in his chest when he thought about her these days. Maybe because he had told himself so many times since February that this day was coming.

Still, he couldn't hide out in the barn forever.

It was getting worse even as he turned up the collar of his coat and dashed back toward the house, thinking about his childhood when they still had a milk cow and fresh milk. That was a treat having it every day, but in the winter, it was hard going out twice a day to milk the Jersey. He was not that old, really, but his family liked being self-sufficient. He did too, but self-sufficient didn't mean taking in stragglers.

He couldn't get over her age. Just looking at her anyone would think that she was in her teens. But her eyes gave her away. They were such a sparkling blue. An impossible blue. Improbable. They were full of life and dazzle, but they also showed a pain lurking there. He knew. He recognized it as the same pain he saw in his very own eyes every morning. She might not have lost a loved one to death, but every person's tragedy was their own.

Now she was stranded with him. At least for the night.

It was the last thing he wanted.

It was the last thing *she* wanted.

But what could be done about it now?

He let himself into the house, immediately feeling less chilled as the warm air hit him.

She rushed over. "Thank goodness you're back."

Had he been gone that long?

Her tiny hands began to brush the snow from his coat. Off his shoulders, off his arms. She had placed a towel on the floor by the door to trap the falling moisture. She was like a delicate hummingbird fluttering around him. He just wished that she would stop touching him.

Then, as if she realized what she was doing, she stopped and took a step back. "I guess the buggy—"

Simon shook his head as he removed his coat and muck boots. "It'll have to stay where it is for now. It will be full of snow by the time this ends, but I don't think there's much we can do about it now."

She bit her lip but nodded understandingly. "You should go stand by the fire. I made some coffee. I'll get you some." She rushed into the kitchen.

She had made coffee? Maybe he had been gone a while.

Simon shook his head. Then, in only his sock feet, he padded over to the fire. He held out his hands to warm them. The skin prickled as the heat touched his fingers.

"When can I go play?" Jacob asked. His son was perched on the couch with his boots nearby at the ready.

"You can go upstairs and play in your room right now," Simon replied.

"Outside," Jacob clarified.

"When the snow stops. Maybe tomorrow."

"Tomorrow?" Jacob screeched.

"Upstairs is still open."

Lily Kate picked that moment to hustle back into the room. She pressed the coffee cup into Simon's hands, then stood back, almost vibrating with the need to do something.

Jacob looked over to his teacher. Lily Kate was still biting her lip and contemplating her next move.

Simon could almost see her brain working, turning over every possibility that would lead to her getting what she wanted: Christmas with her family.

"No," Jacob finally said. "I'll stay here with you." But he was looking at Lily Kate when he said the words.

"I just hope Jamie isn't upset. About the buggy," Lily Kate mused.

"You're worried Jamie King is going to be upset? Your cousin?"

"It's his buggy and horse," Lily Kate replied.

"I've never seen Jamie King get upset about anything," Simon countered. The man was about as even-keeled as they came.

"I was supposed to leave the buggy at the bus station for Ada."

"I'm sure she's not still waiting for you if that's what you're thinking."

"I don't know what I'm thinking." She sighed.

If it was anything like what he was thinking, her thoughts were all about why this had to happen today. Why today, of all days, did Jacob forget his scarf at school? Why did she have to be so nice and bring it to him even though he had another one he could've used until school went back in session? And worst of all, what were they going to do for the next few hours?

Snowed in.

"Are you okay?" Lily Kate asked. He wasn't sure what was worse: her fussing angrily or fussing anxiously. Both were endearing, er. . .he meant annoying. Jah, annoying.

She stepped toward him as if to brush the remaining moisture from his beard.

He set the coffee cup down on the end table next to the couch and captured her hands in his own. They were soft hands, and so tiny, easily disappearing into his. He looked up and caught her gaze. For a moment, the briefest moment, he thought she might have felt the same jolt, but she looked away and the feeling was gone. Had it ever really been there?

"Let's play cards," Jacob chirped.

Simon let Lily Kate go, and the moment was well and truly broken.

***

"Are you sure you don't need help?" Lily Kate asked from the doorway of the kitchen.

Simon grabbed two pot holders off the counter and opened the oven. He removed the bubbling casserole pan and set it on top of the stove. "I'm going to pretend like you didn't say that," Simon said.

He shouldn't be acting like he had cooked the meal. It was the last of the food that his mother had brought him this week. There was only enough left for the three of them, which wouldn't be a problem if the roads were clear in the morning. With the snow still coming down, he had a feeling that wouldn't be the case. Without the snow, he and Jacob would have finished off the dinner and then in the morning they would've driven over to his parents' house and spent the night. That way they could be there on Christmas morning.

But there was snow. And things changed. Simon and Lily Kate set the table, and then he called Jacob in to eat. They said their prayer and served their plates, and dinner turned into a quiet affair.

Simon was a little confused, maybe even a little lost, since he wasn't upset with Lily Kate still. He didn't really know what feelings to have toward her. Though he knew he shouldn't have treated her that way.

"I'm sorry—" Simon started.

"I'm sorry—" Lily Kate said at the same time.

They both chuckled uncomfortably at each other. Jacob looked from one of them to the other, but the boy didn't say a word.

"You go first," Simon said.

"I just wanted to say I'm sorry," Lily Kate started. "I'm sorry for interrupting your holiday. I didn't mean to get caught here, and I do appreciate your hospitality."

"I'm sorry too," Simon said. "I'm sorry for yelling at you that day. I guess I tend to get angry when I get really scared, and you nearly getting hit by the car was terrifying." Thankfully she didn't ask why. Maybe she knew. Maybe Ada had told her.

Lily Kate merely nodded and said that all was forgiven.

"And I'm sorry you can't go home for Christmas."

"Maybe the storm won't be as bad as they are saying, and maybe I can go to the bus stop tomorrow. Maybe then I'll be able to go home."

Simon didn't tell her how unlikely that dream was. But since their apologies for one another, the air seemed different. Quieter. It seemed like something between them had shifted.

Supper was over, and Lily Kate walked Jacob to the bathroom to help him wash up. It wasn't that Jacob was too young to wash up himself. She just needed to get out of the same room as Simon. This was the only excuse she could find. She couldn't stop thinking about him, Simon. That moment when he came back into the house. He was standing in front of the fire, and he grabbed her hands. Then she had felt like she had the time that she touched a damp battery. There was a zing and a whoosh, and then—oh my!

"I prayed for this," Jacob said.

His quietly spoken words brought Lily Kate back to the present. "What are you talking about?"

His green eyes met hers in the mirror, and he smiled that gap-toothed grin. "I prayed for this snow. I prayed for something to happen to bring all of us together."

It took a moment for his words to sink in, for their meaning to become clear and for them to make sense. Then she realized the truth: Jacob wanted the two of them—her and his father—to fall in love and become a couple. They may have formed an uneasy truce, but love was completely off the table. She hated to dash the boy's dream, but she couldn't let him go on believing that something like love might grow between her and his father.

"It doesn't really happen that way," she started as gently as she could.

Jacob shook his head. "Prayers work." he said.

"I'm going back to New Wilmington soon. You know that, right? That's where I'm from."

Drying his hands on a towel that had been laying on the bathroom counter, Jacob nodded. "I know."

She would go back home to New Wilmington. Sooner rather than she really wanted to think about at the moment. Not because she was afraid that she would run into Joseph, but because she had been enjoying her time in Lancaster. She hadn't come here to enjoy herself, but there it was. She wanted to hang on to it as long as possible.

The evening went from bad to worse, as far as awkwardness went. They might have apologized to one another, and they might have formed this ceasefire of sorts, but that didn't mean he had stopped intimidating her. He was just such a large man. And quiet. No one in her family was quite that quiet. Well, except for maybe Jamie King. Then again, he was only quiet about the love that everyone suspected he'd had and then lost. No, most of the men in her family talked about things at night, what they had done during the day, what they were going to do the next day, what their wives had done, etc., etc. But Simon had just sat in a rocking chair and stared into the fire with a contemplative look on his face as he studied the flames.

Lily Kate wished she had brought her bag in when she came into the house. Her purse was still out in the buggy, though now it probably had snow in it from the blowing drifts. She also had a suitcase in the back, the one that she had packed to take home for the weekend. Inside that was the book she had been reading. She would like to read some more right now. But the snow was still falling outside, the wind still blowing. She suspected the storm had been downgraded from blizzard to just a regular storm. Still, there was no going out and grabbing her book just because she was bored. Instead, she found a book on the shelf in the alcove downstairs off the kitchen and took it upstairs to the spare bedroom, well before a normal bedtime.

The snow blanketed everything and forced a hush over the land, over the house. Jacob was in bed, Simon was staring at fire, and she retired upstairs with nothing more to do.

But even as she tried to read the words, she kept thinking about this broken family. She had her own broken heart, but it was nothing like what this family had had to endure. One, at least her Joseph was still alive. He might not really be hers any longer, but he was happy and healthy and safe.

One could argue that Catherine Bontrager was in a better place, but that didn't heal all the wounds and heartaches of those who were left behind. Lily Kate could see the pain in Jacob's eyes even though he was too young to fully comprehend it all. He was told undoubtedly that his mother was never coming home, but he seemed too young to understand what those words meant. Forever was just a word, and not a concept he could grasp. But Simon...Simon was a man, and he could comprehend. The sadness and pain she saw in his eyes, lining his face, was heartbreaking. He was heartbroken, he was devastated, and he had no cause to believe his life would ever change from that.

Lily Kate closed her eyes and sent up a small prayer for the family. "Dear Lord, make it whole and healed once again."

Jacob had said he had prayed for a new mother, and Lily Kate said a prayer for him, for his prayer to come true. "And Lord, please give Jacob a new mother. Amen."

⁓

The next morning Lily Kate woke to more snow than she had ever seen in her life. Well, maybe not her entire life, but the amount was certainly impressive. If she had to guess, she would say there was at least two feet on the ground with six- to eight-feet drifts. The sky was still gray, and the clouds were fat as if more snow was on the way. In fact, it looked like perhaps it could snow again at any moment. If she was leaving, now would be the time, before it kicked up again.

She dressed and skipped down the stairs to find Simon in the kitchen leaning against the counter and sipping a cup of coffee. "Good morning," he said. And there was that awkwardness again.

"Good morning," she said in return. She stopped a few feet from him, trying to decide the best way to announce her intentions of leaving without making herself sound ungrateful for the shelter overnight.

"Would you like some coffee?" Simon nodded toward the pot sitting on the stove. "Cups are right above on the left," he said.

Lily Kate nodded and moved, slower this time, toward the cabinet to get a coffee mug. She filled the cup then took a tentative sip. Somehow, she managed not to grimace. It was awful. But it was warm, and had caffeine in it, and would surely do right to get her started this morning.

"Good morning." Jacob smiled up at her, his mouth full of the breakfast Simon had prepared. Though she couldn't tell exactly what it was. She could make out the lumps that were biscuits, and the yellow spongy-looking pieces had to be scrambled eggs, but the black strips...? Who knew?

"Good morning."

"I was just about to head up and get you," Simon continued. "I have biscuits and some bacon."

So that was what the black strips were.

"Danki." She nodded and a small moment passed between them. She had no idea what it meant. It was just there.

She cleared her throat and took another sip of the terrible coffee. "I was wondering if you could get my horse out for me?" It wasn't exactly how she wanted to approach the subject, but there it was.

A frown drew his dark brows together. "You're not thinking of going out in this?"

Well, she had been until he said it like that.

"It's Christmas Eve," she reminded him. It was Christmas Eve. She had missed her bus yesterday, but she could catch one today and be home by this afternoon. Maybe.

She looked out the window over the sink at the snow blanketing everything in sight. Maybe not.

"I know it's Christmas Eve," he said. His tone indicated that he knew better than anyone what day it was. "But that snow is wet and not packed down, and there's no way you can get a buggy to the road, much less the bus station."

She was afraid of that. There was no way she could debate with him. She had no means of finding out road conditions. But she did so want to hop on a bus and go home.

"The roads are closed. I went out to check on the horses and called the direct hotline of weather and traffic updates."

"You have a phone in the barn." She practically breathed the words. How had that slipped her mind? She still wasn't used to the differences between home and Lancaster.

"Jah." He gave a curt nod. "I told you yesterday, we could go out this morning and call your family, let them know that you are safe."

"I want to do that," she said excitedly. "I need to do that. Call my family." With the storm that bad, even her family in New Wilmington had heard about it. But they needed to know that she was all right.

"I'll go out there and call for you." He took another drink of his coffee and set his mug upside down in the sink.

"No." Lily Kate's voice came out sharper than she wanted. "I mean, thank you, but no. I need to do this."

"I've already been once," he said. "And you don't have boots."

It was a fair point.

"Why can't she wear Mamm's boots?" Jacob picked that moment to chime into the conversation.

That was a bad idea on so many levels. She didn't want to give Jacob any ideas about the time she was having to spend there on the farm, but she couldn't traipse around in the snow without muck boots.

"They'll be too big for her," Simon said. He was watching her closely, his brown eyes searching her face. For what, she had no idea.

"Just do like you did mine last year and put paper in the toes," Jacob suggested.

Lily Kate couldn't read Simon's expression at all. It was as if his entire emotional system had shut down. She wanted to protest, to say it was okay. She didn't need boots. She wouldn't go outside in the snow, and Simon could go call for her. But that was not what she wanted. There was a chance, albeit a very small one, that someone would be close to the phone at the edge of their yard. If that was the case, she might get to hear her mother's voice today. Such wishful thinking, she knew, but she couldn't get it out of her thoughts.

"I suppose that will work," Simon said.

Lily Kate couldn't bring herself to protest. She would wear Catherine's boots with paper in the toes and go cross to the barn and call her family. It was as simple as that.

Jacob clapped his hands together in glee. "Jah. We'll be able to go out and play in the snow."

She almost protested. She almost told him that she didn't want to go play in the snow, but that wasn't the truth. All she wanted to do first was call her family. Then playing in the snow sounded like a great idea.

"I like the way you think," she told Jacob with a cheeky smile.

"Let's go." He started to get out of his seat.

"Not so fast," she told him. She laid one hand gently on his shoulder and urged him back into his chair. "You need to finish your breakfast before we can go outside and play."

He made a face, then leaned toward her conspiratorially. "Dat doesn't make good eggs."

"Well, your dat made you eggs, and that is something to be thankful for, jah?"

"Jah," he said, ducking his head over his plate.

Lily Kate leaned closer to him. "My dat's not good at making eggs either."

Simon took his coffee mug from the sink, rinsed it out, and poured himself another cup. How he was drinking the stuff, Lily Kate had no idea. "If you guys are going out, I don't see any reason why I should have to."

Jacob bounced up and down in his seat even as he chewed on what appeared to be very rubbery eggs. "Please, Dat. Please, Dat. Please." The last word had four or five syllables.

Simon just shook his head. "All right then," he grudgingly agreed. "But Lily Kate is right. Finish your breakfast first."

❧

Lily Kate picked up the receiver in the barn and dialed the number for the phone shanty closest to her parents' house. Just as she knew it would be—even though she was hoping against hope that it wouldn't—no one answered, and she got the recording they used. She waited for the beep before she began to speak. "This message is for the Troyers, Rebecca and Chris. This is Lily Kate. I'm still in Lancaster. The snow has it so I can't get out." No need to tell them where she was stuck in Lancaster. She wouldn't want to raise eyebrows over nothing. "But I just wanted to tell you Merry Christmas." Suddenly her eyes filled with prickling tears. She was not going to get to see her family this Christmas. She could feel it in her very bones. She needed to whip herself up into shape. Crying about it every five minutes wouldn't change the situation at all.

She blinked back those salty tears and started once more. "Merry Christmas and I love you very, very much. And I wanted to make sure you got the package I sent. The one that had the carvings." She didn't want to say more in case for some reason the packages had been delayed, but she hoped not. She really wanted her mother to have the beautiful doe and buck set from Reihl's Quilt Shop early so Mamm could set it up with her other holiday decorations.

As she stood there in the barn in the workroom, Lily Kate couldn't help noticing the blocks of wood and other carvings that were in various stages of being complete. They looked strangely like the set she had bought for her mamm. But how was that?

Lily Kate hung up the phone and couldn't keep herself from thinking about Simon and the buck and the doe. The room she stood in had to be a workshop. In fact, he had even called it "the workroom" when he told her where to go in the barn to call her family.

Did Simon make those beautiful carvings? A person could almost see the love and heart that was put into them. That was what drew her to them in the first place. Though Simon just didn't seem to be that sort of person, one who could express his feelings through art. Or maybe that was the only way he had to express emotions too big for anything else. He surely wasn't good at doing it in person. He was so stern and unsmiling. She supposed he might be a little angry at the lot *Gott* handed him, though she would never say those words out loud. But these carvings showed there was more to Simon Bontrager than she had originally thought. If he was truly the one who had carved them.

She waited a moment and called Allen and left a message. He would get his long before her parents did. Like Simon, her uncle had a phone in the barn. It was just something she wasn't used to yet.

After she left that message, there was no reason to stay and stare at the wood that would someday be beautiful replicas of deer and perhaps other majestic animals. Who knew what else he could carve with those clever fingers?

She left the workroom and headed for the door of the barn, still contemplative, thinking about Simon and the carvings. How he just didn't seem to be the kind of person to do something like that. Yet it appeared that he was. She stepped outside the barn, still musing on the subject and fully planning to ask Simon about it when—whack!

A snowball hit the barn door near her head. Snow cascaded down her neck and into the collar of her coat. She jumped as the coldness slithered down her warm skin.

Jacob doubled over laughing.

"Oh jah?" She chuckled, then bent down and scooped up a handful of snow to join in the play.

CHAPTER SIX

*S*imon couldn't stop himself. He couldn't keep from thinking about this woman who had crashed into his life, this feisty being who seemed sad one minute then decided not to be the next. When she had walked out of the barn, she looked near tears. One snowball later, and she was smiling, even laughing. How could a person get through emotions so quickly?

He hated to admit it, but he was stuck on "sad" and didn't seem to be able to get off it. He wanted to.

Did he want to? He didn't know. He claimed he did. Maybe he really did. He stopped, lost in his thoughts.

Suddenly he was pelted with snowballs. He lifted one arm to protect his face from the hurtling snow. "Stop! Stop!" he cried. "I give!"

Thankfully no more snow came his way, and he lowered his arm in time to see Lily Kate and Jacob whispering to each other.

"What are you talking about?" Simon demanded.

"Just trying to make sure that you're sincere in your surrender," Lily Kate said, continuing to pack a snowball as she talked.

Jacob stood right next to her, grinning. They truly were having way too much fun out there.

"I said I give, and I give." They had caught him thinking and not paying attention. See if he let that happen again.

"Jah?" Lily Kate arched one brow in his direction. Her cheeks were already pink from the cold, the winter adding beautiful color to her sweet face.

Wait...what? Okay, she had proven that she could be sweet. It just wasn't a thought he was yet comfortable with. And beautiful? Well, he supposed that fit too. Just as Jacob had told him a couple of weeks ago, she was nice and very pretty and sweet and nice.

"Let's make snow angels," Jacob cried, stirring Simon from his own thoughts.

Lily Kate caught Jacob's arm before he could fling himself down in the snow. "Wait," she said. "Don't you want to build a snowman first? If you get all wet now, we have to go in, and there won't be time to build a snowman."

"A snowman!" Jacob's voice was excited and yet a hushed whisper all at the same time. He fairly breathed the word as if he'd never heard it before.

"You know what to do first?" Lily Kate asked him.

Simon watched as his son nodded so vigorously he almost knocked himself down into the snow. "First, you get a snow-ball, and you make it bigger, bigger, bigger, and then again and then again."

Lily Kate laughed. And Simon decided he liked the sound even though those words sounded entirely too goofy.

But he did like her laugh. There hadn't been enough laughter around his house, not for a long time. Not since Catherine had died, for sure.

"Simon!"

He turned as Lily Kate called his name. He had a feeling she called him more than once as he had been contemplating the sound of her laughter. Goofy. "Jah?"

"We need stuff for the face. What do you suggest?"

"Let me think about it for a minute." He thoughtfully tapped his chin.

"The nose needs to be a carrot!" Jacob cried.

Lily Kate shook her head. "Remember we don't have any carrots."

Jacob's mood seemed to crumble. "I know."

There was no way Simon could let today's fun be ruined by his poor grocery practices.

"I got this," he said and headed toward the barn.

He could hear them outside, laughing and talking and playing in the snow as he poked around the barn looking for something to serve as a nose. The best he could do was an orange-handled screwdriver. At least it was orange. Surely Jacob would be happy with that. He also found two hockey pucks to use for eyes, and then he headed back outside.

"Dat!" Jacob cried. "Dat!"

He still wasn't sure how they built such a big snowman in such a short period of time. Lily Kate was a tiny thing, and he was sure she'd had to lift the top ball over her head to get it up onto the other two. As far as snowmen went, it was gigantic.

"How about this?" He held out the screwdriver and the hockey pucks.

"Perfect." Lily Kate plucked the things out of his hands and pressed them into the snowman's face. It was nearly a head taller than she was.

"What's that?" Jacob asked, pointing to the deer antlers Simon held.

He raised them where they could see. "I don't know. I was

just thinking about things we could use for the snowman."

"You want to put antlers on it? It's not a snow deer," Jacob said, an edge of laughter softening his voice.

Simon gave a small shrug. "It can be whatever we want it to be," he said.

"Like Bigfoot?"

Simon caught Lily Kate's gaze over Jacob's head. "Bigfoot?" he mouthed to her.

She shook her head and gave a shrug. He knew what she was thinking: She had only been his teacher for two weeks. The boy hadn't learned about Bigfoot from her.

"Can I do it?" Jacob asked.

"You gotta be careful. You don't want to break the head open," Lily Kate warned him.

He nodded. "Be careful. Got it."

Simon came over and handed Jacob the antlers, and then he lifted his son in order for the boy to press the sheds into the side of the snowman's large head.

They all stood back to admire their handiwork.

"You know what it needs?" Lily Kate asked, tapping one finger against her chin.

"A bulldozer?" Simon jokingly replied.

Lily Kate shook her head sadly at him. "It needs a scarf."

Simon really didn't know what possessed him. He tromped up onto the porch. He did his best to knock as much snow off his boots as possible, and then he opened the front door and peered inside.

Right next to the door was a coatrack, and on that coatrack was Catherine's scarf. The one that Jacob had taken to school yesterday. The one he had left. The one that Lily Kate had been delivering when she got snowed in with the two of them. The one that started it all.

Her eyes lit up when Lily Kate saw what he held, but she made no comment. He brought it over and wrapped it around the neck part of the snowman, and they all nodded in agreement. Yes. Now the snowman was perfect.

"Did you kill that deer?" Lily Kate asked.

Simon nodded. "Not this year but last," he told her.

"Do you have any venison left in the freezer?"

He nodded, still not sure where she was going with this. "Jah."

"Well, if you're interested, I make a mean venison stew."

Oh, he was interested all right.

"Venison stew? Whoo!" Jacob jumped up and down with excitement. Then he fell back in the snow to make his snow angels with a large grin spreading across his winter-reddened cheeks.

⁓

After the snow angels, they were all soaking wet. Simon grabbed Lily Kate's suitcase out of her buggy, and together they trudged into the house.

Now they were all dry and warm. Lily Kate was standing at Simon's stove putting together her venison stew. Simon looked on, sipping cocoa. Jacob was at the table working on some coloring pages and activity sheets that Lily Kate had pulled from somewhere—he was thinking out of her suitcase—but he was glad that his son had something new to do. Had it not been for the snow, they would be at his mamm's house, and there would be children and grandparents to play with. Jacob needed something to redirect his attention.

"It looks delicious already." Smelled that way too.

"You know it's better with carrots," she told him. "But it'll be all right this time without them, I suppose." It wasn't accusatory or anything, just a matter of fact. That seemed to be Lily Kate. She just rolled with the punches, as they say.

"But you came all the way to Lancaster from New Wilmington just to teach school for a couple of months?" It wasn't something he had planned on asking. But the question had its own ideas.

She continued to stir the stew even though it looked plenty mixed up to him. Though he realized his question had made her uncomfortable. He had just opened his mouth to apologize when she spoke. "I broke up with my boyfriend."

She continued to stir, and then she tapped the wooden spoon against the edge of the pan and laid it across for future use. "That's not entirely true. He broke up with me. I just needed to get away."

"I'm sorry," he said. And he was. He was sorry that he asked. He was sorry that had happened to her. He was sorry for anyone who had to suffer through a loss.

She gave a negligent shrug. "It is what it is, I suppose," she said. "No going back now, right?"

Simon studied her for just a moment and gave a quick nod. "Jah. I guess that's right." Without another word he turned and went to the pantry.

Simon grabbed a jar of canned carrots and brought it back over to her.

"That'll work," she said, her tone enthusiastic. But he couldn't help thinking about the carrots. From last year. It was all last year. The venison was from last year. Everything. It was all about last year, and that made him feel like he was living in the past. But that was impossible. A person can't live in the past.

It wasn't his fault that all these things happened a year before and yet nothing seemed to get done this year. He hadn't carved anything since Catherine died. He had stopped living when he was still alive. He played in the snow today, and he went to the Christmas pageant. He was getting better, but he knew that he wouldn't have gotten out in the snow if it weren't for Lily Kate. For her teasing. For her smile. He would've gone out for his son, but her smile made it easier and that was something he wasn't comfortable with.

The stew was bubbling merrily on the stove, and Lily Kate had switched from cocoa to coffee, making a pot that tasted much better than the one they had that morning. She and Simon had sat down at the table while Jacob had gone into the living room. She could just hear his soft snores as he lay on the couch. She was content. The snow had left a hush over everything. The day was bright even though the sun wasn't shining. Hopefully, tomorrow it would be gone. But even if the thaw started, it wouldn't melt off enough for her to get home in time for Christmas. That was what was keeping her from being completely happy.

She was trying her best to look on the bright side, and there must be one. Even if she was snowed in with a grumpy man she hardly knew and a student who would love nothing more than for her and his father to somehow fall in love. . .

But that wasn't happening. Yet there was no way she could tell Jacob that. She couldn't tell him that she was never falling in love again. He was seven. He would never understand that love was just nothing but heartache. If they didn't leave, they died, and what was the purpose in all that?

She pushed those negative thoughts away and concentrated on the mug in front of her.

"What's wrong?" Simon asked.

But she couldn't answer. She didn't have an answer. Instead, she turned to him. "What's the thing you'll miss most this Christmas?" She shook her head. "Beyond the obvious. You said normally you would go to your parents' house. What will you miss?"

"Mamm gets up on Christmas morning and makes cinnamon biscuits."

"That sounds delicious. Have you tried to make them?"

"I don't know if you realize it or not, but I'm not much of a cook."

Lily Kate chuckled. "Do you have a recipe?" Talking about food was so much better than talking about all the things she was missing at Christmas at home.

He shook his head. "What about you? What will you miss?"

"Sticking with food, my mom makes the best Jell-O mold." Simon made a face.

"No no no, it's good. So good, and it just doesn't seem like Christmas dinner without it." And that was the moment she realized that they wouldn't be having a Christmas dinner. Neither one of them. They would be snowed in together away from the houses where they went for that meal. If they didn't make it happen here, it wouldn't happen at all.

"What about tomorrow?" she asked.

It was as if he made the realization at the same time she did. "I don't have a turkey or anything. Not even a ham."

"How can we have Christmas without Christmas dinner?"

"I can't cook," he told her again.

That much was apparent after witnessing this morning's breakfast.

"I can."

But he was already shaking his head. "That's a lot of work for one person."

"It's just three of us." Perhaps a slightly more elaborate meal than a normal day since there weren't cousins and grandkids and a bunch of other folks to feed.

"I don't know, Lily Kate."

Well, she did. They had to have a Christmas dinner. Even if it was just the three of them. No, Christmas was not about the food that was eaten or the desserts and company. It was about Jesus, but it was also about being together and experiencing such a special day with loved ones. Or in this case, snow buddies. "Think of Jacob."

That did it. It was his son's first Christmas without his mother, and it needed to be as special as possible regardless of how much snow had fallen the day before.

"Come on," he said, rising from his chair and motioning for her to follow.

He led her down a dimly lit staircase into the basement, then over to the chest freezer that occupied one corner.

"What are you after?" she asked as he began to dig around inside.

"I'm not sure," he told her. "Whatever I can find, I guess. Maybe a whole tenderloin of venison..."

He rustled around a bit more, then brought out a whole chicken. "I have this. But—" He didn't seem sold on the idea.

"That's perfect," she said. "We can have chicken and filling and as many fixings as we can make."

He looked at her, those usually unreadable brown eyes expectant. "And you're really going to do all this?"

They might not have been able to be with the ones they love. And some of the others that they loved had left them behind. But that didn't mean they couldn't celebrate the birth of Jesus in a new way this year. It could still be just as wonderful, just as sweet, and just as meaningful.

CHAPTER SEVEN

*S*omehow in a miracle that might have rivaled Jesus feeding the multitude with five loaves and two fishes, Lily Kate managed to make spaghetti for supper. Simon didn't even know that he had the items to make spaghetti until she set it on the table. She had used old hamburger buns as garlic bread and, he supposed, some of the ground venison for meat. It was delicious, and such a treat to eat food that hadn't been heated over twice.

He mentally chastised himself. He was blessed to have food and grateful that his mother and sister tried so hard to make sure he and Jacob had everything they needed, but somehow having Lily Kate there made everything seem…right. Even when there was no Italian bread and she used hamburger buns for garlic toast. It was perfect. Somehow it was everything it was supposed to be.

But Simon didn't have time to figure it out. He wasn't sure he even wanted to. With any luck she would be gone from his house the day after tomorrow. Then when Mabel Esh came back to the classroom, Lily Kate would go back to New Wilmington.

"Can we open presents after the dishes are cleaned up?" Jacob asked. He was hopeful, Simon could tell, since his son was already on his way to the sink with his plate when he asked.

"It's not Christmas until tomorrow," Lily Kate said before she could stop herself. "Unless that's what you always do..." She turned to Simon.

"We used to open our family Christmas presents here on Christmas Eve," he explained. "Then in the morning we took the presents for the rest of the family over to my parents' house and had the rest of Christmas there."

But they weren't going to his *eldre's haus* in the morning. They were all snowed in.

"Doesn't that make it what we always do?" Again, Jacob's voice was full of hope and excitement. Not that Lily Kate could blame him.

Christmas was such an exciting time, and she would rather the child be excited over the holiday than grieving the fact that his mother was not there. She was certain Simon felt the same.

"If we open the presents today, we won't have any to open tomorrow," Simon said.

Jacob seemed to think about that for a moment. "Can we open one today?"

Simon nodded. "That sounds like a good compromise."

"Compromise," Jacob repeated.

Lily Kate grabbed the rest of the dishes and headed to the sink. "You two can go ahead," she started, hating the fact that her voice sounded a bit choked. But their banter made her miss Mary Kate and Stevie. She was certain they were having a wonderful Christmas. Without her. How she wished she were there.

"No, we are going to clean up the mess," Simon said. "You're our guest, and you cooked our supper twice now. Seems only fair."

"I'm hardly a guest," she said, but she allowed him to go in front of her. It was his house after all.

"I tell you what you can do," Simon said, a twinkle in his eyes. "You could make another pot of that tasty coffee."

Lily Kate nodded and started for the stove and the enamel pot waiting there.

In no time at all, the coffee was made and the dishes were washed and put away.

"I think I'm going up to bed," Lily Kate said. She could read her book up there while they had their family Christmas down here. She wasn't a part of it and felt like an intruder. She gave them a smile, but even to her it felt forced.

"No," Simon and Jacob spoke at the same time.

"You can stay down here. Right, Dat?" Jacob looked up at his father.

"Jah," Simon said.

She started to shake her head, but she was beginning to suspect that they wouldn't take *no* for an answer. She hated being the odd man out, the one who didn't belong. Yet what choice did she have? She sat down in the rocking chair opposite the fire, and Simon made himself comfortable on one end of the couch. Jacob excitedly ran over to the stack of presents in one corner.

"I get to pick which one?" Jacob asked. He threw an encouraging smile over his shoulder to his father.

"Only if it has your name on it," Simon said.

Lily Kate couldn't help but laugh.

"And I need to find one for you too, jah?" Jacob asked his father.

"I suppose," Simon returned.

Lily Kate wondered if there were any presents over there that he hadn't wrapped himself or even one that he didn't know what was inside. Maybe. Jacob might have made him something at school and brought it home to him. Something from Mabel's era of teaching. Lily Kate had been too wrapped up in trying to get the Christmas pageant done. Otherwise, she was certain Simon knew every present that the colorful paper and bags hid from view.

Finally, Jacob was done riffling through all the wrapped boxes and bags stuffed with brightly colored tissue paper. He had a huge smile on his face as he bypassed his dad and walked over to Lily Kate. He held the package out toward her.

"What's this?" she asked. She reached up and took the present from him, though she didn't understand why he was giving it to her. It was a strange shape and had enough tape on it to wrap around the barn, but somehow that made it all the more special. It was all Jacob.

"It's a present." Jacob grinned. "For you."

"For me?" Lily Kate asked. "How do I have a present here?"

Jacob shifted from side to side as only a seven-year-old boy could. "I forgot it on the last day of school. That's why I'm extra glad you're here now. That and you make really good spaghetti. But it's the present I wanted to give you."

Lily Kate still couldn't comprehend what she was hearing. "It's a present for me?" she repeated.

Jacob nodded again.

Lily Kate looked at Simon. He shrugged, and the smile on his face told her that he was as lost as she was.

"Open it." Jacob dipped his head again as if urging her along.

Lily Kate felt strangely sentimental as she started to tear open the wrapping paper. It was a little tough going with all the tape, but she managed to pull it free. Inside was a handmade basket, perhaps the kind that she could fill with spare change or even wrapped candies. It was slightly lopsided but impressive all the same.

"Did you make this?" she asked. Her voice was thick with

unshed tears. For some reason this seemed to be the most special thing she ever received. Because she knew this seven-year-old boy had made it just for her.

"Jah. At Dawdi's."

Lily Kate remembered when she was at Jake and Irene Bontrager's that Jake made baskets in the workshop in his barn.

"Turn it over," Jacob commanded. He actually took the basket from her hands and showed her the bottom of it.

Written there was *Jacob Bontrager* and the date. *Made for Lily Kate Troyer.* Lily Kate didn't know what to say.

"Dawdi said I had to sign the bottom of it. That's what he does to his baskets. That way a person knows who made it and where it came from and when they made it."

Lily Kate nodded, but she couldn't say a word. It was just too special.

"Thank you, Jacob," she finally managed.

He moved in close and gave her a big hug. He squeezed her tight and whispered in her ear, "I'm glad you're my teacher, and I'm glad you're here for Christmas."

Lily couldn't hold her tears at bay any longer. She brushed them aside as Jacob pulled away and skipped back over to the stack of presents.

"I'm sorry, Jacob," she said. "But I don't have a present for you." Her heart was breaking because of it. He'd given her such a special gift. He had made it just for her, signed it and everything.

Jacob turned around and cast a smile over his shoulder. "You made dinner." As if that was the greatest accomplishment of the day.

"Here, Dat," Jacob said, handing a package to his father.

Simon took it, then nodded toward another package off to one side of the stack. "Give that one to Lily Kate too."

Lily Kate was already shaking her head. "No, it's too much."
But Simon wouldn't hear of it. "It's just enough," he said.

Lily Kate didn't know what to make of it all. She accepted the package and waited for Simon to open his.

As suspected, it was a handmade gift from Jacob to his father. A picture frame with all sorts of natural items glued to it. Sticks and rocks and the like. Actually, it was kind of neat, Lily Kate thought. And she realized that Mabel Esh must have a creative bone. (One could only hope she didn't fall and break it in the shower with her arm and her leg.) Inside the frame was a picture of a snow-covered barn complete with a wreath decorated with a red bow to celebrate the Christmas season.

"Danki, Jacob," Simon said, giving a sigh. "Which one are you opening?"

Jacob proudly held up the wrapped box. To Lily Kate it looked like a shoebox.

"Going straight for it, jah?" Simon chuckled.

Jacob sat on the floor and tore the paper off the box with a child's enthusiasm for Christmas.

She was right. It was a shoebox, but more than that. Jacob opened it with an expectant grin, and there were cleats inside.

"You got them!" Jacob's eyes were wide.

Lily Kate realized Jacob had been hoping that there were cleats in the box, but now that he was actually holding them in his hands, he was more excited than ever.

"You don't get to start practice until spring," Simon said. "Sometime in March. And they need to stay in your room, in your closet until that time. You understand?"

Jacob nodded. "I understand, Dat." He jumped to his feet and threw himself at his dat, hugging him around the neck so tight that Simon coughed. "They're just what I wanted," he said. "Exactly what I wanted."

"I've been listening to you," Simon said.

"Danki, Dat. Danki. Danki. Danki!"

"You're welcome," Simon returned, and then they both turned and looked at Lily Kate.

"What?" she asked. She was too caught up in the emotions. So much love and so much gratitude in such a small space. The two of them had been through a lot together, more than she even knew, and they were going to be okay. She could see that. Even if Simon couldn't cook.

"Open your gift," Jacob said. He slid down from his father's lap and walked over next to her. "Do you need some help?"

"Would you mind?" Lily Kate asked.

Jacob shook his head.

She handed the package to him.

He tore it open to reveal a beautiful scarf, hat, and mittens set in a dark, dark green.

"Oh," Lily Kate gushed. "It's beautiful. But does this belong to someone?"

Simon shook his head. "We always do this Santa gift exchange thing at Mamm and Dat's. All the presents get a number, then everybody draws a number, and you get the present with the corresponding number, you know. Well, that was my gift for tomorrow, and since we're not going, it seems like it would be appropriate to give it to you."

Overcome, that was all there was to it. Lily Kate was overcome. "It's gorgeous. Thank you."

Simon nodded, then swallowed hard. "It was one of the last ones that Catherine made."

She shook her head. "Oh no, I can't take it then."

He nodded. "Yes, you can. I think she would want you to have it."

⁂

Lily Kate was still smiling when she made her way up the staircase to the spare bedroom. It was perhaps the smallest Christmas she'd ever been party to, but it seemed so special all the same.

She was thankful to Simon for getting her suitcase out of her buggy, and tonight she could actually sleep in a nightgown instead of her dress minus a few pins. In fact, it was good to have all her things: her brush and kerchief to cover her hair.

She got ready for bed, still smiling, and drifted off to sleep not long after. But sometime later, she woke with a start, realizing someone was standing over her.

It was Simon.

"Simon?" she started.

He shook his head and held one finger over his lips. Then he beckoned for her to follow. They eased out of her room and down to the end of the hall next to Jacob's room.

Simon pointed out the large window, which looked out over the backyard. The same spot where they had built the snowman this morning. Two deer were walking through, no doubt searching for food with all the snow on the ground.

They weren't that far from the heart of town, and Lily Kate supposed that the lovely beasts were all over.

As they silently watched, the pair of deer moved toward the snowman, sniffing at it as if they knew it was supposed to have a carrot for a nose. They seemed almost disappointed to find a screwdriver there instead.

"I wonder what they think about it having antlers," Simon

said, his voice close to her ear.

Lily Kate resisted the urge to shiver as his breath stirred the tiny tendrils of hair around her ear.

"They're probably thinking that's the ugliest deer they've ever seen."

The deer must've heard her, for they stopped and then bounded away out of sight.

"That was beautiful," she said. "Danki for showing me." And she realized he was not at all the man she thought he was. He woke her up at. . . Well, she had no idea what time it was.

"What time is it?"

"Almost five," Simon answered. "You can go back to bed if you like. Sorry for waking you. I just thought you might like to see them."

Lily Kate nodded. "I'm glad you woke me. I'm glad I got to see them. They're magnificent."

Simon just nodded.

"Have you been up long?" Lily Kate asked.

"A little bit." He shrugged.

"Have you already made coffee?"

He shook his head. "I think my coffee-making days are over."

She frowned. "What are you talking about?"

"After having your coffee, I can't stomach mine at all."

Lily Kate laughed and headed for the stairs. "Come on down here, and I'll show you how to make it."

～❦～

There was a part of Simon that wanted to tell her that he had no interest at all in learning how to make coffee, that he'd rather she come by every morning and make it for him. Or even—he slammed the door on that thought. There was not a second chance at love for him, and he surely couldn't see marrying someone because they made the best coffee he had ever tasted. His choices were to learn how to make coffee or keep drinking it as it was.

As she made the coffee, rattling off all the instructions, he was trying to pay attention, but all he could concentrate on was the coconut smell of her hair. Was it coconut shampoo that she used? He had no idea. But it made him think of the summer-like days when his family went to Pinecraft after Christmas one year. It was perfect there, warm low eighties with sunshine and beaches and shuffleboard. He had been sixteen at the time, all out in his *rumspringa*. Not that he got to get into too much trouble. His parents had a tight rein on his movements, and he had to stay close. It had been a really good two weeks, and the smell of that shampoo brought it all back.

"Simon?"

He turned to face her, and he had a feeling that she had called his name once before that. "Jah?"

"Are you all right?"

He nodded, unable to get out another syllable. His throat was tight, his brain confused.

She gave him a concerned look, then turned back to finish making the coffee. He would never remember all of what she said. Not because it was so involved but because he couldn't help but just think about her the entire time. He hated that she wasn't able to be with her family for Christmas, but for some strange reason, he was glad that she was there with him and Jacob.

It was about that time when Jacob came tripping down the stairs, grinning and excited that it was Christmas Day. "When can we open the rest of the presents?"

"After breakfast," Simon said. "Just like at Dawdi's house."

Jacob looked slightly disappointed, as if he had held a hope that his father would forgo tradition this one time, and Simon merely shook his head.

"What's for breakfast then?" Jacob looked from him to Lily Kate. He obviously expected his teacher to cook. True, Simon would have preferred her food over his and not just because he wouldn't have to expend the energy to make it. She was an excellent cook. "I don't know," Simon said. "I'm gonna have to get in the kitchen and see what I can find."

Lily Kate shook her head. "Let me," she said. And Simon was grateful for the offer, though he had a feeling she did it more for self-preservation than anything else. Surely, she would rather eat her own cooking than his. "You just stay in here and play a game or something. I'll have breakfast whipped up in a jiffy."

Simon smiled his thanks to her as Jacob set up the checkerboard in front of the fire. Lily Kate disappeared, and Simon watched her go. He wasn't sure what was wrong with him this morning. Maybe it was Christmas or being shut in with all this snow. He almost felt like he was living in another world. Maybe there was nothing wrong with him at all. Maybe it was just a feeling of contentment, and it had been so long since he felt that way, he had forgotten what it was like. Still, with all the snow outside it did feel otherworldly. A different world from the one where his wife died and his son was motherless. One not so filled with grief and sadness.

After their second game of checkers, a wonderful smell began to emanate from the kitchen.

"That smells good," Jacob said, a grin on his face.

Simon nodded. "It sure does."

"I'm glad Lily Kate is here," Jacob said.

"Me too." And Simon was just slightly surprised, just a little bit shocked, at how much he meant it.

CHAPTER EIGHT

*Y*ou did all this?"

Lily Kate was not sure how to take Simon's words. She nodded and bit her lip, trying to come up with a reason why she'd overstepped in his wife's kitchen. Why she'd invaded it for her own purposes. Well, she had made breakfast for all of them, her version of the cinnamon biscuits that he had talked about the day before. Then, while she was making the icing to go on the biscuits, it occurred to her that it could hardly be Christmas without Christmas cookies. So, she scrounged around and found all the ingredients. Poked around until she found cookie cutters, and then she proceeded to start making cookies.

"Do you mind?" she asked. "I didn't mean to overstep, but one thing led to another and. . . Christmas just isn't the same without Christmas cookies."

She watched the myriad of emotions cross his face. And for a moment she thought he would be upset that she had helped herself to his wife's things. She supposed that they were technically his things now, but that wasn't the point she wanted to bring up.

Thankfully, he nodded. "I suppose it's not."

"I didn't have anything to give you. So, I thought I would bake you something."

"You didn't need to give us anything," Simon told her.

She couldn't read his closed expression. Perhaps she shouldn't have. She shouldn't have tried to make cookies and make the holiday into something that it would never be for the three of them: a family get-together. His words were telling her that it was okay. His eyes were saying something different.

"You're supposed to say danki," Jacob corrected his father.

"Danki," Simon and Lily Kate said the words together.

He laughed, and Lily Kate thought perhaps that was the first time she had ever heard him make that sound. Maybe it was going to be all right after all.

Lily Kate rushed to take the last batch of cookies out of the oven and turned to face the two of them. "I'll set the table if someone gets drinks. Do we have milk?"

"Maybe," Simon said, making his way to the refrigerator. He pulled out a bottle of milk and smelled it. "I think it's still gut."

Lily Kate set the pan of cinnamon biscuits in the middle of the table then added the side of bacon and bowl of applesauce to the fare. Simon poured everyone a big glass of milk, and they sat down to say their prayer.

"I wasn't sure how your mother made them, so I just took my own biscuit recipe and added the cinnamon and sugar. Then I rolled them up, and now we add icing."

Simon nodded. "I do believe that's how she makes them."

Lily Kate pressed her napkin into her lap. "Well, hopefully these will be half as good as hers." It was the most she could ask for. But they were very tasty, and Lily Kate enjoyed such a special treat for breakfast. Normally she wouldn't eat anything that had that much sugar in it, especially not when cookies were waiting to be frosted as well. But they must've been pretty good, these sweet biscuits, because only one was left when they got up from the table, and Jacob called dibs on it as an afternoon snack.

Lily Kate shook her head and laughed at the boy. Then she tousled his hair. "Are you ready to decorate cookies now?"

Jacob jumped up and down. "Yes! Yes!"

"Tell you what," Lily Kate said. "Why don't the two of you go finish opening your gifts, and I'll get the icing ready. Then once you've got your gifts all taken care of and the mess cleaned up, you can come back in here and we'll put the colorful icing on the cookies. Deal?"

Jacob jumped up and down once more, crying, "Yes! Yes! Yes!"

Lily Kate enjoyed puttering around in the kitchen. Or maybe it was puttering around in the kitchen and listening to the two of them out in the family room. They were opening gifts and talking about different things. Things Catherine would have liked, things that Irene would've liked, and things that another woman might like. Lily Kate had never heard her name before, and she supposed from the conversation that Tamsyn was Simon's sister.

But in no time at all, Jacob was running back into the kitchen to help her decorate cookies. If she had been at home, she would have probably been doing the same thing with Mary Kate and Stevie. It made her a little sad to think that they were having their Christmas celebration and she wasn't there to see them. Still, there was something very satisfying about being there with Jacob and Simon.

"Now that the cookies are all decorated," Jacob started on a rush of sugar, "let's go outside and play in the snow again."

As fun as that sounded, Lily Kate only had one change of

clothes with her. She hadn't taken all her clothes when she went from New Wilmington to Lancaster. She hadn't taken all of them with her when she went back for Christmas. One dress had barely gotten dry. She really didn't want to soak another so soon.

When she said as much, Jacob shook his head. "It's okay," he said matter-of-factly. "You can wear one of my mamm's dresses."

The quickly spoken words had been released without thought behind them. Jacob was seven, after all, and buzzing around after eating way too much sugar in one morning. But the words made Lily Kate feel conspicuous. She didn't want to wear his mother's dress. She wasn't there to take his mother's place. She didn't like the thought that he might feel that's exactly what she was doing. Though he didn't sound the least bit upset about it. And that made her wonder even more.

"Well?" Jacob asked.

"No," she said. She grabbed her coat off the rack by the door and shoved her arms into the sleeves. Just a few moments later, she was dressed for outside. "Let's go play."

The first thing they did out in the snow was touch up the snow-man. Simon and Lily Kate shared a moment when Jacob found a spot where the deer had left it in the night. Simon's eyes met hers, and he couldn't help but smile as Jacob headed around and pressed new snow into the spots. Something had shifted inside when they were decorating the cookies. Simon wasn't sure what had happened. Things between them seemed to be changing fast. This was the woman he had been fussing about a mere two days ago. One minute, one feeling was coursing through his veins like white-hot lava, and the next, a different emotion would overtake him. It was confusing and. . .confusing.

"Look," Jacob said, pointing to the icicles hanging off the edge of the barn. They were dripping, a slow steady plop. Simon hadn't realized it until that moment, but Lily Kate was standing in the fringes, and he wondered if something was wrong. Well, something more than it was Christmas, and she was spending it with two males who were practically strangers to her.

"It's melting," Simon said. Wouldn't be long now. Maybe even tomorrow the roads might be clear enough to travel. It was Pennsylvania, after all. But he hadn't been thinking about her leaving. Not since that first day. Just the fact that they were snowed in together was what had consumed his thoughts. But tomorrow it looked like she would be leaving. He would be back to drinking his own coffee and heating his own food, the food that his family would provide. School would continue and maybe he would get to see her a couple of times before Mabel Esh took her classroom back. Maybe then he would get back to carving. Maybe. Or maybe he would just miss her smile and wonder what she was doing. Wonder what she was doing back in New Wilmington.

"What's the matter?" he asked her. She hadn't seemed like herself the entire time they'd been outside playing. She had lain down and made snow angels with the two of them, and now they were back in the house dripping wet.

Lily Kate just smiled, and the motion was forced. He could tell. It was nowhere near a real smile. He knew because he had seen one of those in the time that she had been snowed in with him and Jacob. "I'm fine." She looked at her dress, which was thoroughly soaked. "I'm gonna go change."

He nodded. What else could he do?

Lily Kate started for the stairs, Jacob right behind her. It was dripping outside, all starting to melt. Which was exactly what she wanted. So why wasn't she happier about it?

It was strange, but she felt pulled toward Simon. And that was even stranger, because not two days ago she would've crossed the street rather than walk next to him. Now here she was lamenting that tomorrow the roads would probably be clear enough that she would be able to go home.

Well, not *home* home. That chance was gone. She wouldn't be able to go back for Christmas and be back in time for school to start on Tuesday. But she would go back to her cousins' house. To sleep in a borrowed room. Like the borrowed room she was heading into now. She would hitch up her borrowed horse to her borrowed buggy and head back to her borrowed home. Everything she had was borrowed, even the bed she slept in last night. Even the family she was caring for today. None of it was hers, and it would never be. She pushed the thought away, lest it bring tears to her eyes. She shouldn't care. It shouldn't be that important. It had only been two days.

"Be sure to hang your clothes up to dry," Lily Kate reminded Jacob before he went into his room.

"Jah, Mamm." His words almost stopped her in her tracks.

He didn't even realize he said it. Or if he did, he didn't bother to stop and correct himself. He just went into his room and quietly closed the door.

Lily Kate ducked into the spare room and shut the door behind her. She leaned against it wondering when exactly everything had gone sideways.

She couldn't pinpoint it, but it didn't matter. She pushed off the door and changed out of her wet dress and into the dry one. The one that had just dried from the play in the snow yesterday. She quickly brushed her hair and pinned her prayer kapp back in place. Then she made her way downstairs.

A strange noise met her ears, and it took only a moment to realize it was Simon outside shoveling the driveway. He couldn't wait for her to be gone.

Not that she could blame him. She hadn't exactly been nice to him in those first days, though they had managed to be cordial, maybe even a little more than cordial, since they had been snowed in together. But she had a terrible feeling that it was somehow some sort of magic caused by the snow. Even though she knew magic wasn't real, she also knew that the snow made everything dreamy and otherworldly. Nothing seemed quite as real as it did right then with him shoveling snow out of the way.

As she listened to him scrape and clear the drive, she decided to make the best of it all. She would make their Christmas dinner, and it would be a wonderful dinner. So wonderful, one day they could both look back on it and smile.

⌒

"Just take it slow. Stop if traffic is coming behind you. Don't pull off the road. You might not be able to get back on."

She nodded and shot him a cool look. "Thank you for your hospitality."

Who was this woman? Something had definitely changed in her demeanor. Last night they had had their Christmas dinner, and it had been marvelous. Never before had chicken and filling tasted so good. Somehow Lily Kate had managed to pull out a sweet potato casserole to go with it as well as green beans and corn on the cob she had found in the freezer. Then she added fluffy, yeasty rolls that he knew she'd made from scratch.

And there was the Jell-O mold.

First of all, it was green. Though she said it was usually red, but all she could find was lime Jell-O. She said she couldn't find any walnuts, like her mamm usually used, so Lily Kate had substituted pecans. Other than that, it was. . .strange. Pieces of celery and bits of mandarin oranges. It had good flavor, he supposed, but he had never been one for foods that were molded and refrigerated before they were consumed. It just didn't seem natural to him, but he had eaten a chunk of it to make her happy. She had smiled at his effort, and that had been worth it. But today. . .

"The driveway's clear, but the road may not be as much. You might run into some ice at the end, so be careful pulling out."

She nodded and waited for him to continue. He supposed he had been barking instructions at her like an overprotective father.

After he had shoveled the driveway, he had thrown a little bit of sand down and then headed back into the house. He found her holding her dress close to the fire as if she wanted to set it ablaze instead of merely drying it.

"Will you call?" he asked. "When you get to your cousins' house. Please call so I know you got there safely."

"I will." Her blue eyes were guarded, sweet and cool. Not available at all. *Not too close*, they seemed to warn. They had not been like that before. But he knew that if he asked her, she'd tell him that nothing was wrong. He had already questioned her several times this morning, but it was as if she had woken up a different person. She told him it was all in his mind. That he had somehow twisted everything around until it no longer made sense. So he just hadn't asked any more.

"Okay," he said. Just like that, there was nothing more to keep her with him. He patted the horse on the neck and backed away.

"Bye, Lily Kate," Jacob called, waving to her. "I'll miss you."

She shot Jacob a smile, and Simon saw at once that it was a genuine curve of her lips. It was just him that she was blocking. He didn't understand it at all, but did he even have a right to ask?

"I'll miss you too," she said to Jacob as she flicked the reins over the horse's back and started down the road. She followed Simon's instructions carefully—he could tell as she pulled the buggy out onto the main street. A few seconds later she disappeared from view.

⁓

"What's wrong with you?" Ada asked Lily Kate the next day. "You've been moping around ever since you got home."

"Nothing," Lily Kate said, and then she immediately regretted the lie. How could she admit the truth?

"You act like someone took away your favorite puppy," Ada said. Her hands were propped on her hips as she eyed Lily Kate suspiciously. "What happened at Simon Bontrager's house? And don't tell me 'nothing' because I know that's not the truth."

Lily Kate frowned. She might not normally live close to Ada, but they seemed to be on a similar wavelength. Somehow it was as if Ada knew her thoughts before Lily Kate did herself. "I guess I'm missing Joseph."

"Pfbtt... Whatever." Ada shook her head. "You're not missing Joseph. You're missing what he represented to you."

Lily Kate opened the tin of cookies that Simon had sent along with her. Jacob had brought them out to her as she waited in the buggy, ready to go home and yet not ready to leave at all. "Cookie?" She held the tin out to Ada.

"Stop trying to change the subject," Ada groused. "Did you hear what I said?"

Lily Kate nodded, somewhat defeated. She couldn't get around Ada, no matter how hard she tried. Instead, she took out one of the cookies and nibbled on it as she replaced the lid on the tin.

"You know what I think?"

She was afraid to even guess.

"I think you're in love."

Lily Kate scoffed. "That's ridiculous," she protested. "A person doesn't fall in love in three days."

As Lily Kate said the words, Ada took a cookie out of the container and replaced the lid. "Maybe. But I believe a person can fall in love in an instant, given it's the right person. And if it's what God has planned for you."

"You really think that?"

Love at first sight?

But it hadn't been at first sight. At her first look at Simon, she had. . .well, she had been a little too wrapped up in her own problems to look at him that closely. Then when she had stopped and given herself a moment to take him in and, yeah, well. . .

No, she couldn't admit it. Not even to herself. It just was too far-fetched. A person didn't fall in love in an instant or even a day and not even three days. She wasn't in love with Simon Bontrager. She was just displaced. And that was all there was to it. Because even if it was God's will and He had a hand in it all, how were mere humans supposed to know if that was the right person for them?

Teach me Your way, O Lord. . .

⁐

"I can't believe she's coming back early," Ada grumbled.

Lily Kate was packing up her schoolroom, just the things that she had brought with her. It wasn't a whole lot, but she was having a hard time gathering her things and leaving. Displaced. That was all there was to it.

When she'd first come to Lancaster, she had held onto the small hope that she might be able to start a new life there. She might get to teach school for a couple of years—given that Mabel Esh was in her sixties and could possibly decide to retire instead of continuing on.

Then she would meet that special someone, and it all depended on eight weeks in Lancaster. But she wasn't going to even get a chance to see if anything could come of it, because her eight weeks had ended after three.

Apparently, Mabel Esh was a force to be reckoned with. She had managed to talk the doctor into okaying her return to work. Honestly, Lily Kate didn't think there was any such authorization in place, but Mabel wanted to come back, so they were letting her come back.

"Do you really think she wants to come back early?" Lily Kate asked.

Ada nodded. "It sounds just like something she would want to do. She's very possessive of her job. And I'm guessing that got back to her that the kids liked you better. She can't have that."

"Who said the kids liked me better?"

Ada shrugged and started putting the picture books Lily Kate had brought with her into one of the storage boxes. "You've met Mabel one time, so trust me on this. They like you better."

Lily Kate was just sad. There was so much that she still wanted to do with the class. She wanted to celebrate Valentine's Day and have red and pink hearts all over the classroom, but none of that was going to happen now. She would never see Jacob again.

Or Simon.

At the end of the school day on Tuesday, just after the return from Christmas break, a member of the board had come to her. He'd explained that it was better if she immediately turned the classroom back over to Mabel.

At first, Lily Kate had been worried that someone in her family had gotten hurt, but that wasn't the case.

When she had started this job, she knew the board had been worried about her size. And the kids had tested her, no doubt. But she had done her best, and a bang-up job it was. Not that it did any good now. She was going home.

CHAPTER NINE

$\mathcal{T}$here was no sense moping around. Well, Lily Kate kept telling herself that for the rest of the day.

"Are you okay, *liebschdi*?" Jodie King had asked her when Ada and Lily Kate had arrived back at the house.

Jodie was Allen's second wife, his new beginning. There was an interesting family dynamic involved. Allen had been married to Helen. They had four children: Jamie, Ada and her twin Amelia, and Silas. Ten years or so after Helen passed, Allen married the much younger Jodie Lapp, and together they had additional children. Susie was fifteen, Jonathan twelve, Anna ten, and Barbara eight. It was a joyous household, to be sure.

"I'm fine," Lily Kate said. But it wasn't exactly the truth. She *would* be fine.

Ada caught her eye, her own expression sad. "Maybe you can stay longer," she said, slipping into one of the chairs around the dining room table.

Lily Kate sat in the chair opposite her cousin and propped her elbow on the tabletop, her chin in her hand. "I don't know how I can do that without a job." Truth be known, she did miss her brother and her sister and her niece and her nephew. Not to mention her mamm and dat. But still she was wistful, almost sad that her time in Lancaster was over.

"Why don't you get a job in town?"

Lily Kate gave a small shrug. She supposed she could work in town, but she didn't have her own means of getting places. At least when she was working at the school, they knew there was a beginning and an end to her tenure there. Even though it ended much sooner than expected.

"Sure." Ada perked up at the idea. "You can get a job at the pretzel shop. You love the pretzels so much."

Lily Kate shook her head. There was no way she could get a job at the pretzel shop. Jah, she loved them very much and would probably stuff herself with pretzels every day. But she also knew that Simon loved their pretzels too. Eventually he would come in there, and then what would she do?

"Or the quilt shop," Ada continued.

Lily Kate didn't even bother to shake her head. Instead, she sighed. She couldn't get a job at the quilt shop. One day soon Simon would come to terms with his grief, and he would start making those wonderful carvings once more. Then he would come in to sell them, and she would be wishing again for things that were not hers. Things she could never have.

Ada continued to rattle off places where Lily Kate could go to work, but she knew that none of them were right. She couldn't go to work at the Bird-in-Hand Bakery or even Kitchen Kettle Village. Because there was more to it than just finding a job. Lily Kate didn't have a place in Lancaster. It was time for her to go home.

Simon eased down in the chair in his workshop, his mind still focusing on Lily Kate, even though she was no longer there. She had unknowingly encouraged him to carve again.

He hadn't carved anything since Catherine died. Her death just took it all out of him. But Lily Kate... She had bought those last carvings that he had made. It was bizarre to think about. But there it was.

"Dat?"

Simon whirled around at the sound of Jacob's voice.

"Someone is here to see you."

"Okay," he said. "I'll be right there."

He waited for Jacob to let himself out of the barn, before he rose from his seat. If he hadn't been so lost in his own thoughts, he would've heard his son come in. He would've heard the buggy drive up. But he had been thinking about more than carving. He had been thinking about Lily Kate.

He gave one last promising look to the blocks of wood that would one day soon be a carving of a deer or maybe even a bison—he'd always wanted to try to carve a bison—then took himself outside.

Ada King was perhaps the last person that Simon had expected to see. And it appeared as if this was the last place that she expected to be. She shifted from one foot to the other as he drew near.

"Simon," she started on a huge breath, "I was wondering if maybe we could talk for a moment."

He immediately frowned. "Lily Kate? Is she okay?"

Ada gave a nervous chuckle. "Jah. Of course. She's fine. But can we go inside? It's a little cold out here."

"Jah," he said and motioned for her to go into the house.

Together they walked into the living room. Jacob was there flipping through the pages of a book. A book that Simon didn't recognize. So it must've come from Lily Kate. Then once again she was in his thoughts.

Ada perched on the edge of the sofa, while Simon took up the place closest to the fire.

"Would you like some coffee?" he asked. "I'm not very good at making it, but it's warm." And he still had those cookies that Lily Kate had made at Christmas. Though Jacob had to have one after every meal, and so they were starting to dwindle. Who knew how long it would be again before he had Christmas cookies? Certainly at least until next Christmas, if even then.

Ada shook her head. "No, I just needed to come in and say what I came to say."

She seemed nervous, and that in turn made Simon shift uncomfortably in his seat. Once again, he wondered if Lily Kate was okay. If Ada King hadn't wanted to tell him while they were standing outside.

"I'm sorry for meddling," Ada began.

Simon held up one hand. "Jacob, why don't you go to your room and play?"

The boy looked up innocently from the book he held in his lap. "Do I have to?"

"Jah," Simon said. It was as if his son knew that the conversation they were about to have was about Lily Kate. In the last couple of days, Jacob had made it increasingly clear how he felt about Lily Kate. It was obvious he loved her. He was nearly beside himself that Lily Kate was no longer going to teach at his school. She had told him that once she was done teaching, she was going back to New Wilmington. Jacob was even less happy about that.

Simon was still trying to figure out how he himself felt about it all. "Go on," he urged as Jacob continued to sit there stalling.

With a barely suppressed sigh, Jacob pushed up from the chair and trudged over to the stairs.

Simon waited until his footsteps stopped before nudging again. "All the way into your room," he added.

This time Jacob didn't bother to hide his aggravation. He huffed, and then the door shut, and all was quiet once more. Jah, he might've closed the bedroom door, but Simon had a feeling the boy was hovering at the top of the staircase. Still, he didn't call him out for it.

"So," Ada started again, "I don't know what happened between you and Lily Kate, though I'm pretty sure something did."

Simon started to interrupt and tell her that nothing untoward happened. Nothing but Christmas dinner and snowman building and Christmas cookies and. . . "I also know that the two of you didn't spend much time together," she continued. "I mean, you spent days together, but you haven't spent *a lot* of days together."

Simon could agree with that. So somehow in it all, he had grown very close to Lily Kate. Perhaps because it was the Christmas season. Perhaps because they spent twenty-four hours a day together for three days. Or perhaps it was—

"And because of that, I believe the time you spent together had to be special," Ada said.

He was having trouble gathering the right words, though Ada suffered no such affliction. He had a feeling that most of what she was rattling off she had practiced in the buggy on the way over.

"It's almost like a miracle."

A Christmas miracle.

"And miracles should never be taken for granted," Ada continued.

Simon could just stare at her.

"Lily Kate came here because her heart was broken, did you know that?"

"I did," he replied. His voice sounded rusty and rattling, choked with emotions he dared not name.

He had seen the heartache in her eyes, though she had tried to hide it, smoothing it over with a light tone and a forced smile.

"Jah," Ada sadly continued. "She was engaged to be married. In fact, she was supposed to get married in January."

"January coming up?" Simon asked.

"Jah. But her boyfriend. . .fiancé, Joseph, fell in love with Lily Kate's best friend. That's why she was so willing to come here at the drop of a hat. She wanted to get away for a while. I can hardly blame her."

Nor could he.

He had known that she'd had a failed relationship. But she hadn't disclosed the details. Only that she needed time away from it all. No wonder.

"But since Mabel's coming back to teach. . . I'm assuming with crutches so I'm not sure how that will work with her broken arm, but anyway, Mabel's returning and Lily Kate's going back to New Wilmington."

Simon knew all this, but it still made his heart pang as he heard the words.

"I suppose she'll come back, some time or another. To visit. Someday. And maybe if she does come back. . .some time or another. . .someday. . .to visit, then the two of you might be able to see if maybe there was something special between you. Someday. Truly, I suppose, you've got all the time in the world," Ada said.

But did he really? He had learned with Catherine that

nothing was a given. Jah, he had been taught that his entire life, but being *told* and *experiencing* were two very different things. Catherine's death surely made him realize that life was shorter than any of them knew.

"But why would you wait if you could be with her forever starting today?" Ada asked. Her voice was quiet, near fleeting. "Why would you let a miracle pass you by?"

Lily Kate stared out the window of the King house, waiting for the driver to come pick her up. Today she was going back to New Wilmington. Her bags were packed, and now she was just sitting there. . .waiting. And waiting.

Ada was sitting next to her, twisting her fingers in her lap.

Another storm was coming in that night, and Lily Kate knew that if she didn't get on the road, she might not get home until that storm was cleared off. She could be stuck here for a couple more days. Maybe even a week. And that was the last thing she wanted. It was time to go home.

"What's wrong with that?" Ada asked. "What's wrong with staying a couple more weeks?"

Lily Kate had tried to explain it to Ada several times over the past couple of days, but her cousin just didn't understand. Ada was stronger than Lily Kate. She knew where she fit in. And Lily Kate. . .well, there was a time when she had thought she knew where she belonged. Then Joseph had blown that all to pieces. Now she was just trying to find her way, and it seemed as if it wasn't destined to be in Lancaster.

"Nothing's wrong with that," Lily Kate said with a sad smile. "It's just I've been living someone else's life. Sleeping in a bed that's not mine, working a job that really belongs to somebody else." Pretending to be wife and mamm to a broken family that wasn't ready to move on. But she couldn't tell her cousin that. No, that knowledge was just for herself.

Lily Kate heard a rattle from outside.

Before she could even look out the window and see who was coming up the drive—because it had to be someone Amish and not the Englisch driver in his car; the sound of a horse and buggy was unmistakable—Ada started clapping her hands.

Simon. Simon was driving toward the house.

"Oh, Ada. What have you done?" Lily Kate asked in a terrified whisper. But a part of her tightened with a bit of excitement.

"I just pushed along a miracle." Ada gave her a self-satisfied smile.

"A miracle?" Lily Kate asked.

But Ada ignored the question as she rose and made her way over to the door. To her credit, Ada waited until Simon actually got out of his buggy and knocked on the door before opening it. And still, somehow, she managed to sound surprised as she greeted him. "Simon," she gushed, "so good to see you today. What brings you by?"

Simon stepped into the house and pulled his hat from his head.

Lily Kate stood and wiped her hands down the sides of her dress, as Ada shut the door behind their visitor.

"Simon," Lily Kate said. His name sounded scratchy on her lips, but it felt good to say it.

"I was hoping we could talk," Simon said.

"I—I suppose," she stuttered. "I mean, I've got a driver coming. I'm going home today."

He nodded understandingly. "This won't take long."

Lily Kate turned to Ada, hoping her cousin would serve as a

buffer, but somehow in the last few seconds, Ada had completely disappeared.

"Would you like to sit down?" Lily Kate invited.

Simon shook his head. "I'll just stand, if it's all the same to you." He looked nervous, almost scared. For a moment Lily Kate wondered if she had offended him in some way during their shared time together. Why else would he appear so antsy?

"Something happened," Simon started, and Lily Kate's heart sank in her chest.

She had. She had offended him in some way. The time had been so special to her. So precious, but she had ruined it for him.

"I—" She started to apologize, but Simon held up one hand.

"Just let me finish, please." He closed his eyes as if gathering strength.

Heavens, what had she done?

"Something happened," he started once more. "Something shifted during those two days. And I think we should discover what it is."

"What?" This had not been at all what she had expected him to say. Not at all.

"I think we should get to know each other better." The words came out in one rush of air all strung together, each syllable nearly on top of the last. "See where it leads us. I mean, if you want to. I don't believe in love at first sight," he said. And once again she felt like he was rambling nervously. "But something happened."

"I believe in love at first sight," Ada called from wherever she had disappeared to. To Lily Kate it sounded like the kitchen.

Simon turned back to Lily Kate and gave her a smile, this one with trembling, growing confidence. "Okay, so maybe I might believe in love at first sight. And if maybe you do too—"

Lily Kate couldn't allow him to finish. She launched herself at him and wrapped her arms around his neck. "Jah! Yes," she cried. "I do believe in love at first sight."

It was simple when she had figured out what God wanted from her. From the two of them.

Simon held her close as, from a distance, Ada started clapping.

EPILOGUE

Christmas, one year later

"Well," Ada said, nudging Lily Kate in the ribs with her elbow. "How does it feel to be married?"

How did it feel to be married? Lily Kate wasn't sure yet. She had been married for less than three hours. But she was confident that she would love being married. Love being married to Simon. Love being a mother to Jacob. The past year had been nothing but bliss.

She had ended up taking a job in town sewing for Englisch and Amish alike. Lily Kate had always enjoyed sewing but had never thought about it being a job until Jodie King brought it up. Though now that Lily Kate and Simon were married, she figured she would at least go down to part-time. Until, God willing, they started to fill their house with more children. Jacob had already been asking for a brother or sister, though neither Simon nor Lily Kate wanted to explain to him that it might be a while. Probably close to a year, at least, until there was another Bontrager in the house.

"I'm just glad that it's not as cold and snowy this year as it was last year," Lily Kate mused.

Ada nodded. "Though that snow last year was something of a miracle." She gave Lily Kate a knowing smile. And Lily Kate felt heat rising to her cheeks.

Jah, some folks claimed it was a Christmas miracle that brought her and Simon together. Simon, whom she had argued with heatedly during those first days after they met. One snowstorm and a year later, they were married. Strange how the Lord worked.

Lily Kate's heart began to beat heavily in her chest as she saw Simon break away from his father and head in her direction. "Are you ready to go?"

Her pounding heart was filled with love for this man. She was nervous but ready. "Jah."

Simon gave a small nod.

Lily Kate turned to her cousin and hugged her tight. "Come see us off?" she whispered in her cousin's ear.

"I wouldn't miss it for the world."

Lily Kate took her husband's hand, and together they walked out the front door of her parents' house.

The shiny black buggy looked so beautiful and festive with pine wreaths and red bows. Someone had even woven a red ribbon through the horse's bridle and tied a bow next to his ear. It was clear that Christmas would always be so special to them.

As tradition dictated, they had married in New Wilmington. Her father had loaned them a buggy for the evening. When they returned to Lancaster, there was a new staid-gray carriage waiting just for her. But for now, this was perfect.

Lily Kate couldn't say that it was a miracle that the man fell in love with her or that she fell in love with him. Or even the family she was gaining. Maybe not a miracle, but it was definitely God's plan for the two of them. Three, she corrected herself. And maybe one day, four.

She blushed at her own thoughts.

"What are you thinking about?" Simon asked as he helped her up to the buggy.

She shook her head. "I'm glad that Ada stuck her nose in our business."

Simon chuckled as he walked around the front of the horse and over to his side of the buggy. He pulled himself up beside her, then spread the blanket over their legs to keep them warm. "Me too."

They waved goodbye to family and friends and received cheers and waves and whistles in return.

"I have to admit," Simon said once they were on the road—their first ride as a married couple—"I was coming to see you anyway."

"Jah?" In the last twelve months, they had talked about a lot, but he had never told her this. "Why is that?"

Simon nodded solemnly. "Because you make the best cookies I've ever tasted."

He held the reins over the horse's back. The mare simply ambled along in front of them.

"And that's the only reason?" she asked him with a small pout.

He turned to her, holding up his finger and his thumb about an inch apart. "Maybe this much," he told her.

"And the rest of it?" she asked.

"Because I love you without question."

Lily Kate smiled and laid her head over on his shoulder. There was no one around to see. "I love you too," she said on a happy, happy sigh.

And she loved that she was right where she was supposed to be.

Amy Lillard loves nothing more than a good book. Except for her family. . .and maybe homemade tacos. . .and nail polish. But reading and writing are definitely way up on the list.

Born and bred in Mississippi, Amy is a transplanted Southern Belle who now lives in Oklahoma with her deputy husband and two spoiled cats. ^..^

When she's not creating happy endings, she's an avid football fan (go, Chiefs!), an adoring mother to an almost adult son, and loves binge watching television shows with the hubs.

Amy is an award winning author with more than sixty novels and novellas in print. She loves to hear from readers. You can find her on Facebook, Instagram, Twitter, Goodreads, Tik-Tok, and Pinterest-not necessarily in that order. Or you can email her at amylillard@hotmail.com or check out her website http://www.amywritesromance.com.

LEAVING
LANCASTER

by Mindy Steele

Dedication

For in Him we live, and move, and have our being.
ACTS 17:28

Acknowledgments

While writing is a solitary profession, a novel is never completed alone. First, to the One who created a hope in my heart to share inspirational stories, and to the readers who continue to enjoy them. To my Barbour Publishing team, you are all a solid foundation for us authors. Thank you Becky Germany for taking a chance on me. To Vicky, my first-reader extraordinaire. To Julie, for keeping the ball rolling and Rachel Good for painting a more vivid picture for me. And last but not least, to Mike, for feeding me through the long hours of writing, revisions, and research.

CHAPTER ONE

$\mathcal{A}$s the sun peeked through her upper east-facing window, Louise Wickey awoke with a smile and stretched her long legs under the warmth of two heavy quilts. Staying up late to finish nine more Christmas jam orders had earned her a later-than-normal waking hour. If business continued to grow, *Daed* would surely build her that kitchen she had been petitioning for since summer. Her smile deepened at the thought.

Today was Friday, which meant a routine hike across the nine snowy acres to her neighbors, the Kings. Clare King was her dearest friend, and ever since Louise had been old enough to trek the farmer's fields alone, it had been their day of catching up and was now time to start sewing Clare's wedding dress. Louise found January weddings too cold, but she couldn't wait to see Clare get her happily ever after.

One more friend to wed, and here you are twenty-five and single yet.

Mammi Iolene said God's timing was perfect, especially for the pickiest of His children. The comment had been directed strictly at Louise. Louise wasn't picky. She was precise. One wrong ingredient or too much sugar, and then nothing set firm.

A disturbing odor floated upward, reaching the second floor. Leah was obviously helping ready breakfast this morning. Leah's talents in the kitchen were a work in progress, *Mamm* often argued in defense of her daughter. Leah's twin, Beth, took to anything tried, but Leah, well. . . Louise giggled. Leah simply needed more practice than others.

Slipping from her quilt, she reached toward the end of the bed for Blinkers. Startlingly she found the large red tabby—which wasn't red at all but a buttercream orange—gone. Blinkers always slept at her feet.

"Blinkers," Louise called out in that childish voice reserved only for him. She slipped out of bed. The cat must have woken early in hopes of a quick game of hide-and-seek, but a quick search under the bed revealed nothing of her furry companion. That meant only one thing. One of her younger brothers must have locked Blinkers in the bathroom again.

Hurrying into her newest dress, Louise worked her hair into a bun, placed her heart-shaped prayer covering over it, and fetched her wool socks. Who knew how long he had been in there.

Rushing two doors down, Louise discovered the bathroom door open and no Blinkers. A search of the remaining upper rooms her three brothers could have possibly stowed him in produced the same result. Temper flaring, she hurried downstairs to inspect every dark corner.

"*Mariye*, sleepyhead," Beth greeted as Louise stepped into the kitchen.

"Have you seen Blinkers?" The worry in her voice was evident.

"Not again." Beth was equally concerned. Blinkers did enjoy napping in Beth's lap in the evenings, whereas he had never showed an interest in curling up with Amos, Caleb, or Mitchel.

Brothers were a thorn.

"Mamm, why did you give us *bruders*?" Beth questioned as she peeked behind the washroom door.

"To do the milking when it gets *kault*," Mamm replied with a sly grin as she placed a heaping bowl of cheesy scrambled eggs and potatoes on the table.

"This is why I don't do pets," Beth grumbled and strolled into the neighboring bedroom belonging to their parents. Returning, she shook her head. Blinkers wasn't in there either.

"Those three need a dog. Need me to help you look outside? He could be prowling the feeders again." Before Louise could answer, the door blew open, bringing with it a brisk wind of approaching December in Lancaster. Taking off their ear warmers and knitted caps and kicking their boots off by the door, the men entered and aimed straight for the long family table.

"Sure smells. . .good," Daed quickly offered up, floating an encouraging smile Leah's way as she plated another dark circle onto a plate of other burnt circles. Whatever she cooked, he never complained. Daed simply appreciated any of his children's efforts, even if it was a threat to everyone's health.

"Best we eat now, and find Blinkers after," Mamm advised and urged the rest of her family to the table.

Louise didn't find it best at all but took a seat in the chair she'd claimed long before siblings came along. She narrowed a glance at Amos. At seventeen, he was quite the prankster despite his laid-back demeanor. *If he put Blinkers outside in the cold. . . Nee*, Louise didn't want to start a fresh day with bad thoughts, and she lowered her head for the silent prayer. Surely God could convince her brothers to fess up to their mischievousness.

When heads lifted, food immediately was passed to the left. "I see you finished all your new jam orders," Daed said, noting the boxes stacked near the back door.

"Louise needs a kitchen of her own. She could make twice the jam and jellies if she didn't have to work so late in the night from sharing this one. Candy too," Beth put in. Louise appreciated her sister's help and looked to their father in hopes he would finally agree.

"She has created a livelihood for sure and certain." Daed winked and resumed eating. Louise's shoulders dropped as she took her share of eggs and pancakes. At least they weren't as hard as bricks this time.

"Sol Martin put in another large order for his shop as well." Mamm smiled at her.

"It wonders me why he buys so many jars at all. It's a leather shop," Mitchel commented. His sandy-brown hair curled at the neck but lay flattened on the forehead. "Maybe he's sweet on ya," he teased.

"He's older than Daed," Beth quipped.

"He sells them all nonetheless, and talking and eating are two separate things," Mamm said in a motherly tone. "Best you finish up or you'll be late for school."

Louise appreciated her mother's faith in her regardless that every woman in Lancaster County knew how to make jelly and jam. Well, not Leah, but that was beside the point. Sol Martin was a faithful customer who also happened to be courting the widow Byler in the next community.

Louise was certain it was the eye-catching logo Beth had conjured up that made her jams stand out among others. Louise refused to add the horse and buggy like most did. She was selling jam, not her religion, but the red barn drew your attention with Louise's Fresh Homemade Jams written underneath. No matter what had enticed customers, the wages she'd earned had been better than Louise could have hoped for. Maybe she should invest some of her savings on a dog to keep her brothers occupied to prevent further pestering of Blinkers.

Poor Blinkers. She glanced about. No telling where he was. Louise attacked her pancakes with both fork and knife and urgency. It was best to hurry through breakfast and resume her search. One of these innocent-looking boys kidnapped her cat, and Blinkers could be anywhere this time.

"Did you see JoJo and Beast tussling this morning?" Caleb at only fifteen was on his second helping already. He was the tallest of the lot and was growing yet. All too quickly, talk of deer began filling conversational gaps between chewing and swallowing, leaving any further chatter of a shop for Louise's jam business behind.

"The rut has started," Daed said in a warning tone. "Best you all keep a distance for a spell longer." They each knew raising deer came with precautions. Some days one could hand-feed a buck, and other days just looking at one too long created too much stress. While it was an uncommon livelihood compared to most of the Amish families in the community, raising deer had provided well for the whole family. Louise loved watching the graceful creatures, though seeing them caged always made her wish her family stuck with carpentry instead.

"I think the pumpkins have been a real treat, Beth," Daed addressed another of his *kinner*. It was a statement to the man he was, always saying something positive to each of them at the start of every day.

"I was glad Jep suggested it. I didn't even know deer like pumpkins." Beth had spent the last year working for the Kauffmans at the farmers market, which earned her a few out-of-season extras.

"You live on a deer farm and don't even know what they eat,"

Mitchel scoffed and rolled his eyes.

"Beth continues to learn. You'd be wise to follow her example." Daed narrowed Mitchel a fatherly scowl. Where Beth was outspoken, Mitchel was annoyingly blunt. He dropped his focus to his plate. Repeating his last year of school hadn't gone over well with Daed.

Mamm cleared her throat. "Kinner, your daed has news to share with each of you." All eyes shot toward the head of the table.

"I found us a farm where we can expand and grow."

Louise was so caught up in swallowing burnt pancakes smothered in maple syrup and eyeing the corners for Blinkers to suddenly appear that she'd only caught half of what followed.

"Kentucky will be good for us." He gave mamm an endearing glance. "We've prayed long on what is best for our family. I feel *Gott* is leading us in this direction as an answer," Daed finished.

Did he just say he bought a farm? Moving? Louise sucked in a breath causing a piece of crusty bread to lodge in her throat.

"But we can't leave!"

Louise jerked upright at her younger sister's sudden outburst, dislodging the pancake. She set down her fork for safety and tried to contain her own shock. She was none too happy about moving either, but she wasn't prone to displaying her thoughts openly. She was prone to getting Leah's crusty concoctions stuck in her throat. No amount of butter in the world was going to help her through this meal.

"Now Leah," Mamm soothed as she often did when one of her kinner was unraveled. "Land in Kentucky is cheaper than here, and you will have no trouble finding a new job if that is your concern. Your *onkel* Willis could use help at the Bulk Store, and many *maedels* have taken up to being mother's helpers."

Leah wasn't as concerned with her job at Dienner's Country

Restaurant as she was with Conner Bricker, whom she'd been courting for three years now.

"*Jah*," thirteen-year-old Mitchel seconded. His hazelnut-colored brows tended to mimic a flock of geese flying in formation when someone sat on the opposite side of his way of thinking. Louise adored the youngest among them but had to admit he too had been stitched together with a tight thread for the dramatic.

"You should probably consider an apprenticeship in cooking." Mitchel cocked his head toward his half-eaten pancakes. "We get to expand."

Louise was almost certain this one was her catnapper, and he wasn't the only one smiling about the news. Amos and Caleb were beaming, but would they still be smiling once reality hit them? Could they so easily leave this farm or their *freinden* just to raise more deer for antlers, bottled scents, and breeding stock? Didn't Kentucky have enough deer already?

Beside her, Beth leaned forward on her elbows, eagerly anticipating the details. It was no secret that, to Beth, adventure was always a stone's throw away, and moving to another state classified as an adventure. Her blue eyes glinted with excitement.

"Those deer!" Leah scoffed and stood. She began clearing the table with a quiet fury. Having no appetite left either, Louise moved to help.

"She's just sore because Conner don't want no *fraa* who'd burn his supper," Amos jested, causing Mamm to send out another warning in proper table manners and three grown boys to chuckle.

"Enough, Kinner," Daed said sharply. "It's done. Amos, Lilly, and I will leave tonight with the driver. We'll be gone for a few days meeting the new community. Bishop Graber and your onkel Willis are already getting the *haus* ready, but much more will need to be seen over by myself."

Daed's brown eyes landed on Louise. "I know you have your orders to fill, but you will see to start packing up what won't be needed each day. Better to get ahead of that than waiting for the last minute. The boys will help and see to selling off a few things we can buy later. No sense in paying to haul so much when much can be purchased later. There will be changes to be made under the new bishop. Even our buggies will not be the same."

Not even their buggies would be accepted.

"Mammi Iolene is sewing new *kapps* for each of us, but we can worry over the rest once we get moved. We have a year to comply with all the changes." Mamm pushed her food around her plate. Was she considering how different their life might be?

Every community had its own set of rules. Louise expected that, but she wasn't a fan of change, especially life-altering ones such as this. She didn't want to give up her heart-shaped kapp or the room facing sunrise that always made her days extra special. To some it was a small sacrifice her parents were asking her to make for the greater good of the family. Would they have to wear those long heavy sleeves even in the summer months like some communities she'd heard of down south?

This was happening, and Louise wasn't sure if it was breakfast or the rush of life flipping upside down that twisted into her stomach. She nodded faithfully, doubtful Mitchel and Caleb were capable of either selling off anything for a good price or helping unless their parents were around to enforce following through on their assigned jobs. No matter, she knew the way of it. As the eldest it was her duty to watch over her siblings and finish chores in the wake of one of them being distraught, tired, or forgetful.

"Cannot we wait until spring? Packing will take a long time, and Louise is helping Clare with her wedding. Mitchel has school yet, and what of Beth and her job at the market? They will never find anyone to replace her so quickly. Alma asked me to cover two of her shifts at the restaurant. What do I tell her?" Leah put in one last plea to hold on to their life. She too was no disciple of change.

"Life will go on as it always has." Daed pushed his plate aside. "We will not move before the new year, beating the heart of winter. They haven't seen snow yet. Which is good." Daed smiled.

Kentucky was lower on the map, but Louise was surprised to learn they had barely seen winter yet when a foot of the white stuff had already packed hard outside.

"As soon as all the proper paperwork is finished, I'll have the deer stock moved. I sure hope those fences down there will hold," he mumbled to himself. Was he second-guessing his own decision, or perhaps checking off a list he stored mentally? But just as quickly as his voice wavered, he regained his head-of-the-family composure and looked to his kinner. "I know this is sudden, *Dochdern*, but it is what is best for our family. You will have one last Christmas to say your so-longs."

Louise swallowed her selfish hopes and nodded. Daed would never make a decision that wasn't the right one even if it felt as if he was making a huge mistake to leave behind years of memories and community. "But you still will need to find a buyer, will you not?" Such could take months even. So there was time. Her shoulders relaxed.

"That part was easier. I already sold it."

"We were blessed with a fast sale," Mamm said, equally pleased.

"You did?" Beth was as shocked as the rest of them.

"Our neighbors have been hoping to expand." Daed put his thumb in his suspenders and leaned back in his chair as if he hadn't added more stress to her already-hectic morning.

Louise's breath hitched. Of course the Dauleys living beside them were not buying the farm. They were almost eighty. That meant only one other family could be responsible for buying her home: the Kings.

"Marcus King grows cabbage, not livestock," Amos said.

"Now he can grow plenty more," Daed returned.

Louise had a sudden attack of hiccups at the news. Clare hadn't mentioned anything about her brother buying their farm. Had they not just spent Wednesday together, shopping for supplies? A thick trail of saliva coated her mouth, and she swallowed.

Louise had known Marcus all her life. She had once had a crush on him when they were *youngies*, but Marcus never noticed. His focus was on crops, not people.

"Clare will soon wed. It's only expected Marcus is ready for a family of his own now too. He has provided well for his family since their parents' passing." Louise agreed, Marcus had seen over their needs, but that was his place as eldest, was it not?

"Best be getting the day started." Daed stood from the table. "After chores, I'll phone the driver to be certain he isn't late this time."

"I'll see to packing a few things for us for the days ahead. Leah can help me today since it's her day off." Mamm peered at Louise. "I'm sure Louise is eager to visit with Clare."

Louise would be if her head wasn't spinning right now. They were moving, her best friend failed to mention her own bruder had purchased the farm, and Blinkers was still missing and possibly a victim to the cruelties of having three younger brothers.

Louise closed her eyes and took two calming breaths. *One thing at a time, Louise.*

As soon as the kitchen was tidy, Louise fled outdoors. She did want to speak to Clare, but finding Blinkers was foremost.

"Blinkers," Louise called out. When Blinkers failed to respond,

Louise inspected the woodpile. Her cat often hunted there. Shoving her hands into her pockets as a cool southerly wind blew over the flattened landscape, she searched the yard and along the deer fencing where bucks were playfully testing each other's strength in a match of "my horns are wider than yours." Her precious Blinkers was gone. They were moving. Life was never going to be the same.

Reaching the porch again, a cardinal darted from the lawn to one of Leah's many feeders. Louise lifted the lid on the bird-feed container nearby and offered a generous helping of seed to the barn-shaped bird feeder hanging closest. It was normally Leah's chore, but this morning Leah was in no shape for the task.

At the sound of the feed container being snapped shut, Louise noted a buttery blur move swiftly behind the sitting-room window. Sure enough Blinkers appeared to be watching the feeding frenzy.

Sneaky feline. The familiar sound had prompted him out of hiding.

"Are you feeding *birds* at a time like this?" Leah said in a shaking voice. Her watery blue eyes were indication enough she had been crying.

"Birds must eat no matter how upset you are." Louise turned to find the twins standing nearby.

"*Ach*, Leah," Beth said. "Kentucky sounds wonderful. We might even make a special friend there." Her brows wiggled playfully.

"Some of us already have. . .a special friend," Leah sobbed.

"Imagine all the fun things we will see, new freinden we will make," Beth continued, ignoring her twin.

"I'm not happy either, but I understand. I just hope they like jam," Louise sighed.

"I don't understand at all." Leah sucked in a distraught sob.

"It's not the end of the world, Leah." Beth wrapped a shawl around her twin's shoulders as the morning chill bit at her pale cheeks. "I think you should see this as a blessing. God—"

"Directs our path," Leah finished Beth's comment. The twins had a habit of finishing one another's sentences often. "Are you saying God doesn't want me to be a fraa?" Leah was appalled at her twin's comment.

"Nee, but maybe you are meant to be someone else's fraa."

Louise had come to the same conclusion during the last gathering when she'd witnessed Conner chatting it up with newcomer Sybil Lambright, but she wasn't one for pointing out the obvious.

"Conner Brinker had three years to ask you," Beth said bluntly.

Leah fled into the house, an emotional torrent of tears and wails.

"Perhaps you could have delivered that a little softer," Louise said disappointedly.

"A good lesson isn't a thing you spread your Christmas jam on, Louise."

Perhaps it wasn't.

CHAPTER TWO

*Y*ou got a hair in your lunch or something?" At the sound of Daniel Fisher's voice, Beth finally swallowed the apple slice she had been chewing on so long it had become applesauce in her mouth. She hadn't bothered to test the cheese and crackers tucked in her lunch bag or take one sip of the *kaffi* from her thermos despite having barely touched her breakfast.

Any other day Beth's enthusiasm for meeting new customers and making friends had made working at Kauffman's Orchards the perfect job for her. The U-pick farm offered her as much sunshine as it did interesting people. But as she sat between a tree made of wooden crates filled with holiday pumpkins and the table of greenery that would soon be wreaths for Christmas, it was guilt for speaking to Leah in such a way that had spoiled her appetite. She didn't like upsetting others and needed to make right the wrong she had done.

"Hello." Daniel waved a hand in front of her. He was tall, his hair always trimmed dangerously shorter than most of the Old Order Amish men in the district, and he had the strange ability to smile and make maedels go doe-eyed. Beth found him a nuisance who spent more time chatting it up with customers than ringing up the next sale.

"What?"

"You've been staring at that stack of potatoes for five minutes," Daniel said. "I assure you, they ain't going to start sprouting no matter how long you will them to."

Had she? Beth shook her head. She was in no mood for his common pestering. Her whole life was playing a fast game of tug-of-war with her heart. Moving to a new community was a great opportunity, but when you were a twin, sadly you didn't get to feel only your emotions, and Leah was dulling her sunshine. How could she be excited about what lay ahead, while Leah was struggling to stay behind?

Beth gave Daniel her full attention. He wasn't even smart enough to wear a coat...in winter. She suspected it was to show off his muscles or make folks think he was thick skinned or something. Beth found him a boy who'd rather waste his days than grip life's adventures. He was...typical.

"If you must know, Daniel Fisher, I have a lot on my mind today, and I'm on my break...you're *naet*. Aren't you supposed to be putting out more apples?" Ten large crates still waited in the back, and from the looks of the produce tables, he'd not even carried out a bushel yet.

"Not much of a break, and your head's smaller than those baking pumpkins." He sat down beside her. "Can't be too much going on in there." He leaned back and watched the customers browse. A good employee would ask if they needed help.

Beth let out a sigh. "You're so sweet, Daniel Fisher. It's a wonder you ain't married yet with all those sugar-coated words you know." His laugh sent a parade of goose pimples over her.

If Beth wasn't mistaken, Daniel only riled her for his own amusement.

"I've been practicing." He winked. "Nee, really. What's got you looking like you lost your best friend?"

"It's a family matter." To another, that would be the end of it, but not Daniel. His brows gathered in a sudden look of concern.

"I'm a good listener, and prayers are free," he prodded, giving her shoulder a light bump with his own. "Is Lilly ill?"

"Nee." Beth was a little surprised he asked about her mother. It was almost sweet.

"Your daed?"

"Nee, my family is well, mostly. Mamm is fine. Daed is fine. We are all fine." Weren't they? The look on Louise's face this morning had Beth wondering if Louise wasn't happy about the move either.

"'Bear ye one another's burdens. . .'" Daniel lifted a sharp brow.

"So you do listen to Sunday sermons," Beth jested. But Daniel was right. Beth considered the same sermon, but could she apply it when it came to Daniel Fisher?

Beth shook her head. It wasn't like a family secret would be exposed. Soon enough all would know of her father's plan for them to leave Lancaster. "I made Leah cry and now she's inconsolable."

"I'm sure you didn't mean to, and Leah has always been a little. . .sensitive." That was true.

"We've always had the ability to—"

"Finish each other's sentences," Daniel chuckled. "Sorry, but it's fun watching you two do that."

"It's not for showing off. We're twins. Twins have the ability to feel each other's emotions and finish each other's thoughts," Beth informed him, thankful there was only one Daniel Fisher to deal with. "Hers are making me miserable. She and Conner have been courting for three years. She hates the deer farm, and I know she'd rather stay here in hopes they marry instead of moving with us to Kentucky. She's not one for new adventures." Beth let out a sigh. It was a problem for certain sure. How could she be happy with what lay ahead while feeling all these negative emotions from her twin.

"You're moving?" Daniel shot to his feet. Beth flinched at his sudden reaction. Folks moved, did they not? So why was he looking as if someone just stole his courting buggy and he might have to stay home next gathering?

"Jah, after Christmas."

"Kentucky?"

"It's not a big deal, but you know my sister," Beth said with a sideways smirk, considering Daniel had once asked to take Leah home from a gathering. Unfortunately Conner had asked first. It had always been that way. Men seemed more attracted to Leah and her quieter demeanor than Beth's chatty one.

"We may look plenty alike, but she dislikes change. I, on the other hand, can't wait for something new." Beth collected her uneaten lunch and stood. Perhaps talking to Daniel wasn't such a bad idea after all, because now Beth knew what she had to do. She had to help her twin get the marriage proposal she had been waiting for. Sounded easy enough, she thought as she tucked her thermos back into her lunch bag and worked the zipper closed.

"You'd really leave?" Daniel questioned. Beth stared at him for three long seconds. Why was her future any concern to him? Perhaps he was coming down with a viral infection.

"I'd never let my family go without me, and it's twice the land.

Our family depends on the deer, and we can't expand here." It made perfect sense. "Winters aren't as cold either, and when it snows, there will be plenty of hills for sledding."

"But won't you miss. . .your freinden?"

"I can write them." She would write plenty to keep up with the comings and goings. "I can visit too, once we are settled." It would be more traveling, taking in more places she would have otherwise never seen.

"I will miss Mammi," Beth said despairingly. Hopefully they could convince her to come along. "She taught me all about the importance of getting the most out of your day." Perhaps Beth was much like her grandmother in that way. Mammi's stories of long trips to the west and north had fed Beth's wandering urges over the years.

Beth looked to Daniel again. His deep frown said he didn't like Daed's decision, but it was none of his concern. He was always trying to confuse her. Just yesterday he had convinced her to deadhead all the poinsettias when it had been his duty all along. "And it's not about moving. It's about me upsetting my sister. I shouldn't have said what I did. Leah's one for habit, and she loves Conner."

"Well, Conner is certainly a habit," Daniel mumbled under his breath. "He's helping my bruder all week to rebuild the rest of the Yoders' barn in Ronks. I could talk to him."

"I don't need your help with my *schwester*'s private life." She didn't mean to sound so harsh. Daniel was offering to help her sister after all. "I mean, it can't be too hard to convince him to ask her to marry. He obviously loves her."

Daniel laughed, and Beth bristled. "What's so funny?"

"You're daft, Beth."

She wasn't daft. She didn't even know what daft meant. Daniel

Fisher was just opinionated.

"What do you know about love?" He gave her kapp string a flick with his finger. Beth opened her mouth but soon closed it again. Nothing, she knew absolutely nothing about love. Of course Daniel presumed himself an expert.

"And you do," she finally responded with a hint of sarcasm.

"I'm starting to." Daniel grinned in such a way Beth suddenly felt like a hare in a snare. "I'll speak with Conner. We're all playing basketball tomorrow night at the Kings'."

"Basketball," Beth mumbled and pulled her gaze away. "I'll see to my own. You should tend to the customers." Beth pointed to the nearest checkout station.

"I don't mind helping out a. . .friend. You clearly need help the way I see it. Four weeks," he said, in a low tone that surprisingly sent goose bumps up Beth's arms again. How did someone so bothersome stir such effects? Beth felt oddly uncomfortable. She didn't need his help.

Daniel pinned her to a spot and smiled. "A lot can happen in four weeks," he said before walking away. Why would he care about Beth's future, and why was he looking at her that way?

Beth Wickey feared few things in life. A buck in rut, snakes, and Daniel when he grinned like he had a secret needing to be told. Beth wasn't afraid, but Daniel's behavior today did surprise her enough to make her wonder what secret that might be.

CHAPTER THREE

*L*ouise tramped across the snowy field separating her family's parcel from the Kings' produce farm next door. She was mindful of the frozen and uneven earth. She didn't want a twisted ankle.

Darkened clouds loomed in the distance. Stuffing her gloved hands into her coat pockets, Louise marched across the yard, leaving a trail of booted footprints behind. Clare King had a lot of explaining to do.

The plain, two-story gray house had no adornments. Not since the passing of Clare's mother had the siblings even considered growing a path of flowers that once welcomed visitors to the door. Louise gave two hard knocks, announcing her arrival. After a few seconds, she knocked again. *Odd*, she thought, leaning closer for sounds of footsteps inside. Nothing but passing cars on the nearby road.

When a third attempt still hadn't produced Clare, Louise looked about. The Kings owned a vast ninety acres in cropland, but only one acre was spared for the house and the red metal barn used to store produce in season and buggies when room was to be had. There was the old toy shop, but it had lain dormant for years.

Marcus King, like his father Malachi before him, believed dirt was meant to be seeded and nurtured. Louise had to agree. From the time she was old enough to drop seeds into a freshly hoed row, watching bounty bloom out of hope gave her a sense of accomplishment and satisfaction. It was the same with making jam. Just a few ingredients and you had something sweet that made others smile.

Perhaps Clare was helping her bruders in the barn this morning. While Marcus had continued the family's livelihood, Fred only helped when he could be spared from the hat shop.

Inside the barn with shiny concrete floors and painted lines for monthly basketball games, Louise found no sign of anyone but horses munching on hay in a faraway corner and kittens dashing into the shadows. The buttery blurs made Louise giggle. Blinkers wasn't a wanderer, but the markings on the kittens proved that at some point he had tested exploring the area.

Louise was just about to leave when she heard the noise like furniture being scooted across a wooden floor. Facing the white-washed building with the red sign reading Kings Wooden Toys and Furniture, she wondered if Clare was fetching something from inside.

It had been years since Louise had been in there. Malachi King was a man who loved his children more than firm ripe tomatoes ready for market. It was no wonder that between harvest and planting, he'd begun creating toys for them. It took no time for orders to start coming in, and soon a second King business was born.

"Clare," Louise called out as she reached the shop door. If Clare was in there, Louise feared she might be dealing with another bout of missing her parents. Surely her upcoming wedding was making her miss her mamm all the more. As much as Louise wished to talk to her friend about her own upturned life, nothing compared to what Clare had lost.

The door sprang open quickly, but instead of Clare, Marcus stood in the dark doorway. Under one arm he held a potted poinsettia, but it was the smile on his face that had Louise taken aback for a moment. He was capable of smiling. Louise had seen him do so before, but here he was smiling, holding a poinsettia, and making her feel like a clumsy twelve-year-old all over again. "Where's Clare?"

"Hello to you too." Marcus' smile flipped into a familiar frown before he turned and disappeared inside.

Louise rolled her eyes. When she was finishing up her last two years of school, there had been a time, a brief one, when Louise found Marcus King. . .handsome. Well, he was still handsome, she concluded. He wasn't as tall as his younger brother Fred, but Louise never liked being looked down upon. His light brown hair had been in need of a trim. She liked his blue eyes, rimmed in black with streaks of soft white forming galaxies she once saw pictures of in a book. But her brief schoolgirl crush ended the day Marcus scolded her for being a terrible sister when Mitchel slipped out of her sight. He was also Clare's bruder, which made her infatuation seem foolish.

Unfortunately, he was right. She had been in charge of watching over Mitchel that day, but in her defense, Mitchel was five and prone to disappearing. Still, it had left a sore spot in Louise's heart to be considered a bad sister.

No matter. Marcus never so much as showed an interest in anyone. He didn't go to gatherings or smile at anyone special. He did however play basketball, hosting a game each month in his barn for all the youngies. In cold winter months it had spurred quite a crowd, or so she'd heard. Louise would never attend a basketball game uninvited.

Amos and Caleb loved sharing the latest gossip of who won those games and who left with his head down. Amos and Caleb would do well to learn that one could have a good time without making a sport out of it, Louise thought. Louise never boasted she was better at sewing than Beth or could make the fluffiest pancakes by the time she was ten when Leah was still struggling.

And this was the man who had bought their farm. The house she never wanted to leave. Despite her internal agitation, Louise stepped inside and forced a smile. "Hiya. I've *kumm* to speak to Clare, but she didn't answer the door."

"Because she isn't here," he replied. "Thought maybe you came out here to talk to me."

Louise did have plenty to talk to Marcus about. Like why would he buy their farm so quickly, hurrying them along. Louise opened her mouth to address the topic when she noticed what he was doing. It was a familiar piece. The toy ran by cranking a wheel on one side, allowing a marble to run its course over curved shapes moving up and downward in the motion. He was making toys just as his father once had.

Closing her mouth, Louise took in the rest of the room. There were new toys strewn about the shop, older ones dusted off and displayed on shelves. The room had been swept. Cobwebs had been taken down, and the air hinted of pine and vanilla. It was as if Malachi King was open to tourists again and Ada was giving away fresh *kichlin*.

"Your daed's shop looks just like I remember." Louise reached down and picked up a plastic bag filled with wooden puzzle pieces.

"That's what I hoped for, but I reckon it's my shop now," he said with a thread of longing catching in his throat. Surely he missed his parents as much as Clare did. She set down the puzzle and noted his gaze aimed directly at her.

"Is that a new dress?" Louise didn't respond, taken aback he'd noticed such a detail. "You used to bring your brothers here all the time," he remarked before returning to his work.

"Jah, when they were young. Caleb taught me a lesson not to take them anywhere alone after that."

He chuckled. "I suppose when one swallows a handful of marbles, it can hand out lessons to others too." Louise cringed. Was he about to remind her once again of her shortcomings as a sister?

"Clare tried swallowing one of the rubber bands from the toy guns." He ran a long wooden rod into holes bored in five egg-shaped pieces of various sizes. These would move the curved blocks above in rhythm to keep the marble moving. "I was to watch her, and froze."

Louise found it hard to believe he froze at such a time, but she was more shocked Marcus shared such a personal memory with her. He wasn't one to put his vulnerabilities at the center of a table.

"She does bounce back and forth a lot," she added with a timid smile. Everyone made mistakes, did they not?

"She does." He grinned. "I learned a hard lesson that day, to never take my eye off her too. I don't think I would have managed five siblings. Clare and Fred were plenty enough for me."

Louise warmed in the compliment. Perhaps he didn't find her completely lacking. "What made you want to reopen the shop?" She hadn't remembered a conversation between them lasting more than three seconds before.

Marcus shrugged. "Gives me something to do when I can't farm, and I guess in part I did always hope for a house full of kinner of my own to enjoy them."

"Well, you now have a house big enough for a dozen." It came out harsher than Louise meant for it to.

"Jah, but a man can't fill it alone, Louise. Gott's timing, and all of that," he said before tapping the rod into place. "I was glad your daed came to me first, though I will say, as much as I was looking forward to purchasing the land, it will be hard to see you all go. We've been neighbors a long time."

"All our lives." Louise glanced in a dark corner where more toys were being unveiled. "It just came as a surprise to us too. Usually daed doesn't make such quick decisions without us talking about it as a family. I was just as shocked that you bought it." Was he considering marrying soon? Clare had not mentioned Marcus having a special friend. Then again, she hadn't mentioned her bruder had bought the farm either.

"I was glad for the land, but I'm not eager to move into an empty house yet."

"Then why buy it?" Who spends that much money for a home he didn't plan on living in?

"Will you go. . .with them to Kentucky?"

The question jerked her attention back to him. "Of course. Family stays together," she said, and he agreed with a nod.

"But we are to start our own families, are we not?"

"I have no plans for such. Leah on the other hand is a little upset."

"Conner." Marcus shook his head.

"Jah. She had hopes. It will be hardest on her."

"She doesn't own her own business," he quickly inserted. "Leah could stay. See how things work out with him."

"Why would a woman stay if he won't declare his love for her?" Louise said sharply. "I mean—" she cleared her throat,

"Conner has yet to even talk of marriage, family, or a future with her. I can't imagine what that is like for her."

"Perhaps he will come to his senses soon enough," Marcus replied. "Some of us take longer than others to tell others how we feel."

"I just wish there was something more I could do," she admitted.

"You can be her sister, but Gott knows what will come of it."

That was true. God knew every story, though it would be nice if He left hints to help a person along the way. "Mitchel can't wait. He's thrilled to wear a wider brim. Says he'll feel like a cowboy."

"Beth too I imagine." He chuckled, knowing her family well.

But he didn't know her. If he had, he would know it was more than her jam business she feared for—it was leaving the home she was born in.

"Clara is over at Issac's this morning, planning her wedding with Carol and Kathy," he informed her, setting aside the finished toy and taking up more pieces to start another. "She'll be back soon enough."

"She ditched me for Issac's schwesters?"

"Weddings are a big deal, so I'm told, and everyone wants to help. Can you hand me those stacks of blocks there?" Marcus motioned to a pile of flat wooden blocks with curves carved into them. Louise had never really considered her own wedding.

"Take one of each size and hold them here," he instructed while holding the side in place for her to slide them in.

"I never made a toy before," Louise said, concentrating on the task at hand. "Malachi once let me and Clare glue jar rings in the candy dispensers, but he had a big order."

Marcus gazed over her face as if his lost father was somehow rekindled behind the whites of her eyes. "You always were smart enough to figure out most things."

Louise slid the blocks in place, her finger lightly brushing his knuckles. She quickly let go and took a step back.

"*Danki,* Louise. I reckon a helpmate could save a man loads of troubles."

"I should go and see if Leah needs help with laundry." She had the sudden urgency to put some much-needed space between them.

"Be sure to tell your brothers we're playing ball tomorrow night. Figure we'd get in a game or two. . .before—" He left off the rest of the sentence, but Louise knew what he meant: "before we are no longer neighbors."

"I'm sure they'll like that. I caught Amos and Caleb practicing in the barn a few nights ago. . .with Beth."

"Amos needs the practice." Marcus chuckled before casting her a mindful glance. "You should kumm."

"Me?"

"Jah. It can be a show when some get to losing." He laughed again. Louise had always enjoyed his laugh, deep and slow moving like the dark waters of the Muddy Run flowing into Mill Creek.

"Though I can't say there will be any treats. Clare seldom offers to fix supper anymore, and the last time one of the guys brought something, it had raisins in it." Marcus made a face. He was not a fan of raisins.

"You're inviting me to a game if I bring kichlin, aren't you?" Louise placed a hand on one hip. How long had she waited for such an invite, and yet the need for cookies spawned the invitation.

"I am," Marcus said with a hint of pink on his face. "I'd deny it if asked, but yours are better than Clare's. Here it is December and not one kichlin in the house." Marcus placed a hand on the back of his neck and rubbed some tense muscles. "And. . ."

"And?" Did he want her to make tea too?

"Fred brought over a lot of boxes for me to pack up my things. I'm in no hurry to do that." He locked gazes with her.

Was there a question in his words?

"You are welcome to them, for your family."

"I am in no hurry to pack up either." A fact as true as her socks being a yucky brown and not black, since Beth rushed through laundry without paying one bit of attention last week.

"That's good to know. I'm in no hurry for you to leave either." Another awkward moment of silence sliced between them.

"Go on inside and set a few boxes out and warm up a bit. I can deliver them over to your place once I'm done out here."

Louise turned to leave.

"And you don't have to bring cookies." The melancholy of his tone smothered out any crushed feelings she had that he had bought her home. Christmas was less than four weeks away, and Louise sensed Marcus was thinking of Ada, his mamm. Ada never let a December day linger without the King house smelling of fresh-baked goods.

Pausing in her own memories of the woman with strawberry-kissed hair and pronounced dimples when she looked at her kinner, Louise understood well enough how Marcus was feeling. Ada had taught Louise many tricks to protect garden vegetables from pests and how to make oatmeal whoopee pies and the best apple bread. A sudden hunger for both had her mouth salivating.

Christmas didn't feel like Christmas anymore at the Kings, and Louise felt it too. Inhaling a quiet breath, she let it out slowly as his expression tore at her chest. It was Friday, and Fridays were for spending the day next door, but this Friday Louise would spend it helping another. Gott would expect no less from her.

"Apple bread?"

Marcus' eyes lit up, and the saddest smile Louise imagined anyone could produce aimed at her.

"I'll go set aside a few boxes. Please tell Clare I stopped by if I'm gone before she arrives." Louise slipped back out into the cold and aimed for the back door of the King's home. She knew the way.

CHAPTER FOUR

$\mathscr{P}$oor Marcus," Louise snickered as she entered the kitchen. On the center of the table sat two bags of apples and a loaf pan. It seemed he had left the hints for his sister to bake their mamm's apple bread, but Clare's focus was stitched tight to her upcoming wedding. So much so, she'd forgotten their Friday too.

Boxes were stacked to her left just as Marcus had said. Louise could begin packing a few of her own things tonight. It wouldn't be much, she considered. She only had six dresses, and Marcus had noticed one of them. Her cheeks warmed at the fact, but she quickly shifted away from the thought. She had her hope chest and a few knickknacks cluttering her dresser top. How had she lived twenty-five years with so little to show for it?

The warmth of the kitchen hurried her out of her gloves and cape. She was in no rush to go home. Marcus was deep in toy making. That left her plenty of time for baking apple bread.

Gathering all the needed ingredients, Louise made quick work of mixing up a thick batter. She folded in two diced apples, slipped everything into the bread pan, and slid it into the oven. She went to the propane fridge, hoping for a glass of tea while the bread baked. Unfortunately, the pitcher was empty. She quickly set a pot of water on to boil and fetched the tea bags from the pantry. She knew this kitchen as well as her own.

In the next room she began setting boxes near the back door. After a few minutes, she returned to the tea boiling on the stovetop. Louise added the appropriate amount of sugar and gave it a lazy stir as scents of cinnamon and fresh bread lifted into the room. It was a routine chore, and she didn't mind helping out another. Soon she would be baking in a new kitchen, and the thought unsettled her.

Mamm said their new home only had three rooms for now. Louise dreaded to think she might have to sleep with Beth and Leah. Beth snored and Leah tended to thrash wildly in her sleep. Poor Leah. Louise wanted to understand what she was going through, but Louise had never been in love before.

The front door opened, followed by giggling and shuffling footsteps. "Oh Issac, you really should get on now," Clare's voice giggled. "You're gonna get one of Marcus' frowns for sure."

"I cannot wait to marry you, Clare King."

Louise rolled her eyes at the sound of kissing in the next room and quickly poured the sugary concoction into a pitcher and began adding water from the faucet.

"I knew I smelled apple bread," Clare said, stepping into the room with her face aglow. Envy sparked embers in Louise's chest.

The front door closed, revealing Issac's leaving. "I can't believe you made Mamm's apple bread. Marcus is going to love you!" Clare slipped off her bonnet and cloak, hanging them on the fourth peg by the laundry room door.

"I. . .I. . ." Louise was speechless. She had only baked the bread to make Marcus feel better over the loss of his mamm. It was the neighborly thing to do. She hoped her friend didn't get the wrong impression.

"He's been missing holidays with our parents something terrible. I'm sorry if he talked you into. . ."

"He didn't." Louise let out a breath. "I wanted to. I understand the holidays can be hard and I did have to find something to do this morning since you weren't here."

"I'm sorry Louise, really, but Issac's sisters showed up this morning and I couldn't *verra* well tell them no." Clare moved to the stove and peeked into the oven. "Looks done."

"It should be. Here." Louise slipped on an oven mitt and pulled the perfectly golden loaf from the oven.

"That smells just like. . ." Clare sucked up her next words, but Louise knew. Memories had scents, just as they bore pictures in one's head.

"Danki, Louise. You are the best friend a woman could ever have." Clare folded her into a hug. Oh how she would miss Clare. No more Christmas meals or Second Christmas visits. No more days sewing or making jam together while they talked about who was courting whom and who was on the verge of making Bishop Martin frown.

"Instead of my dress, which is almost done by the way," Clare said with a hint of pride, "I hoped we could have some hot chocolate while you help me sort through mamm's quilts. I've got to tell you all about Kathy's idea that we should serve carrot cake at my Christmas wedding." Clare rolled her eyes as she took two cups down from the cabinet. Kathy was known for her fanciful ideas. Louise hoped Clare wasn't letting her plan the whole traditional meal.

"Marcus will need half of these cups, even if he isn't married yet. He hates doing dishes," Clare remarked, closing the cabinet door.

Once the hot chocolate was done, Louise filled both cups and followed Clare into her nearby bedroom. The bright blue walls had always reminded Louise of soft spring skies, accompanied by lacy white curtains and doilies on her dresser stand. Louise always found Clare's room more pleasant than her own drab walls of ivory. Perhaps in Kentucky she could have blue walls. Suddenly she wondered what else she might do differently. Would she finally meet someone who could make her heart beat a little faster than the slow pace of normalcy?

On the bed were at least a dozen handmade quilts. "Why are you going through them?"

"It's time," Clare said somberly. "Marcus said I should choose which I wanted, and which to give Fred, but he should have part of them too, I told him. I mean, he will not have anyone to quilt one for him unless I find the time. I don't like when he leaves such tasks for me to do."

"You're his only sister, and he has made many decisions," Louise defended him absentmindedly. Being eldest, she knew the pressures, and Clare, being the youngest of her lot, tended to be a tad spoiled by her brothers when it came to a great many things.

Clare let out a sigh. "He hates sifting through memories as much as me, and Fred avoids them altogether. It is hard to see all the beautiful things Mamm created and know she can never again create another. I had always hoped we would sew my wedding quilt together."

"But we made a beautiful quilt for Issac this summer. Your mamm would have loved it."

"Danki, Louise." Clare wiped her face. "Don't be sore at me for not being here. I hadn't any idea Issac's sisters were coming until they knocked on the door this morning. I should keep this one," Clare said, confiscating a beautiful blue-and-green wedding ring quilt. "It was our parents. Perhaps you can sew one for Marcus yourself." Clare snuggled the quilt greedily.

"Or he can let a fraa do it. I don't mind making apple bread, but that wouldn't be proper."

"I guess by now you know Marcus is buying your family's farm," Clare said in a low voice.

"I found out at the breakfast table, but a little forewarning would have been nice," Louise replied as she admired a tulip design with pale pinks and blues. She loved tulips and their spring welcoming.

"I would have told you if *mei* bruder wasn't so good at secret keeping. He's always been that way, keeping his thoughts to himself. I do hope his plans for his future work out. He is a *gut* bruder, and deserves to be as happy as Fred and me. You aren't moving with them, are you?" Clare lowered the quilt, her brown eyes pleading. "Oh, Louise." Clare rested the quilt on the sitting room couch and grasped Louise's hand. "You must stay. We were supposed to marry and have kinner together."

"Where would I stay, Clare? I don't have a home anymore. We both know I have to go with my family."

"You're of age to decide so," Clare scoffed.

"I may be of age, but mamm needs me. The boys tire her out quickly, and Leah isn't very helpful, especially now. Beth will be seeking freinden and fun instead of making sure Daed and the boys have supper that isn't ham and mustard relish sandwiches."

Clare made a face. "Beth sure has funny tastes. That apple-and-pumpkin dish she served at the last gathering had so many spices in it, I had to drink two cups of milk to make it go away."

Louise laughed. "Jah, she does like to try on new things. I think Leah hopes to stay though, if things come out right."

Clare paused as she was folding a brown-on-brown block

quilt. "If Conner Brinker wanted to marry her, he would have by now. You know I speak the truth. Marcus always says he's not good enough for Leah."

"Marcus says that?" Well, he did know a lot about her siblings.

"He and Daniel Fisher sat in the kitchen just last week eating all my apple dumplings saying so," Clare's voice hitched. Louise was surprised to think *menner* chatted like old spinsters.

"Leah loves him, and he must love her too for as long as they have courted."

"Or he is just stringing her along. I agree with mei bruder. Leah and Conner are no match. She deserves a man who isn't too slow to show he loves her. Issac would never make me wait three long years to tell me he loves me."

"Nee, he told you on your second date," Louise reminded her.

"But we had been freinden since we were young," Clare defended him with a lifted chin. "Sometimes loves grows slowly. It doesn't come to everyone quickly. Leah will soon learn this, but you I'm not so sure. I think you should tell your folks you want to stay."

"I can't do that. I have no reason to stay."

"What about your jam business? You don't want to give that up, do you? You can live with Issac and me."

"I'm not living with you and Issac, here." She glanced at the room. Couples needed time alone, to get to know each other, not to have a best friend sleeping in the next room. Louise blushed at the idea.

"Marcus is in no hurry. You could stay in your house, until things change."

Clare was always full of quixotic ideas. "Marcus won't think that a good idea."

"You'd be wrong to think you know him more than me." Clare

smiled cleverly. "We should ask him."

"Nee!" Louise didn't mean to raise her voice, but help from Marcus would only make an uncomfortable situation more uncomfortable. Especially now that the strange effects of her fingers brushing his still lingered.

"Marcus will want to start a family of his own one day. He can't do that if I'm living in my—his—house!"

"Oh, he won't mind," Clare insisted, picking up another quilt. This one was white with tight stitching. In the four corners lay a small rose embroidered in pinks.

"I saw he is opening the toy shop again." Louise hoped to change the topic of conversation.

"Nee, me and Issac agreed to open it. Marcus just wants to get things in order and continue making toys like daed did. Fred has no interest in it, and it will give me and Issac an extra income. I can't keep working at the coffee corner once I'm a fraa, and Issac doesn't get much work in winter building houses."

A silent pause lingered between them as Louise wondered if Marcus might turn daed's feed room into a woodshop. It had potential, the extra lighting from all five windows. It had been the perfect place for her jam business, she thought despairingly. It was selfish, the thoughts she was having. The house deserved a family. Perhaps Marcus would marry and be blessed to fill it, and years of love and laughter might continue to fill the halls and rooms.

"Marcus is a gut bruder," Clare said with a little added mischief in her eyes.

"If you compare him to mine, he's the best bruder ever. I'm certain Amos stole Blinkers this morning."

"Again." Clare harrumphed.

"All I know is that he wasn't on the bed when I woke, and

I searched everywhere for him. He suddenly popped up at the window just seconds after they headed to the barn."

"Well, Marcus likes *katz*. Says they keep rodents out of the seed. He suspects all those in the barn now might be Blinkers. He found him out there twice already. Carried him back to your house and dropped him off."

Louise hadn't known that.

"I think you and my bruder have much in common. You both like katz and apple bread."

"Lots of folks like those things," Louise replied, wondering what point Clare was trying to make.

"Not Katie," Clare giggled. "She and Alma have eyes for him, but I don't think Katie likes katz." Clare looked at her curiously. "Do you find mei bruder to have a look to him?"

Louise did, but she would never admit to that out loud.

"*Vell?*" Clara insisted.

"He's your bruder and my neighbor. I never really gave it much thought. Besides, it doesn't matter what I think. Alma and Katie like him. I will be leaving." The thought of Marcus settling down with either woman made Louise's stomach twirl.

"Unless you sweetened Marcus up. Leah might not get her happy ending, but you could."

"Clare King." Louise slapped Clare's arm playfully. "You are just rotten to the core."

"I am," Clare admitted proudly. "But anything can happen at Christmas. You may turn his head yet, and don't pretend I don't know you want to."

"Marcus is not interested in me." If he had been, surely he would have said something by now. "He thinks I have no common sense and clearly is only nice to me now because he's buying our home."

"Not everything is what you think." Clare snickered. "And I fear you have missed so much making jam and not looking about. You worry over Leah's happiness. What of yours?"

"I—"

"You don't even know, do you?" Clare shook her head and smiled, revealing dimples she'd inherited. "Don't you want to be as happy as Issac and me?" Louise did, but love didn't find everyone the same.

"What I want doesn't matter. Gott will send me where He wants me to go."

"What if Gott has plans for you to stay right where you are?"

"You're talking nonsense." Louise slipped the tulip quilt into a box.

"She does that a lot." Louise let out a gasp when Marcus spoke from the doorway. Embarrassment riddled over her in a hot wave. She was going to die in her best friend's bedroom.

"Sorry if I startled you, but I'm ready to take those boxes over to your place if you are."

"Boxes?"

"The ones you came in here to fetch. . .two hours ago."

"Jah, the boxes."

"I'll see to loading these while you put on a coat." He grinned. "Clare, don't you have something to do?"

"I thought I was doing plenty." Clare shot him an arrogant smile.

Louise had never been more flustered in all her life. Well, not since the time Beth wet herself at church while sitting on Louise's lap. Nothing topped that.

"Danki, Louise," Marcus said as he worked a handful of boxes into folds to downsize them.

"For what?"

"The house hasn't smelled this wonderful since. . .our last Christmas as a family." With that the room went quiet, but the look of total appreciation from Marcus before he slipped outside caused Louise's heart to start racing an unnatural rhythm. Even still, he had that effect on her.

"See, you never know. Gott's plan is smarter than yours," Clare said and snickered from behind her.

CHAPTER FIVE

After saying so long to her parents and Amos, Louise filled Blinkers' food bowl and strolled through the house seeing all the doors were locked and the lamps extinguished before making her way up the stairs.

Glancing into her parents' room, she hoped they wouldn't be gone for more than the week. In the next room, she cautiously peeked inside. Any other season, Mitchel insisted the door remained closed, but even though winter had just begun, the cold outside always seeped into this room the most.

"Don't let that fur ball in here, or he'll end up outside again," Mitchel warned, his gaze never leaving the pages of his newest hunting magazine. He looked silly sitting in the dark, his headlamp aimed at the pages and his hair wildly arrowing to the north. Where had the little boy gone who once beamed to search her pockets for candy?

"*Gut nacht*, Louise," Caleb said, pulling two thick quilts over his head.

"Nacht, Caleb, and you too, Mitchel."

Slipping on down the hall, she paused at the twins' door

with an unbidden thought. Did Marcus see his siblings tucked in at bedtime as she did? Of course not now. They were older. But before. She suspected he had. The sound of sobbing pulled her from her thoughts. Louise cautiously opened the door, and Blinkers rushed inside.

"Beth, Leah, is everything all right?" Leah had her face buried in her pillow on the bed. Blinkers immediately went to her, sensing her emotional upset. Her long blond hair had strewn around her without the first braid attempted yet. Beth sat upright reading, as if Leah's tears had no effect. Louise knew different. Despite Beth's strong personality, she had a tender heart.

"Conner forgot to drive her home from work today," Beth said indifferently and set down her newest mystery novel. Her infatuation with such stories had been the current topic of family breakfasts, until daed announced the move. With both parents gone to Kentucky, Beth was obviously getting in all her last-minute reading before donating her scant collection to the nearby consignment shop.

"He had a delivery," Leah defended and sat upright. Poor Leah, it seemed the more she loved Conner, the less he loved her back.

Louise moved over to the bed and sat down. Without their kapps, hair hanging over opposite shoulders, the twins looked even more alike. Louise remembered when they were born and how Leah was so easily content, while Beth cried over the tiniest sound.

"You always think the worst of him," Leah scoffed.

Louise stood and began the task of braiding her hair.

"I don't think the worst of him," Beth protested, "but a man who makes you cry isn't worth sparing kind words on."

"I love him, and I want to be his fraa. You shouldn't say

anything bad about anyone."

"Well, she says the same about Daniel Fisher. It's just her way," Louise soothed. "I'm sure Conner didn't mean for you to be without a ride home."

"I had to ride home with Marcus King." Leah sulked. "He was getting boxes from the store nearby and saw me."

Had not Marcus insisted he had plenty of boxes, so much so he shared them? "He's our neighbor and I'm glad he was there to see you home safe," Louise said.

"I don't know what to do. I tried talking to Conner when he came in for lunch, but the restaurant was so busy, and he had Silas with him. What if he never asks?"

Louise passed a look to Beth. She too had her doubts.

"If I go, Conner might forget about me. He might. . .marry another," Leah whimpered. "I've dropped so many hints I'm surprised he doesn't have a headache listening to them."

"Does he know we are leaving in a few weeks?"

"He was upset when I told him. Said fathers ruin everything." Leah rolled her swollen eyes. "It's hopeless. I will never marry."

"You will. . .eventually." Leave it to Beth to be blunt. "I have an idea."

Louise didn't like Beth's cunning look. She liked her plans even less, because they often ended in them all getting in trouble.

"We can go watch the basketball game. Conner can't ignore you then."

Louise and Leah stared at her critically.

"Basketball?"

"Daniel says they are playing next door tomorrow, and Conner is happiest when playing basketball."

"Daniel Fisher. Didn't you say he's a flirt and spends more

time chatting with customers than working?" Louise folded both arms over her chest. "Should we be taking advice from someone like him?"

"He knows about these sorts of things. He spends time with Conner, since Conner works for his bruder, Jesse. If you don't like my idea, then tell us yours." Beth crossed her arms over her chest and glared at Louise. "You're the oldest and know more about how to get a man's attention, I reckon."

Louise sputtered out a laugh. She was the plainest of plain, which is why few men ever glanced her way. She couldn't even turn the head of the one man who knew her the longest.

"We are not to strive for attention," Louise scoffed.

"Levi Yoder is always saying sweet things to you," Leah corrected.

"Nee, he says I can set a good table and he likes blackberry jam. His stomach may be flirting, but not his heart."

"Well. . ." Leah tapped her foot stubbornly. "Marcus has always thought you pretty. He told Alma that a pretty maedel like you would be snatched up faster than a ladybug in a bird's beak. Or was it a grasshopper?"

Louise was speechless. *Marcus said what?*

"Anyways, that isn't important." Beth waved it off, though Louise suddenly found the surprising revelation a little important. Since when did Marcus King think her pretty?

"This is possibly our last Christmas here. I think you should tell him how you feel. He might follow you all the way to Kentucky." When Beth was hit with an ounce of passion, she beamed like a snowflake on a frosty window.

"You think so?" Leah perked up.

"I say we go. We can talk you up to him." Louise had no

intention of going—just seeing Clare deliver snacks for the break—but somehow Beth had encouraged it out of her.

"But that's a *buwe* thing," Leah said. "Amos says they can get really competitive. It's not like volleyball at all. You've not been to a gathering for too long, Sister."

"And the last time I was, maedels weren't seeking after the buwe, but the other way around." She inhaled. "I was invited, so no one will mind you both going too. Besides, it might be fun," Louise said unconvincingly.

"Invited to watch them play basketball? By who?" Beth questioned, a stickler for details.

Louise reached out for Blinkers and cradled him in her arms. "Marcus said I should kumm." Louise felt her cheeks warm at the admission. "He's hoping I bake a few things for it," she confessed, "but it's still an invite."

"Did he now?" Beth chuckled.

"It's not like you think. He was just missing his mamm's baking. It's the least he could do since he bought our house."

"He'd give it back to you if you'd only ask," Leah continued to tease.

"You're baking for Marcus." Beth looked at Louise, not letting the little detail slip under what was really important here. Then she looked at Leah. "You can even borrow my evergreen dress. It makes your eyes look prettier."

"Oh, that would be wonderful. Danki, Schwesters, for understanding. Mamm and Daed just don't appreciate how much I love him." Louise suspected they did, but it was more the lack of love being shown by Conner that didn't convince them to pay much mind to Leah's courting beau.

"Change can be gut," Beth said. "No matter how it comes.

But I hope you both always see it as a blessing like I do."

Louise considered Beth's words as she slipped under her quilt that night. Change was a part of life, but suddenly Louise wondered if change might disrupt everything she loved.

CHAPTER SIX

$\mathcal{T}$he Kings' barn wasn't a barn really, but a huge metal building, complete with concrete floors marked in red, white, and yellow lines, with two goals at each end. In years past, it had held seed and produce and machinery too large to fit in Malachi's woodshop for making toys. Now all that was left of Kings' toys was tucked away in the small wooden shop nearest the house.

Beth loved get-togethers next door when she could ride her scooter across the floors faster than Fred and the other boys her age. The Kings had been wonderful neighbors, and she was going to miss them.

Louise insisted on being late. Beth hated tardiness, but older sisters did know best as all eyes landed on them when they entered the side door carrying two trays of Louise's best walnut-and chocolate-chip-cookies and peanut butter blossoms.

"I thought when you said we were going to a gathering tonight, you meant something different," Alma whispered to Leah. Alma reminded Beth of a goldfinch with her light hair, small features, and passion for bird-watching.

"It's a gathering." Leah waved a hand.

"I had Marcus put out a table," Clare said as she led the gaggle of awkward maedels to a far corner where three buggies rested out of the weather. The table already held cups and lemonade and what Beth suspected was cocoa in a tall green thermos.

Whoops and cheers echoed over the space. Perhaps she could talk the *maeds* into a game too. Beth liked volleyball, and after playing with Amos and Caleb, who both clearly cheated and took advantage of her smaller size, she found basketball to be just as fun. Who didn't like learning something new?

"Might as well get used to that. They make a lot of noise." Clare rolled her eyes.

"Kumm, let's sit over there by the buggy so we can see better," Clare prodded. "Marcus promised they wouldn't play long tonight so we could enjoy what Louise baked."

"How did he know I'd even come?" Louise asked.

"Ach, Louise, why do you ask me foolish questions?"

Beth couldn't ignore the flicker of surprise on her sister's face. They all found a seat where they could see the game unfold. Beth nestled next to Louise, who watched the game with unprecedented interest. Beth wondered if something was going on between her eldest sister and Marcus lately. They had been neighbors all their life, but as far back as Beth could recall, neither Marcus nor Louise ever showed an interest in anyone. Beth felt a grin emerge. Louise might be the best secret keeper ever.

"When Issac and I marry, we agreed no more youngie games," Clare said, giving Issac a wave.

"One must grow up," Louise replied.

"Not if they don't have to," Beth added swiftly. With that thought, her gaze landed on Daniel Fisher.

"Oh, now Conner has the ball." Leah sat on the edge of her seat. Her twin was ridiculous. No way could Beth ever be so smitten with a man her whole future depended on his next move. Conner was very athletic according to Leah, but as Beth watched him move between Silas and Enoch and push hard against Marcus to reach the basket, she found his pushiness a little unsportsmanlike.

Craning her neck, she watched Daniel move from the center of the court at lightning speed to steal Conner's next score. *If only he moved that fast at work*, Beth mentally grumbled.

With ball in hand, Daniel weaved through Allen and Adam, Conner's team players, and was at the other end of the court before she could bat an eyelash. He didn't even look like he tried to jump, but he reached an amazing height as he forced the ball into the red circle rim roughly. Shouts echoed the whole room, bouncing off walls, and causing Beth's adrenaline to match it. Basketball was a much more exciting sport to watch than to enjoy with two younger bruders.

Daniel smiled his typical wide-brimmed smile as cheers rang out in his favor. He had a nice smile. Then he looked her way and winked. Not once, but twice, as if he wanted to be sure she saw him. Jah, basketball was very addictive, Beth concluded as she restrained herself from moving, flinching, or cheering for a pest like Daniel Fisher throughout the rest of the game.

"At least he's good at something," she mumbled.

"Marcus says if he wasn't Amish, he could be a professional. Too bad he'd rather use his mouth to make a living," Clare informed them with a sarcastic tone.

Before Beth could inquire how one used their mouth to make a living, Daniel had the ball again and her attention was gone again. She held her breath as Daniel smacked the ball against the floor and passed it to Marcus. His height gave him an advantage over the younger men, but Conner was working his way to a stealthy steal when Marcus tossed the ball to Isaac, who in a split-second decision, put it back in Daniel's hands. Daniel dodged around Conner and did what Clare called a layup. Beth didn't know all the names for maneuvers but was impressed.

Daniel made a few baskets and missed a few more, but one thing she noticed throughout the game: Daniel didn't boast about the points he earned, and he didn't grumble at shots missed. He simply focused on the next move. Something about that spoke to her in ways she didn't understand.

"Finally, break!" Alma made her way to the snacks first. For a little thing, she always had the healthiest appetite. Daniel and Marcus marched to one corner, feeding the wood barrel stove once more. They too seemed ready for a break, a snack time taken after an event. Conner stalked behind the others a few paces. No one liked a sore loser.

"These are my favorite," Issac said. "Did you make them?" he asked Clare.

"Nee, these are Louise's. You know I haven't had much time for such. My dress is almost done."

"Have your parents left already?" Marcus asked as he approached, his eyes roaming over the table greedily.

"Jah. They left last night with a driver. Mamm is hoping to see the house and determine what is needed, and Daed wants to ensure fencing is ready," Leah offered.

Conner moved into the clutch, and Beth wondered just how this plan of hers was gonna work. Did she just blurt it out? Remind Conner of all the fine qualities her sister had? *Just don't mention baking or cooking*, she told herself.

"I thought this was no hens allowed." He glared at Marcus.

"And miss a bunch of pretty maeds in new dresses?" Daniel laughed. Beth floated him a thankful smile.

"Louise and Beth thought it would be fun. You play really well, Conner," Leah said shyly. "Let me pour you some hot cocoa, or would you prefer lemonade?"

"Lemonade and some kichlin."

Leah hurried to pour his cup and snatched three cookies, placed them on a napkin, and folded it over before handing them to him.

"Conner, you should give Leah a ride home. Louise and I promised Clare we would help tidy up. I'm sure Leah would much rather ride home with you than us after working all day."

"I can do that, but I told John Denton and the fellas I'd meet up with them later."

Beth flinched at the name. John Denton was Englisch and was known to throw wild parties that many of the Amish youth attended. Beth had even attended one, but after watching others drink and dance, she swore never to attend another. There was having fun, and there was being reckless with one's body and soul.

"It's the least you could do since she had to get a ride home from Marcus the other day," Alma said boldly.

"I had to work," Conner defended, shooting Marcus another sharp glare. "Come on, Leah. I'll take you home first." Conner motioned to her sister to follow.

"Conner," Daniel called out to him. "Make the right one." The men simply stared at one another for a good three minutes, words passing between them Beth wished she could hear.

"I have." Conner turned and marched toward the door, Leah scampering to catch up.

"I don't know what she sees in him," Alma muttered.

"Did he even notice her dress?" Louise whispered.

"I doubt it." Beth felt something jab in her gut. Her twin was not protecting her heart. Turning, Beth found Daniel still standing at arm's length. He slipped a whole peanut butter blossom in his mouth. The tip of the chocolate on top smashed against his upper lip.

"You are so smart, Daniel Fisher. I'm glad we followed your advice." She glared up at him. He looked a little silly with chocolate on his face like that.

"I was trying to help you. I cannot help how it all works out." Daniel's brows knitted into a frown. "I don't like to think about Leah with him either or that he still acts like a youngie," Daniel said with an angry look.

"Wipe your face Daniel Fisher, before someone sees you." He made an attempt and missed the mark altogether. Out of pity, Beth reached up and swiped her thumb across his mouth. "There, now you don't look like a *boppli* stealing from the jar." She grinned.

"I like kichlin and bopplin, and now you have chocolate on your fingers." He reached out and latched on to Beth's hand. For one quick instant, Beth wasn't sure what Daniel was going to do. She let out a breath when he wiped her hand down the side of his trouser leg. "Now we pass as grown-ups." He winked.

A knot formed in Beth's throat. Not from the unease of her sister giving her heart to the wrong man or because Louise was ogling Marcus as he followed Leah and Conner to the door to speak to them. Beth's heart was pounding so fast she wondered if she might drop dead right there on the concrete floor because, unexpectedly and against her best judgment, some of Daniel's well-known charms had spilled over on her and *that* couldn't happen.

"Wait here. I'll fetch us some hot chocolate." Daniel hurried off before she could even decline. What made him think he could tell her what to do? Before Beth could gather her thoughts,

Daniel returned with two cups of steaming hot chocolate and a napkin of Louise's kichlin.

Beth accepted the hot chocolate on impulse and studied the man. "Don't you own a coat?" Suddenly Beth hoped he did. If not, Beth was going to have to sew him one to keep him from freezing to death.

"I do, but basketball warms you up. Thanks for being so concerned. A man likes to know when he's in a woman's thoughts."

"I don't think about you, Daniel Fisher." They both turned back to the door as Marcus strolled back inside. Beth felt for her twin. Love had failed her, or at least what she believed love to be.

"She'll be heartbroken and in turn, I'll be—"

"You'll be miserable," he finished. "He's not for her," Daniel mumbled.

"He might be," Beth defended. "He might," she repeated.

"Beth—" Daniel turned, taking up her other hand. "We make time for who and what is important to us. Remember that."

"I could never love a man who didn't hear a thing I had to say."

"Nee, you could not."

"You could talk to him."

"I've talked to him. Yelled at him," Daniel admitted. "He's using her so his folks don't suspect he's might jump the fence."

"Why would he do that?" Beth gawked up at him as if he'd sprouted horns.

"That, I can never answer."

"I don't understand it. He has someone who cares for him, despite his flaws." Did not love conquer a multitude of troubles and shortcomings? Did not the birth of one child change the whole world?

"He's struggling, Beth, between his faith and his freedom."

"But how can one be free without faith to guide you? It would be like walking with nowhere to go! He is turning his back on Gott." It was a serious matter, they both knew.

"A man must choose a side, and he has. You don't go back on your choices, that's why you make sure to make the right ones."

"But it could be a mistake. You could talk to him. Tell him he has someone who loves him. Someone who will help him through this."

"Oh, Beth. You see her love for him, but you're missing the whole picture. Do you see his love. . .for her?"

"Only Gott can see the whole picture." Beth shrugged, hating how smart Daniel Fisher suddenly sounded.

"I love how much you care for her, but you're not blind, Beth. You see what we all see. Leah deserves better."

"She does." Beth surrendered. "But I see things from being her twin."

"I see a lot too." Daniel moved closer. Were they talking about Conner and Leah still?

His nearness sent a shiver up her spine, but when he reached out and boldly latched three hooks of her coat, Beth was certain she was being chastised because a sudden race of gooseflesh riddled over her.

"You really need someone to follow *you* about in the cold too," he said with a chuckle. "Want to go skating?"

"Huh?"

"For a woman who likes adventure, you sure question having any."

"Right now?" He was a *dummkopp* who had no common sense. So why was her chest thundering at his question? "It's freezing out there, and it's dark, and—"

Daniel laughed. "Next Saturday, after my shift at the market."

Daniel reached into his pocket and pulled out his gloves. Beth was momentarily stunned by the way his eyes could smile along with his lips. Daniel worked the green knitted gloves over her fingers. She should be concentrating on her sister, not letting Daniel touch her.

"Folks may think us. . .courting." Beth had never courted before. Most men found her too talkative, and her idea of fun was not common for a maed hoping to marry and start a family, but suddenly the thought carried some appeal. With the right man of course. Not Daniel Fisher. No, not him, but maybe a man who shared her idea of adventure and trying out new things. Someone who would let her be a mamm and try on new hobbies. Kentucky might produce such a man, if Gott willed it.

"Folks don't pay no mind to friends hanging out together, Beth Ann."

Daniel had never called her by her full name. She wasn't even sure how he knew what it was, but the way he said it sent a second run of shivers over her.

"Besides, I thought we were not to care what others think." He lifted a cocky brow.

"I like ice-skating." He smiled as if he already knew that too.

Daniel opened the door leading outside. "Let me give you a ride home." A waft of frigid air splashed over her cheeks, but upon his request, Beth paid it no mind.

"I have to help Louise. I came with her, remember?" Poor fella, he had the mind of a cantaloupe.

"Marcus will see Louise home. She knows I'm seeing you home."

"She does?" Beth stared through the small crowd for Louise. She was nibbling on a cookie while Marcus spoke with her.

"I told her earlier."

"You did not," Beth slapped his arm, helpless against it.

"She said that was a good idea. I think I'm growing on her." There came those winks again. He was insufferable.

"Like mold on cheese," Beth added under her breath.

"Last one to the buggy has to drive."

Beth barely had time to respond to Daniel's childishness, when he took off toward the buggies waiting in the dark outside. Well, she may be small, but she was fast yet.

CHAPTER SEVEN

*T*he annual school Christmas recital began at noon. Mamm always prepared treats for the occasion, so Louise started early despite not having kinner of her own participating. It was the way of it. Community supported community, no matter what the day delivered. The kinner always did a wonderful job memorizing their lines, and often a joke would bring everyone to laughter before songs were even sung. Louise looked forward to the event each year.

Staring down at the sugar cookie with green icing, she was supposed to add little red berries to give the cookie wreath a more Christmassy look. She tried to muster up a little holiday cheer. No matter how sweet the kitchen smelled or how perfect the little wreaths were turning out, Louise didn't feel very Christmassy at all.

Mamm had left a message on the phone answering machine on Tuesday, saying they would be delayed an extra week, which meant Louise needed to get started packing while filling her newest Christmas jam orders. Two local shops were adding them to baskets, doubling their regular order. Hopefully Beth could bring home more cranberries, as Louise was running awfully low.

Then there was the matter of Marcus King. His strange behavior lately was leaving Louise perplexed. First he invited her to a basketball game, trusted she would come bearing cookies, and then fussed over Leah like she was his own. He even thought to see her home, despite her having her own buggy.

Marcus was filling her head. He was simply everywhere since buying their farm. Currently he was just outside, helping Caleb and Mitchel get a good price out of the contents in the barn. Why after all these years was he inserting himself into her life? Was he simply being neighborly, or was he hurrying things along so he could take over?

The washroom door burst open, snapping Louise back to the present.

"Your boyfriend is bossy," Mitchel grumbled as he ran into Daed's office to fetch a few papers. "I had a good price for the buggies, but Marcus is demanding more. Don't see why it's any of his concern."

"Daed asked him to come." A fact Louise still hadn't understood. "Make sure you get the blue notebook—it holds the herd breeding records." Mitchel grumbled a few unrecognizable words and ran back into the office. He emerged with the blue notebook and swiped a cookie from the cooling rack.

"If you didn't bake so well, I might find a way to embarrass you by telling him you snore." He grinned.

"He's not my boyfriend," Louise called out, but he was already out the door. "And I don't snore."

"Little cookie thief," Beth fussed, closing the door behind him. "He shouldn't have skipped school today. I'm never having sons of my own. Too much trouble."

"Only when they're grown." Louise smiled. Mitchel had been an adorable toddler and always the most eager to taste her new jelly flavors first.

"Do you think three dozen is enough?" She counted the cookies already cooling. The Christmas recital was one of the biggest events of the year for scholars. No one missed it, and each family always brought their share of treats for afterward.

"Do you remember when we were kinner and reciting our lines for the Christmas recital?" Leah slipped cookies into boxes and covered them with plastic wrap. She had drawn little snow-flakes and stars on them with silver and blue food markers. Her baking needed work, her definition of love needed to be redefined, but she always made everything around her more beautiful. The little cardinal stickers were a nice touch, Louise noted.

"I remember you throwing up when it came your turn to speak." Beth nudged her twin's arm playfully.

"I was eight, and not everyone has your confidence in leading songs. Life was less complicated—"

"When we were kinner," Beth finished. "I'm sorry, Leah." Beth gave her twin a worried brow.

"Conner isn't the same." Leah sulked. "He's changed."

"People change." Louise was discovering how true that was. Marcus, for one, had changed. "I never would have guessed Beth would ride home with Daniel Fisher. They even had a foot race to the buggy."

"You did?" Leah's eyes bulged wide with joy. "I knew you two would make a match."

"We are not a match." Beth rolled her eyes. "He wants us to go ice-skating though." She turned a smile on Louise. "I'm sure you and your special friend can kumm."

"Who?" Leah begged.

"Marcus King. He's got stars in his eyes for our Louise," Beth informed her twin.

"He does not." Louise slung the icing bag in her hand toward Beth instead of a finger point. A blob of red icing flew into the air and landed on Beth's cheek. Leah snickered, covering her mouth. A lot of good that did when, seconds later, she burst out into outlandish laughter.

"What are you laughing at?" Beth asked her twin, perturbed. She lifted the blob with her finger and turned the accidental icing mishap into an intentional attempt at quieting her twin by smearing the blob down Leah's arm.

"Ach! Beth! What's wrong with you?"

"Louise's condition must be catching." Beth reached out and collected another finger dip of icing from the bowl, holding Leah hostage to quiet her amusement with the smear still on her finger.

"How old are you two?" Louise scoffed, tapping a spoon on the table to gain control. If it wasn't her brothers wrestling, it was the twins battling their scant differences. "No wonder neither of you are married yet. You're acting like kinner."

"Jah." Beth turned her sly grin onto Louise. "We are. We"— Beth pointed to herself and Leah—"have no plans of becoming sour old spinsters. And we love you."

"We do," Leah put in, reaching for her own ammunition.

"What are you two doing?" Louise took two steps back. Those sweet faces weren't fooling Louise.

"We are going to sweeten you up schwester," Beth replied.

"You will not!"

Leah cocked her head, and Louise could see she was considering her next move. "If she refuses to let Marcus do it, then—"

"Leah and I must see to the task ourselves," Beth finished.

Louise knew those looks, and before either sister swiped the bowl of green icing still resting on the table, Louise turned to run. She was still plenty able to outrun them.

Unfortunately her escape ended abruptly. Colder weather meant shutting doors like the one leading to the washroom. Louise smacked the door with her face, hard. So hard, she bounced back, landing on her bottom with a solid thump that jarred the dishes in a nearby cabinet.

"Ouch!"

"*Ach du lieva*! Louise!" Beth cried out.

The pain was indescribable—something between a hornet sting and a hoof to the face. And there was blood. So much blood. Louise quickly brought her apron up to her nose to try to stop the flow. She could feel the onset of swelling. Her eyes already watered from pain, so crying was no use. As sore as her backside felt from her hard landing, Louise was certain her nose had taken the worst of her misadventure. Surely it was broken.

"You're bleeding *baremlich*," Leah said. "Lay your head back some. Beth, get ice!"

Sounds of shoes smacking the linoleum floors told her Beth was fetching ice while Leah rushed to collect dish towels.

"The kault will help stop the flow of it. Here, let me apply some pressure," Leah said, kneeling on the floor next to her.

Leah's natural instincts surfaced, but her not-so-tender touch immediately sent a fresh wave of pain to Louise's nose. "That hurts." Louise tried to hold it in place herself. If not for the nausea threatening, she might have been able to apply more pressure. She closed her eyes. It was her own doing, running as she had. How many times since they were toddlers had Mamm fussed at them to never run in the house?

"It's still bleeding, Beth. Hurry up!"

The door that had been the tool to Louise's current mishap suddenly flung open. Louise opened her watery eyes to discover her bruders staring down at her. With them. . .Marcus. All three were out of breath and looking at Louise as if she had just been shot.

"What happened?" Marcus said gruffly and quickly came to her side. Yanking off his gloves, he knelt. "Let me take a look," he insisted. Mortified, Louise tried covering her injury as best she could. What woman wanted to be bloody and sallow when being looked at by her handsome neighbor?

"*Veck*! Don't touch it." Those big hands would surely bring further pain.

"I'll not let go. You're hurt."

"She was fine like three minutes ago," Mitchel said, as if that was of importance. "Did you hit her?" His glare shot straight to Beth.

"Now why would you think I'd do that?" Beth knelt, offering Marcus a fresh towel. "Here's some more ice. She smacked into the door, really hard."

"Did you push her?" Caleb fell to his knees on Louise's right side. "Louise, let us see how bad it is."

Louise would have shaken her head no if such movement was an option.

"Kumm now, *schatzi*." Marcus urged her hand away, revealing the true face of being a clumsy idiot. He winced, proof it looked as horrible as she felt.

"Leah, gather more towels?"

Behind her, Leah scrambled to the drawer and raced to the sink. The water turned on, but it was blue eyes with forever galaxies holding Louise's attention. At least it helped the pain lessen. . .a little.

"It's swelling fast," Marcus informed her.

"It's crooked," Caleb added. "It's *gebrochen!*"

"As broken as your thoughts," Beth muttered. "Why would you think I'd push her?"

"I dunno. You have a. . .temper." Louise tried not to smile, but when Marcus' lips curved slightly, so did hers. He'd probably dealt with siblings quarreling at times too.

"Let's try to clean some of this up and see what we have to work with," Marcus said.

"We might better *geh*," Caleb said. "She needs it seen to."

Having Marcus tend to her sent a fresh awareness through her. It was probably best if she just fainted.

"Mitchel, run and call a driver. Tell them it's an emergency." Mitchel rushed out of the room. Thankfully the landline phone was not far from the house.

"It's bad, jah?" Even talking hurt, so Louise decided she wouldn't do much of that.

"Nee, Sister," Beth said with a forged smile. "It's just messy. We need more towels."

Louise groaned. She hated being so much trouble. She would have been better off covered in red icing. *And what of the Christmas recital?* One act of stupidity, and she had ruined everything.

"You remember when Fred broke my nose with a baseball?"

Louise did remember, but looking at him now, she could see no evidence of it. He let off some pressure but quickly applied it again when more blood rushed out.

"It feels worse than it is, but we best get it seen to." He leaned closer. Close enough Louise could smell peppermint on his breath.

"A nose this cute can't be lopsided forever."

Louise's eyes widened at the admission. Well, if Marcus had ever thought her nose cute, he'd soon change his mind. Could this day get any worse?

"Caleb, you stay here. Mr. Bolton is on his way to look over that stack of doors and windows in the barn, and Ammon said if we didn't sell all three buggies, to give him a call."

"I can handle calling Ammon," Mitchel announced, entering the room again. Louise opened one eye to find him looking down at her in shock from a safe distance. Not everyone could handle the sight of blood. Who knew he had a weakness?

"You best get to school. Your folks won't like you missing the whole day," Marcus ordered before turning back to Caleb. "Don't let him get that wagon for less than we talked about. He likes to talk down to a fella. You gotta be firm."

"I can do that."

"What about the kichlin for the recital?" Leah asked, looking to Marcus for a reply. Since when did Marcus King make decisions for her family?

"The recital," Louise groaned.

"Mitchel can take them with him and tell folks"—he glanced down to her again—"tell them Louise is home with a stuffy nose and is being seen after." Louise narrowed a look at him.

"Good one." Mitchel laughed. "I'll get them right over." He was best known for arguing. So why didn't he listen to her as obediently?

"I called our neighbor, and he's pulling in now," Mitchel announced.

Louise made a motion to move. "Hold on," Marcus said as he got to his feet. Without warning, he bent forward. "Put your arm around mei neck." Effortlessly, he lifted her from the floor.

It was her nose that was hurt, not her legs. Fainting was surely going to come to her now. Louise was no dainty woman. Her height alone contributed to her weight, even if she didn't pack on any extra pounds. Out of instinct, she wrapped a tight arm around Marcus' neck and glanced about the room. Beth stood with her mouth open, while Leah smiled, holding a pile of soiled towels.

"Beth, you help Caleb. Between the two of you, I reckon Ammon won't get a practically new buggy for a few bills. And please put the money up until Louise returns to see to it." Marcus shifted his body toward the door. "Leah, could you gather her cloak and bonnet. You should kumm along with us."

"Jah." Leah hurried to collect those things.

And just like that, Marcus King had come to her aid, organized the chaos she had created foolishly, and carried her out into the cold. With the pain of the fall matching that of her nose, dizziness took over. It was strange to be carried.

"Keep this." Marcus handed her his handkerchief, a simple blue-and-white design, after seeing her safely inside the back seat. He closed the door and climbed into the front.

Eighty-six-year-old Mr. Dauley looked back. "I got here as fast as I could. Cold weather and this old car aren't friends. You just sit back and rest, Louise. I sure hate that you got hurt."

He was a gentleman. A huge fan of Louise's Christmas jams. But Louise was almost certain Mr. Dauley no longer carried a license to drive.

"Thanks for coming out with such short notice," Marcus offered.

As the car began to pull out of the drive, Louise leaned her head back and felt her shoulders sag. She was suddenly grateful Marcus was there. Someone would have to be strong enough to pull her and Leah out of the impending crash if Mr. Dauley forgot how to navigate, she thought as she closed her eyes.

CHAPTER EIGHT

*O*nce Beth saw Louise safely tucked in bed, she slipped down the hall to her shared bedroom. The wind outside howled angrily, but with the medications given her, Louise would sleep through it.

"Is she resting?" Leah asked as she climbed into her side of the bed.

"She is. She looks so miserable and the bruises are more noticeable now."

"Poor Louise. I just hope we get her to the next church service. She will likely hide in her room until all the swelling and bruises are gone."

"Especially around Marcus King," Beth added. It was fun to jest about the sparks growing between Louise and Marcus, but Beth feared if they kept sparking, Louise might have second thoughts about moving to Kentucky.

"Or that tape. I wouldn't want anyone to see me like that either I guess."

"I shouldn't have teased her," Beth confessed. "This is all my fault."

"It was both our faults, but you're right about Marcus. Did

you hear him call her *dearest*?" Now that Leah mentioned it, Beth did recall the endearment.

"When the doctor went to tape her nose, I was sure I'd get ill and left the room. But when I returned, Marcus was holding her hand."

"Whatever. You have never gotten sick before, even when I cut my finger slicing peaches last summer." Beth still bore the scar of the mishap. What was her twin up to?

"Jah, but Marcus and Louise didn't know that. The way he looks at her, is how I wanted Conner to look at me."

"Are you playing match meddler?"

"Someone needed to. It's so plain between them. Marcus didn't say hardly a word the whole time, just sat by her. He did say something about strawberries being good medicine." Leah's nose scrunched, sharing the detail.

"Sounds like he hit his head." After changing into her gown, Beth slipped under the warmth of the heavy quilts.

"Sounds like a farmer. I've always liked Marcus and think he'd make a good brother-in-law."

"But we can't let her stay behind. We are a family," Beth quarreled.

"We will still be family. Don't you want her to be happy? She loves this house, her business, and him. She just won't admit it. Marcus is perfect for her. He sees her. He hears her." Leah stared up to the ceiling, her hands gathered over the quilt tucked around her. "It says more than someone with lots of fancy words."

Beth agreed that Marcus was a man of few words and believed he would make a good brother-in-law. "Jah, some men say too much while others say nothing at all."

"I won't be staying," Leah confessed, surprising her. Beth sat up quickly.

"You're not?" Beth felt elated at the news. She wanted Leah happy, but being so far apart from her twin was going to prove difficult.

"Conner doesn't want to marry," Leah said in a tone Beth had never heard before. She didn't seem upset. She sounded like a woman who just accepted she was the shortest member of the family. "I think he wants to jump the fence."

Daniel had revealed just as much. "I hope you are wrong about that. He could be shunned."

"I told him that, but he doesn't care. He blames his daed for many things. He doesn't appreciate all they have done for him." Leah turned to her twin. "I'm not sure if my heart understands how someone can love you, but love the world more."

Beth didn't understand either. Love was forever. It was devoted and set in stone. Their parents were a great example of what love was.

"I want to still be his friend—I think he needs one right now—but I'm not sure he will listen to what I have to say."

"You can only try, but what can one person really do to change the heart of another?"

"One birth changed everything. One friend might change his plans. He is a good man. Conner just has too many people around him that are bad influencers."

"Just promise me one thing, Sister." Beth turned to face her. "If Conner jumps the fence, don't follow him."

"I wouldn't. I will never abandon my faith. I've already accepted that I will leave. Gott's plan for me isn't here. I knew that for some time. I only had to accept it."

Beth was glad her twin had come to this conclusion herself. They held hands like they did when they were but toddlers waiting for a storm to quiet so they could sleep.

"Will you promise me something too?" Leah asked, looking tightly at Beth.

"What do you want me to promise?"

"Promise me you will follow Gott's plan for you too, even if you are afraid to do it."

"I will." Beth hugged her twin and knew whatever the future held, they would always face it together.

CHAPTER NINE

*T*he next day Beth breathed in the cool crisp air as Daniel veered the buggy into the small lot next to two other buggies at Ronk's Pond. The sky had dumped a fresh bed of snow over the crusty earth overnight, but the temperatures held to a comfortable forty degrees.

"Guess we aren't the only ones out today," Daniel remarked, helping her from the buggy. He gathered up their skates and led her to a fallen log near the water's edge.

Beth brushed snow from the log, then sat and began working on her skates. They were a little tight, considering she had worn two pairs of socks to keep her feet warm. "Aren't you skating?" Why was he hesitating? "You don't even have your skates on yet." She wrinkled her nose.

"I'm getting there." Daniel pulled his gaze from the pond back to her, a look of concern on his brow.

"Something wrong?" Beth stood, waiting.

"Nee." He regained his confident smile and began working off one boot. "Nothing is wrong now. I'll hurry, but don't forget, I'm not very sure-footed on ice."

"Then don't break a leg," Beth said as she made her way out onto the frozen pond. The blades connected, and her feet found wings. She needed to put a little space between herself and Daniel. Those long looks made her head fuzzy.

Adding a little more speed, she didn't want to think about this being a date, the kind she often read about in her mystery novels. Mamm thought too much reading might influence her thoughts about love, so Beth settled for mysteries instead. Unfortunately, most of those had elements of love buried within their strategic plots, and currently too many romantic notions about Daniel Fisher were filling her thoughts.

Two young girls with red hair tucked under black scarfs moved in slow motion. One flew out her arms to regain her balance, while the other tiptoed forward at a snail's pace. Their father latched onto both girls' hands. Beth skated around them, tossing an encouraging smile over her shoulder.

She recalled the feel of the frosty air and a sore backside from her first time on Ronk's Pond. Daed had taken each of them out alone, as Mamm, much like Louise, never enjoyed the thrill of gliding over ice. When Beth's turn came, Daed told her how good she was, and how he imagined she would be good at a great many things. It had born in her an itch to try out new things—an itch that often needed scratching.

With the wind on her cheeks, Beth reached the starting point again. Daniel had finally moved onto the ice. He looked like a new deer, fresh on its legs, forcing a giggle out of her. He was so good at everything he did. It was nice seeing he too knew what it was like to wobble on both legs.

"Need a hand?" She slowed up beside him, spinning backward, and showing off a bit. When his gaze met hers, Beth felt a flutter of newness, warming her internally.

"Jah." Daniel reached out, clasping tight to her right hand. Spinning around, she set the pace and wondered if hand holding was allowed among friends.

"You best keep me steady or we will both fall," he said.

That's why Beth didn't let go.

The lake was beautiful under a noonday sun. Snow shimmered over the tilted landscape. Old cedars hung heavily in new fallen snow. They noted a clutch of young boys moving onto the ice, long sticks in their hands. Surely a hockey game was about to commence.

"Thanks for not abandoning me." Daniel winked.

"I have no choice. Friends help friends who struggle." She smiled playfully.

"You always have a choice with me, Beth. Remember that. I'm just glad today, I'm yours." Another comment to send her head swirling and heart racing.

They moved around the shallow end as a few more youngies moved onto the ice. Henry Reihl yelled out to his cousins to hurry and fell hard on his backside, causing Beth to snicker.

"Well, guess I'm not the only clumsy one out here." Daniel chuckled. "Tell me something," he said, working the toe of his blade to gain momentum.

"You really aren't so bad at skating. I think you tricked me into holding your hand."

"I have a few more tricks up my sleeve," he admitted shamelessly.

"You may grow up yet." Beth had meant it as humor, but when Daniel looped her gloved hand around his forearm, her laughter stalled in the unexpected security.

"I will never stop my tricks. . .with you." He winked. "I have plans, if you want to know. Plans for the future. It's near time I head toward them."

What plans? "What of your job at Kauffman's?"

"I'm only helping them part-time since their *sohn* had that buggy accident. I don't take a wage for it."

"You don't?" *He works not for a wage.*

"It was the least I could do since Dillion was with me and Silas the night he raced his horse with a car. Of course we both told him it was a bad idea, but his ears were closed to our thoughts on it."

"I didn't know that." It had been the highlight of gossip when a group of youngies decided to race a car, ending with a horse dead, a buggy destroyed, a car sunk in a field of mud, and Dillion Kauffman with two broken ankles and a fractured skull.

"Why have you never mentioned that?" Friends mentioned such things, did they not?

"We are not to be proud, but a servant to others. Jesse wanted me to work for him, but I've been helping my onkel at the auctions and it's only part-time for now. It allows me to do both. I have found auctioneering suits me."

He wants to be an auctioneer. Now Clare's comment made sense. A job using his mouth. "You are a fast talker, but doesn't he leave for weeks at a time?"

"There's a lot out there to see, and I don't mind working my way around to see it."

Beth's thoughts scattered to the four corners at this revelation. "You're not staying in Lancaster are you?" Her feet suddenly clipped a dip in the ice. To add further shock to her system, Daniel swung an arm around her protectively and tightened it. They were moving a little fast for a fall. Thankfully Daniel had quick reflexes.

"I'm leaving Lancaster just like you." The arm around her waist loosened slightly, but he didn't let go. Instead, Daniel guided her beyond a clutch of young maedels now on the ice.

"Come spring I'll start my own adventure. I'll be auctioneering for my onkel in different places."

And probably meet a dozen different maedels. Beth's heart felt its first stab. She couldn't recall when her heart had opened to him, but somewhere between working alongside him and racing him to the buggy and taking up the reins, it had.

"What kinds of places?"

Daniel veered them out to the center of the pond as the hockey game widened. "Onkel William has folks wanting us from Gordonville to Shipshewana. Come spring we'll be traveling western Indiana, southern Wisconsin, Illinois, Missouri, Montana." He slowed, knowing full well the effect this was having on her.

"Montana." Beth hated how her voice sounded, but Daniel would see the great mountains she'd only read about. He would see it with someone else.

"And Kentucky," he added, creating an unexpected hope that maybe, just maybe, she would see Daniel Fisher again.

"Then I hope you'll come visit. I might even bake you a raspberry pie."

"I was hoping you'd say that. Raspberry is my favorite." He flashed that smile she had come to find endearing, encouraging, and only meant for her.

Beth could see him, the auctioneer. His voice did carry a cadence that lulled you. His command over others came gentle but firm. Her own strong will had fallen victim to it as well.

"I don't think you oughta move." Beth crossed her right foot over her left to make the slight turn and Daniel did the same.

"You're moving." A fact she hadn't forgotten.

"I'm going with my family. You'll be alone. You'll have no home, Daniel Fisher," she said, hiking her voice. "You'll be homeless." He was chasing adventures, and she couldn't quarrel with that, but he'd be alone. She always had her family close at hand.

"I will have a home, a place to go to if all comes out right."

There went his annoying confidence again. How could he know all would come out right? Nothing felt right at all. He weaved them toward a shallow edge where tall cedars reached the water's edge. Within the bosom of their heavy arms, wild things hid and thrived.

"I don't plan on being alone either." He spun around, facing her under an awning of wide green drapes and steel-blue juniper berries. "Do *you* not want to see more, Beth?"

"I do before I marry." She wasn't ready to marry, become the confirmed fraa and mamm just yet, but he was making it terribly hard to not see a family in her near future.

"So you want a family?" His gaze lowered to their joined hands. His thumb was making small circles on her gloves.

"I want a great many things, jah. Gott knows I do. I want life, adventure, and security first." Honesty was the best response, Daed always said. Hers often gifted her a few perplexed looks. Daniel wasn't looking perplexed. He looked. . .like Beth had just handed him a challenge.

"Family is life and safety. It can also be an adventure," Daniel added with a wry grin.

"Don't I know it." She glanced out, seeing families laugh alongside one another. Perhaps they shouldn't be under snowy branches on a romantic day.

"Love is an adventure."

So she was discovering, or at least the sparks of it, as Daniel Fisher held her hands in his and stared all starry-eyed down on her. Beth felt the slow changes over weeks, embraced the warmth of a heart opening wider. She knew love in various ways, and now she was discovering the love that grew between a man and woman.

"Your pretty head is thinking too hard."

"You think I'm pretty?"

"That is not a real question. You have always been beautiful, Beth, but even more when your eyes light up watching kinner skating and young boys get a little rough playing hockey. You smile every time a new face walks into the market, like you're about to make a new friend. When the sun comes up through the main store windows, you watch it like it's not the same sun every day."

"It's not," she replied. "Each new day is a gift and worth watching."

"It is. So is watching you smile when you think I don't know how to skate." He brushed his knuckles over her cold cheek.

"I knew you were faking." She gave his arm a playful pat.

"Tricks, Beth. I have a whole pocketful of them." He reached out and tucked her left ear underneath the black scarf covering her head. He was a master at tricks, and with each new touch, each new compliment, he was ruining all her plans.

"I don't like tricks. I like honesty."

"Honesty, huh?" Daniel placed his hands on her shoulders and simply gazed at her for one long minute.

"Then I will be honest with you now. You worry about your twin as if she is you, yet you are nothing alike. She never shares her thoughts, and you never hold back."

"Are you telling me I talk too much? I already know that, Daniel."

"I love listening to you talk, even about deer and Leah's sorrowful baking or how Mitchel cheats at basketball. I know more about a cat named Blinkers than anyone in Bird-in-Hand should. I know you can run like the wind since you beat me at a footrace in the third grade."

"I'm sure you've gotten faster since then."

"Oh, I have." He leaned closer. "You see Gott's love around you and appreciate it. You drink it in like Mamm's sunshine tea." He stared long and hard at her once more.

"Sunshine tea?" Was he trying to compare her to tea?

"It's sweet and bitter and"—his eyes fell to her lips—"tastes of peppermint and warm sunshine." His gaze lifted and rested there. The sounds of laughter, of voices, faded under the rapid beating in her chest. No way was Daniel Fisher about to kiss her. Yet he remained stone set. Not inching closer, not backing away.

And he looked nervous, which struck a chord in Beth's heart.

"I love mamm's tea." He leaned closer, his breath blending with hers, and Beth was certain she caught a whiff of. . . peppermint. She studied his eyes for secrets and tricks, his brows for cockiness. She didn't like being made a fool of, but somehow she knew in her heart and from the glint in his eyes that he meant what he said. Not only had love found her, it had found him too.

"I sure hope those hills and critters down there are worth it." He leaned closer, so close Beth felt the warmth of his breath fan her lips.

There were moments in life when a woman had to make big decisions. Sometimes they were scary, oftentimes easy, and sometimes they changed the course of everything.

Beth had a decision to make, and Daniel was giving her a chance to do so in his reluctance to close the short space between them. She appreciated his patience while her mind raced through scenarios and her heart raced with angst. This was a man who raced her to buggies, fooled her on ice, and made her heart ache for more. She wasn't afraid of new things, and this time, Beth was going to be first.

In the quiet of snowcapped cedars and two hearts wildly beating in a strange yet perfect rhythm, Beth met him the rest of the way, and sure enough, he tasted just like peppermint. It was her first kiss, and it was everything she'd read about in books, matched with every hope she imagined. The only thing Beth would have changed was the duration.

"You may have just complicated things," Beth said, staring at him.

"You started it," Daniel replied.

"It's Leah's heart I've been so worried over, and now..." Beth stepped back.

"It's yours you're going to have to listen to because I know my heart already." It was a declaration, and Beth felt the newness fill her veins with a fast-pumping adrenaline that caused her to shiver.

The day had grown colder. They would have to leave soon enough. She'd rather stay on the ice, in the warmth of Daniel's hand.

"We should head back before you freeze." Daniel smiled and helped her onto the bank and to the log. She removed her skates and traded them for her shoes.

"Are we ready?" Daniel stood, offering her a hand.

"Yes, Daniel, I am." She let him help her to her feet.

"Say that again," Daniel said in that low tone.

"What?"

"Say 'Daniel.'"

"Daniel."

"Race ya." He took off. The cheater.

CHAPTER TEN

$\mathcal{A}$s a new week presented itself, Louise tackled the laundry with renewed vigor. It was a rare occasion when she had the whole house to herself. Her sisters were working, and Caleb was waiting for the veterinarian to arrive for the inspection of the herd that was required before moving out of state.

Her fingers were nearly frozen by the time she finished hanging clothes. Hopefully the sun would soon be brighter than it was right now, winking behind clouds. She added two more sticks of kindling to the fire, thankful Caleb packed in plenty, stacking it in the washroom for easy fetching.

Louise had resolved to spend today packing the rest of the boxes Marcus had gifted her, but hopefully she'd have time to fill three more jam orders. Then there was figuring out what to cook for supper. Mitchel had been begging for Louise's chicken casserole, but Caleb and Leah had requested Mamm's baked spaghetti. Mitchel should have packed wood too, Louise thought as she slipped out the side kitchen door to fetch a package of sausage from the nearby icehouse. While sausage thawed in the sink, Louise took up where she'd left off in the packing. Even on quiet days, there was plenty of work to be had.

After a couple of hours, her arms ached from muscling boxes and stacking them neatly against the long sitting-room wall. Blinkers moseyed into the room to perch on the windowsill. "Those cardinals are laughing at you," Louise mocked, filling another box with warm-weather shoes. No one would dare wear flip-flops in this weather.

Trinkets and candlesticks, recipe books and mamm's collection of devotionals, all filled another box. With a grunt she slid the box across the room and lifted it on top of another. Releasing an exasperated breath, she wiped her brow.

Though much of the swelling had gone down, breathing through her nose was still a chore. Now she would be a mouth breather like Mr. Dauley. Her poor neighbor had risked a lot seeing her to the hospital. A basket of jams and those pecan bars he was so found of would make a more appropriate thank-you than the one she'd offered while in a medicated stupor.

Glancing about the room, she knew she'd never finish packing before her folks returned tonight. That left Louise with only two options. Not fill her Christmas jam orders today or ask her siblings for more help. Neither was a good option, but she couldn't think of a third.

Delegating some of the tasks meant nothing would be packed right. She sighed at the thought, but she'd simply have to be okay with that. Time was running out.

Time, she pondered, carefully wrapping mamm's clear crystal plates and glasses in old newspapers and pages torn from magazines collected over too many years. Twenty-five years in just a handful of blinks. And what did she have to show for it? *Two boxes and a chest full of things never to be used. That's what.*

Louise wasn't looking for fresh starts like the rest of her

family. She was perfectly content with life as it was. This house, like her life, had been filled with a thousand moments and cherished memories. Memories that also included her neighbors. Marcus King had finally noticed her. Why would God give her all these feelings, all these hopeful thoughts, if He didn't want her to explore them?

"Peaks and valleys." That's what mamm would call her indigestible life right now. It was one thing to grow real romantic notions for someone you'd known all your life. It was another when they held your hand while you had your nose taped into place. She touched her nose and smiled at the memory. Marcus didn't even laugh when the doctor slipped three long pieces of white tape over her fracture. She never knew Marcus to be so. . .attentive. She never knew a heart could want something so much.

The clock in the kitchen did its hourly chime. Three times the bells rang, moving in a counterclockwise circle. She was wasting the day, letting her mind wander when there were chores to be had.

"We've jam to make. No more feeling sorry for ourselves." She wiped her face tenderly of any leaking emotions. Blinkers meowed. "You need to go out? Don't be long. It's too kault for even you." Louise let him out the door to do his business. He'd return soon enough.

"You're talking to a cat," she quipped, closing the door. Maybe she was addlebrained as Clare insisted.

Louise went to the basement and fetched the boxes of pint jars. She washed them fully in soapy hot water, collected lids and rings, and dropped them in a pan of hot water on the stove.

Gathering all the necessary ingredients, a fresh reality jolted her. What would she do if her jams and jellies weren't profitable in Kentucky? Lancaster was a large tourist area, and many of the local stores were happy to help sell them for her, but

Mamm mentioned that the nearest town from their home was a whole thirteen miles away and they would never have to suffer the onslaught of picture-taking tourists again. Louise wasn't sure what she would do if she couldn't make jams and jellies.

It was a fresh despair, having the dream of owning one's own business threatened. So many changes were overwhelming her senses. As she collected the cranberries and strawberries, someone knocked on the back door. Hopefully it was Clare. Louise needed her best friend. So much had happened over the last couple of weeks.

Clare. She would have her happily ever after while Louise spent her last days in Lancaster packing boxes, possibly making her last jams and jellies to sell, and hiding away from Marcus because she couldn't trust her own heart.

"Marcus?" Louise said in surprise. More surprised at how happy she was to see him. There was something to be said about a man holding a cat to make a woman forget she had tape on her nose and confusion in her heart.

"Someone took to wandering again." He shrugged. "We have enough katz, no matter what mei schwester says."

Louise reached out to take Blinkers and suddenly felt self-conscious. At least now the tape was only one piece, and shorter, not covering all of her cheeks.

"I have a mind to have a talk with your bruders," he said, cocking his head to peer behind her.

"Why?"

"I found a can of tuna on my front step, and that fella was eating it up."

"They never stop pestering him." Louise cradled Blinkers affectionately. It was one thing to get her upset, but they had no business involving Marcus in their pestering.

"Making jam?" He peered around her, noting the ingredients strewn over the table.

"Seems I can't make it fast enough lately." She sighed. "I should still be packing, but you know." She shrugged, suddenly lacking the ability to know what to say next.

"I do." Marcus shifted from one foot to the other. The cold outside gave her a sudden chill, but Louise was in no hurry to see him go.

"Christmas morning won't be the same without seeing you cross our field to deliver a basket of goods."

Did he truly cherish all her efforts? "I could leave some for you, or share the recipe with Clare. I'm sure she could see you have some for future Christmases." Christmases he would most likely have with his future wife. Her shoulders lowered at the thought.

"I may have to visit Kentucky sometime, see my shelves plenty full." He smiled bashfully, and there went those same dizzy feelings again.

"You'd travel all the way down there. . .for jam?"

"Well"—his ears grew a little red as he looked to his feet before lifting his gaze to her face—"not just for the jam."

How was she supposed to respond to that? This time the chill that ran over her had nothing to do with standing in the cold doorway.

"Daniel told me he took Beth ice-skating." He made a motion to step inside. "I'm surprised you didn't go."

"Are you kidding? Me on ice skates would certainly call for another trip to the hospital." Louise took a few steps back and closed the door behind him before any more cold air leaked in.

"I reckon so." He chuckled. "Want help?"

"Making jam?" Taken back, Louise simply stared at him. She'd been making jam for years without the need of help.

"A stove can be dangerous." One brow lifted, taking a corner of his mouth with it. Why was she looking at his mouth? Louise lifted her gaze.

"I've been making jam since I was eleven. It's not dangerous."

"You never know. I should stick around, just in case." He winked, working out of his coat and boots.

Awkwardly Louise followed him into the kitchen. Marcus King was offering to help make jam. Her heart did a little gallop just as it had the day she'd helped him assemble a wooden toy. She wanted to spend more time with him, but his timing couldn't be worse. All these years, and now he'd decided to notice her. There wasn't much Louise could do about that. At least she could enjoy the time they had, giving her cherished memories she could call upon when needed on her lonely days ahead.

"I've never made jam, and I'm all yours," Marcus announced. "What do I do first?" he asked, rolling up his sleeves. He still bore a deep leathery tan though his fields had been put to rest months ago. It was best to stay focused on making jam, not on how handsome he was standing in her kitchen, awaiting her instructions.

"You can wash cranberries and strawberries and put them in the pot there."

"That I can do." Marcus moved to the sink while Louise added spices to the pot. "How many orders do you have?"

"Three, but I want to make one extra just in case," she replied, slicing two oranges in half and tossing them in the pot next.

He was staring. "What? It's what makes it taste so good."

"I know what makes it taste so good," he said, his gaze unwavering. He was making this hard, looking at her in such a way.

"You should see Leah when it's her day to cook." Louise pulled from his gaze.

"She'll learn." He moved to wash cranberries next.

"Not from me," she informed him. "She does better when Beth helps her. I don't have twin thinking." Louise rolled her eyes.

"I imagine you are a good teacher, but they are close for sure."

"They know each other's next thoughts, and I'd rather keep mine to myself."

He poured the berries into a bowl and moved to the stove. Louise tried to focus on something else, but having Marcus at hand was making it mighty hard.

"Your thoughts aren't that hard to read." He began pouring the berries into the pot. "But it's something hearing them finish each other's sentences or seeing them eat the same things. They always did make Mamm smile."

Louise warmed at the memory of his mother and the kindness she had always bestowed on everyone around her, especially the twins. "They were adorable bopplin, but like kittens, they grow up and some of their adorableness disappeared."

"That is the way of it." He smiled. "Being oldest isn't easy. We have that in common." He turned to her once more, and Louise felt as if gravity was resting. He was so handsome, like chocolate-covered strawberries on Valentine's Day, which Louise had never been given.

"We have to let this all simmer a bit. Then we add sugar, and finally the pectin." When the pot came to a rolling boil, Louise added sugar as Marcus began stirring. Then she lined the jars on the table nearby. Surprisingly the man who couldn't cook was a great help in making jam.

"Did you hear Leah and Conner decided they were best being friends?" Louise was glad to know they would all be together still.

"Leah is better off without Conner Bricker as a husband."

"Why do you think so?" Louise asked and added the pectin

to the pot. "Let that come to a boil."

"She's got a kind heart," he replied quickly. "She tries, which is better than giving up. She'll make a fine fraa and *mudder* I think."

"She still can't make pancakes without burning them," Louise mused.

"Jah. But that can be remedied with practice. She'd do better with someone who wasn't so restless."

Like him? Marcus was as steady as pine, even in high winds. It was one of the first things she noticed about him all those years ago. He never wavered from doing what was right and never rushed into a matter.

"Beth is restless—and Mitchel," she said. "You are right, though. Leah deserves better."

"If she would look up just once, she'd have half a dozen men proposing marriage to her."

Louise began ladling the jam into jars while Marcus worked the lids and rings on. Suddenly a picture formed in her mind, a collection of comments over the last few weeks. Her hands trembled, splattering jam over the side of the jar. Had she read everything all wrong? Had Marcus only been sweetening her up because he had feelings for Leah? She wiped up her mess and continued filling jars, but Louise had to know. "Marcus, do you have feelings for. . .my schwester?"

He stilled and lifted a befuddled gaze upon her. "What makes you ask that?"

"Well," Louise swallowed, "you bought our house."

"Not for Leah's sake, I assure you."

"You know Leah wants nothing more than to marry, and you said you are ready to settle down. You drove her home and had her ride along to the hospital." Still he stared at her blankly. She was out of line with such questioning, but sometimes the heart led before the brain could catch up.

"You don't have to answer. I shouldn't have asked, but it makes sense."

"How does that make sense?" Now he was irritated. Louise could tell by the way his jaw tightened. She had ruined a perfectly good day and couldn't seem to stop.

"You helped Caleb get a good price on the buggies and helped me when I got hurt. I've known you all my life, and suddenly you are everywhere."

"I've always been here Louise. You just haven't noticed." He resumed putting lids on the jars, but she had soured everything with her runaway thoughts.

Louise had noticed, but when it was apparent Marcus had no interest in her, she practiced daily to not notice him at all. It had worked well enough until he bought their farm.

"She is your schwester," Marcus explained. "You have much to see to, and I didn't mind talking to Conner about how to treat her or helping your family when they needed it. I asked her to come to the hospital for your sake, not mine."

"You did?" Louise paused in pouring the next jar, noting how the tips of Marcus' ears were turning a pretty shade of poinsettia red.

"I know how much you love selling your jams and jellies, and Clare has told me all about your hopes for your own shop." He turned to her and inhaled a breath, letting it out slowly. "I think you should stay. If that's what you want," he added.

Louise wasn't sure what he was asking, but she was sure she couldn't stay in Lancaster, not with her family leaving as they were. "I can't stay, and this will be your home soon enough."

"I told you the land is all I needed, but what I want and what you want isn't so different."

"How do you know what I really want?" There was no way he could ever know what her heart truly desired.

"I know everything there is to know about you, Louise Wickey." Marcus leaned closer, and Louise's heart began to speed up. Marcus, her girlhood crush, was going to kiss her in her mamm's kitchen while making Christmas jam.

A truck engine roared, shredding the moment into a thousand shattered pieces.

"That would be the vet," Marcus whispered and slowly backed away. "I should see to helping Caleb with the chore."

Louise was speechless and frozen to the spot as she watched him slip back into his boots and coat.

"I'm going shopping tomorrow for a few things. I'd like it if you'd go with me." He didn't wait for her reply but simply walked out the door. When the latch clicked, she lowered herself into a chair and burst into tears. Jah, Marcus King had the worst timing ever.

CHAPTER ELEVEN

*L*ife was almost normal again now that her whole family was under one roof. The morning dawned bright, and an unwilted blanket of puffed-up snow lay undisturbed outside the kitchen window. With the scent of cinnamon bread filling the air, Louise finished sealing her newest jam order, careful not to make too much noise while mamm rested in the next room. Since returning home, she'd been resting a lot more than usual, proof the trip had been hard on her.

The sound of a motor roared up the drive. It would be Mr. Pramberger with the special trailer for hauling their precious deer to their new home. Leah craned her neck to peer out the window, her grim expression confirming it.

"Our bruders chatted like old hens again all night," Leah said, peeking into the oven. Louise knew it wasn't time to remove the bread. The scent hadn't grown yet. Something she had learned long ago on instinct.

"I heard. They are just excited about the new haus." Louise slid a fresh label over the front of the jar she had been working on and picked up the next jar.

"Amos said the sun rises through the trees and sets behind a hillside. I will sure miss seeing it come and go slower." Leah shrugged. She had accepted leaving well enough, but Louise knew parts of her would always miss home too.

"Oh, you're almost out of cat food," Leah informed her before collecting a pile of towels and heading up the stairs to get ready for work.

Louise glanced in the corner. Sure enough, the clear plastic container had a scant amount of cat food visible. Had she not just purchased Blinkers a new bag while shopping with Marcus?

Shopping with Marcus had been the most fun Louise had had in years. She'd purchased a new set of candlesticks for mamm, and for Beth a new set of Emma Miller books. For Leah, Louise spotted a hand-carved American finch on a limb. Marcus insisted the Amish wood maker was well known for taking a block of wood and turning it into a thing of natural beauty.

Her heart was stolen, and when Marcus placed a hand on her back, guiding her through crowded stores, she had never known such safety or care before.

And he wants to write me, she recalled him asking, but a bond based on letters couldn't produce a real relationship.

"I smell cinnamon cake." Daed entered the kitchen. He slipped out of his boots, leaving them on a mat of cardboard Louise laid out in hopes of catching some of the moisture.

"It's almost done, and I made more jam too," Louise added. "Just figure the more ingredients I use up, the less I have to pack."

"Smart like your mamm." He winked. "Is Lilly resting?" The tip of his nose was red from the outdoors. Under one arm was a rectangular box.

"She is. Leah is getting ready for work, and Beth is tackling the attic today, but we can be ready to help now that the trailer is here." Louise hurried to the oven as the bread was done.

"I don't envy her. Lots of forgotten things up there, but don't fret." He waved a hand. "I've plenty of help today." Daed set the box on the table. It was a shiny rich brown with gold ribbons and rather thin. Mamm was blessed to be married to a man who never stopped courting her after all these years.

"If you don't mind, make more kaffi. Those fellows out there will need warming when we finish up. I just came in to get my checkbook for the driver." He slipped into his office briefly and slipped back into the kitchen.

"Never knew it would cost so much to move a few deer between one state and another." Daed had filed for his Wildlife Transportation permit before leaving, and now that the deer had all been inspected for diseases and the paperwork was final, it was time to see them on their way to Kentucky.

"Will Amos be going with the driver?" With Christmas only one week away, surely Amos would not leave.

"Nee, there's a man named Joe I met when we were introduced during church down there. He and his kin have offered to see to the chore for now. I reckon he knows enough to keep them alive until we get there. I promised you all one last Christmas, and I keep my promises." Daed winked.

He slipped his knitted hat back on his head and motioned to the box. "That's for you."

"Me?" Louise stared at the box in quizzical surprise. "What is it?"

"I have no clue, but I'm guessing something sweet. I was asked only to deliver it." He met his eldest daughter's gaze and held it for three long heartbeats. Louise didn't know what to say.

"I reckon I saw this coming. Him buying the farm and all." His expression was blank, and without another word, he slipped back outside, leaving Louise afraid to step forward or back. Did she really want to know what was in the pretty box, or was it best to return his gift and say goodbye before things got harder?

Louise remained anchored to the spot as Leah returned, dressed in her pale blue dress and white apron frock.

"See ya." She collected her bonnet, coat, and scarf and raced out the door, but Louise's attention never left the gift on the table. Oh, this was ridiculous. A grown woman afraid of a box. Taking three steps forward, she lifted the lid and felt her insides immediately dissolve into a liquid mush. She remembered telling Clare they were her favorite, but never had she thought her friend would share that fact. Twelve chocolate-covered strawberries sat in the box, as well as a small card with three little words that made her heart thunder: The Best Medicine.

"He knew." A laugh bubbled out of her.

With sweets in hand, Louise ventured upstairs to the cold attic where spiders lived without fear of a broom or boot stomp. She weaved past the wooden cradle, a sheet of clear plastic draped over its sides. An old green chair once belonging to her grandfather held stacks of old newspapers. Daed was known to save things he hoped to read again. Perhaps Beth's love of reading stemmed from him as mamm never much cared for the pastime.

She found Beth bent over, exploring the contents of an old suitcase. "Daed was right. There is much clutter here."

"You scared me," Beth squeaked out before noting the contents in Louise's hand. "What is that?"

"Chocolate-covered strawberries." The best chocolate-covered strawberries she had ever tasted.

"Daed trying to sweeten Mamm up again?" Beth giggled. Pulling a book out of the dusty suitcase, she wandered to the window and, under better lighting, perused the cover.

"Nee, they're mine." Louise laid hold of another strawberry, took a healthy nibble, and peered out the frosty window. Why wasn't she surprised to see him out there alongside the men of her family? *Because he has always been at hand*, she reminded herself.

"I won't guess who. That's no secret, but are you going to eat them all?"

Louise offered up the box, and after a quick study of each one, her sister snapped up one from the middle.

They both stood, watching as the men maneuvered along the stretch of fencing to begin the daunting task of pushing deer toward the barn. Louise noted an unrecognizable shadow among them.

"Who else is helping them?"

Beth chewed slowly and swallowed before replying. "That would be Daniel Fisher."

What a turn of events, Louise mused. "Well, that was. . .nice of him." Unsure what to add, she plopped the other half of the strawberry in her mouth and let the flavors burst.

"He said Leah told him we needed the help," Beth huffed. "She need not try her hand at match meddling for me."

What a turn of events for sure. Thankfully, Louise didn't have a twin to interfere with her life. "Many hands make light work. I made jam with what was left from the market. I'm thinking of taking some to Widow Dienner and Mr. Dauley."

"We can wait for Leah and sing Christmas songs like we used to with all the youngies. Caleb and Mitchel can kumm too."

"That could be fun." Just like they did when they were kinner. So much had changed since then. While she shared her sweetheart gift with her sister, they watched as Daniel and Amos went left and Marcus and Caleb moved to the right. Only one buck raised his head, alerted by the extra bodies moving about. They had been caged so long, most were less jittery with human encounters.

Once the men were in place, Marcus raced to one end of the long lot, his straw hat in his hand. Like the evening of the basketball game, he moved easily for a man of his size. He slipped around the base of a tree at the far end of the lot, Caleb on his heels.

Daniel and Amos moved into place next. Beth leaned into the window, her breath forming a ring of white fog on the glass. Louise wasn't the only one struggling with her heart right now, she suspected.

While the four men herded the deer, waving their arms and hats in the air, Daed leaned leisurely on the outside fence, watching with the driver, who was enjoying the process. It didn't take long for the animals to know they needed to return to the barn. In a lazy race, one by one, they crossed the width of the southern lot and slowly disappeared inside the barn before emerging again into the narrow aisle constructed of high gates, creating a temporary trail into the trailer.

Louise popped the rest of another strawberry into her mouth and chewed slowly as the trailer swayed under uneven weight.

"They are going in," Beth said solemnly. "They didn't even try to turn back."

It was not a natural thing for the deer, yet they followed. Louise empathized with the wild animals. Were they afraid of what lay ahead of them or ready to go as long as they were all together? She wished she knew the answer.

"They trust Daed to see them safe," Louise said. Her eyes trailed back to the man challenging her own trust in what lay ahead of her. As if sensing eyes on him, Marcus closed the cattle trailer door, slid down the large metal latch, and glanced up at the small third-floor window. Heat crawled up her neck. Her heart was his, but she couldn't stay. Surely he knew that.

"He has eyes for you, in case you haven't noticed." Beth reached for another treat.

"And Daniel Fisher has eyes for you," Louise returned. Change was inevitable.

"Soon we will all leave, and it won't matter."

Louise sensed her sister's internal struggle. It matched her very own. "Will it not?" It mattered.

Quiet slipped through the low-ceilinged room as they watched their father thank both men with handshakes and a firm pat on the back.

"He invited them to stay," Beth observed when Daed waved them toward the house.

"I can see that." Now she would have to face Marcus since receiving his gift. A gift she and Beth had half eaten.

"Ach, Schwester. We are in trouble," Beth said, her eyes following Daniel's movements toward the house.

"Jah, we are."

CHAPTER TWELVE

$\mathcal{B}$eth sat next to Alma on the eve of Jesus' birthday as Deacon Lenchager led everyone to sing "Joy to the World" in German. Across the room Daniel Fisher sang above the rest of the menner, his gaze tight on Beth's. If he was trying to get her attention, he'd succeeded. Beth frowned, but it didn't dissuade him from tossing her one of his signature winks.

Alma nudged her shoulder and grinned knowingly. He was making quite the spectacle of himself. Who knew he had a passion for singing, auctioneering, and adventure? Who knew he didn't give three licks about causing a scene today?

Beth tried not to let him distract her, but it was no use. He was a distraction. She looked at her bruders. If anything could remind a woman of her place it was having bruders who tended to forget theirs. That's when Beth noticed it. Or didn't, for a better word.

Conner always sat one seat away from Daniel, but today he wasn't. She scanned the clean-shaven faces and stopped to note Conner's bruder Ivan not singing and his head hung low. Craning her neck as one Christmas hymn blended into another, she caught a glimpse of Conner's mamm slumped over, the arm of the minister's fraa around her shoulders. Who missed a special church service, unless...

Throughout the fellowship meal Beth tried to keep a distance from Daniel. The last thing she needed was someone to ask her if she was sweet on him. Beth wouldn't lie. So it was best to avoid such talk altogether.

She hustled upstairs in the large Eicher home to fetch the stack of four gray dishpans to help tidy up the tables. A clutch of women surrounded Conner's mamm, who sat staring at the floor. Beth heard the whispers before they all quieted in her presence, and sure enough Conner had left in the night. Leah had feared he would, despite all her attempts to sway his decision.

Beth had never paid much mind to her twin's special friend. She often found Conner too boastful, too flighty—and one whose eyes always looked back while his feet moved forward. Now, her heart felt for him. Pity for what lay ahead. She sent up a silent prayer. Only God knew what Conner needed now.

Once families began to leave, Beth collected mamm's favorite casserole dish and quietly slipped from the Eichers' house. She didn't want to visit with friends or think about how many people she would soon miss. She didn't want to think about Daniel Fisher and the way his smile made her heart gallop.

Late-December air chilled her through her coat and shawl. She should have worn gloves, she thought as she slipped between two buggies in search of the one belonging to her family. There was barely room for each of them this morning now that they had sold all the other buggies, but she'd welcome the warmth going home even if she had to be pinned between Caleb and Mitchel again.

"You'll be leaving soon."

Beth spun about. He stood there lurking in the shadows of the barn opening. She allowed herself to take in the look of him in his long black coat and hat. He looked older, wiser, and more handsome than the boy who'd worked alongside her at the market for the past year. She'd store this to memory and never forget it, she told herself.

He moved out of the shadows, chivalrously taking the dish from her hands and slipping it on the buggy seat nearest them.

"Aren't you as well?" Answering a question with a question might buy her a few more minutes of this. Of him. Soon, it would be over. Her heart ached at the thought.

"I'm waiting until spring, but"—he moved closer, looming over her as if fearing she might bolt away—"I'd like it if I didn't go alone. I hear a man can get mighty lonely out there." He smirked and fingered her kapp string.

"Sounds like you listen to wise folks." Beth grinned, but the seriousness of the matter made her take a step back and straighten. It wasn't fair to let him love her. It wasn't fair to let her heart fall any further.

"Daniel, you should know that my family means so much to me and—"

"We'll make a home in Kentucky once things get going. Spend a few months traveling, seeing new places, making freinden, and saving up." He was serious, if the determination in his eyes was any indicator. "Then we'll build a haus." He moved closer, taking up her hand. "Beth, I care for you." He cleared his throat. "Nee, that isn't right. I love you. The only thing worse than watching you leave, is leaving without you."

It was strange, the things that came to a woman's mind at such times. Beth had just finished a new book she had found in the attic. It hadn't been her typical choice of reading material, but the cover had drawn her in. She had always wanted to see snow-capped mountains and trees so large cars drove through them.

The story had centered around a man who survived a snow-storm. She shivered, recalling the character's plight and the decisions he made along his perilous journey. If not for wearing new shoes, he could have frozen. Using one of his shoe strings to work wood in a spinning motion, he started a fire. With the other shoe string, he tied branches together to hold tight for a shelter. He had worn a hat his wife told him not to, but the material and shape helped catch fish for nourishment, and that driver's license he thought unimportant those first days, made cleaning a fish a simple task and whittling wood possible.

Everything he had, which wasn't much, saved him. It had been enough. Gott had not made his lost days easy for him, but He had provided him enough for the journey.

Beth didn't have a license or need to catch any fish, but she did have to make a decision. Could she trust herself to make the right one? Was Gott asking her to trust Him?

Each choice she had made in her life had led her to the person she was...and the person Daniel found worthy. Gott had provided her with everything she needed, had He not? She didn't want to be like Leah, trusting her future to the wrong person. She was nothing like Louise, afraid to admit where her heart truly was.

"You want to live...in Kentucky?" she repeated. Did he truly know what he was saying?

"Home is where you are, the haus can be wherever you say it will be. I can make a living anywhere. It's a simple life, for sure, but it's all I have and it's yours." He held her hands firmly and bent to meet her at eye level.

"Are you asking. . ." Beth sucked in a breath. Daniel wasn't asking to court her over distance and scant visits. He was asking for her to choose him as her future.

"We both want the same things—sunrises over new places, kinner who will make us crazy." He chuckled. Beth couldn't help but laugh too, as she could see his future, her future, unfolding like a picture book. That's why the tears came.

"I'll earn enough to set up my own auction house, and you can help me. We make a great team. Marry me. Marry me so I can take you on an adventure."

Those pesky tears simply kept coming, blurring her vision. Who knew joy brought forth such uncontrollable emotions. Who knew how much one heart could love another. Oh, how she loved this man. A man willing to give her the life she'd been craving all along. A man who knew all her heart wanted.

"I've already told Mamm and Daed I was marrying you," he added to sweeten his proposal.

"When did you do that?" She swiped her face and hoped he didn't think her an overly emotional girlfriend.

"A year ago. My first day at the market. You were explaining how to make applesauce to an Englisher." He grinned.

Beth remembered that day and the woman who sought her out for her recipe.

"We can marry as soon as you want. Marcus has offered to let you stay in your home until we can. It's your choice to make. I've already made mine."

Beth was speechless. Not only that Daniel wanted a life with her, but that Marcus wanted to help them achieve their future together. She had always thought he was a better bruder than the ones Mamm gave her.

"Well, I guess I have to now." She faked an exasperated tone.

"Marcus clearly is giving his blessing, and we can't let you make a fool of yourself with your parents. I won't marry a liar, Daniel Fisher." She put both hands on her hips and cocked her head.

Daniel smiled as bright as the sun on a snowflake before wrapping his arms around her and lifting her up. His lips smacked into hers with the same fury as her heart was beating. Jah, Beth was certain this choice was the best decision she would ever make.

Now to tell her parents.

CHAPTER THIRTEEN

reenery filled the Wickey house as thick as a summer forest, hanging from window sashes and adorning tables. Beth wasn't the only one shocked that her brothers had made an extra effort to have their last Christmas in Lancaster the best one yet, tying red ribbons on stair railings and doors. Warm aromas of fresh-baked pies and a sweetened ham filled the air, while white candlesticks trimmed in gold sat waiting to be lit.

Celebrating the birth of Jesus was Beth's favorite day of the year, and this year she felt more thankful. For change may have come into their lives, but Gott would add to their family now that she had agreed to be Daniel's fraa.

Mammi Iolene arrived before the sun rose, bringing their cousins Martha and Julie, who had recently come for a long visit. It was common to exchange gifts at Second Christmas, but Mammi Iolene had never been particularly patient, thankfully so.

Pinning on a fresh apron, Beth entered the kitchen where the Christmas meal was still being prepared. With fewer chores to see to now that the deer had been moved, Daed and her bruders had taken over loading the box trailer outside with many of their belongings. Thankfully they hadn't gotten to the upper bedrooms yet, for her things would only remain where they were for now. She needed to remember to thank Marcus, although Beth was sure he wasn't sacrificing much by letting her stay. Marcus was in no more of a hurry to live here than Louise was to leave. If only those two would confess their feelings, she mused as she sought out a large jar of walnuts.

"You know we have plenty of room. Reuben and I don't like knowing you're so far away." Mamm tried once more to convince Mammi to go to Kentucky with them, all the while instructing Leah how to finger pinch a pie crust for beautiful edges.

"I plan on seeing those hills and blue grass," Mammi Iolene replied. "It wonders me how one makes grass turn blue," she said, floating Leah a mischievous smirk. "Besides, how else will you get these kinner married without me?"

"You're kumm'n with us!" Mamm's voice pitched happily. Beth set down the food chopper and abandoned chopping walnuts for her much-loved cranberry salad to watch Mamm's relief. It would be good for her, since one of her kinner was staying.

"I reckon one can be happy anywhere if they choose it," Mammi confirmed. She worked the heavily seasoned bread chunks into balls for baking. A strong scent of sage filled Beth's nostrils, and she warded off a sneeze.

Happiness was a choice, and Mammi Iolene would be happy to know she had one less *grosskinner* to marry off.

"I always look forward to your stuffing," Louise said. Beth did too because of how Mammi made it with bits of turkey, celery, and onion.

"Who's gonna tell you all about the time Lilly climbed into an old well to rescue a crow? God is with me, wherever I plant my feet. My happiness will be wherever my kinner are."

Noting Louise's solemn expression, Beth moved to her side. As hard as it had been for Beth to know where her heart belonged, it was harder yet for Louise. She had dreamed since she was young of opening her own jam-and-jelly shop, and now she was facing a very uncertain future.

"Are you okay?"

"Jah, I just. . .I love this kitchen. Its every scratch and dent is a memory," Louise murmured.

"Is that all you love?"

"Nee, but you heard Mammi Iolene. Family is everything."

"You can choose to make your own family, can you not?"

Louise narrowed two perplexed brows.

"All this time you have taken care of us, this house, and right next door love has been waiting for you. It's not easy deciding," Beth said with sympathy. "But you have to choose."

"What's next door?" Mammi quizzed. Her hearing was impeccable for a woman her age.

"Ach, nothing. Just wondering where Blinkers is, that's all," Louise quickly inserted.

"I'm sure he's around someplace." Leah moved to the sink where she relieved their cousins Martha and Julie from dish duty. She was no longer sulking, but her quietness had grown in the wake of Conner's leaving. She would heal, in time. Beth felt certain her twin was much stronger than she believed she was. Beth also knew when a woman wanted to be alone, washing dishes was a job that allotted her the time. No one liked doing dishes.

Louise lifted tinfoil off the top of two pies. Pumpkin. "These look good," she complimented.

"It's my recipe," Mammi Iolene spouted. "Your cousin Julie is getting an early start on baking. You know the best way to catch a husband." Mammi winked at each of them. "A good recipe."

"You shouldn't be encouraging them." Mamm waved the potato masher, a steaming bowl of sweet potatoes in front of her.

"And why not? Not a one in the lot married yet. I say they could use the encouragement." Mammi Iolene pinned Leah with a sharp glare. "Got that recipe from one of those *Taste of Home* magazines. You should start a subscription, dear. Who knows how many young menner there will be in our new community," Mammi Iolene added.

"There are many from what I saw, but no one is rushing you kinner. These things take time." Mamm turned to Louise. "Your *Aenti* Verna has a spot for you at the store, and the new boppli your cousin Joel has is adorable."

"I haven't seen Joel or Lydianne in ages," Louise said. "It will be good to be close to them."

A lie if ever Beth heard one. "Has it not been years since Lydianne wrote you?"

"And almost ten years since we last saw them," Leah added.

"But you were once close. You can be again. You will adore her kinner," Mamm continued. "She has two, and if my thoughts are correct, another one is coming soon. She has the look of a woman blessed."

"I'll enjoy seeing them," Leah put in. "Louise has jam to make," she reminded everyone.

"I cannot find the tray. The one with the little snowmen on it." Leah opened a few cabinet doors, then closed them again in frustration.

"Louise," Leah asked. "Did you remember the tray from Clare's? The one we delivered kichlin on weeks ago?"

"It was a paper plate," Louise said, unamused. Without the tape on her nose, her beauty was more defined today. And why did Leah suddenly care about a missing tray?

"Well, it would have been perfect for the cheese dip and crackers. Perhaps Clare has one we can borrow."

"I'm sure we can manage without borrowing from the neighbors," Louise replied, but no one missed the way her voice trembled.

"Louise?" Mamm started to speak, and though Beth wasn't ready, she knew Louise would appreciate her rescue.

"Mamm, what if—"

"What if what?" Mamm lifted a questioning brow.

"What if one of us...wanted to stay." Finally Beth has said it, but clearly mamm didn't think the question was arrowed at her.

"Leah," Mamm said in a sorrowful tone. "I know you have feelings for Conner, but—"

"Conner made his decision, and I have made mine. I dislike deer more than baking pies, but I'm leaving Lancaster with you."

"Ach, my heart." Mamm clutched her chest. "I knew you would come to your senses about that one. I have prayed for it. Gott knows what is best for us, even if it's hard for us to understand." She enveloped Leah in a hug.

"Conner Bricker jumped the fence," Julie announced in case anyone was clueless.

"He'll be back, but he was not a match for our Leah. The heart knows, even when the head isn't convinced. You must trust Gott as I did. Your dawdi and I never saw it coming." Mammi smiled, turning a pretty shade of pink. "He followed where the Lord aimed him. We raised cows and kinner, owned two shops, and saw ice blocks in Alaska with your cousin Anna Mae. When you put your trust in Him, you find—"

"Icebergs." Beth giggled.

"Whatever." Mammi waved a hand. "You find life is sweeter.

Now I can live in a whole new state with all of you." Mammi Iolene swiped the bowl clean, forming the last stuffing ball. "I'll see you kinner meet some fresh faces."

"Stop encouraging them," Mamm said.

Beth swallowed hard and looked at Louise. Her heart collected an extra beat. "Mamm. . ." Beth cleared her throat. The time had come, and Daniel would be here in an hour to share the Christmas meal with them.

"I want to stay."

It was Beth's words, but it was not her voice. Beth turned sharply and faced her sister.

"Louise?" Mamm's voice pitched.

"I mean, I can go with you, but I'm coming back once you are settled."

"Louise, I don't understand." Mamm was beside herself. Her eldest, the one she depended on the most, was asking to stay. Beth and her twin couldn't stop smiling.

"Mamm," Beth quickly interrupted. "I'm staying too. Marcus has offered to let us both stay here, for now."

"Both of you?" Mamm clutched her chest and plopped in the nearest chair.

"They are in love." Mammi Iolene clapped her hands together. "Ach, this is wonderful news. A Christmas present for sure and certain."

"How did I not know this?" Hurt, Mamm put her hand to her head.

"It just happened." Beth shrugged. "It wasn't like we meant for it to. Leah needed help. . ."

"With Conner," Leah said. "And while they tried a hand at helping me, they—"

"Found our match," Beth said. She couldn't contain her smile.

"With who?"

"Must you ask that question?" Leah giggled. "Our neighbor."

"Marcus King?" Mamm's tone could be heard all the way to the end of Church Road.

"And who is the blessed man who's won our sweet Beth Ann's heart?" Mammi Iolene prodded.

Beth rolled her eyes. She hated to confess it, not after spending a whole year complaining.

"Daniel Fisher," Leah spit out in a laugh. "She is in love with Daniel Fisher."

"But I thought you didn't even like him. That he was *faul* and rude and. . ." Mamm was counting on her hand all the offenses she recalled Beth complaining about.

"He's not so lazy, and he makes me laugh. He loves me and I. . .I love him. I agreed to be his fraa."

"It's a season for miracles, Lilly! Gott has brought us two already."

CHAPTER FOURTEEN

*L*ouise watched from her upper-room window as the buggy pulled into the narrow, snowy drive. Clare and Issac jumped out first, but it was the man who took extra care, seeing his horse unhitched and warm inside the barn, who held her attention.

Until this minute, Louise hadn't known what had come over her to tell her folks she was staying. Daed wasn't surprised at all, but Caleb was. It would be hard to see her family leave, but Beth was right, it would be harder to leave her heart behind. Her roots were here, buried deep within the bones of this house.

Downstairs she heard doors open and close, warm welcomes commence, but she wasn't ready to join them. Not until she told Marcus the truth. Not until she knew he felt the same way.

Footsteps on the stairs caused the hairs on her neck to bristle. Leah had most likely come to fetch her, but she wasn't ready. Not yet. She had to know the right words to say.

"Louise?" His voice sent a shiver over her, but she remained still at the window. It was now, she knew. No more time to practice how to explain her heart. She took a deep breath of frosty air. She was a grown woman, capable of handling awkward situations, was she not? She needed to shore up some courage. When his footsteps halted at the door, she finally spoke.

"I love this house. Did you know that I was born in this room? The midwife barely arrived in time with all the snow that year. After Beth and Leah came, Mamm and Daed moved to the room down the hall. It has always been mine."

"It's a fine room," he said, holding his place by the door. Louise turned to face him. Her heart overflowed with what she felt for him.

"Your folks said to fetch ya," he said and started to turn.

"Don't go."

"I love them, you know." He did. If ever a person understood the love of family, it was Marcus King. "From what I hear, Beth is staying put for now." He grinned.

"Jah, and you gave her a place to stay until her and Daniel wed."

"I always knew he had a thing for her."

"You did?"

"Leah told me she didn't have to pull any teeth to get him to come around." He took two steps into her room. "She told me this morning, when she came to apologize for putting cat food in mei barn, it was a chore."

"She's a good schwester." Louise laughed. He made his way to the window, his shoulder brushing hers.

"I offered you the same. You could stay here, Louise. Keep running your business. If that is what makes you happy."

Louise wanted that, but she wanted him more.

"It's a fine room. I'd love it if you'd keep it."

"But I want more. I want a family. I cannot do that alone," she said without a hitch in her throat.

Turning to face her, Marcus took up her hand. "I tried waiting for the right time, but time is something we are short of now.

Clare says I'm always late. That I should have told you when you were thirteen, that I knew you had eyes for me, and I had eyes for you. I wanted to wait until we were older, but then. . ."

"Your parents passed," Louise said. It was true. He had so much responsibility with the farm and his siblings that he didn't have time to worry about trying to start a family of his own.

"We both had so much happening in our lives." He studied her hand as if it had words etched on it. "When you broke your wrist helping Amos catch that buck that got loose, I threatened him."

"You threatened him? It wasn't his fault, and I couldn't let Caleb go. He was barely ten."

"Jah, I told him a real man would come fetch me and not ask you to wrangle a full-sized buck! And I cried after hearing you crying to Clare the day your dawdi passed. I know how close you were to him. Your eyes twinkled every time he was visiting."

Louise had no idea he had heard her, or that it had moved him to tears. He ran his fingers slowly up her arm, revealing flesh under her sleeve.

"You burned your arm with bacon grease teaching Leah to cook. You twisted your ankle chasing down Beth that day she jumped on Penny and thought she'd ride her to town." He smiled.

"It was her pony, so she thought she could do whatever she wanted. Malachi caught her before she reached the end of the lane." Louise warmed at the memory. Their lives had always intertwined. A connection Louise didn't want to sever.

"He knew her spirit just as I know your heart." He kissed her forehead. "I bought the land to grow my future. I bought this house so you could have yours. I want you to be happy, raise a family here. Even if that's not with me."

What words he had penned in honesty. Her heart didn't race as it had when he first touched her hand. Instead it beat steady and strong. It was God's blessed assurance, His affirmation that this man was created for her just as she was for him.

"We have taken a long time to know what Gott has tried telling us for some time."

"We have," he replied.

"If I stay, I want a jam-and-jelly shop," she said with a sneaky grin.

"And I want the bed next to this window." His lips found hers as his arms wrapped her up tightly. Louise clung to him too, as she would for the days ahead. He tasted like Christmas, warm fires, and home.

CHRISTMAS JAM

Winter's Delight

INGREDIENTS:

6 cups frozen strawberries
2 cups fresh or frozen cranberries
1 orange, seeded and separated
5 cups sugar
1 teaspoon cinnamon
1 teaspoon ground ginger
¼ teaspoon ground allspice
¼ teaspoon ground cloves
2 pouches liquid pectin

DIRECTIONS:

Puree strawberries, cranberries, and orange. Pour in large pot and add sugar and spices. Bring to a full boil where it cannot be stirred down. Stir constantly for 1 minute. Remove from heat, add pectin, and stir well. Return to heat and bring to a boil. Stir for 3 minutes. Skim off foam. Ladle in sterilized jars. Place in water bath for 10 minutes. If at high altitude, adjust cooking times and length of water bath according to recommendations from local extension service.

Mindy Steele was raised in Kentucky timber country and has been writing since she could hold a crayon against the wall. Steele writes Amish Romance peppered with just the right amount of humor, as well as engaging Suspense, using rural America and the residents as her muse. Steele strives to create realistic characters for her readers and believes in engaging all the senses to make you laugh, cry, hold your breath, and root for the happily-ever-after ending. A hopeless romantic, with a lyrical pen, Steele wants her readers to find themselves somewhere within her pages. A mother of four and grandmother to a half dozen blessings, Steele enjoys hiking and gardening, coffee indulgences and weekend road trips, and is personally doing all she can to make peanut butter its very own food group.

THE HEART OF THE AMISH

Full of faith, hope, and romance, this new series
takes you into the Heart of Amish country.

AVAILABLE NOW:

The Flower Quilter by Mindy Steele

Barbara Schwartz struggles to find what brings
her artistic joy and purpose amidst traditional
expectations of her Amish community.

Paperback / 978-1-63609-642-1

Ruth's Ginger Snap Surprise by
Anne Blackburne

Amish widow Ruth Helmuth seeks a way to
keep her family farm while discovering that
love accepts who we are, not who we think
we should be.

Paperback / 978-1-63609-689-6

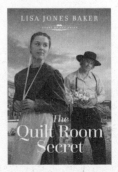

The Quilt Room Secret by **Lisa Jones Baker**

Trini Sutter seems to have her life all lined
up—but secret dreams threaten to force her
to choose between her independence and love.

Paperback / 978-1-63609-775-6

Courting an Amish Bishop by
Mindy Steele

Stella Schmucker faithfully uses her herbal knowledge to help her Amish community while neglecting her own desire for romance—until she meets the bishop.

Paperback / 978-1-63609-815-9

Mary's Calico Hope by **Anne Blackburne**

Mary Yoder is happy with life despite her disability, but then a Mennonite doctor comes into her life, challenging her contentment and offering hope.

Paperback / 978-1-63609-855-5

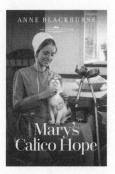

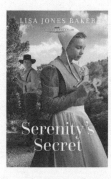

Serenity's Secret by **Lisa Jones Baker**

Serenity Miller is content with her life, until a brush with danger and a taste of romance make her question the secrets she has always held close.

Paperback / 978-1-63609-958-3

JOIN US ONLINE!

Christian Fiction for Women

Christian Fiction for Women is your online home for the latest in Christian fiction.

Check us out online for:

- Giveaways
- Recipes
- Info about Upcoming Releases
- Book Trailers
- News and More!

Find Christian Fiction for Women at Your Favorite Social Media Site:

 Search "Christian Fiction for Women"

 @fictionforwomen
